CROSSROADS OF GRACE
BOOK TWO

Speak through the Wind

A NOVEL

ALLISON PITTMAN

Multnomah Books

SPEAK THROUGH THE WIND
published by Multnomah Books
A *division of Random House, Inc.*

© 2007 by Allison Pittman
International Standard Book Number: 1-59052-625-2
Cover design by James Hall
Interior design and typeset by Katherine Lloyd, Sisters, OR
Multnomah is a trademark of Multnomah Publishers,
and is registered in the U.S. Patent and Trademark Office.
The colophon is a trademark of Multnomah Publishers.

For information:
MULTNOMAH BOOKS
12265 Oracle Boulevard, Suite 200
Colorado Springs, CO 80921

07 08 09 10 11 12 — 10 9 8 7 6 5 4 3 2 1

Praise for the Crossroads of Grace Series

"In *Speak Through the Wind*, Allison Pittman guides her heroine down the dark alleys of New York and through the bustling streets of San Francisco on a harrowing journey toward wholeness. Carefully chosen details and realistic dialogue bring the gritty scenes to life as Kassandra spirals downward, even as her day of redemption draws near."

LIZ CURTIS HIGGS, bestselling author of *Grace in Thine Eyes*

"While *Speak Through the Wind* is beautifully written, wonderfully moving, and a testament to God's love, it suffers from the following: It is highly incompatible with mascara (waterproof or otherwise), getting one's children to school ahead of the tardy bell, and putting dinner on the table. I simply could not put it down."

TAMARA LEIGH, bestselling author of *Perfecting Kate*

"Allison Pittman's *Speak Through the Wind* is a heart-wrenching saga of betrayal and redemption and a young woman's struggle to find herself, against all odds. Poignant and unforgettable!"

KATHY HERMAN, author of the Seaport Suspense
and Phantom Hollow series

"Through this moving and insightful story, Allison captures some of the crippling lies we all encounter on our journey to trusting in the character of God—such as being enticed away from His protective authority by empty promises of something more satisfying, and believing He is responsible for the consequences of our choices. She reminds us that, no matter where the lies have led us in our own lives, no matter how broken and bruised we have become, it's never too late to 'come home' into the arms of our ever accepting and loving heavenly Father."

JULIE FERWERDA, author of *The Perfect Fit:
Piecing Together True Love*

"Allison Pittman gives us another powerful story of action and grace. *Speak Through the Wind* tells a spine-tingling tale set in a harsh and brutal time, but it's gloriously lit with laughter, courage, hope, and love. An absolute must-read."

KAREN ROTH, author of *Found on 16th Avenue*

"*Ten Thousand Charms* is a terrific debut for writer Allison Pittman, a tale of love and redemption that grabs you and won't let go. It will leave you like it left me, anxious to see this author's future work."

JAMES SCOTT BELL, bestselling author of *Presumed Guilty*

"Once I started my *Ten Thousand Charms* journey, I couldn't turn the pages fast enough. Pittman's literary eloquence provides a sidesaddle perspective into one woman's life journey, love struggle, and eternal conflict. Definitely a keeper! This will be a suggested read for all of my listening audiences."

LINDA GOLDFARB, syndicated talk radio host,
speaker, and writer

"If you took Francine Rivers' classic *Redeeming Love* and merged it with Janette Oke's quaint prairie style, you could almost envision the masterpiece Allison Pittman has created with her poignant tale of God's redemptive power. If you're in need of a fresh touch of God's grace, *Ten Thousand Charms* is the story for you."

JANICE THOMPSON, author of *Hurricane*

"Are you thirsty, weary, or heavy laden? Come—rest and let Allison Pittman take you to another place and time where you will find joy resting in the arms of Jesus."

LAUREN L. BRIGGS, author of *What to Say and Do When Someone is Hurting* and *The Joy of Family Legacies*

"*Ten Thousand Charms* is a moving story of love and redemption as its diamond-in-the-rough characters struggle with faith to leave behind a dark past for a brighter future."

LINDA WINDSOR, author of *Blue Moon*

For my guys—Mike, Ryan, Jack, and Charlie.
It's good to be home!

Acknowledgments

"How can I repay the LORD for all his goodness to me?"

(PSALM 116:12, NIV)

Good question! The blessings God has showered on me are immeasurable.

He has brought my family to a place of healing, comforting our hearts and reassuring us of His presence and His plans.

To my fellow teachers—I miss you. For the first time in twenty years I'm eating lunch alone! And particularly to Jennifer: I've never seen anybody suffer so much fire with so much grace.

To my fellow writers—thank you for Monday nights. I can't imagine my life without them.

Finally, Rod, thank you for holding my hand through all of this. You were, for me, proof that God does give us second chances. And first choices.

Dear Lord and Father of Mankind

John Greenleaf Whittier (1872)

Dear Lord and Father of mankind,
Forgive our foolish ways;
Re-clothe us in our rightful mind;
In purer lives Thy service find,
In deeper reverence, praise.

Drop Thy still dews of quietness,
Till all our strivings cease;
Take from our souls the strain and stress,
And let our ordered lives confess
The beauty of Thy peace.

Breathe through the heats of our desire
Thy coolness and Thy balm;
Let sense be dumb, let flesh retire;
Speak through the earthquake, wind, and fire,
O still, small voice of calm!

In simple trust like theirs who heard,
Beside the Syrian sea,
The gracious calling of the Lord,
Let us, like them, without a word,
Rise up and follow Thee.

Amen.

very Sunday Mr. Maroni built up a fire right on the corner of Mulberry and Bayard. After hauling out the big
black cauldron from the back corner of his grocery, he
tossed in the odds and ends of unwanted food—potatoes with
black spots, limp carrots, turnips gone soft, greenish meat. To
this he added water and whatever broth could be salvaged from
the meat boiled for his own Saturday-night supper. All this he set
simmering in the predawn hours of the city's day of rest. By the
time the first church bells rang, a perfectly respectable soup (or
stew, or hash, depending on the ingredients and consistency)
was available to the public. Mr. Maroni stood at the pot with a
ladle the width and depth of a blacksmith's fist, ready to serve
anyone who came with a bowl and a penny.

On chilly autumn mornings like this one, the line formed
early—sometimes before Mr. Maroni even had a chance to settle
the pot over the flames. The drunks showed up first, reeling
from a night full of rotten whiskey and eventually crumpling to
the street to be trampled under the feet of the less intoxicated.

Then came the rowdy street boys, arriving in line as they
moved through life—together. They whiled away their time in
line knocking each other upside the head with battered and
rusted tin cups. They taunted Mr. Maroni with threats of violence to his wife and his children if their serving was watery or
thin, detailing just how they would torch his entire grocery if
they found another cockroach at the bottom of a cup.

Sometimes a mother would show up with her entire brood

and a handful of pennies—one for every ladle full dropped into her bucket. Later she would gather her children and divide the contents according to each child's age and hunger, until, as it happened every week, there was only the barest broth left for her.

Then there was Kassandra. Small and slight, she lingered at the edge of the crowd, clutching a blue porcelain bowl. It had a tiny chip at its rim and a picture of a sparrow perched on a branch painted in its bottom. The bowl was deep enough to hold two servings of Mr. Maroni's soup, a fact not lost on the rowdy boys who elbowed each other relentlessly in front of her in line.

"Better have yourself two pennies for that," one said, his beady eyes staring hungrily at Kassandra's bowl as he patted his own piece of broken pottery nervously against his leg.

"Aw, leave 'er alone," said another boy. Taller than the rest, his red hair sprang from his head like tiny curled flames. "She's so scrawny, looks like she needs an extra bit."

Kassandra said nothing, but clutched her bowl to her body and shuffled her bare feet closer to the bubbling cauldron. It would be the first meal she'd had in days, and the endurance of a few boys' teasing seemed a small price to pay. She kept her attention focused on Mr. Maroni's ladle as it sloshed its contents into the cups and bowls and jars of the men and women and children in front of her. Kassandra felt today would be a lucky one, that her place in line was just perfect. Too close to the front or too far back and you might get nothing but broth.

Soon, only the redheaded boy stood in front of her. He held his bowl out to Mr. Maroni, dug a penny from his pocket and dropped it into the grocer's outstretched hand. Two heartbeats later, Kassandra stood in front of that same outstretched hand, holding her bowl up until it was just level with her chin, focusing her large gray eyes on Mr. Maroni's deep brown ones.

"Penny?" Mr. Maroni said.

Kassandra shook her head from side to side, then held her bowl a little higher.

"No got a penny?"

Kassandra shook her head, no.

"Well, then." Mr. Maroni balanced his ladle across the top of the soup pot and crouched down until he was eye-level with Kassandra. He brought one long brown finger and tapped his right cheek. On command, Kassandra leaned forward and planted a tiny kiss, feeling the edges of his moustache tickle her lip.

"And again," said Mr. Maroni, tapping the opposite cheek. Again, Kassandra leaned in to give a little kiss to that side.

"And here." Kassandra had to go a bit to her toes to land a kiss on Mr. Maroni's forehead, just between the bushy eyebrows almost equal in density to his moustache.

"Now, you want soup?" he said, flashing a cracked brown smile from beneath the black hair on his lip.

Kassandra nodded and tightened her grip on the blue porcelain bowl. She closed her eyes and leaned forward one more time, placing her own lips on Mr. Maroni's. He tasted, as always, of olives, and she called on all her strength not to shudder against the bitterness.

"Now, *bella*," he said, "give this to me."

He reached for her bowl, hooking one dirty thumb over the rim and cupping it from the bottom in his large hand. Within seconds, the bowl was full of two steaming helpings of Mr. Maroni's Sunday soup—plus a delightful little piece of fat floating on the top—and she offered a small curtsy as the prostitutes behind her in the line laughed and tried to negotiate their own price for a free meal.

Kassandra gathered up her skirt, using the thin material as a shield against the hot bowl. She brought the bowl to her lips and allowed herself one tiny sip of the broth—just enough to burn the taste of Mr. Maroni from her mouth—before heading through the streets to find a quiet corner to savor her meal. Her body had grown dull to its hunger, but that little taste of the salty broth brought it to ravenous life again. An enticing bit of carrot floated near the top, but she had to hold the bowl with both hands, so retrieving it would be impossible before she found a place to settle down. Lately she'd been sleeping in a large build-ing up the street where the peddlers parked their carts for the night. Now, as she looked around, she saw them in the streets, singing their songs and hawking their wares. The warehouse would be abandoned and quiet—perfect for a hot, leisurely meal and a good sleep to follow.

When the heat of the soup began to seep through the fabric of her skirt, Kassandra quickened her pace slightly, careful not to let one precious drop of broth slosh over the side. The anticipa-tion was often more delicious than the soup itself. Somewhere in her blanket at the warehouse was half of a sourdough roll she'd found just yesterday. Left alone it was a flour-crusted stone, but Kassandra intended to plop it into this broth and let it sink down to the little bird, then she would mash great moist bits of it into her mouth.

The thought of it made her insist on one more taste, and without breaking stride, she brought the bowl to her lips. Had she not been so engrossed, so hungry, she probably would have seen the carriage careening down the street towards her. If noth-ing else, she would have heard the terrified cry of the horse as its driver pulled desperately on the reins. Instead, her first knowl-edge of the presence of the carriage or the horse came as something hit the bottom of her bowl. She felt the porcelain rim clink into her teeth and bump against her forehead, and she got one quick glimpse of the sparrow sitting on its branch just before two ladles full of Mr. Maroni's Sunday soup flew into her wide, staring eyes.

She was surprised to hear herself scream. She thought her voice had completely closed up within her; it had been so long since she'd uttered a single sound. Yet here she was, her face alive with pain, surrounded by darkness as her eyes burned within. She fell to her knees, then straight to the ground. Some of the broth had gone up her nose and now choked her. She writhed on the street, calling, "*Mutter! Mutter!*" although the memory of when such a call would bring her mother to her side was a memory all but lost.

However, she did soon feel a presence beside her. A hand took both of hers in its grip and another cradled the back of her neck. Kassandra had been touched enough to know it was a man, and she stiffened against his ministrations.

"Hush, now," a gentle voice said. "Hush, little one. It's going to be all right."

Kassandra let her body go limp. Tears welled up behind her closed eyes, sending new waves of pain. She sensed a crowd had gathered, heard muttered conversations and a few hurled, angry words. The gentle hand that held her own released its grip, and the voice that had been so gentle in her ear now spoke loudly above her.

"She's calling for her mother! Does anyone know where her mother is?"

Kassandra wanted to tell him that she had no mother, but when she opened her mouth to say so, she could only produce whimpers that called again for the woman.

"Well, then," said the voice, "where does she live? What is her name?"

She knew nobody could answer him. Nobody knew her name, and she didn't live anywhere. She wanted to tell the voice all of this, but before she could she was lifted by one strong arm under her legs and another around her waist. Then she was flying through the air until she finally felt a soft cushion beneath her. She tried to open her eyes, but the effort seemed too great and an onslaught of pain a promise, so she contented herself to enjoy the comfort.

She felt her body shutting down, felt uncontrollable drowsiness take over. She thought that maybe she was dying—she'd never felt quite so comfortable and tired ever in her life. Maybe the arms she'd felt were the arms of God Himself, lifting her up to this upholstered heaven. Her mind filled with a sense of relief. What perfect timing this death would be. After a few brief years on this earth, how convenient to be taken at her hungriest. Before the winter came to find her without shoes.

Her reverie was interrupted by the voice speaking softly just to her. "*Haben Sie nicht Angst*," it said, telling her not to be afraid.

And strangely enough, she wasn't, even as her body lurched forward into what was surely a journey into the next world.

2

*T*he constant darkness made it difficult for Kassandra to distinguish between wakefulness and sleep. The washing was real enough—a soft wet cloth scrubbing the top layer of grime off her face. And the ointment was real, as were the thick strong fingers that dabbed it on her face none too gently. She brought her own fingers up periodically to gingerly touch the bandage—seemingly coated in the same ointment—only to hear the now-familiar chastisement of the woman called Clara.

"Put your hands down," Clara said, enveloping Kassandra's spindly wrists and depositing them on the bedcovers.

And oh, the bedcovers. Heavy and warm they settled around Kassandra's body, pouring a sumptuous weight from her shoulders to her toes. Whenever she sensed that Clara was not in the room, Kassandra would gather a handful of the quilted coverlet and bring it to her nose, breathing deeply the scent that she identified only as *clean*.

Clean, too, was the pillow that billowed around her head. This she knew because of its scent, but more so because of Clara's initial complaint about resting "that filthy hair" on such fine linens.

"Sho' to be full of nits," Clara'd said in the voice that sounded as rough as her handling. "She'll have the whole bed crawlin' with vermin, Reverend Joseph."

"We'll heal her first, Clara," said the voice Kassandra recognized from the street and the carriage.

She dozed off and on, making no attempt to decipher how

much time had passed since she'd been in Mr. Maroni's soup line. She listened for Reverend Joseph's soft step into the room, his quiet inquiries.

"Has she spoken yet?"

"No, sir, Reverend Joseph. Think maybe she don't speak English."

When she heard Clara's heavy stomp squeaking the floorboards, she brought herself to perfect stillness, refusing to acknowledge the gruff offerings—"Girl, you hungry?"—waiting instead for the softer, familiar—"*Sind Sie mein Liebling hungrig?*"—whispered just at her ear, at which she summoned from deep within herself a little nod and waited for the miracle to follow. She would be propped up in her bed, just enough to keep the spoonfuls of rich porridge from dribbling down her chin. Once she even felt a cool glass rim press against her bottom lip and was treated to long sips of cold milk.

After that she slept, deep and long and full of dreams. Dreams of her mother, holding her close in a crowded back room. Holding her hand as they made their way through the streets in search of money or food. She never dreamt a face, but a presence—arms wrapped around her, soft words of promise. *Alles ist gut, Kassandra.* You're going to be just fine.

Then Kassandra woke up and remembered that her mother had said the same thing before she turned and disappeared into the crowd on the street, leaving Kassandra, small and bewildered. After a time she cried out to the crowd, "Ich wansche meine Mutter!" But when darkness began to fall and nobody took notice of her pleas, she shut her mouth, dried her tears, and found a place to sleep. She'd lived through two winters since then, in silence, broken only by calling for her mother yet again when Mr. Maroni's soup flew scalding into her face.

She wished her mother could see her now, nestled in a clean bed, a father and a Clara at her side. Occasionally there was even a doctor who stopped by to lift the bandage from her eyes, cautioning her not to open them as he swabbed the discharge and gently patted her skin, making little encouraging noises that she wasn't badly damaged. She was going to heal just fine.

Finally the day came when Kassandra was allowed to see all that she had been hearing. She heard the booming, friendly voice of the doctor downstairs. Clara offered him coffee, but he was in a hurry today. Only had enough time to make a quick check on their little patient, take those bandages off and have a look at those eyes. Footsteps followed. Up the stairs, a creaking on the fourth one, Clara's breath coming heavier as she reached the top. No sound of Reverend Joseph. Must be out calling on a member of his congregation.

Then there was a weight on the edge of her bed and a hand patting her leg.

"Good morning, little girl," Doctor said. "We're going to have a look at those eyes of yours."

Kassandra felt his breath on her face—he'd recently eaten some kind of fish—and then his fingers at the side of her head.

"Close those curtains," he said to Clara. Then to her, "Now, I'm going to remove the bandage, but you must keep your eyes closed until I tell you to open them. Do you understand me?"

"Oh, she understands you all right," Clara said. "She hasn't made a sound since she got here, but she knows everything that's going on."

"Mm hmm," Doctor said, patting his fingers gently along her face.

"Reverend Joseph, he talks that German to her, but she don' fool me. She understan' English just as good as us do. She just don' talk."

"Perhaps she simply doesn't talk to you, Clara," Doctor said, and Kassandra forced herself not to smile at Clara's annoyed *hmph!* as she stomped across the room.

"Lift your head for me?" Doctor said, and Kassandra obeyed, bringing her head just inches off the pillow. The layer of gauze was being unwound, and with each passing of it, her heart pounded between hope and fear. There had been talk at the beginning about blindness if her eyes had been badly burned. Doctor had decided to gauge the healing of her eyes by the healing of her face—keep them closed, covered, protected and assume that when the blisters on her cheeks and forehead healed, the eyes would have healed themselves as well. He used to ask her questions about pain: if it was bad, if it was worse, if it was better. But Kassandra hadn't known how to answer. How could she complain about the burning of her eyes when her body was nestled in such softness? And soon enough, anyway, the burning sensation dulled to a minor discomfort, caused more by the stickiness of the ointment and the irritation of the gauze wrapped around her head.

She'd been tempted several times to test her vision, but the weight of the ointment and the bandage made opening her eyes impossible. And each time the bandage had been changed, there'd been a finger pinning her lashes to her cheek.

Now she stood on the threshold of knowing. Perhaps the last thing she'd ever see would be the little globule of fat from the top of Mr. Maroni's soup flying into her face. She knew what her life would be like, back on the streets, blind. She would have to give up her daily wanderings, relegated to a single corner, a doorway, at the mercy of charity and kindness in a world where threadbare lives made such things impossible. She'd seen what happened to those people who couldn't survive. They simply didn't. She'd stepped over them herself, though she hadn't stooped to checking their pockets like some of the older boys did.

These were the images that filled her head as the final layer of gauze was removed. The bandage lifted from her eyes. A soft cloth dabbed at her closed lids.

"Now, little one, it's time," Doctor said. "Open your eyes."

It wasn't easy. Her lids felt heavy with disuse, and she found herself merely raising her brows.

"Come on now, girl. Open them up."

Clara's direction would not be ignored. Kassandra took a deep breath, stiffened the back of her neck, and forced her eyes to open.

Her first thought was that Doctor was a truly ugly man. Hairs grew in odd spurts over the top of his head, with inches of scabby baldness between them. As Kassandra scanned his face, she must have registered some horrified expression, because he broke into a victorious smile, revealing stained teeth with gaps between them that mirrored the sparseness of his hair. His face was flanked with whiskers growing down below his ears and seemingly straight out of his face, but his chin was bare, save for sparse stubble.

An unfamiliar sound came from just over Doctor's shoulder, and it took a moment for Kassandra to realize that it must be the sound of Clara. Laughing.

"Well now, Doc, seems to me that you mighta given the child something more pleasant to open her eyes to besides yo' ugly mug."

Doctor himself laughed at that, spraying Kassandra once again with his fishy breath. Kassandra leaned to her left, getting her first look at Clara. She was expecting to see a huge woman capable of producing the stomps and squeaks that heralded her every step. But she was small. Round, yes, but her head was barely visible behind the seated doctor who she now shooed from his perch on the side of the bed so she could lean in for a closer look.

"Now, girl, let me look at you," Clara said, holding Kassandra's chin in her hand and bringing her face up close.

But it was Kassandra who was looking, taking in Clara's wide-set deep brown eyes and round face. She had always suspected that Clara was a Negro, and she was right. Clara's skin was a seamless brown—no freckle or imperfection marred it from her jutting chin, across her round cheeks, and up to the wide forehead that promised a high hairline beneath the dark kerchief tied around it. Something told Kassandra that she would not win a smile from Clara as easily as she had from Doctor.

"Well, she still looks pretty sad, Doc. Reckon I can clean her up a bit before Reverend Joseph comes home?"

"I don't see why not," Doctor said. He was splashing his hands in the basin of water on a stand over by the window.

"Good." Clara released Kassandra's chin and put both hands on her wide hips. "Just watchin' her head crawl makes my hair itch. I'm gonna hafta burn the sheets."

A large galvanized tub sat in the middle of the kitchen. On the stove were four pots of boiling water emitting an uncomfortable steam into the room. Kassandra had been led here, her hand firmly clutched in Clara's, at such a speed that she had barely noticed the other rooms in the house. She was vaguely aware of chairs and carpets and books, but this was the first room besides her own that she'd been able to study. And it was wonderful. Even with her mother, Kassandra had never lived in a real house, but rather in dank, windowless rooms in back tenements and basements—often having only a few feet of floor to claim as their own. The only kitchens she had seen were those in the back of pubs and restaurants where she was often granted a scrap of food if she got her hungry look just right.

But here—what a kitchen! It was big, with a counter running all along one wall, a stove that looked big enough to roast a goose in, and a pastry shelf along the back wall. In one corner was a water pump, and in the middle a table on which sat half a loaf of bread, a dish of butter, and a crockery pitcher with grapevines painted on the handle.

Everything was meticulously, spotlessly clean, and Kassandra was more aware than ever of her own filthy state as Clara dragged her over to the tub. She looked down and saw about six inches of water, but Clara hauled one steaming kettle over and dumped it in, squatted to test the temperature, frowned, and went back for a second kettle.

"I can see where you'd be a bit shy of steamin' water," she said seemingly to herself, "but I needs it warm enough to clean you up."

By the time the fourth kettle was dumped in, the tub was about half full. Kassandra watched the entire process with a fascination that quickly turned to horror as Clara made her next announcement.

"All right, girl. Strip."

Kassandra looked at her blankly. She understood English perfectly, but Clara's command may as well have been in another language.

"You heard me, girl. And I know you understan' me. Now take off that gown and get in the tub."

Kassandra grabbed a handful of the white cotton nightshirt and clutched it to her skin. She wasn't about to strip naked and get in that tub of water. Not with winter so close. Not with the chill in the air just outside this steamy room.

"Now listen here," Clara said, backing Kassandra against a wall, "I din' say nothing when Reverend Joseph brings your filthy self into this house. And I held my tongue whiles he carried you upstairs and plops you down on my clean sheets. And I fetched you a doctor, and I fetched you your food, and when he said so I fetched you that very shirt you've been sleepin' in all these days. And as long as I live in this house I'll fetch and do for Reverend Joseph all he wants 'cuz this is his house. But this," Clara flung her arms in a wide, sweeping gesture, "this here is *my* kitchen. And so help me, no little guttersnipe is gon' come in *my* kitchen and tell me what she will and what she won' do. Now, take off that gown."

Kassandra felt the kitchen wall against her back. "*Nein! Ich werde krank! Ich sterbe!*"

"And don' you talk that talk with me. I's born here in

America and it's what I speak! This is for your own good, girl."

Clara tried to pry open Kassandra's clutch on the nightshirt. When that didn't work, she reached down, grabbed the hem, and brought the whole garment up over the girl's head.

"*Bitte! Nein! Clara, bitte!*"

Tears stung Kassandra's eyes as she stood, naked, still clutching the nightshirt in two great fistfuls in front of her. Clara had stepped back and was looking at her with an expression of near kindness.

"So," Clara said, "you know my name, do you? Well, that's a start. How about you tell me yours?"

Kassandra brought the wad of material up to wipe the tears now streaming down her face.

"I know you thinkin' that getting in that tub's gonna make you get sick," Clara said. "But let me tell you ain't nobody ever died from taking a bath." She reached out, gently this time, and took the nightshirt from Kassandra who, defeated, relinquished her grip. "But you got to think of it this way. This here, coming to this house, might be a whole new life for you. Starting a whole new life and all, don' you want to start it off nice and clean?"

Kassandra allowed herself to be led over to the tub. Then, holding Clara's arm for balance, she lifted one foot over the edge. Then the other. The water was deliciously warm and, looking down, she saw its immediate effects as it began to cloud with the grime floating off her feet.

"Now, set yourself down in it," Clara said, pushing Kassandra's shoulders until she had folded herself within the tub. "You just set yourself a minute whiles I heat up some more water."

Behind her, Kassandra heard the pump working and the stream of water hitting the kettle. Clara was humming a song— something Kassandra had heard her do often throughout the house. When she'd set the kettle on the stove, Clara walked back over to the tub and, grunting, settled herself on a small stool. She had a washcloth in one hand, and she dunked it into the water, wrung it out, then ran it across a cake of soap in a small wooden bowl she held in the other hand. Once coated, she dunked it back into the water, worked it into a lather, lifted one of Kassandra's arms, and began to scrub.

"Good heavens, girl," she said, "you han' got nothing on you but skin. Once we finish this up, I'll fix you up somethin' nice to eat. That sound good?"

Kassandra nodded. She allowed her body to respond to Clara's direction, lifting her arms while Clara ran the soapy rag in the hollows. She stood while Clara scrubbed her back, her legs, then sat back down and lifted first one foot then the other. As the water blackened around her, Clara made her stand again, step into a second tub where she stood, shivering, until Clara brought the fresh, tepid water from the stove to pour over her.

The new cleanliness only intensified Kassandra's awareness of the crawling sensation on her scalp. Periodically throughout Clara's ministrations she'd brought her hand up to her hair only to have it swatted away.

"We'll fix that flint in a minute, girl."

When Kassandra had been thoroughly rinsed and stood ankle-deep in relatively clean water, Clara once again ordered her to sit. Oval-shaped, the tub was large enough to allow Kassandra to scooch on her bottom until she could lean back, her head resting on a folded towel Clara had placed on its ridge.

"Now I'm going to try to get a comb through this mess, but it don' look like anyone's tried to do that for a long time. Am I right?"

Kassandra just closed her eyes and gave a small nod.

"And then I gots to go through it with this." She poked at Kassandra's shoulder, forcing the girl to open her eyes and see the small, fine-toothed comb that Clara brandished like some kind of cosmetic dagger. "This is to scrape out the bugs. And the nits. And believe me when I tell you that it's gonna hurt. Like

Satan hisself dragging his pitchfork up and down your head. Burnin' and scrapin'. 'Cuz then I gots to pour kerosene on your scalp—"

At the word *kerosene*, Kassandra sat straight up, fixing terrified eyes on the too amused Clara.

"—and that's gonna burn like anything what with your head being all cut up from the combin'."

Kassandra shot out her hand and grabbed Clara's wrist, stopping the advance of the deadly comb.

"What's this?" Clara's voice was full of mock surprise. "You had enough burnin' for one lifetime?"

Kassandra nodded her head.

"Well, we gots one more option. But I don't know if you'll like it any better."

Kassandra continued to look pleadingly into the woman's brown eyes that were now nearly dancing with amusement.

"We could shave it."

"*Wie der Doktor?*"

"Like the doctor?" Clara laughed. "Yes, girl, like the doctor. Only a little bit cleaner."

She reached over to the table and opened a leather pouch. From it she withdrew a shining, straight razor. She held it in one hand and the comb in the other.

"So what's it gonna be?"

Kassandra gave a small nod in the direction of the razor. Clara scooted the stool over to where Kassandra's head draped once again over the edge of the tub. She began humming again—the same song from the water pump, the same song from all her daily chores—and Kassandra felt handfuls of her hair being gathered together and snipped with a pair of shears until a hand brought gingerly to her head revealed that the tangled mass was gone, replaced by a close-cropped covering of matted hair. Then another bucket was set on the ground next to the tub, and yet another kettle full of warm water was poured over Kassandra's head. Clara continued to hum as she worked up a foamy concoction in the wooden soap bowl, which she then massaged all over Kassandra's head.

The first scrape of the razor was cool and quick. The second, too. And after some time Kassandra quit trying to count the number of times the blade passed over her scalp, focusing only on the idea of being *clean*. Like the bedding upstairs. Like her skin. Like this house. She listened to Clara humming, decided that once she was able to speak, she would ask Clara what song she sang. Maybe even learn to sing it herself.

If she were allowed to stay.

The water she was sitting in grew colder, and she shivered despite the warmth of the kitchen.

"There, there," Clara said, her voice more gentle than it had ever been, "we're done. You can stand up now."

Clara went over to the stove, brought one more kettle full of warm water and, starting at the top of Kassandra's head, poured it over her.

"Now you just the way you was the day you was born. Naked, wet, and bald." Clara laughed again, and this time Kassandra joined her. "And on the day you was born, I know your mama gave you a name. I ain't your mama, but if you don' tell me your name I'm just gonna make up one for you myself."

Clara held out her hand and Kassandra took it, stepping gingerly out of the tub and into the warm, soft blanket that Clara wrapped around her.

"Kassandra," she said, and fell into the softness of Clara's arms.

Later, as Clara busied herself dumping the wash water into the alley, Kassandra sat at the kitchen table. In front of her was a white china plate, its edge painted with a delicate pink pattern of vines and roses. In its center was a baked sweet potato Clara had pulled from the embers of the kitchen's oven. Kassandra had watched with wide-eyed wonder as Clara cut a slit in the potato's skin and filled the new cavity with slivers of butter and brown sugar.

"Now you best be eatin' that down 'fo Reverend Joseph gets back," Clara said on her way to return the empty washtub to the mudroom behind the kitchen, "or he's likely to snatch it right off your plate. I promised him baked yams for his own dinner…"

Clara's voice disappeared, mumbling something about never quite knowing when that man would show up for a meal, never being able to plan nothing, not keeping no schedule.

But despite her admonition, Kassandra continued to stare at the potato on the plate. She'd never had such a treat before. The aroma alone filled her. She dreaded the first bite, knowing it would inevitably lead to the last.

It wasn't until Clara planted both of her massive black hands on the table—rattling the plate on impact—and threatened to throw the whole mess out with the wash water if she didn't eat, that Kassandra picked up her fork, dug around in the orange, warm mass and brought a heaping fork full just to her lips where she tested it, then opened her mouth wide to its sweet, buttery flavor.

Clara was still holding her imposing pose across the table, and when Kassandra took the first bite both faces exploded in great, satisfied smiles.

"That's a good girl," Clara said. "You eat up now whiles I go upstairs and put some clean linens on your bed."

Your bed.

The words brought an even bigger smile to Kassandra's face as she attacked the rest of the sweet potato. She was safe for at least one more night.

No sooner was Clara's heavy step clomping above her than a voice boomed from the front of the house, "Clara! Clara! I'm starved!"

The door separating the parlor from the kitchen swung open and, for the first time, Kassandra got a good look at the man who had saved her. Remembering the feel of being swept up in his arms, carried to his carriage, carried up his stairs, she imagined arms the width of tree trunks suspended from shoulders at least six feet off the ground. And while his height did not disappoint (he fairly towered in the doorway, leaving a scant six inches between it and the top of his head), the arm that held the door open was long and thin, completely encased in the long black sleeves of his coat. And at its tip was a hand that seemed ghostly white against the brown wood of the door. Her eyes traveled up, up a thin torso and a skinny white neck that looked a little like those of the unfortunate fowls that often hung in Mr. Maroni's window on Tuesday afternoons.

But it was his face that held her gaze. Framed on either side by dark blond hair that fell clear to his chin, it was perfectly oval, perfectly smooth and beautiful. His eyes were warm and brown, his nose thin, his lips parted in a surprised smile to reveal a slight gap between his two front teeth.

"What is this delightful creature God has left me in my kitchen?" he said, letting one impossibly long leg bring him, in a single stride, from the doorway to the table. "What have I done to deserve such a present?"

❦ *3* ❦

*B*reakfast was always a great feat of precision and timing. Reverend Joseph liked his eggs boiled for exactly four minutes, so Kassandra kept a close eye on the timer, ready to retrieve them with the long-handled slotted spoon just as the last grain of sand dropped. In the meantime, one drizzle of molasses was stirred into the porridge, tea was steeped to the color of dark oak, and bread was sliced in order to be popped into the oven and toasted the minute Clara gave the alarm that the reverend was on his way down.

Kassandra had begun helping with the breakfast preparation as soon as she was tall enough to cook without needing to stand on the kitchen stool. She took over completely after the morning Clara responded to Reverend Joseph's complaint about his scrambled eggs by dumping the whole lot on his head.

This morning, the table was set and the bread toasting when the kitchen door swung open and Reverend Joseph stood on the threshold. "Good morning!" he said after planting a fatherly kiss on top of Kassandra's head.

"Good morning, Reverend Joseph," Kassandra replied, all traces of her native German tongue nearly erased, save for a slight, harsh tick on the consonants.

The egg cooled in its cup, and she ladled the porridge into the bowl at Reverend Joseph's place. Turning back to the stove, she used her apron to guard against the heat as she popped open the oven door just long enough to jab inside with the long toast fork to retrieve four slices of bread. Two for Reverend Joseph, two for herself. Then she settled in the seat opposite him and folded her hands for the morning blessing.

"Our Father in heaven," Reverend Joseph began in a somber voice devoid of the lightness and humor it so often held, "thank You for granting us another day to live in Your creation. Guide our steps and guard our lives as we try to live this day as a testament to Your love and power and grace."

There was a tiny pause, just long enough for Kassandra to know his prayer was over, and it was her turn. "And Father," she prayed, "again I thank You for the blessings and the family You have given me here. And for the love of Your Son, Jesus Christ. Amen."

"Amen," echoed Reverend Joseph.

Over the past seven years, Kassandra and Reverend Joseph had perfected their breakfast routine, and now they ate in companionable silence, listening to Clara's heavy footsteps overhead as she moved about the rooms making up the beds. Kassandra, as always, had been careful to spread up her own covers, taking special pride and care in keeping her room tidy. But no matter how much attention she paid to detail, Clara always came in behind her and found one crease to straighten or one speck of dust to wipe clean.

Reverend Joseph tapped his spoon around the circumference of the egg. "Tell me, Kassandra, do you have your piece memorized for your recitation today?"

"Of course," Kassandra replied, taking a tiny nibble off the corner of her toast.

"Look at you. You even eat like a little sparrow."

Kassandra smiled. Reverend Joseph always called her his little Sparrow. He said she looked like a baby bird that first afternoon—her head bald, her eyes swollen, her skin a mass of tiny bumps in the after-bath chill.

"I am not much like a sparrow anymore," Kassandra said. "More like a goose. I'm taller than any other girl my age."

"Now, now—"

"And I am ugly."

"Nonsense."

"I have a face like a horse. Everybody says so."

"The most important thing," Reverend Joseph said, dipping his spoon into his egg, "is the beauty that is inside of you. The love of Christ in your heart. Now, let me hear your recitation."

Kassandra brought a napkin up to brush the toast crumbs from the corners of her mouth and stood behind her chair, clasping her hands primly in front of her just as Miss Bradstreet, her teacher, taught her. She cleared her throat, cleared her mind, focused her gaze on the shelf just above Reverend Joseph's head, and began.

"At Christ's right hand the sheep do stand,
His holy martyrs, who
For His dear name suffering shame,
calamity and woe,
Like champions stood, and with their blood
their testimony sealed;
Whose innocence without offense,
to Christ their Judge appealed."

She moved seamlessly through the next five stanzas about those who remained true to Christ despite their afflictions, those who suffered great sacrifice for Him; those who grew in His grace. When she came to the lines—

"And them among an infant throng
of babes, for whom Christ died;
Whom for His own, by ways unknown
to men, He sanctified."

—she unclasped her hands and turned them into a tiny cradle, swaying it with the rhythm of the words, returning them to their proper recitation gesture for the final lines.

"O glorious sight! Behold how bright
dust heaps are made to shine,

Conformed so to their Lord unto,
whose glory is divine."

"Them's sure some fancy words comin' out of that mouth," Clara said, having come into the room in that silent way she was capable of when she wanted. "But this child needs to use her mouth to finish her breakfast so's I can get to cleanin' up this kitchen."

"Yes, Clara." Kassandra took another bite of her toast, chewed it thoughtfully and swallowed before speaking again. "Sarah James gets to do the verses about the pits and sufferings of hell, but I think my part is much nicer, don't you?"

"Of course," said Reverend Joseph, blowing on a spoonful of porridge to cool it.

"Besides, she does not understand what most of the words mean. She pretends to be smart because her father is rich, but she is really quite stupid, and—"

"Now you watch yourself," Clara said. "It weren't so long ago that you wouldn'a known any part of them verses yourself. Don't be thinkin' that because you got some knowledge in yo' head and some ribbons in yo' hair that you're any better than anybody else."

Kassandra wanted to explain that she could never be better than Sarah James, who was dainty and pretty and had not only ribbons but *silk* ribbons in her hair, but she knew that any such remark would be taken as ingratitude, so she chose instead to pick up her spoon and heap a generous portion of blackberry preserves on the remainder of her toast.

"Your recitation was perfect," Reverend Joseph said, sending a pointed and protective glare toward Clara, who turned to busy herself at the sink. "But you shouldn't be so critical of young Sarah. Perhaps you and she can practice together, and you can help her understand the poem's meaning."

"She does not ever talk to me," Kassandra said, dropping a glop of preserves on her chin.

Reverend Joseph smiled and reached across the table to wipe it off with his own napkin. "You should try. Who knows? Perhaps you will be a great teacher someday."

"Do you really think so?"

"Why not? You are quick and intelligent and thoughtful. Look how much you have learned in just these few short years."

He rose from the table and left to his study to work on his sermon for the upcoming Sunday. When he was gone, Clara walked over to the table and stood there until Kassandra looked up at her.

"Reverend's right," Clara said. "You are smart. Know what you need to know to fit in. To survive."

Kassandra squirmed under her gaze.

"But, child, don't you forget where you come from. What you was. And whatsoever the Lord giveth, He can taketh away. And don't think He won't slap down the prideful and send them back to the mud He pulled them out of."

The last crust of toast seemed lodged in the back of Kassandra's throat, and she reached for Reverend Joseph's own teacup to wash it down. But Clara snatched the cup off the table before Kassandra could take hold of it, saying, "No time for tea this mornin', girl. You got a poem to say."

4

*A*lthough he was a humble man and true servant of God, Reverend Joseph Hartmann was not a man of modest means. His parents owned several textile mills in his native town of Heidelberg, Germany, which they sold in order to bring a massive amount of cash to invest upon their emigration to America. Joseph was just fifteen years old at the time, already torn between following in his father's industrial footsteps and his own desire to enter the ministry. His mother died of fever during the voyage, and his father had only enough time to build this home in the fashionable district of New York's Centre Street before following his wife after succumbing to a bad piece of fish. The bright spot in young Joseph's view was that the family fortune was largely intact. He took from it only what he needed to finance an education at a modest New York seminary. Within five years, at the young age of twenty-six, he secured a position as minister at the Tenth Street Methodist Church—the place of worship for some of New York's most affluent Methodists—and as a spokesman for quiet reform.

On Tuesday afternoons, the New York City Abolition Society gathered in Reverend Joseph's parlor to bemoan the tragic injustices of the South and to compose tracts to be distributed to all merchants who participated in trade with known slaveholders. On Wednesdays, several members of Reverend Joseph's church came to his home to have a somber evening of prayer and petition for the needs of his congregation. Every third Thursday, the table in the formal dining room was covered with ledgers and lists of the month's charitable donations, and the elders of the church gathered to discuss their dispensation. And on Fridays, Reverend Joseph sat placidly in his parlor, reading his Bible or some evangelical text, while acquaintances outside his congregation paid social calls.

The Friday morning visitors usually consisted of middle-aged mothers and their marriageable daughters. They arrived sheathed in propriety, managing to carry on conversations bemoaning the plight of the poor without dropping a single crumb of fruitcake, all the while scanning the elegance of the furnishings with wistful, hungry eyes. The mothers hung on every one of Reverend Joseph's words, tilting their heads and eyeing him as if looking through a scope. The daughters kept their eyes downcast, as if entranced by the pattern in the fabric of their skirts.

When Kassandra was still a very little girl, her head still sporting tufts of soft, sandy blondness, the women would fawn over her, admiring her large gray eyes and applauding her ability to carry their emptied cups on a tray twice the width of her small frame.

"You've not found a home for this one?" they asked in sweet soprano voices.

"No," Reverend Joseph would reply. "Families want American children. Her English is not yet strong enough."

As years went by, Kassandra's status grew from being a foundling to an adorable little girl, and the mothers would comment on their own daughters' love for children, to which Reverend Joseph would smile and offer them an opportunity to volunteer in the schools and orphanages supported by his church.

"Now really, reverend," the aggressive matrons would coo, "don't you ever intend to marry?" To which Reverend Joseph would smile and reply that he hadn't yet met the woman who would be content to give away as much money as he did.

Kassandra's very presence in the house became, after a time, a sore spot in the eyes of Reverend Joseph's ministerial and social circles. More than once as Kassandra passed through the rooms, she heard the mutterings and chastisements of his colleagues and invited guests.

"You simply cannot just *keep* her, reverend. Not without a mother in the house."

"She is becoming a young woman. It simply isn't proper."

"People are beginning to talk."

But Reverend Joseph dismissed their criticisms and suspicions with a sweep of his hand, saying, "God brought her to me for a reason. I cannot simply turn her out."

Each time Kassandra heard Reverend Joseph defend his right to keep her, she bowed her head and gave a prayer of thanks to God. But still, she was careful to be as inconspicuous as possible, especially when the Friday morning visits of the matrons and their daughters came with ugly glares and suspicious mumblings whenever Reverend Joseph left the parlor. It was at those times that Kassandra would lift her modest eyes and smile with a ferocity that defended his generosity, her virtue and, most of all, their territory.

The spring that Kassandra turned fifteen, she was summoned away from a particularly stifling Friday morning social call by an insistent pounding on the back kitchen door.

"Clara?" Reverend Joseph called to the house at large, before Kassandra could remind him that Clara was out paying a call on a sick neighbor. When he began to rise from his chair to answer the pounding, Kassandra, loath to be left alone with Mrs. Weathersby and her dull daughter Dianne, leapt from her chair, insisting that the three continue their conversation about the propriety of reading from the Song of Solomon from the pulpit.

The knocking intensified as Kassandra tore through the parlor and the dining room, and by the time she was crossing the kitchen she could hear muted profanities coming through the door.

"I'm coming! I'm coming!" she muttered not quite under her breath. When she reached the door, she yanked it open with all the force of her frustration.

His fist was stilled in midair, ready to administer another blow, his face barely discernable under the cap pulled low on his brow.

"Not a very patient one, are you?" Kassandra asked, opening the door just wide enough to poke her head out.

"Not when it's nearly five minutes I'm out here, frappin' until my hand's nearly thick with blood." He shouldered the door open and pushed past her. Once inside the kitchen he turned to face her and asked, "Where are you wantin' this?" referring to the canvas-wrapped bundle he had slung over his shoulder.

"I am not sure," Kassandra said. Clara was meticulous in her power over deliveries—a duty she had never sought to share.

"Well, until ya are, I'm leavin' it right here." He dropped the bundle on the middle of the kitchen table, causing the crockery vase of freshly cut flowers to jump nearly an inch off the surface. "It's a heavy son."

The young man took his cap off, revealing a mass of tight red curls. He turned to Kassandra, who was still standing in the open doorway, and fixed her with a bright smile that made her feel as if a tiny bird had been let loose somewhere behind her rib cage.

"You know, miss, you might want to shut that door before you bring in too much of a chill into this nice, warm kitchen."

"Of course." Kassandra felt a slight sense of uneasiness when the door clicked behind her, not knowing if it was such a good idea to be trapped alone in this room with this boy. As a matter of precaution—and to keep standing despite the very real threat of her legs buckling beneath her—Kassandra kept her hand clasped on the doorknob, and her eyes fixed on the mysterious bundle on the table.

"It's a lamb," he said with a demonstrative gesture. "My guess is the reverend ordered it for his Easter dinner."

"Of course," Kassandra said again, mentally kicking herself for her lack of originality.

They stared at each other for a minute. At least she was sure he was staring at her—her face was burning so—but she kept her own gaze in constant motion around the familiar room.

"Of course…" he said, his voice tinged with the amusement of echoing her words, "you could just leave it out here on the table. But I suspect it might start gettin' a little green after a bit. Would you be wantin' me to take it to someplace a bit cooler? Like maybe a cellar?"

"Of course!" Kassandra said yet again, thrilled to have a plan at last. "I mean, yes, the cellar. Right this way."

She let go her grip on the kitchen doorknob and walked, head down, into the pantry just off the kitchen. She heard him behind her, grunting as he shouldered the weight of the lamb once again.

"It's just down there," she said, kicking back the mat that covered the cellar door.

"Well, now, do you think maybe you could open it for me? I'm a bit burdened here."

Before she could stop herself, Kassandra said, "Of course," again before stooping to grasp the iron ring and raising it to expose the open, empty blackness.

"And is there a ladder?" he asked.

"Of—yes, there is."

"And is there a light? Or would you rather I broke my neck tryin' to bring you your Easter dinner?"

"A lamp. Yes, I'll get one," Kassandra said. "Wait here."

She stepped back into the kitchen, grabbed the kerosene lamp off the shelf above the stove, lifted the globe—amazed at the steadiness of her hands—lit the wick, and held the burning match while she replaced the glass, remembering to shake it out only when she felt the first twinge of the flame against her skin.

"You all right?" he called.

She scurried back around the corner, holding the lamp in triumph. "You go on down," she said. "I'll hold the lamp for you from up here."

"Scared to go down to the pits of hell with me?" he said, cocking his head and sending her what she was sure was a wink.

Before she could reply, he was descending the ladder, lamb balanced perfectly on his shoulder, leaving her at the threshold of the cellar, breathless.

Dear Lord and Father of mankind
Forgive our foolish ways…

5

In the evenings after supper, Reverend Joseph retired to his study with his pipe, his brandy, and his Bible. He was left there alone for exactly thirty minutes while Kassandra helped Clara clear away the supper dishes and put the kitchen back in order. When all was tidied away, Kassandra went to the study door and knocked softly three times. Sometimes she would be given a muffled, "Good night, Sparrow," through the heavy wooden door, but other nights—and these were the nights she treasured—she would be summoned inside to sit on the thick, soft rug at Reverend Joseph's feet.

It was here that Kassandra first learned to speak English, carefully mimicking Reverend Joseph's pronunciation and intonation as she recited Scriptures in the firelight. Meaningless words at first, but as her understanding of the language grew, so did her comprehension of God's holy Word. One evening, when Kassandra was still a very little girl, Reverend Joseph leaned forward in his big leather chair and settled his Bible on his knees, running his well-groomed finger along the words as he read aloud in slow, clear English: *"Are not two sparrows sold for a farthing? And one of them shall not fall on the ground without your Father. But the very hairs of your head are all numbered. Fear ye not therefore, ye are of more value than many sparrows."*

Kassandra brought a hand up to her hair—just grown long enough to reach the bottom of her ears—and made a joke in broken English about what an easy job God would have counting the hairs on *her* head. Reverend Joseph had laughed gently, then took her small hand in his own.

"Do you understand, *mein kleiner Spatz,* what this means?" he asked her. "It means that God—God, who created all of the universe, all of the world—knows exactly who you are."

"And He sees me?"

"Always. He saw you when you were all alone in the city. He sees you now."

At that, Kassandra had shifted her gaze above Reverend Joseph's head, her large gray eyes scanning the ornate ceiling, much to the older man's amusement.

"No, no, my Sparrow," he said, chuckling. "This is not a cause for fear. Quite the contrary, in fact."

Reverend Joseph let go of her hand and stood to cross the room to a wall lined end to end, floor to ceiling, with bookshelves stocked solid with leather-bound tomes of religion and history with the occasional frivolous novel stuffed in between. The monotony of gilded spines was interrupted occasionally by the odd knickknack—most brought by his mother wrapped in soft cloths to survive the voyage from the old country. He scanned the shelves, as if looking for the perfect title, but his hand instead came to rest on a tiny figurine, a little brown-spotted bird that seemed poised to take flight from the brown china branch clutched in its perfectly painted claws. Reverend Joseph brought the tiny treasure over to where Kassandra sat, still coiled on the rug, and held it balanced in his open hand.

"May I touch it?" Kassandra asked, her hand already hovering.

"Yes," Reverend Joseph said, kneeling, "but be careful. It is very fragile, you see. If it were to fall from my hand, it would break into a hundred little pieces."

Kassandra allowed her fingers to graze over the smooth, cool surface of the wings while her eyes took in the work of such intricate detail. The artist had taken great pains to give the tiny bird texture, with fine brushstrokes creating miniscule feathers on both the outstretched wings and the soft white belly. The sharp black eyes of the bird held a determined glint, as if great adventures were waiting for the moment of flight. She moved her finger to the tiny beak and giggled a bit at its sharpness.

"Now watch," he said, looking down at her. With a quick movement, the tiny bird was in flight, soaring up towards the ceiling, spinning as it flew.

"*Nein!*" Kassandra screamed, but it was too late. The bird was plummeting, wobbling in the air, destined to be shattered on the polished wood floor until—*plop*—it landed in Reverend Joseph's outstretched hand.

"I want you to have this, Kassandra," he said solemnly. "I want you to keep it to remember what you are in God's eyes. You are beautiful and precious to Him, do you know that?"

"Yes," Kassandra said, never taking her eyes off the treasure.

The little bird stared at her now from its new perch on the bureau in her room as she stood staring into the mirror that hung above it. It was a Friday afternoon, and her face was flushed from the run home from school. Teacher had insisted on holding the class until everybody completed their history recitations, and that dull Sarah James seemed determined to forget every detail of the first Continental Congress. Kassandra had torn through the neighborhood, flew through the door, barely able to compose herself enough to give a polite greeting to the assembly in the parlor. This afternoon there were two ladies—the Misses Austine—with their niece visiting from Boston.

"You look like you've been tossed by the wind a bit, my little Sparrow," Reverend Joseph said, peering at her over his cup of tea, seemingly oblivious to the shudder of disapproval the women gave over the affectionate name.

"Yes, Reverend Joseph. School got out late," she said. Then with a swift nod and a smile, she turned and left the parlor, clamoring up the stairs to her room.

The pink tinge to her cheeks, Kassandra thought, was a little becoming, but her hair was another matter entirely. The spring breeze combined with the ferocity of her running had torn much of it from the blue ribbon that secured the mass at the nape of her neck. With one swift motion, she tore out the ribbon, grabbed the bone-handled brush that sat atop her bureau, and dragged the bristles through the mass until it crackled. Her hair was long now, past her shoulder blades, and heavy, though it hung straight from her scalp without the slightest bit of curl. The brushing brought an electric life to it now, and singular strands stood straight out from her head, making her look like she was indeed in flight.

"Jealous?" she whispered to the little bird before crossing over to the basin and dipping the bristles of the brush in what was left of her morning wash water. Returning to the mirror, she once again brought the brush through her hair and pulled back just those strands that framed her face, twisting and coiling them at the top of her head and holding them securely with one hand as she used the other to open the top drawer of her bureau. She searched under the top layer of clean stockings and found the comb, lacquered and ornate, decorated with tiny, shiny stones. He'd given it to her the last time they'd met, said he'd been carrying it in his pocket for weeks, waiting for the right opportunity. She used it now to secure the knot, the rest of her hair hanging down her back. Kassandra gave herself one more scrutinizing look in the mirror. Still not pretty, but different. Older? She turned around and twisted her head, trying unsuccessfully to get a glimpse of the comb adorning her hair.

Sighing, not quite satisfied, Kassandra walked out of her room and tiptoed down the back stairs leading to the kitchen. She was on the third step from the bottom when she heard the first knock, and she had the door open before the third.

Same wool cap, same red curls. But this time the smile was waiting the minute Kassandra opened the door.

"Hello, Kassie."

His name was Ben Connor. She'd learned that after their second meeting when he delivered a package of flank steaks that Clara pan-fried and served smothered in fresh mushroom gravy the next day. When he showed up with a dozen links of freshly ground sausage, she learned that delivering meat for the butcher on North Canal Street was just one of his many jobs—one he said he'd never enjoyed until that Friday afternoon when he walked a lamb into Reverend Joseph's cellar. The next week, when Kassandra complained that the sausage had been too spicy for the reverend's delicate constitution, he tried to make amends with an extra-nice piece of liver and the bejeweled comb that now sat on top of her head.

"You're looking particularly lovely this afternoon, my girl," he said, taking off his cap as he walked past her into the kitchen. "Let's see now…what's different about you?"

Kassandra closed the door and stood for a moment, her back to him, giving him plenty of time to notice her new hairstyle before turning to face him—briefly—and dropping her eyes to study her boots.

"Is that a new dress you're wearin'?"

"No," she said shyly, smoothing the pretty blue woolen skirt, wishing it were new.

"And you haven't grown any taller? Because if you did I'd never see the top of that pretty head of yours."

Kassandra smiled, looked up, and brought her hand up to check that her hair was still pulled back and smooth.

"Well, it is your hair, then?" He deposited his packages on the kitchen table and, placing a hand on Kassandra's shoulder, turned her around once, letting out a slow whistle before bringing her back to face him.

"Does it look all right?" she asked.

"Looks lovely. Like one of them little crowns a princess wears."

"A tiara."

Ben's eyes narrowed a bit, losing their glint, though his smile didn't waver. "What?"

"That is what you call those little crowns. They are... um...tiaras."

"Well, I guess that's one of the benefits of such a fine, fancy education then, isn't it? Knowing all kinds of fine, fancy words."

"Reverend Joseph, he thinks I should finish secondary school," Kassandra said, her gaze once again on her boots. "He thinks I might be a good teacher some day."

"Oh, now, that's a fine thing." Ben reached out his hand and pinched just the tip of Kassandra's chin between his thumb and forefinger, forcing her to look at him. The smile was back—all of it—the gleam in the corners of his green eyes dispersing the momentary chill. "Why would he want to take such a lovely young girl and turn her into some old spinster teacher? Well, I can just see you now..."

Ben let go of her chin and assumed the bent posture of an old woman, shuffling from the table to the stove, rattling pots and cutlery with exaggerated palsied hands.

"We have a nice pork loin for supper tonight, Reverend Joseph," Ben said in a comic high-pitched voice, losing his warm Irish brogue in a nearly perfect imitation of Kassandra's lingering German accent. "And a nice cup of tea to keep away the chill. Let me be sure to fetch you a soda powder. That tea can be a bit too spicy..."

Kassandra tried not to laugh, made a sincere attempt to feel offended by the mockery of her beloved companion, but when Ben whisked the comb out of her hair and planted it in his thick red curls, she could not stop her giggles.

Ben retained his bent posture, wringing his hands, his eyes fixed heavenward. "There was a time," he continued in his comic voice, "when I was a lovely girl. A princess. With a tiara. But thank God the reverend saved me from such a frivolous waste."

By now the kitchen was full of laughter of such great volume and hilarity that Kassandra clasped her hands over her mouth and hissed a warning "shush" lest they bring Reverend Joseph and the Misses Austine in from the parlor. When they had quieted themselves to nearly silent giggles, Kassandra made one mad swipe to get the comb from Ben's hair. He quickly hopped to the other side of the table, pulled out a chair, and held it between them like a lion tamer fending off a ferocious beast. And Kassandra truly had the appearance of a beast at that point, her hair long and loose, flying about her head, obstructing her view.

"Give it back!" she said, her voice full of hushed play.

"I gave it to you once, lass," Ben said, his brogue returned in full force. "And if you ask me, you let it slip away far too easy."

"Give it to me again." Kassandra used both of her hands to rake her hair off her face, her words as measured as her newly recovered breath. "Give it back, and I'll never let it out of my sight."

The silence was now as thick as the laughter had been as Ben, never letting his gaze falter from her, dislodged the comb, grasped Kassandra's hand, and placed the comb within it, closing her fingers and holding them tight until Kassandra felt the teeth digging into her flesh.

"Do you ever ask yourself, Kassie, why you're here?"

"Reverend Joseph. He—"

"Now, we all know about the kind reverend." Ben relinquished his grip on Kassandra's hand. "He's a famous man back at the Points. Snatchin' children right off the streets, takin' them away to nice new families."

"You make it sound like he is stealing them." Kassandra looked down at her uncurled fingers, each of which bore a tiny red mark. Not bleeding, but distinct.

"Do I now? How could it be a crime if there's women on the streets just lookin' for someone to take their child? Everybody knows that poor people don't really love their children, right?"

"That's not what—"

"I mean, you go to the Points and there's people just waitin' to give their young ones away. Sell 'em if they could. In fact, if it's a lucky day and the kind reverend has a dollar in his pocket..."

"I would be dead today if Reverend Joseph hadn't brought me home," Kassandra said, no longer feeling at ease in Ben's company.

"Maybe you would." Ben crossed his arms in front of him and leaned back against the kitchen table, studying Kassandra through narrowed eyes. "But how long ago was that?"

"It seems my whole life."

"And all that time he's keepin' you for himself. To himself. Tell me, did he ever try to find a family for you?"

"I was ugly. And sick. I didn't speak English."

"And heaven forbid some rich, childless couple take in somethin' the likes of that. Just be careful you don't go thinkin' the man has so great a heart just because he's kept your belly full all these years. And if you're not careful," he reached for her then, gently grasping her arms just above her elbows and drawing her closer, "he's goin' to have your belly full of somethin' else in some soon time."

The implication of Ben's comment dawned slowly, and would have escaped her completely if not for the accompanying leer. "That is a terrible thing to say."

"Now, Kassie dear," Ben said, gently shaking her, his voice taking on a jovial twinge, "do you mean to tell me the man's never touched you?"

"Never," Kassandra said, steeling herself against his charm.

"He's never kissed you?"

"Of course he has kissed me. He loves me."

"Where does he kiss you?"

"What do you mean?"

"Does he kiss you here?" Ben asked, dropping his grip on one of her arms and bringing his finger to bounce, lightly, on the top of her skull.

"Sometimes," she whispered.

"Like this?" He pulled her forward until her nose was just an inch from his chest, her vision a blur of the coarse wool of his shirt and the smattering of freckles under his collarbone. "Right here?" She felt his lips on the top of her head, moving slightly against her hair. "Or here?" He moved his hand to the back of her head, tilting it back, moving his lips just to her hairline.

Kassandra fought for breath and balance.

"Does he ever," Ben said, letting go of the back of her head and running a finger along her lips, "kiss you here?"

"Of course not," Kassandra said, jerking her head to the side to dislodge Ben's finger. "He's like a father to me."

"Ah, but he's not your father, is he, love?"

Kassandra said nothing, but looked down in shame.

"And since he's not your father, he doesn't have any real claim to you, now does he?"

"He cares for me," Kassandra said, keeping her eyes focused on the floor.

"But if I kissed you here," Ben grasped her chin and forced Kassandra to look at him, running his thumb along her lips, "I'd have a claim to you, now wouldn't I? Would you like that? Would you like me to have a claim to you?"

"I don't know," Kassandra said, her lips moving against his roughened skin.

"Well, would you like me to kiss you?"

She didn't know that, either, but apparently Ben wasn't interested in her answer, because in the next instant she was drawn full to him, his arms circled around her, his lips on hers, his smile becoming a part of her as he brought her closer.

Kassandra's arms hung limply at her side, her fingers twitching nervously as the comb dropped unheeded to the floor. Her mind raced. She knew she should feel embarrassed or wicked; a good girl would bring up those hands and push Ben away. But she could no more command her hands than she could her heart, which she could feel pounding against her clean white cotton chemise. All the fear, all the discomfort she'd felt when he insulted her education, mocked her life with Reverend Joseph, even the nauseating accusations against the reverend's character disappeared as the sweetness of his kiss took command.

When Ben slowly, gently, teased her mouth to open, just a bit, every drop of blood was drawn from her, leaving her body powerless to stand on its own, on the verge of collapse saved only by the strength of Ben's arms now wrapped tight around her. She fell against his chest, the pounding pulse in her head drowning out every sound except the breathing of this redheaded boy and—somewhere—the click of a door handle and a familiar heavy step.

"Get out of my kitchen."

Clara's steely voice cut through the fog in Kassandra's head. She brought her hands up, pushed herself away from Ben's embrace, and spun to face the formidable figure filling the doorway.

"You must be Clara," Ben said, his voice full of humor and charm.

Clara said nothing, only stepped away from the open door, clearing the way for Ben's exit, never taking her withering glare off Kassandra, who stood frozen in fear, unable to look away.

"All right then," Ben said, his voice never losing its bounce. He crossed the kitchen, but stopped just short of the door. "Oops," he turned and took a step to the side, standing between Clara and Kassandra. "Forgot my hat."

Kassandra looked up, saw the mischievous glint in his eyes, and felt a tiny wave of comfort wash over her. Ben sent her a wink, and she was powerless not to reward it with a smile. Then, with a few quick steps, he was back at the open doorway, his cap nestled at a jaunty angle in his mass of red curls.

"Shall I have Mr. Sampson put the delivery on your bill, Miss Clara? Or would you like to pay me now?"

Once again, Clara said nothing.

"Right then, it's on account."

He was whistling before the door was shut.

"Now, missy, suppose you tell me what I just seen," Clara said once the diminishing whistled tune left the kitchen with a heavy silence.

"I don't know." Kassandra was no longer able to meet Clara's eyes. Looking down at the floor, she saw the comb lying just next to her boot. She gave it a slight kick, sending it skittering under the table, and hoped to retrieve it in secret before the meticulous woman had a chance to sweep it away.

"Well, then," Clara said, "let me tell you what I seen. I seen you in here with some piece of Irish trash treatin' my kitchen like it was some filthy back alley—"

"He just kissed me, Clara."

"His hands all over you. And look at you, hair loose, down your back. Nothin' but shame and filth."

It wasn't the first time Kassandra had seen Clara in the throes of anger. The woman was a mass of unpredictable temper, but this was different.

"Tryin' to raise a good girl. Decent."

"Clara, I am a good girl—"

"An' the first boy comes up them back steps…"

"Clara, please!" Kassandra reached out, alarmed now at the change in Clara. There was an ashen undertone to the woman's brown skin, a sheen of sweat on her smooth, dark brow.

"Please what?"

Kassandra wasn't sure. She wanted Clara to please calm down. Or please rant and rave in a more comfortable, familiar fashion. She wanted her to please not think of her as a bad girl, to please understand how wonderful it felt to be kissed. She wanted her to please not tell Reverend Joseph. This last unspoken plea rang most true as the door to the dining room swung open and the reverend himself stepped onto the scene.

"Ladies?" he said, entering the room. He stopped as the door fell shut behind him, his gentle eyes darting back and forth between Kassandra's pleading face and Clara's ever-present glare. "Is everything all right?"

"Is your company gone home?" Clara asked, her voice dull and flat.

"Yes, finally," Reverend Joseph said. "I was coming here to ask you to clear away the tea, but I must say, Clara," he stepped closer, his face taking on an expression of concern, "you don't look well."

"I was just saying the same thing," Kassandra said, surprised at how easily the lie came. "I think she should go lie down. And rest."

Clara snatched her arm away from Kassandra's grasp. "I feel fine," she said.

"No, no, Kassandra's right. You go to your room. I'll send for the doctor to look in on you."

"I don't need no doctor." The strength of Clara's voice had returned. "But I think I do needs a little quiet." She began walking toward her room, nestled just at the foot of the back stairs. "There's some chicken and pea salad left from yesterday. Looks like you two will have a cold supper tonight," she said, barely looking over her shoulder as she walked. "Think you can take care of yourselves?"

"We'll be fine, Clara," Reverend Joseph said, a touch of laughter in his voice. "After all, Kassandra's practically grown-up now, isn't she?"

Before hearing Clara's reply, Kassandra left to gather the tea things from the parlor.

They did have a cold supper that night—and an early one—as Kassandra complained of not feeling well herself. She knocked on Reverend Joseph's study door after tidying up the kitchen, but opened it only a crack to peek through and say good night.

"Will you check on Clara before you go to bed?" he asked, looking up from the huge leather-bound volume in his lap.

"Of course."

She walked back through the kitchen and stopped at Clara's closed door.

"Clara?" she asked, after softly knocking. But there was no answer. "Clara?" she said again, then opened the door just wide enough to poke her head through.

The early hour still permitted some gray light to come through the small window, and Kassandra saw the woman lying on her bed, a light blanket draped over the form that seemed much less round and imposing at rest.

"Clara? Are you awake?" But there was no answer, just an eerie wheezing sound. Relieved that she would have the distance of night and sleep before facing Clara again, Kassandra softly shut the door and went upstairs to her room.

Sleep came fitfully that night as Kassandra tossed on her clean white sheets. She played the kiss over and over in her mind, trying to remember exactly what it felt like, while simultaneously quelling the guilty joy that coursed through her body at the memory. She rolled up the sleeve of her cotton nightgown and brought her own lips to the soft skin at her wrist, wondering what her lips felt like to him, pressing them tight against her pulse. She tortured herself with visions of what might have happened if Clara had not come home, if there had been time for more. She smiled and curled her body up in girlish glee. Then a sliver of moonlight drew her eyes to the tiny sparrow figurine on the top of her dresser, and another thought entirely invaded her mind.

She and Ben had never been alone in the kitchen. God had been watching. And He was watching her now.

The delightful tumbling in her stomach turned to a dense,

leaden weight, pulling her from her bed and to her knees. Her forehead sank into the soft mattress and her lips, no longer reenacting a lover's kiss, moved against her clasped fingers as she whispered in fervent prayer.

"God, forgive me. Forgive me for showing such disrespect for my home. The home You brought me to. Forgive me for feeling…" She had no words to articulate the way she'd responded to Ben's touch. Only Clara's accusations burned at the back of her mind. Shame. Filth. Yet even now Kassandra didn't know if her sin lay in her body's betrayal or her mind's desire. "Lord, help me to be a good girl. Help me not to think about Ben. I confess my sin to You, God, and in the name of Jesus Christ Your Son, I ask You to forgive me."

She stayed on the floor long after her whispered "Amen," knowing that her confession wouldn't end there. She had to tell Reverend Joseph. His forgiveness and understanding would restore to her some of the peace that she had destroyed. In the back of her mind she knew, too, that he would be much more willing to forgive an indiscretion she confessed rather than one Clara reported.

Clara. Before getting back up into her bed, Kassandra opened her prayer once again, whispering, "And please, dear God, help Clara to not be so angry with me. Amen."

Once in bed, Kassandra forced her thoughts away from Ben, silently reciting her multiplication tables up to twelve times twelve before moving on to the elected terms of the presidents. She was up to the inauguration of John Quincy Adams when she heard the soft knock on her bedroom door.

"Kassandra?" Reverend Joseph spoke from the other side.

Never, unless she was sick in bed with a fever, had Reverend Joseph ever come to her bedroom at night. Even when she was ill, it was Clara who stomped across the threshold with a cup of weak tea and a cool cloth. But here he was now, knocking again, calling again, "Kassandra? Are you awake?"

She wasn't, she decided. She clutched her covers up to her chin, turning onto her side, her back to the door, filled with a terror she could never have imagined even the night before.

Even with one ear buried in her pillow and the other nearly covered with her blanket, Kassandra could not shut out the sound of the turning knob, the slight creak of the opening door. She allowed one eye to open slightly, seeing her own shadow cast on the wall as the room filled with light from the single candle the reverend used as he maneuvered around the house at night.

"Kassandra, *Liebling,* wake up."

She felt her mattress sink as weight was added to it. He was sitting there, on the edge of her bed. His hand on her shoulder, shaking her slightly, turning her toward him.

Unable to keep up the ruse, she turned, saw his face, long and gaunt, the sharpness of his nose and chin exaggerated by the candle's flickering light, his deep brown eyes pools of blackness, each reflecting a tiny dancing flame.

"Yes, Reverend Joseph?" Kassandra said, feigning a yawn.

"Get up, little Sparrow, and get dressed. Come to the kitchen."

He stood then and began to walk toward the door. Kassandra sat upright, still clutching her blanket tightly to her.

"Wh-what's wrong?" she asked, hoping to feign innocence as easily as she had feigned sleep.

"I'm afraid it's Clara."

"Is she sick?"

"No, *mein Spatz.* She's dead."

～ 6 ～

The kind thing to do, Reverend Joseph said, was to offer to hold the funeral in his home; after all, Clara had been a loyal servant and somewhat companion of the family for more than twenty years. But his counterpart—the minister from Clara's own church, equally as tall and solemn and just as dark as Reverend Joseph was pale—politely declined, saying that few of Clara's friends and family would feel comfortable gathering in this fine home, so far removed from their own neighborhoods and lives. Kassandra was quick to note the briefest passing of relief across Reverend Joseph's face at this suggestion, just enough so he could offer what she knew to be a genuine expression of his sadness at Clara's death and a respectful acceptance of the opportunity to speak at the service.

Kassandra herself, through all the visits of Doctor, the coroner, the jet-black minister, and the small Negro man who, surprise of all surprises, was Clara's own husband, sat mutely at the kitchen table, staring at a final crumb of Clara's good corn bread lodged in the grain. Each cup of tea made for each new visitor reminded her of her final words with Clara—the ashen undertone to her face, the fight for each breath and word, the eerie wheezing coming from the shadows. Clara had been in the jaws of death at that moment, and Kassandra had done nothing. Doctor and the coroner emerged from her tiny back room, both in agreement that the poor woman's heart had just stopped in the night, a phrase that sent Kassandra's hand to such shaking that it sent a few scalding drops from the kettle scurrying across her thumb as she tried to fill the china teapot. She did not cry out in pain, undeserving as she was of the least bit of sympathy or attention from her old friend the doctor. Reverend Joseph heard her gasp, though, and draped his arm across her shaking shoulders, saying, "There, there, child. It was a good heart that stopped."

Any plans Kassandra had for confessing her behavior with Ben in the kitchen that afternoon stopped cold with this tragic turn of events. She was whisked up to her room to be spared the sight of the young men commissioned to carry Clara's body out to the coroner's wagon parked in front of Reverend Joseph's home, though she parted her curtains just enough to witness the scene from her window. The rest of the morning was a steady flow of visitors—wailing women who worked in neighboring houses, wringing their handkerchiefs while tears flowed unchecked down their dark faces; a long-estranged sister who came to claim Clara's best Sunday hat and coat, just as Clara would have wanted; and the husband, quiet and meek, who wanted, if it wasn't too much trouble, whatever salary was owed to her.

Each of these was received in the parlor, treated with the same respect and tea as any of the reverend's friends. The wailing women were given clean, crisp handkerchiefs, which Kassandra found in Clara's top drawer, each embroidered with a different floral border in perfect tiny stitches that Kassandra would have never thought the woman's thick fingers capable of producing. The hat and coat were brought from the small cedar-lined pine wardrobe after Kassandra—following Reverend Joseph's careful instructions—tucked a few "forgotten" coins into the pocket.

She was, however, hustled out of the kitchen and up the stairs when the husband arrived, knocking at the back door as all the others had. But unlike the others, there had been no discernible sign of grief on his haggard face. In the brief moments Kassandra had spent with him, she decided he looked positively hungry, turning his hat over and over in his hopeful hands. Poised at the top of the landing, unable to resist her curiosity about this never-mentioned husband, Kassandra listened as Reverend Joseph counted bill after bill into what she imagined was an outstretched, shaking hand, until he had counted up an amount nearly twice what Kassandra imagined Clara's salary to be. Then there was a loud admonishment not to spend the money on liquor, and a whispered promise, "No, sir," before the door shut on the final visitor of the morning.

"Kassandra?" Reverend Joseph's voice called up the staircase. "Kassandra, darling, I know you are up there. Come down here, please."

Kassandra gingerly took the steps down into the kitchen where Reverend Joseph stood, his arms outstretched.

"Come here," he said, and his voice was full of such kindness that Kassandra felt pulled into his embrace, falling against him, her face buried in the dark wool of his vest. She hadn't yet cried at Clara's death, and even now tears wouldn't come. Instead she wrapped her arms around the reverend's thin body, felt his long arms fold themselves over her shoulders. This was the second time she'd stood in this kitchen, wrapped in the arms of a man, only this time instead of an insidious shameful panic lurking at the edges of her spirit, she felt only comfort and love and strength. She wanted to lift her head, look up into Reverend Joseph's face, and tell him that she'd killed Clara—as much as if she'd gone into the room and ripped the failing heart right out of the woman's breast.

The silence was punctuated only by Reverend Joseph's soothing murmurs until Kassandra, her face smashed against him, not fully aware that she was speaking aloud, said, "You are a good man, aren't you?"

"What did you say, darling?" Reverend Joseph said, pulling himself away to look down at Kassandra's face.

She looked up into those kind brown eyes, not nearly as far

away as they used to be, and spoke with strength and conviction. "I said, you are a kind man. A good man."

Reverend Joseph chuckled a bit. "I try to be a good man, yes."

"You gave those people all of her things. And that man money…"

"Well, now, Sparrow," Reverend Joseph eased himself away and pulled out a chair, indicating that Kassandra should do the same. "I'm not sure if that was exactly the right thing to do, the money. Sometimes we take actions and hope that God will make something good come out of them. He can do that, you know, take any horrible event and turn it into a blessing."

"What if," Kassandra said, studying the fabric of her skirt, "what if we do something bad? Can God make something good come of that?"

"The Scriptures tell us that all things work together for good for those that love God. Now, my dear," she felt his finger on her chin, lifting her face to look at him, "is there something you want to talk about?"

"I—" *killed her*, she wanted desperately to say, but her courage failed her. "I am not always good."

"Of course you're not." He smiled that warm smile, and the sight of it brought such a load of guilt to her heart that she had to look away. Not down, but just past him, to the small wooden cross hanging on the wall.

"None of us are good all of the time," he continued. "God knows that. That's why His forgiveness is part of His divine plan, so when we do sin—whether it is something big or small—we need not carry the weight of it on ourselves. Now, what do you need to tell me?"

Kassandra didn't answer right away, but pondered what Reverend Joseph had just said—*big or small*.

"It isn't your fault, you know."

His words jarred her out of her reverie, brought her eyes directly back to his own.

"My fault?"

"I know you and Clara were quarreling yesterday afternoon."

"How did you—"

"You and Clara often quarreled. I know right now when you remember her, you are thinking of all the warm and loving times you shared. It's natural and good to remember those things."

"She was very angry with me."

"But her anger didn't stop her heart, Sparrow. She had a hard life before she came to live here. And she worked very hard taking care of me. And us."

"I should not have—" she searched for the words. "I think I made her work too hard."

Reverend Joseph laughed softly. "Nonsense. She was happy. Oh, she may have grumbled a bit, but I know the woman she was when she showed up on my doorstep looking for work, and I know the woman she became over the years. She felt safe and protected here. We gave her a good home, Kassandra. A kind family. That's all any woman really wants."

Kassandra looked around the cozy kitchen. Spotless as always, the only dishes piled on the counter were the stacks of teacups and saucers from the morning's parade of visitors. Hidden in the bread box was half of Clara's last loaf of bread, and in the center of the table where they sat was a little tray holding three jars of her good jam.

"She always said this was her kitchen."

"And so it was. But now she is in the most beautiful house imaginable. Safe with God, and happier than she has ever been in her life. We can be sad at her passing, but she spent a lifetime here waiting to be with God. She's probably sweeping the streets of gold right now, grumbling that the angels track in too much heavenly mud."

Now it was Kassandra's turn to laugh, softly, and Reverend Joseph seemed to take her laughter as a great reward. She couldn't rob that joy from him now. She didn't want to drag his thoughts away from this celestial vision to the mire of what she and Ben had done in this very room—Clara's kitchen. Instead, she brightened her smile and said, "Thank you, Reverend Joseph," and stood to place a sweet kiss on the top of his head, where his thinning blond hair revealed a pink scalp.

Before she could walk away, he grabbed her hand, stopping her by his side.

"Can I ask one thing of you, Kassandra?"

"Yes, sir," she said, turning.

"There's an empty crate just outside on the back porch. Would you please take it into Clara's room and pack up her things? I'll take them to the funeral service and give them to her minister. I'm sure there are many needy people in his congregation who could make good use of them."

As it turned out, there wasn't much for Kassandra to pack. Two skirts, four blouses, half a dozen aprons, all laundered crisp and clean, even those she'd worn the day before. She'd taken the time to wash out her shirt and socks before lying down to die. One pair of shoes showed all the signs of her heavy step; a wooden-handled brush played host to springs of gray hair.

There was a well-worn Bible on the small table beside the bed. Kassandra opened it, flipped through the pages now soft with years of touching, turning, but not reading. Clara had many tricks to hide her illiteracy, often making excuses for Kassandra to read aloud. What did she do with this book? Hold it? Look at the words scattered across the page? It seemed unfair, somehow, that Clara would have this book while Kassandra still didn't have one of her own, reading from Reverend Joseph's huge leather-bound volume in his library when it was time to have her daily Scripture lesson.

She folded each item one by one and placed it carefully in the crate, thinking about all the trinkets that had already been given to Clara's loved ones and hoping that these few items would be put to good use. That's what Clara would have wanted; she was a generous soul in her own way. The Bible was laid on the top of the pile, surrounded by a nest of starched, clean aprons.

An entire life packed in one small crate.

She took the crate into the kitchen and set it on the table—Clara's table—and was suddenly overcome with exhaustion. It was just after two in the afternoon, and the sleepless night and busy morning finally had the best of her. She was hungry, too, having only had the smallest nibble of toast sometime earlier that morning. But fixing a snack seemed like far too much work, and she hoped to be upstairs and in bed before Reverend Joseph returned from his visit with the funeral director and Clara's minister with yet another chore for her to do. She started toward the stairs, but paused to run her fingers over the pile of worldly goods Clara left behind.

"I loved you, Clara," she spoke into the empty kitchen, and almost heard Clara's impatient *hmph* at such frivolous speech. Her hand rested now on Clara's Bible—gripped it, really—and without much thought she lifted the book, clutched it to her breast, and fairly ran for the stairs.

Clara never would have allowed much weeping in her kitchen.

7

*C*lara's funeral would not be the first one for Kassandra. As a member of the minister's household, she was often expected to attend the services and burial of his parishioners. It would, however, be the first time for her to face a corpse of her own creation, and the thought of doing so churned her stomach so that she used the illness as her first excuse to stay home.

"Nonsense, Sparrow," Reverend Joseph said as she stood at his elbow, clutching her stomach, hoping the slight squint to her eyes would enhance her greenish complexion. "It's just nerves. And a little sorrow. You'll feel better on Monday."

Then she pointed out that she didn't have a black dress; Clara always said it wasn't proper for such a young girl to wear black.

"It won't be the first time you wore your good dark blue to a funeral," Reverend Joseph told her, surprising Kassandra that he could catalog her wardrobe. "You'll look just fine."

In the end it was the Misses Austine who provided Kassandra sanctuary from her final confrontation with Clara. As she and Reverend Joseph were walking out of their front gate on the way to the funeral that Monday afternoon, the sister spinsters were just arriving with a pot of baked beans.

"We assumed that with your Clara dead, you may need some help in the kitchen," one of them—the taller one actually holding the pot—said.

"Well, that is very kind of you indeed," Reverend Joseph

said, putting an awkwardly protective arm around Kassandra. "Isn't it, Kassandra?"

Kassandra nodded.

"Are you on your way to the funeral?" asked the other sister who had a dish towel-covered pan of what Kassandra really hoped was some sort of cake.

"Yes, we are," Reverend Joseph said, turning back toward the gate. "But we can spare a few moments to walk into the kitchen with you to leave the food."

The Misses Austine exchanged a glance between the two of them, making no attempt to hide their disapproval.

"Now, really, Reverend Joseph," said beans Austine, "do you really think that's a good idea?"

"Yes," chimed her sister. "To take this young girl to where those people—"

"Now, Miss Austine," Reverend Joseph said. "Clara was a good Christian woman."

"Really?" twittered beans. "I thought she was a Baptist." The sisters shared a giggle, and Reverend Joseph graced them with a slight smile. "But honestly, Reverend, the church is in a very unsavory neighborhood, I'm sure. And she is just a young girl. Mightn't she feel a little uncomfortable, out of place?"

"It is a funeral, Miss Austine," Reverend Joseph said, swinging the gate wide open, "not a church social."

Kassandra had been listening to every word, turning her head back and forth with each addition to the exchange. She didn't want to capitalize on the Misses Austine's prejudice, but she couldn't ignore this final opportunity.

"Reverend Joseph," she said, tugging his coat sleeve, looking up at him plaintively, "Clara never wanted me to go to her church."

"What are you saying, Sparrow?"

"I always wanted to go and see. Her church sounded so different from ours," Kassandra said, drawing a slight snort from the Misses Austine. "But she never wanted me to. Said that it wasn't a place for a young white girl like me."

"Kassandra," he said, moving his body to create a barricade between her and the Misses Austine, "you never told me this."

"It was quite some time ago," Kassandra said, shifting her feet. "But maybe they wouldn't want me to be there."

Reverend Joseph gave a sigh of resignation and held out his arm, gesturing for the ladies in attendance to go through it into the house. "If you really won't be comfortable there, I suppose there's no harm in letting you stay home. We may have more people in to pay their respects."

"Oh, thank you, Reverend Joseph," Kassandra said, hugging him tight around his waist.

The Misses Austine exchanged yet another disapproving glance as their skirts brushed past her on their way to the front porch.

And so it was that Kassandra found herself completely alone in Reverend Joseph's house. She couldn't remember the last time she'd been wholly alone—Clara and the reverend were rarely gone at the same time—and she wasn't completely sure what to do. The kitchen was no longer comfortable, with so many memories of Clara in every corner, and her upstairs room was uncomfortably stuffy in the late spring afternoon. Reverend Joseph's study was out of the question, leaving only the formal dining room or the parlor in which Kassandra could settle down with her schoolbooks. After all, Reverend Joseph had been quick to point out, she had been given permission to miss school to attend the funeral. Now that she wasn't going, she needed to keep up with her day's lesson.

So, trying very hard to concentrate on the Battle of Waterloo, Kassandra curled up on one end of the parlor's sofa (how Clara would have hated seeing her stocking feet up on such fine upholstery), making herself read and reread whenever her mind trailed off to the circumstances that had brought her to this afternoon alone.

When she heard the knock at the door, she sighed and put her book down. Her back popped a little as she stretched before crossing the parlor to the door, and she got her face ready to register polite gratitude for the offered flowers or food.

The image she saw through the clouded glass door, however, stopped her dead in her tracks. She recognized the silhouette of that cap and the cocky posture—shoulders thrown back, hands in jacket pockets—and the familiar whistled tune. Her hand went cold as it reached for the knob and opened the door to Ben.

"I saw the reverend leave a while ago," he said by way of greeting. "Without you with him."

"What are you doing here?"

"Went to the back door like always. Guess you didn't hear me knockin'."

"You should not be here," Kassandra said, but even as she spoke Ben was shouldering his way past her into the entryway, never looking back as he walked straight into the front parlor.

"Blast, but this is a fine house," he said, never turning to look at Kassandra. He walked the perimeter of the room, his eyes taking in every inch of the furnishings, the paintings on the walls, the carpet. "And you with this all to yourself?"

"You should not be here," Kassandra repeated, following him. "It is not proper, us being here alone."

"Oh, now, Kassie," Ben said, moving toward one of the high-backed chairs facing the sofa, "aren't you going to ask me to sit down?"

"No."

He sat anyway, stretching his legs out in front of him and settling himself back in the cushions.

"I was just worried about you is all," he said, his eyes still roving around the room. "I heard about what happened. Poor woman. I thought she didn't look well."

"How could you have heard?"

"People talk. One maid tells another, who tells another, who comes to the Points to visit some relative. I hear things. Now sit down, Kassie girl. You're makin' me nervous standin' there."

Kassandra wasn't sure whether she should feel flattered or frightened that Ben took such pains to know what was happening in her life, so she forced herself to ignore the cautionary knot forming in the pit of her stomach. She picked up her abandoned history text from the sofa and clutched it to her as she perched nervously on the edge of the sofa.

"So tell me, darlin'. How are you holdin' up?"

"Just fine."

"You don't look fine, Kassie. You don't look fine at all. You look a little…scared."

"Not at all." She clutched her book more tightly to her.

"I saw how angry that woman—Clara, wasn't it?—looked when I left here the other day. You two must have had quite the argument."

"Not really," Kassandra said, Clara's accusations ringing in her head.

"That kind of anger? And the woman not feelin' well to begin with?" Ben punctuated his thoughts with a shrug that made the conclusion obvious.

In that one simple gesture he expressed every thought that had been haunting her since Reverend Joseph came to her room. For just a moment she felt relieved, grateful for a chance to unburden her soul to somebody who understood, but she stopped herself short of a full confession, knowing that voicing the suspicion would make it undeniably true. She hadn't been able to even look at herself in a mirror since awakening to Clara's death, being unable to face her accuser, and every silent second spent in that parlor took Ben from confidant to conspirator, and she was suddenly unable to face him, either.

"Please, Ben," she said, her eyes closed against him, "do not say that."

"Now, don't fret about it."

She couldn't see him, but his voice was coming closer, until it was just outside her ear, and his hand was resting on her shoulder.

"It can't be entirely your fault, can it? For a heart to just stop like that—no matter how agitated a person might get—there was probably somethin' wrong to begin with."

"No, no." She trembled under his touch, and the tears that needed to be shed for days finally began a slow, painful course down her face.

"I'm just tryin' to make you feel better. Don't cry, Kassie. Hush now."

Kassandra's arms went slack around her book as Ben's arm snaked across her shoulders. The tome was lifted out of her grip and dropped to the ground, and his other arm brought her into a full embrace. She felt the coarse material of his shirt against her skin, her tears soaking his shoulder. When he spoke again, softly just above her ear, she felt the vibrations of his throat against her face.

"You didn't tell him, did you," he said. "About what we— why Clara was so angry."

She shook her head against him.

"Of course you didn't. And why should ya, knowin' how he'd feel?" He scooted back from her, held her at arm's length, and she opened her eyes. "Do you remember what it felt like? To kiss me?"

"Stop it," she said, worming out of his arms and standing to tower above him. When he, too, stood, she turned and started to walk away.

"Ah, Kassie," Ben said, grabbing her arm. "I loved you the first time I saw you. Don't you love me, too? Just a little bit?"

"How could I know that?" she said, not turning around until the slightest twist of her arm forced her to.

"Kassie, come away with me. Right now."

There was no glint of humor in his voice or in his eyes. No impish grin of a little boy planning an adventurous lark. Until this moment, that was exactly how she had thought of him—childlike and fun, always quick with some silly joke to make her laugh. But now she saw him as a man, a man with an entire life lived beyond this house and their playful encounters in the kitchen. A life he was offering to her.

"Go upstairs," his voice intensified. "Get your things."

"I could never leave Reverend Joseph. He needs me to—"

"To what? Waste your life shufflin' around here? Breakin' your back servin' him for the next twenty years until your heart just stops in the middle of the night and you die in your little room off the kitchen?"

"And what would my life be with you?"

"Whatever you want it to be, Kassie girl. They're pullin' gold out of the ground in California. Got ships leavin' the docks every day takin' people there to find their fortune."

"I've never been on a boat."

"We could leave the city. Buy a little farm. Have hundreds of cows and dozens of children and breathe in that sweet country air doctors are always screamin' about."

The ghost of the imp was back, and she giggled despite the growing discomfort of his grip on her arm.

"Or we could go down south. I've spent a few winters workin' down there. The place is bustin' with—"

"Reverend Joseph is an abolitionist," she said. "He'd never allow—"

"He won't be part of it! He's got no claim to you, Kassie. He doesn't love you like I do."

"He does love me."

"Yeah," he said, finally releasing her and gesturing grandly about the room, "like this fine furniture and these fancy carpets. You're a thing he has, one he doesn't know what to do with."

He stopped dead in the center of the room and adopted a perfect pose of Reverend Joseph, somehow transforming himself to the reverend's height and making his compact, muscled body take on a gaunt bearing. He brought one hand to his chin, stroked it thoughtfully, and spoke in a voice devoid of his slight Irish brogue and rich with the deep tones of her beloved companion.

"Should I adopt her? Marry her? Better move her down to the kitchen before I forget myself and creep into her bed one night—"

"Stop it," Kassandra said, offended at the reverend's portrayal, but strangely fascinated and amused at Ben's ease of imitation.

"He wouldn't fight for you, Kassie," Ben said, very much himself again. "Not like I would."

He bounded across the room to the large marbled fireplace against the far wall. Above the mantle, two ceremonial swords hung on the wall, crossed in a grand elegance. In a swift heroic gesture, Ben grasped the handle of one of the swords, sliding it off of its perch with a screech of steel across iron and swung it through the air in a frantic simulation of a duel.

Kassandra burst out now in full laughter. Ben hopped around the room, fully lost in his mock thrusts and parries, making *"clink, clink"* sounds as his sword contacted that of his imaginary foe. She had been to the theater with Reverend Joseph, had seen trained actors on stage engaged in the ballet of battle, and the sight of this redheaded, freckled comedian attempting to capture that fervor was immensely funny, until the blade came hazardously close to the drapes, threatening to tear a nasty snag in the heavy silk brocade.

"Ben!" she called out through her laughter. "Ben! Stop it."

"By God, Kassie," he said, breathless, but not pausing, "I swear I would run him through if he came between us." He punctuated his words with a final, brutish jab. "But tell me, darlin', can you see him fighting back?"

"Just put the sword down," she said, unwilling to tell him what she thought.

Ben walked back to the fireplace and rose up on his toes to return the sword to its resting place, not bothering to adjust it to its original angle.

"You should leave him, Kassie," he said, leaning against the marble wall, crossing his arms across his chest. "For his own sake."

"What do you mean?"

"Don't you think he'd like to get married someday?"

She glanced to the side, to the sofa where her history book lay forgotten on the floor, and envisioned the parade of Friday afternoon visitors—all those hopeful women vying to be mistress of this house. Most were rather sour-looking or timid, but there had been a few, young and pretty, just the type to be a faithful minister's wife, with sweet dispositions and an aura of kindness that would match Reverend Joseph's own heart. Sometimes, when these would leave after finishing their tea and cake, it seemed Reverend Joseph lingered a little longer at the closed door, sighed just a bit as he turned to carry the tray back to the kitchen.

"No woman is going to join herself to this household as long as you're in it," Ben said, invading her reverie. "You're a beautiful young thing. What woman would want to share her husband with the likes of that?"

"I am his family," Kassandra replied, a territorial edge to her voice.

"No, darlin', you're not." He crossed the room and stood close to her again. "No potential wife is going to see it that way. You're a woman, sharin' his home. You're not a daughter, you're not a servant. You're not a spinster sister or some distant cousin. You're a seedlin' he plucked off the street that grew into something beautiful." He brought his hand up and stroked her face. "Does he ever tell you you're beautiful?"

"It wouldn't be proper," she said, trying to turn from his touch, but his other hand was there to capture her, and she remained, locked into his gaze.

"You deserve to be with someone who thinks you're beautiful," he said, "who'll tell you every day that you are. Ah, Kassie," he whispered and brought his lips to hers, kissing her with exquisite softness.

She kept her eyes open and stood, rigid in her boots, unwilling to bend. But her staunch resolve only intensified her longing as Ben's lips scattered kisses across her face, fluttered against her eyes, trailed sweet promises just outside her ear and then back to her lips, questioning, wondering if they had paid their due, made their case.

Kassandra welcomed Ben's mouth to her own, wondering why she would rob herself of this feeling. The memory of their first kiss had been the only thing powerful enough to keep her mourning of Clara at bay, and now here that feeling was again, boldly expressed in the middle of the parlor, in the middle of the afternoon. The scandal of it made it that much more enticing, made her less resistant to Ben's advances as his hands worked their way across her back, to her waist, laying claim to her body. There were promises in his hands and in his lips, promises more enticing than all the gold in California.

"Come with me, Kassie. Will you?"

She knew right then that he would never ask her again.

"Yes."

The next moment was lost in an elated, victorious *"Whoop"* as Ben lifted Kassandra clean off the carpet, twirling her around the room. She clutched her arms tight around his shoulder, pulling in her feet lest they knock some priceless artifact off the end tables, and watched the room spin around her. Her mind was floating every bit as much as her body, full of the thoughts of endless days just like this afternoon, locked in passion, safe in the arms of this boy—this man, really—who wanted her beyond all reason.

Too soon, and breathless, Ben set her down again, both of them dizzy from their whirlwind. They laughed and kissed and laughed again. Once he had regained his breath, Ben took Kassandra's hands in his and looked into her eyes until her breath was as steady and sober as his own.

"Go upstairs now and get your things," he said. "I'll be waitin' for you at the back door."

"Don't be silly," Kassandra said. "I have to talk to Reverend Joseph. I have to tell him I am leaving."

"He'll never let you go, Kassie. No more than he'd let me walk out the door with a handful of his silver."

Kassandra felt the room spinning again, even though she was locked stock-still in Ben's grip. "It seems wrong. So sudden."

"That's when we get the best out of life, darlin'," he said, smiling the smile of that first afternoon. "When we take a chance."

Kassandra closed her eyes. Hadn't Reverend Joseph said that very thing just a few days ago? She felt a brief, gentle kiss on her forehead, and opened her eyes.

"Like I said, I'll be waitin' at the back door. For just about ten minutes." He pulled a gold watch from his pocket—a very nice piece for a butcher's delivery boy. "After ten minutes, love, I'll be leavin'." Another brief kiss on her cheek. "And you'll never see me again."

Precious minutes ticked by as Kassandra stood alone, frozen to the parlor's Persian carpet, her own eyes drinking in every bit of this home, seeing it for the first and last time simultaneously. She would come back soon, maybe as a Friday afternoon visitor, and explain everything.

She crept up to her room, moving in unnecessary silence as she opened her drawers, taking out her clean undergarments and stockings, laying them on top of the skirts and shirtwaists that covered the bed. In the center of the pile, she placed Clara's Bible and her bone-handled hairbrush. Her hair was plaited into one single braid that hung down her back; she coiled it into a knot and secured it with the pretty tiara comb. Finally, she took the tiny porcelain bird and wrapped it inside her winter night-gown, hoping the soft flannel would keep it safe on whatever journey lay ahead.

"*Are not two sparrows sold for a farthing?*" she said to the dark-ening room. "Please, God, if I am falling, promise to catch me."

Re-clothe us in our rightful mind;
In purer lives Thy service find,
In deeper reverence, praise.

assandra hadn't known what to expect as she followed Ben, trotting to meet his stride, through the backstreets and alleys of Reverend Joseph's neighborhood.

"We don't want anybody to think I've just come in and nabbed you," he'd said, hoisting her little bundle of belongings over his shoulder and grasping her arm to keep her close to his side. "We'd best make our way outside the pryin' eyes of the windows."

It seemed they walked forever, but Ben kept her amused and entertained with every step. He knew the family and story behind most of the houses they passed. There was a state senator with a mistress on the side. Ten blocks later—in a much seedier neighborhood—was the house of the actual mistress. There were mansions built from secret profits of the slave trade and humble cottages built with the sweat and dreams of the hopeful.

"Think about it, Kassie," he said pausing momentarily at a gated yard. "There's a story behind every door."

"How do you know them all?"

"I talk to the people. No man's too rich to tip my cap to." To prove this, he offered a friendly greeting to the obvious owner of the home. "An' if I don't talk to the owners, I talk to the servants. When nobody talks to me, I listen. You see, when you're poor, you become invisible. Them rich folks, they don't see me as bein' much more than a lump of dirt doin' their biddin'. We blend into the bricks."

"That is not true," Kassandra said, trying to keep his face in focus as she bounced beside him. "You completely captured *my* attention."

"How many times you reckon you walked right past me in the street? With your little hair ribbons and your snooty friends, gigglin' and carryin' on?"

"You—you saw me?"

"Stay there." He let go of her arm and walked ahead of her about twelve paces, then turned back. "Can you see me?"

"Of course I can, silly."

"I'm not too far away? Not hidin' behind a bush? It's not too dark?"

"What are you saying?"

"I was workin' day labor, buildin' the livery at the corner—"

"I remember."

"You remember the construction, maybe. But you don't remember me. You passed by every mornin' and afternoon on your way to school. You and that other girl—"

"Sarah James," she whispered.

"I remember you recitin' some poem about the saints gathered round Christ in heaven—"

"That was nearly two years ago!"

"And I'd hear your voice from half a block off, stop workin'—got in trouble for it more than once, I'll tell you—and watch you. Heard that poem so many times I learned some of it myself. There was one day you forgot a line, and I said it for you. You weren't any farther away from me than you are right now."

Kassandra felt her very breath go ice-cold. "I—I did not hear you."

"Nor see me, either. Like I said, us poor, we blend in."

"I am sorry, Ben."

"I'm not," he said, planting a quick kiss on her temple without breaking stride. "It gave me time to learn all about you. Where you're from. The poor little girl who got kicked by the horse and brought back to life in the reverend's fine home."

Kassandra stopped. "You know all about that?"

"Darlin' Kassie," he said, shifting the weight of her bundle higher on his shoulder. "Do you see? You were nothin' more than another cobblestone. C'mon, it's gettin' late."

They walked in silence through the duration of Park Avenue prosperity and shared a snack of roasted peanuts and lemonade bought from a street vendor at the edge of Union Square. There wasn't much opportunity for talk, either, as they battled their way south on Broadway where the tangled mass of carriages, carts, and horses made any form of conversation a dangerous distraction.

When they did talk, however, Kassandra continued to marvel at Ben's ease with the city. Just as he knew the stories behind the mansion doors, he could narrate the story behind the massive structures that lined the wide, paved streets of the city. He knew the name of the architect, the foreman of the construction crew, the legitimacy of the construction cost. He narrated—with exquisite detail and drama—the fiery circumstances behind piles of burned rubble. Block after block he brought life to every brick and stone, pointing out the passersby who lived in them, worked in them, built them. The tone of the stories shifted with each intersection. Eleventh Street, Tenth, Ninth—as the numbers descended, so did the evidence of economic prosperity. Fourth, Second, Third—and the numbers ran out.

"I have to stop," Kassandra said.

Some time before they hit the intersection of Broadway and Second Street, the city had gone full dark. Lamplighters were igniting the street torches, but Kassandra and Ben were the only motionless forms in a bustling block of shadows. Skirts swished by, heedless of the girl collapsed—exhausted—on the walkway, her aching feet spread straight out into the street, heedless of the carriage wheels passing precariously close to her pointed toes. She leaned her shoulder against the lamppost and sighed.

Ben dropped her bundle on the sidewalk and sat next to it.

"It's not much farther now, Kassie. We're more than halfway home."

Home.

"You did not tell me how far away you lived. You worked for Sampson's Butcher. I thought you lived…closer."

"What? On Fifth Avenue? You think I went back to my castle every day after droppin' off two pounds of bratwurst and a beef tongue?"

Before she could respond, Kassandra was jostled into Ben's lap as a man wedged himself between her and the lamppost, clumping his heavy boot in the lowest protruding rung and climbing to the top.

"Hey, watch out for the lady!" Ben reached across the bundle to put a protective arm around Kassandra.

"Shaddup," replied the lamplighter, without much energy or anger at all. In just a second he was gone, and Kassandra and Ben were bathed in the eerie glow of the gaslight.

"You walked this far?" Kassandra asked. "Every day?"

"Not every day, love. Just on Fridays. Just to see you."

"I just do not know if I can go back there." She gazed past Ben, down the dark narrowing street.

"Back to the Points?" he asked. "Or back to bein' poor? 'Cause there's no shame in poverty, my love."

"I know that—"

"And for all that fine house, the kind reverend never took you out of it. He may have brought you out of the Points, but he never made you rich. That's nothin' one man can do for another. Now," he stood towering over her, blocking the steady glow of the streetlight and casting her in shadow, "you can come an' be poor with me, or stay here on this street and go it alone. But I've got a home waitin' for me—for us—an' it's not as fancy as what you've known, but it's not as dire as what you're thinkin'."

He held out his hand, and even as she allowed him to pull her up from the street, she wasn't entirely sure of the choice she would make. But as Ben once again shouldered the bundle containing all her earthly possessions, there seemed to be little option but to take the first, then second step behind him, joining the flow of humanity as they headed further south to Canal Street.

She was back in Five Points, but at least she wasn't alone.

Ben and Kassandra picked their way carefully, stepping over bundles of drunken rags and dodging both flying fists and staggering revelers. Kassandra's relief at arriving at the place Ben called "home" was tempered when she looked up and saw the swinging placard above the door. Mott Street Tavern. Inside, the cavernous room was dimly lit by a series of lamps lining three of the four walls. The entire length of one side was taken up by a wooden bar with shelves behind it holding a variety of glass bottles and large wooden barrels stationed at each end. In between the bodies of milling men and women she saw glimpses of tables and chairs, but they were mostly abandoned as the crowd engaged in a frantic display of dance, desperately trying to match the tempo of the musicians on a platform in the far corner. There was no grace or fluidity to their movements—how could there be when notes of the straining fiddle and the rhythmless jangle of the tambourine could barely be heard above the raucous laughter and shouted conversation of what had to be nearly two hundred human souls?

Ben gripped her hand tighter and led her through the crowd, which parted for him much as she imagined the Red Sea did as Moses led his people out of their bondage. Men on either side clapped Ben's shoulder, shouting, "And who've we bagged tonight, eh, Bennie?" Women in brightly colored skirts and scandalously low-cut blouses stepped out of the sea entirely, standing square in front of him, leaning in to whisper. Kassandra couldn't hear what they said, but whatever it was, it brought Ben to smile like Kassandra had never seen before.

As they made their way to the back of the room, the notes of the musicians became clearer, the tune distinct, and Kassandra recognized it as one Ben often whistled to himself on the path between Reverend Joseph's back door and the gate. When he came to a door at the far end, he turned and motioned to her to stay put while he opened the door just a crack and peered in. Seeming satisfied, he opened it wide and ushered her through into utter darkness.

"The stairs are right here," he said, still needing to raise his voice above the barely muffled din behind them. "Stay close."

He needn't have warned her. Kassandra wished there were some way to meld her feet to his, lest she be left alone in this blackness. With one hand she grabbed a handful of his shirt and braced the other against the wall as they made their way up a narrow passage. When they got to the landing on the second floor, she was relieved to see a dimly lit hallway.

"You stay off this floor," Ben said, not pausing in his stride. "This is where some of the girls from downstairs bring their men."

"Their men? Oh…" The warning was clear when she saw three women clad only in chemises and pantalets lounging in open doorways.

The hallway on the third floor was completely dark, and the noise downstairs had diminished to a low, consistent rumble. Kassandra stepped onto the landing, never letting go of her grip on Ben's shirt, and allowed him to lead her down, down, down the narrow hallway. She followed so closely that when he did stop, she nearly knocked him over.

"Sorry," she said.

"Wait here." He reached behind him to pry his shirt out of her grip.

Kassandra heard the sound of a doorknob, then found herself alone in utter darkness for just a moment, until the sound of a striking match brought welcome illumination.

"Now then," Ben said, returning to her at the door's threshold, "seems only fittin' that I carry you across."

The entire room could fit within Reverend Joseph's parlor. Ben nearly ran the few steps it took to cross the room to the opposite wall. "We got two windows. *Two!* We'll get sunlight durin' the day, and a nice little breeze at night." As if in response, the thin fabric hanging on either side of the pane gave a faint ripple.

A shelf ran the length of the shortest wall, holding Ben's meager supply of cookware and dishes, and in the corner opposite the door was a small cookstove. In the middle of the room sat a small table covered by a faded floral cloth and two chairs. In the middle of the table, a single kerosene lamp now burned, bathing the entire room in warm light.

Then, in the farthest corner, the bed. It had an ornate iron headboard and a colorful quilt. According to Ben's current chatter, his mother had brought it over from Ireland. Next to the bed stood a dresser—four drawers and a washbasin on top—but Kassandra's eyes fell back on the bed.

"Where am I to sleep?"

"Ah, now, Kassie dear, surely you know the answer to that."

She did, of course, although all the fantasies stemming from Ben's kisses fell short of the piece of furniture glaring at her from the corner of the darkened room.

"Right now? Tonight?"

"Ach," he said, uttering a noise that captured a mixture of amusement and frustration, "you're spent now. C'mon. Sit."

He pulled one of the chairs out from the table and gestured to it grandly. Kassandra sank down in it, comforted by its sturdiness. She scooted down until her head came to rest against the chair's back. "I could just sleep here," she said.

"Give me your foot."

Kassandra opened one eye to see Ben kneeling at her feet, her boot propped on his knee. He untied the laces, then gently slipped it off.

"Stockin', too." He reached up her skirt to find where the top of her stocking was cinched tight, just above her knee, and peeled the stocking away, then repeated the gesture with the other foot.

"How's that?" He held her foot in his hand, gently massaging first one and then the other, and the sensation was nothing short of heaven.

"Now, let's find your nightgown and get you into bed. You're exhausted."

He gently set her foot onto the floor and began to go through her things. The first item brought out of the bundle was Clara's Bible. "This'll be handy," he said, fanning through the pages before placing it in the middle of the table right next to the lamp.

Next he unfolded her blouses and skirts and walked to the wall next to the bed where a blanket hung from a rope spanning corner to corner. He pulled the blanket back, revealing a series of hooks where two shirts and a pair of trousers hung. Ben moved some of his clothing aside, making room for Kassandra's, then closed the blanket back over the lot.

"Quite fancy, eh?" he said with amusement as he pawed through her underthings before opening the top drawer of the dresser to deposit them.

Finally, he came across her nightgown.

"Careful," she said. "There is something wrapped inside it."

"Is there now?" Slowly he turned the bundle, until the top of the little china bird popped out of the fabric. "Well, isn't this a pretty?"

He lifted the figurine out of its flannel nest, and Kassandra let out a grateful breath knowing it was intact.

"This'll go right up on the dresser," Ben said.

In just a few minutes, every item that was a part of Kassandra's life was placed away neatly in Ben's world.

"Come now, love. Let's get you undressed."

He took her hands in his and pulled her to her feet, guiding her the few steps across the room to the bed. He kissed her once, softly, then went to work unfastening the row of delicate bone buttons down the front of her bodice. She brought her hands up to grip his wrists.

"Stop that."

Ben smiled, lifted his hands up and kissed Kassandra's fingers until she loosened her grip. A little. He took her face in his hands and kissed her deeply, once, then gently, twice.

"Listen to me," he said, his voice a more serious, intimate tone than she had ever heard from him before. "I won't do anythin' to hurt you. D'you believe that?"

Kassandra nodded.

"An' I'll be good to you. And gentle. Have I ever given you any reason to fear me?"

Kassandra broke her gaze away and looked around the room, sparse and foreign and throbbing with the sounds of the saloon downstairs and the laughter of those women on the floor below.

"Not this place," Ben insisted, commanding her attention again. "Me. Ben. You trusted me enough to come away with me, didn't you now? You can trust me here."

"But Ben, we're not... Should we not get married first?"

"All in good time, my love. All in good time. Now, I'm goin' downstairs to have a drink. Let you settle in."

He gave her one last peck on the cheek before turning and walking out the door. Left alone, Kassandra sank onto the mattress, unable to take any comfort in its softness. Something told her she should cry, but tears seemed childish as she sat on this bed that she would share with this...man.

A sense of calm resolve overtook her as she resumed undressing, hanging her clothes on one of the hooks behind the blanket and dropping her summer nightgown over her head, loving the feel of it as it settled on her shoulders and billowed protectively around her. She picked up her brush from its new home on Ben's dresser, took down her hair, and sat on the edge of the bed, brushing it thoughtfully just as she had every evening of her life.

"Genesis, Exodus, Leviticus, Numbers..." she recited with each stroke. It was a game she'd played with Clara, a way to prepare herself for Reverend Joseph's Bible lessons. She wondered if she would ever again be called upon to recite these books. By the time she reached "Jude and Revelation," she was so tired it seemed a heroic effort to be able to replace the brush on the dresser top. She did, though, just before pulling back Ben's mother's Irish quilt and sinking beneath it.

She was in bed. Ben's bed.

Kassandra had vague ideas about what it meant for a man and a woman to share a bed together, pieced together mostly from sly passages in forbidden novels and giggled conversations in the school yard. Sarah James was a particularly fertile source of information, having accidentally walked in on her Uncle Stephen James and the third-floor maid one afternoon, but her account of what she saw was fraught with such comic implausibility that Kassandra had dismissed it.

She got out of bed and padded across the room to turn out the lamp, and it wasn't until she was alone in utter darkness that the enormity of her decision hit. Her knees buckled beneath her, and she fell to them and crawled until her outstretched hand met the intricate Celtic stitching. Instead of climbing into the bed, however, she remained on the floor.

"Holy Father," she said, then stopped. Had she fallen to her knees earlier in her own room, by her own bed, would she be here now? "Forgive me, Lord, for not seeking Your will." But surely she wasn't the first person ever to act on impulse. Did Jonah not flee from God? She opened her eyes and was able to make out a few shapes in the room with the little light let in through the small window. It wasn't exactly the belly of a whale.

"Please, dear Father, hold Reverend Joseph close to you."

Right now he was probably mad with fear, calling her name, searching the neighborhood, calling on friends, anyone, asking if they had seen his little Sparrow. "Help him to find peace and comfort. Speak to him, Lord. Let him know that I am...well."

She climbed up into the bed and pulled the quilt up to her chin. She turned her eyes to the ceiling beams above her and whispered, "Please, dear God, keep me from harm. Amen."

She must have fallen asleep, though she would have sworn that the noise downstairs and the fear in her heart would have kept her awake. But sometime in the night she was awakened by the sound not of an opening door, not of a footstep, but of the rustle of a mattress and the whisper of her name.

"Kassie, my love. Turn to me."

Strong hands willed her to obey.

"I have never—"

"Ssh, ssh now, darlin'. I'll be easy."

She should have panicked. Should have pushed him away, run screaming from the room. Thrown herself into the crowd downstairs hoping that at least one soul would take pity on her. Take her away. Should have cried out through the window for Reverend Joseph who, for all she knew, had followed them every step of the way and was waiting outside right now—his carriage ready to once again take her out of this place and back to his safe, chaste home.

But she did none of those things, because on that first night Kassandra came to two conclusions. For as much as he promised to be gentle, Ben was a man of his word. And Sarah James was right about everything, down to the last detail.

~ 9 ~

The stench reminded her, in the first hours of every new day, that she was once again a creature of the city. The tiny apartment window, thrown open to alleviate the stifling heat of the summer night, ushered in some semblance of a breeze, but with that came the fetid evidence of the teeming life three stories below. She had lived in this filth as a child—scavenged through it, fought through it, bedded down in it—without ever giving any thought to its source. Now, though, her senses could pick out each element in isolation. Putrid, rotting food left for the foraging pigs that roamed the streets and alleys. Animal carcasses left too long at the slaughterhouse. Piles of muck left from the countless beasts that pulled the countless carts of vendors and artisans mingled with the sewage seeped out of overburdened outhouses. It clung to her skirts and stuck to her shoes, wormed its way into her home, swarmed, inescapable, over every inch of her life.

Except, perhaps, their bed.

Long before daylight would revive the relatively quiet streets, Kassandra would lie in bed, eyes closed against the predawn shadows, and search for something clean to smell. If she'd had a chance to do a washing, she would bring a corner of the bedsheet to her face, cup it around her nose and mouth, and breathe in deep the odor of the cheap soap that lingered in the worn fibers. When she could, she would buy a small bunch of violets from one of the wide-eyed little girls on a street corner and sleep with it under her pillow until its fragrance became little more than a faint hint of green.

Most often, though, it was Ben himself who provided her with a brief respite from the foul odors of the city. Sleeping beside her, one arm pinning her to the mattress, Ben never seemed to carry an assaulting scent. He reminded her of Reverend Joseph's black oilskin coat, which repelled the harshest raindrops, sending them into harmless rivulets snaking down the sleeves. On these mornings, she would turn to him, carefully maneuvering under the weight of his arm, and sneak her cheek across his shoulder until her nose just touched the hollow at the base of his throat. There she breathed. Deep. His skin smelled of ginger, though she could never trace the source. In the early days she had followed behind him, sniffing the cake of soap he slivered and worked into a furious lather before shaving each evening, but it smelled like glycerin and lye. Not like Ben. On particularly hot nights, the ginger mixed with a thin sheen of sweat that evaporated under her breath as she buried her face in his skin, drinking in that sweet, warm scent.

Soon she would feel his arms draw her closer, the first kiss of the day planted on the top of her head. She would look up, know that his eyes were still hidden behind his freckled lids and dusky lashes.

"Mornin', Kassie, my love," he'd say, his voice heavy with dozing.

And she knew she would be able to hold her nose and plunge through another day.

In the first weeks after their arrival, Kassandra had been too fearful of the squalor of the neighborhood to venture far from the little apartment above Mott Street Tavern. Leaving only for the most necessary excursions, she spent long afternoons sitting at the open window, looking out on the raucous lives below. She felt a little like one of those princesses in the fairy tales Reverend Joseph used to read to her as a child—trapped in a tower, waiting for rescue from an uncertain fate. But in the end it was the tower keeper himself who saved her from exile, as Ben took her hand one afternoon, saying, "Come on, Kassie love, it's not as bad as all that," and began to introduce her into his world.

There was a clamorous volume to life on the streets. Men and women, standing not eight inches apart from each other, shouted their conversations over the constant noise of the jangling harnesses and rumbling wheels of the ever-present wagons, carriages, carts, and cabs that jockeyed for a clear path on the narrow streets. The street vendors—proprietors and drivers of many of those vehicles—shouted even louder, hawking their wares and services to the masses. Chimney sweeps strolled the sidewalks singing, "Sweep-o, sweep-o your chimbley today; sweep-o, sweep-o the black soot away!" Ragmen drove their wagons, shouting offers of two cents per pound of "good, clean rags" and two bits a bushel for bones.

At the corner of Mulberry and Canal, a fat man with a blond beard sold baked pears. After pocketing Ben's nickel, he lifted two of them, dripping with syrup, from the shallow metal baking pan. Kassandra took her pear by the stem—as the man had demonstrated—and brought it to her mouth, sinking her teeth into the warm, sweet fruit. After weeks of nothing but bread and cheese and coffee in Ben's apartment, it was the nicest treat she could imagine. So consumed was she with her snack that she failed to hear all of the conversation between Ben and the purveyor of the pear and was surprised when she saw the man reach into the same pocket where he had deposited Ben's nickel and draw from it a handful of bills which were handed back over to Ben.

"Why did he give you that money?" Kassandra asked, wiping a drizzle of syrupy pear juice from her chin.

"Just a matter of business, darlin'," he said, devouring half of his own pear in three bites before tossing the core into the street as a contribution to the pungent smell.

There were, it seemed, several matters of business all along the blocks that Ben and Kassandra strode together. As they made their way down Mulberry Street, across Bayard and back up Mott towards home, Ben stopped at several establishments, met their proprietors at the door, and left with his pockets considerably richer for the conversation. With some patrons there was a genuine affection to their greetings, but others spoke through tight-lipped resentment. He shook the hands of well-dressed, well-groomed businessmen who would offer Kassandra a gentlemanly nod in greeting, though Ben never formally introduced her. He also offered chaste kisses to brazen women of low reputation who eyed Kassandra with a leering grin before giving Ben a wink and a nudge, saying, "Popped you a good un, eh, Bennie?"

When he wasn't conducting a matter of business, Ben was waylaid on the street, caught at the elbow by some young man or another. She'd seen many of them before, as they were regular visitors to Mott Street Tavern. Each doffed his hat in polite greeting to "Miss Kassandra," revealing close-cropped hair that defied the style of the time. They all had clean-shaven faces—not a moustache or beard among them—and seemed, in comparison to many of the other men on the street, meticulously clean. Most wore green kerchiefs tied around their necks, and Kassandra had heard enough conversation about them to know they were called Branagans. Ben's Branagans. Whenever one of these men came up to talk to Ben, Kassandra leaned in to listen, curious to know what matters needed to be discussed with such urgency. But she was usually disappointed when Ben would clap his arm around the shoulder of his confidant and take several steps away.

It was one of these men—tall and strong with piercing black eyes, jet-black hair, and a face with continuous stubble that would sprout without effort into a beard if ever allowed—who stopped Ben just outside a shoe repair shop. His name was Sean, Kassandra recalled, and he wasted little time tipping his cap to her before letting flow a stream of language, speaking syllables that sounded like they were delivered through a mouth full of cotton. Kassandra could not understand a word of it, but knew from hearing some of it tossed about in the streets that he was speaking Gaelic. Then, to her utter surprise, Ben responded in kind, allowing Kassandra to listen to every word. Though the topic was unclear, the feelings behind it were not. By the end of his talk with Sean, Ben was furious in the stony, jaw-clenched way that often made Kassandra reach down for her quietest self, disappearing until the anger passed. Within the space of an afternoon Ben became a complete stranger before her eyes.

When Sean finished his conversation, he clapped Ben on the back, received a reassuring return gesture, and actually offered a polite smile to Kassandra before leaving. Ben started again on his trek up Mott Street, seemingly unaware that Kassandra was not following. He was at least ten paces away before turning, signaling for her to join him, and finally walking back to her side, where he reached for her wrist and gave it a strong tug.

Kassandra refused to move, standing as if mired in the street. Indeed, glancing down, she saw there was plenty to be mired in, as her boots were precariously close to a steaming pile of horse dung.

"Tell me about Sean," she said, forcing authority into her voice.

"He's a friend. That's all you need to know." He gave a more forceful tug of her wrist. "C'mon."

"No, Ben," Kassandra said, finding the courage to refuse to take another step. "Tell me what is happening. Why are these people giving you money? Are you collecting some kind of rent?"

Ben laughed and dropped her hand. "What? D'ya think I'm a secret millionaire, hidin' my fortune in my cap?" He turned and bowed to her, taking off his cap as if to prove its lack of fortune. "No, Kassie. There's no money ownin' a buildin' in the Points. One minute y'have a thrivin' trade, the next a pile of ashes."

To punctuate his point, he nodded toward a structure

scorched by fire, having lost only its topmost floor while its neighbor was nothing more than a blackened foundation.

"Then wh—"

"It's the people inside," Ben interrupted, quickening his pace. "Let the landlords own the property, take their rents and sit back, fat and rich off the lives of the poor man livin' and workin' in it. Me? I own the people. Just a bit of 'em—" he said, holding up his hands in a gesture of defense against Kassandra's indignation, "—not enough to tear the flesh, but enough to make 'em feel the pinch of it."

Kassandra felt her own flesh prickle at the utter calm and seeming humor behind Ben's words. Even with this she didn't fully understand his meaning, and she was still deciding whether or not she really wanted clarification when a voice called from across the street.

"Connor! I gotta piece with you!"

The voice scattered the people gathered around the front of the property—a grocery store that sold produce and daily goods stocked on floor-to-ceiling shelves, and a barrel of uncertain liquor set up on the counter from which customers could siphon a nickel shot before leaving with their purchases. The man himself looked rather like a barrel, with his tiny feet and a smallish head that capped a large, round middle.

"What's your problem, Kinley?" Ben asked.

"You're not getting a dime from me this week, Connor. You hear me? Not a dime!"

"Now, Kinley, you know that's not true," Ben said, the compassionate tone of his voice a far cry from the implied threat of his words.

"Oh, it is true." Mr. Kinley nervously fumbled with the apron that covered a pair of stained, brown striped trousers and a sweat-soaked shirt. He wore small round spectacles, and try as he might to hold eye contact with Ben, his gaze was soon darting past him, to the small gathering of Branagans, all with shorn hair and jaunty caps, who seemed to have come from out of nowhere to gather in a loose semicircle behind Ben. "It's just—uh—I been robbed, Mr. Connor. Three times this week."

"I know you have, Kinley. My boys told me." Ben gestured grandly behind him. "My men haven't caught up with him, yet."

"Well, ha!" Kinley said, like a man taken with a sudden draught of courage. "Guess what? I got him! Myself! Got him locked in my cellar!" He rubbed his hands together in pudgy glee. "Gonna take him to the police! I just been waitin' for you to come around so I could tell you to your face."

Kassandra, in wide-eyed shock, watched as the grocer brought his sausagelike finger up to emphasize the last three words, its tip landing just short of Ben's nose. Her gaze landed on Ben's eyes, green and narrowed to mere slits. Then they crinkled, just at the edges, the way they always did when he smiled. But this wasn't the smile that could warm her heart and make her laugh when the world around her seemed frightening. This was the smile that sometimes made it so.

"Bring the boy out to me," Ben said, and although he did not break his gaze with Kinley, the message was clearly intended for the young men behind him. Two of them broke rank, walked through the grocer's open door, and emerged minutes later dragging a ragged, bony, barefoot boy who shook his head to clear away a shank of dirty brown hair to shoot Ben a look of utter defiance.

"Take 'im to Mott's. I'll be there directly."

In one swift movement, the two men half dragged the boy toward Mott Street. Kassandra watched them go, but when the boy turned his head and sent his hatred into her own eyes, she looked away.

Mr. Kinley, meanwhile, had lowered his hand and was once again fumbling with his apron. He seemed to have grown shorter in the intervening moments, his courage completely dissipated, leaving him with a deflated demeanor.

"Now, Kinley," Ben said, his voice still controlled, "you know I don't want police takin' care of my business."

"He robbed my store three times!"

"Whose store?"

"Listen Connor, this here is *my* place."

"Maybe so," Ben said, edging closer to the little grocer, "but it's on *my* street. An' me and my boys handle the business on my street."

"And just where were your boys when this hooligan was stealing my inventory?" Kinley said, his jaw set, his jowl quivering.

Ben turned his gaze upward as if in deep thought. Then he shrugged and said, "You have a point, Kinley. The boy's a sneaky one—got away from us. Tell you what. For your inconvenience, I can forgive this week's payment. Sound fair?"

Mr. Kinley clutched and unclutched his fists, dangling at his side, as if trying to pump himself full of the strength he would need for his reply. "No disrespect, Connor, but I don't think I want to fall in with you no more."

Ben chuckled. "Are you quite sure? Because you do have a fine establishment runnin' here. I'd hate to see any harm come to it."

For the first time, Ben looked away from Mr. Kinley, turning his gaze behind him to the burned-out pile of rubble just over his left shoulder. Kassandra followed suit, as did Mr. Kinley.

"You just think on it, Mr. Kinley," Ben said, holding out his hand, "and I'll check back with you personally in a few days."

Mr. Kinley held out his hand to shake Ben's. "Yes, thank you, Mr. Connor," he said, before turning on his heel and walking back inside.

For all Kassandra knew, Ben had forgotten that she was even there as he set his jaw and strode, arms tensed and swinging at his side, back to Mott Street. His remaining men followed suit, and Kassandra had to push her way through their ranks to get close to Ben.

"What are you going to do to that boy?" she asked, practically running beside him.

"Not now, Kassie." He didn't stop or speak again until he was swinging open the door of the Mott Street Tavern. He turned to address his men, saying something in Gaelic, which they repeated back to him in one solemn voice before dispersing into the street.

Although the people of the neighborhood thought nothing of spending entire afternoons drinking in the tavern, on this day the place was practically empty. The usual permanent fixtures kept their place at the bar, and some of the women Kassandra recognized from their silent passing on the stairs occupied the tables, but there was no warm greeting of Ben as he burst across the threshold. In fact, no one was speaking at all—not even Hamlet, a regular at the swill barrel who could recite any Shakespearean sonnet at the drop of a shot.

Kassandra followed Ben through the large room to the closed door at the back. She had never seen this room before. She had walked through it several times, as it was necessary to do so to get to the stairs, but, windowless, it had always been drenched in black. Now, though, several sconces lining the wall were lit, their glass bowls tinted to give the room a dim red light, revealing that it was larger than she had expected it to be—nearly half the size of the tavern at the front. The walls were roughly plastered and irreverently whitewashed; the floor was nothing but hard-packed dirt. Besides the odd, mismatched chair, there wasn't a stick of furniture in the room. At its center was a round, raised platform, bordered on all sides by three-foot fence pickets, each cut to a sharp spike at the top and placed so close together that she doubted even her tiniest finger could wedge between them.

Standing in the center of the platform was Mr. Kinley's little thief, his hands clasped behind him as if bound. Just behind him was Sean, his trademark cap pulled low over his dark eyes, his hand clapped firmly on the boy's shoulder.

"Go upstairs, Kassandra," Ben said, not looking at her.

"What are you going to—"

"Now!" He turned to face her then, his lips curled to a snarl.

Kassandra hesitated just long enough to look at the boy one more time before she turned and ran up the stairs. Once she was safely on the third-floor landing, she turned back and descended again, walking on the balls of her feet, the worn leather of her shoes silent, just as she had many an afternoon when Ben was waiting for her in Clara's kitchen. She stopped on the third step, far enough down that she could, by craning her neck, watch the scene unfold, but back far enough to remain undetected.

"Now what's your name, son?" Ben was asking. His back was to Kassandra, but she could tell by the tone of his voice that he was wearing the friendly face.

"J-James," the boy said. Kassandra's view of him was blocked by Ben's wide shoulders, but she could hear a hint of fear in his voice.

"An' tell me, James. How old are ya?"

"I dunno…twelve?"

"Go get young Ryan," Ben said, directing the order to his man, who immediately cleared the fence pickets with one long stride and left the room. Kassandra flattened herself against the wall, lest a causal glance up the stairwell reveal her presence.

"Here now, James," Ben said, "let's get you out of there to come talk to me." He reached his arms over the fence and lifted the boy up and over it, as if the child weighed no more than a puppy. Once the boy was deposited on the packed earth, Ben bent at the knees, bringing himself eye level with the boy, who shrank back.

"You stole from Mr. Kinley."

The boy said nothing, only looked at the ground.

"Did no one ever tell you that stealin' is wrong?"

As if infused with newfound strength, young James looked up with narrowed eyes. "Don't tell me you never stole nothin', ya

lousy mick. Everyone knows there ain't an Irishman alive what
ain't—"

"We're not talkin' about me right now, James," Ben said, his
voice cool, controlled. "You're not from this part of the neighborhood, are you?"

"You think you know every kid on the block?"

"I do, James. I make it my business to know. Now where do
you live?"

"Bowery."

"So what're you doin' in my neighborhood? Too scared to
rob the stores down there?"

"I ain't scared of nothin'!"

"Ah, but they know you there, don't they? Know you for the
little thief that you are." Ben laid his hand in the thick mass of
the boy's hair, giving it a comforting tussle. "You're just hungry,
aren't ya, James?"

Kassandra didn't need to hear the boy's voice to know his
answer.

"Listen, son, there's no shame in bein' hungry," Ben said. "But
stealin' from another man? There's no honor in that."

Just then the door leading to the tavern opened, and the man
called Sean came back in. With him was another boy, probably
no more than twelve or thirteen, sporting the same style cap and
green neckerchief as did all of Ben's men, walking with his
abnormally broad shoulders thrust back, his fists balled .

"You sent for me, Mr. Connor?" the boy said. The high pitch
of his voice made all of his outward bravado that much more
startling.

"Ryan, this is James," Ben said, as if making introductions at
a social gathering in a formal parlor. "James has been stealing
from Mr. Kinley's grocery. Offer your hand."

Kassandra had assumed that the boy's hands were bound
behind him, but when young Ryan held out his hand, James
brought his own out from hiding and engaged in a friendly greet-

ing while his eyes darted between Ben and Sean.

"Now," Ben continued, "it's important for young James here to understand that I have an obligation to Mr. Kinley, and to the other shops on my block. Can you guess what that obligation is, James?"

James, fast losing his defiant edge, said nothing.

"That obligation," Ben continued, pacing now in a series of little steps that cast a rhythmic shadow across the boy's face, "is to keep louts like you from harmin' their business." He gave an almost imperceptible nod to Sean, who moved behind James and grabbed the boy's arms just above the elbow and held him so tightly that James emitted a quiet gasp of pain. "Ryan, show young James here what happens to a thief on my block."

Ryan, the tip of his cap barely clearing Ben's elbow, gave a quick jump of glee before landing a solid punch right in the middle of James's stomach. The blow seemed to suck out every ounce of breath in the boy's body. Sean let go of his grip and moved away from the boys, taking a guardian's stance at the door. James doubled over in pain, and young Ryan's left hook caught him square in the mouth—unhinged by the shock of the first hit—and sent him reeling for two or three steps before he fell, face-first, onto the dirt floor.

"Stop it!" Kassandra cried, hurtling herself from her hiding place in the dark stairwell. She headed toward the boy, writhing and moaning on the ground, but Ben's strong hand caught her, jerking her arm until she felt it would be snapped from her body.

"I told you to wait upstairs."

"You cannot do this!" Kassandra continued to struggle despite the pain.

"Take her," Ben said, shoving her into Sean. When she made another attempt to run to James's aid, Sean gripped her hard across the waist and lifted her nearly an inch off the floor so that her feet—still running—treaded helplessly in the air.

In the meantime, James had somehow found the strength to

stand up, though his thin shoulders still hunched. Blood trickled, unchecked, from his swollen lip. Ryan stood poised before him, shifting his weight from one foot to another, looking like a cat ready to pounce on its prey.

"Can I hit 'im again, Mr. Connor?" he asked, his voice full of hope.

"Let him get his breath," Ben said. "Make it a fair fight."

"I ain't—" James started, then spat a mouthful of blood before continuing, "I ain't gonna fight no lousy Catholic, Mary-prayin'—"

Ryan flew at the boy, his open palms flat against the caved-in chest, sending James flat on his back. Ryan pounced on top of him, his knees pinning James's arms to the ground as he delivered a series of blows to the boy's face—his own face red in the room's eerie hue and his mouth spewing spittle and curses.

"That's enough, Ryan," Ben said, but the boy may not have heard him, as Kassandra was screaming the same command. The boy didn't stop his assault until Ben walked over to him and caught his blood-smeared fist in midair. His other hand grasped the back of Ryan's collar, and he lifted the boy off his victim. "Go on now, boy. You've done your bit," he said, almost affectionately, and Ryan stalked out of the room without so much as a glance back.

"Now for you, son," Ben said, squatting to the floor and peering into James's face. "Can you get up?"

He held out a hand to help James off the ground, but the boy slapped it away.

"I don't need no help."

He valiantly stood to his feet and brushed off his pants, as if he had experienced little more than a trip over a loose floorboard. His face, however, told a different story. Bright red continued to spill from his mouth, from his slightly altered nose, and from a gash just above his left eyebrow. The eye below it was swollen shut, the first tendrils of purple bruising creeping along his cheekbone. The other eye, while still open, was caught in a series of fluttering spasms, though none of the defiant glare was lost.

"He just got me by surprise is all. Let me have at him in a fair fight, and I'll show—"

Ben held up his hand, laughing, and said, "There, there, son. You've proven yourself plenty this afternoon. Not many a boy could take a beatin' like that and get up from it."

There was a decided break in the tension of the room, and Kassandra felt Sean's grip on her go slack, allowing her to twist out of his arm and walk over to where James and Ben stood. She reached into the pocket of her skirt and took out a white handkerchief and brought it up to dab up some of the blood flowing over the swollen eye. James took the handkerchief from her to staunch the flow from his nose. Kassandra reached for the boy, wanting to pull him close and pat him the way Clara sometimes had, but just as her fingers grazed his shirt, James pulled away, shrugging off her attempted embrace, radiating pride behind the blood-seeped cloth.

"Tell me, son," Ben said, resuming his earlier stance, hands on his knees, bent to look into James's eye. "D'you have a mother?"

"Course I got a mother."

"What I mean to ask," Ben said, calmly and patiently, "is if your mother is still livin'. Does she take care of you?"

"She's sick." James broke eye contact for the first time, looking at the ground.

"I see."

Ben stood to his full height, reached into his pocket, and pulled out the handful of the bills he had so diligently collected on his route that afternoon. At the sight of the money, James's good eye fluttered as wide as it was able, though the reaction seemed to bring him considerable pain. Ben continued to manipulate the bills until satisfied with a particular amount, which he folded into a compact bundle and slipped into the boy's front pocket.

"There's ten dollars there," he said, bending low again and grasping James by the shoulders. "You take it home, give it straight to your ma. Tell her the truth. Tell her you were caught for a thief and you paid for your crime. D'you understand me?"

James nodded, apparently on the verge of shedding the first tear of this incredible afternoon.

"An' the next time you're hungry," Ben said, standing, "you come and find me. I'll put you to work. Are we square?" Ben held out his hand and waited patiently while James transferred the handkerchief from his right hand to his left in order to shake it. "Now, d'you remember my name?"

"B-Ben Connor."

"Good. Now, Sean here is goin' to take you up front and get you a bite to eat." Sean nodded and stepped aside to open the door. "Then he's goin' to see you home."

"I don't need no one to—"

"If that other eye swells up the way it looks like it's goin' to," Ben said, his patience coming into play again, "you won't be able to see your way home. Plus, you're walkin' 'round with a fortune there. You need someone to guard it."

Sean gently, almost fatherly, laid a hand across the boy's back and ushered him through the door.

Ben and Kassandra faced each other in the room's red light. Every bit of the gentle tolerance Ben had exhibited was immediately erased as he glared at Kassandra through eyes narrowed to green slits, his lips set and narrow. His expression, though, however intimidating he intended it to be, would not deter her. She set her hands firmly on her hips and gave back an equally icy stare, barely needing to tip her chin to meet his gaze directly.

"That was awful, what you did," she said.

"I told you to go upstairs." He turned away from her and

walked over to the sconce on the wall, reaching up to turn down the wick and kill the flame.

"He is just a little boy," Kassandra said, keeping just half a step behind Ben as he made his way to the next light. "How could you beat him like that?"

"First of all, he's not a little boy. He's not much younger than you. What's more," Ben continued, turning toward Kassandra after extinguishing another flame, "I'm not the one who beat 'im, was I? Rest assured, Kassie, if I take it to my mind to knock someone down, I'll see to it he never gets up again."

He leaned over to place a gentle kiss on the tip of her nose, then doused the final three lamps. The room was now black as pitch, and the only hope Kassandra had of escaping it was through the clutch of Ben's warm, dry hand.

10

It was Ben who first realized that Kassandra was pregnant. Not because of the early morning retching into the porcelain bowl tucked under the corner cabinet or the overwhelming fits of fatigue that sent her up to the bed on stifling August afternoons for hours on end. He simply noted one September afternoon that she hadn't had a "woman's time" since she had come to be with him.

"What can you mean?" she asked, mortified to be having such a conversation with a man.

Back at Reverend Joseph's, the advent of her menstruation meant a supply of soft, white cloths placed discreetly in her top drawer, and just as quietly whisked away by Clara, who would return them, washed and bleached, ready for the next month's use. Even after two years Kassandra had never developed a sense of calculating her regularity—simply taking for granted that Clara would meet that need—and she had never given thought to the connection between sharing a bed with Ben and the consequences of what happened there.

Now, here they sat, sharing a simple lunch of tart apples and buttered bread—the only thing she seemed capable of keeping down these days—and Ben was speaking about her most private bodily function with a smattering of crumbs on his lower lip and a delighted gleam in his green eyes.

"Ah, now, Kassie," he said, washing down his last bite with a swig of beer from the keg downstairs, "certainly y'aren't so innocent as to not know what's happenin'."

"This is just not something you should—we should talk about together."

"Well, my love, I think we made a baby together, now didn't we?"

Slowly, the truth of her nights with Ben and the truth of his words right now formed a realization that, just days or minutes ago, would have seemed as unimaginable as the idea of sprouting wings and flying away. She shifted her gaze away from Ben, across the room to the china bird figurine perched on the dresser next to their bed, then, letting out a cry, "Oh, God," clenched her fists and closed her eyes.

"You didn't know? Seriously?" Ben planted his elbows on the table, his face hovering just inches from her own. She felt his breath on her hot, embarrassed cheek. "Clara never talked with you about it? Or the girls at school?"

But they had talked about it—ceaselessly it seemed. There were constant whispered tales of horrid cousins and shameful servants sent packing with red-rimmed eyes and rounded stomachs. These were wretched, nasty girls who did unspeakable things with filthy, disgusting men in dark corners and back alleys and attic rooms. Kassandra's mind flipped through the catalog of conversations. Sarah James hissing and giggling behind her white lace gloves. Clara showing her how to fasten the clean white cloth to the belt around her waist, looking up at her with a furrowed brown brow, saying, "Don't you let no boys mess with you now, Miss Kassandra. There's nothin' but trouble in it for you if you do." But the warning then had seemed pointless. There were no boys to speak of, only the gawky, spot-faced ones whose attention amounted to little more than the calls of "horse-face" and "stork-legs" on the way through the school doors in the mornings.

Now, though, the ominous message of all those rumors and murmurs was patently clear.

"I am a bad girl," Kassandra said quietly, hanging her head

and opening her eyes to stare at the four remaining apple slices on her plate.

Instantly, Ben was up and out of his chair, kneeling beside Kassandra. He grabbed both of her hands in his, brought them to his lips, and placed tiny kisses on each finger.

"You're not, Kassie love," he said, holding her hands tightly. "How can you say such a thing?"

"But I am." Kassandra tried to wrench her hands out of his grip, but no vise could have held them tighter. "I am a horrible, dirty girl. That's why you won't marry me—"

"Hush now—"

"No," she said, quelling the hysteria that threatened to overtake her and calling upon every ounce of her strength to appear calm and strong. "No, I won't hush. You are always saying that. 'Quiet now, Kassie, me love. Go back to the flat now, Kassie, wait for me, Kassie, wake up now, Kassie girl.'"

Ben seemed amused at her mimicry. He loosened his grip, laying his hand across hers as they rested in her lap, and settled back on his haunches, looking up at her with an indulgent expression, like a man doling out just enough rope to a desperate swimmer floundering just off shore.

"Now look what you have done," she continued, her voice quiet. "You have turned me into one of those shameful girls. I will get all big and fat, and my baby will be a bastard—"

There was a clattering of wood as, in one swift movement, Ben rose to his feet, grabbing Kassandra's wrist and bringing her to stand with him as the chair tumbled out from underneath her. She was brought up hard against him, her right arm twisted behind her back until her wrist nearly touched her left shoulder blade. The pain made her cry out, but any maneuver she made only increased the intensity until she was sure the next clattering sound would be that of her very bones ripped from her and tossed across the room.

"Don't ever say that." His breath, laced with apples and beer, spread hot across her face.

"Ben, you are hurting me…"

"Don't you ever use that word about my child again."

"But it is so, Ben. We aren't married."

"Stop with your talk of that!" He released her then, letting her arm drop to her side. "Can I help it, Kassie? Haven't we been through it a hundred times? Or have you suddenly become a good Catholic without my knowin'?"

"You know I'm not."

"Then how am I to marry you?"

"You did not think of that before you brought me here? Just look out there." She pointed toward the open window. "There are countless good Irish girls out there you could have. Why me?"

"Ah, Kassie." He was pacing now, short circuits like he'd done in the parlor the day he convinced her to come away with him. "How can you ask me that? The moment I saw you, I knew it had to be you." He stopped, just in front of her, reached for her and took her hand. "Those sluts out there—all of 'em givin' themselves or sellin' themselves first chance they get. I couldn't have no chance of that. But you—I knew the reverend plucked you up, took you home, kept you pure. Like he was savin' you just for me."

Ben wasn't really talking to her anymore. He'd drawn her close to him, his hand tracing abstract patterns on her back as he held her close, his words spoken just over her head. She could feel his breath in her hair. Both his hands and his breath stopped as soon as Kassandra spoke her next words.

"And now I can never go back."

"Would you want to?"

"I think about it sometimes."

"When you're with me?"

Kassandra smiled against his shirt and pulled away just enough to look up into Ben's face.

"No, not when I am with you. But when I am up here alone,

or I have to go out. Sometimes I think about how noisy and dirty everything is here, and I miss—"

"Bein' rich?"

"Do not start that, Ben. You know I have never cared about money. I just feel far away."

"From what?"

She took a full step away from him, trying to collect her thoughts, and brushed up against the table. At the sound of the rattling dishes Kassandra put out her hand to steady whatever was in danger of crashing to the floor, and her fingers brushed against something smooth and warm. She looked down and saw her fingers absently caressing the cover of Clara's Bible. When had she last opened it? Kassandra closed her eyes, having an answer to Ben's question.

"From God."

"What do you think?" Ben said with an air of disgust. "The only place you can be near God is if you're in the sainted company of the good reverend? Didn't Jesus Himself live among the poor?"

"I only meant that sometimes it feels like when I came here, I left God behind."

"And you're blamin' me for that? Have I ever kept you from Him? I suppose next you'll be sayin' that I've been stoppin' your prayers, hidin' your precious Bible." He picked up the book, brandishing it just inches from her face. "Well, it's been sittin' here since the day you came, Kassie. It's no fault of mine that you haven't picked it up."

"Of course not," Kassandra said. "But you have to realize that I am quite a different person since I came here. Before you, I never dreamed any of"—she gestured helplessly—"this for myself. I never did anything, well, wrong."

Ben chuckled. "Well, now, love, what's the use of havin' the Son of God die for your sins if you never have any sinnin' to speak of?"

"This is not funny, Ben Connor. Not to me. Not at all."

"*Tsk*, my girl." Ben drew her into his arms again. He kissed the top of her head, lifted her face, kissed her nose, her cheeks, her lips. "D'you really think God loves you any less because you love me?"

"I don't know," she whispered.

"You've never told me that you do. Tell me now, Kassie. Say it."

His hands gripped her shoulders now, the throbbing pain from moments ago long subsided and nearly forgotten. With each breath of hesitation, however, the grip grew stronger, willing an answer.

"Of course I do," she said at last.

"Say the words."

"I love you, Ben."

"And I love you, Kassie. And as long as we love each other, there's no harm in the life we're livin' here together."

Kassandra looked deep into Ben's eyes, now full of the warmth and humor that could so draw her into whatever web he deemed fit to spin. True, sometimes those eyes were cold and flat, and she learned this afternoon that those arms could be used to hurt as well as hold. But the man himself was a haven from the squalor just outside their tiny apartment. She would hide in him—abide with him—set upon crafting a new life for herself and for the new life she carried within her.

She cupped her hands against her stomach, looked up at Ben, and asked, shyly, "Do you really think I am going to have a baby?"

"Well, I'm hardly an expert, but I know enough."

"You know more than I do. Ben, I—I am not sure if I can do this."

Just when Kassandra thought there was nothing Ben could do to surprise her—no side of him that she hadn't already seen, whether it inspired fear or laughter—he fell to his knees, right there in front of her, and laid his head against her stomach, wrapping his arms around her legs to hold her steady.

"This means the world to me, Kassie. D'you understand?"

"Of course, Ben," she said, too afraid to say anything else.

"Just give me a son," he said, still on his knees but looking straight up into her eyes. "Give me a son, and the day after we'll marry. I'll give you and him my name."

"Do you mean it, Ben?"

"Just give me a son, Kassie. That's all I ask."

She knelt down with him then, right next to the forgotten toppled chair, their hands clasped, their heads bowed. *Dear God,* Kassandra prayed, neither knowing or caring if Ben was praying too, *I'll never get through this alone. I am frightened, dear Lord. I don't know how to have a baby…*

She waited for a rush of comfort to fall around her. Instead, only tiny phrases swirled through her confusion—*Trust in Me. Abide in Me. Look to Me.* She hoped it would be enough, but when she opened her eyes, all she saw were Ben's own green ones, looking at her with a mixture of pride, acceptance, expectation. The tiny voice inviting her trust a mere echo of a long-forgotten promise.

"I will not be able to do this alone, Ben," she said, gripping his hands.

"You won't be alone, love. I'll be right here with you. You know that."

"That is not enough." She was pleading, hoping to convey the sheer terror she felt.

"I know, Kassie. I know," he said, pulling her into an embrace. "No fears, love. I'll fetch Miss Imogene to you directly."

Imogene Farland was quite a legend in the Five Points. A miniscule woman—just over four feet tall and weighing less than the largest fish tossed in the market on any given day—she moved through the streets largely ignored by men. Her hair was sparse and gray, worn in two loose braids that she occasionally pinned to the top of her head, her skin an indeterminate cocoa color that defied any explanation of her origins. She might claim, in a single day, to be a slave escaped from a Virginia plantation, or the product of a torrid affair between a Jamaican sailor and the captain's daughter, or a Pawnee squaw hiding from her insane French trapper husband. Her age could have been anything between thirty and sixty, for she claimed to have memories of events that predated the turning of the century, but she conducted herself with a youthful gait—spry and quick—like a homely, ragged sprite weaving through a sea of lumbering humans.

But if the men of the city passed over Imogene with little more than a slightly bemused expression, the women of the Points sought her out, following her every move as she passed through doorways and under lampposts. They listened for her distinctive tiny step in the dark stairwells of their tenements, strained to hear her voice—high-pitched and rasping—with its undefined accent floating through their crowded halls. She lived in a tiny wooden structure, squashed between a dry goods store and a brothel that specialized in luring (and robbing) foreign businessmen, on Water Street. Any passerby would know when Imogene was home to receive callers, because there would be a gathering of women just outside her door, huddled in groups of two or three, some furtively searching up and down the street as if in terror of being found here, others proudly displaying a burgeoning figure, their bellies high above their hips, hands resting on their majestic mounds.

Imogene was a midwife. Or an abortionist, depending on the state of mind and body of the woman in question. She excelled at both, never having had a death of both a mother and a child at any single birthing. Or abortion, for that matter. She kept her secrets close at hand, but those women who gave themselves over to her ministrations reported a mixture of powders and potions with chanting and prayer—all very mysterious and well worth the fee, which varied with Imogene's innate ability to know how much a woman could afford.

Of course Kassandra knew Imogene Farland just as anybody might know a local legend, but the two women didn't meet face-to-face until the following day when Kassandra was spending a rare afternoon downstairs in the Mott Street Tavern enjoying a baked apple tart with cream—a special Saturday treat from the baker at the corner. When the door burst open, ushering in an onslaught of late autumn sunshine, Kassandra could make out little more than silhouettes in the doorway. At first glance it seemed to be a small, bent child swathed in an impossible amount of skirts holding the arm of a man whose cap seemed to dangle nearly two feet above her own small head. When the door closed and Kassandra's eyes had a chance to readjust to the dimmer light, she realized the tiny creature was this woman of legend. And she was not holding the arm of the taller man, but rather was being held by him, for it was none other than Sean who clutched the arm of Imogene Farland in much the same way as he had the young James nearly a month before, with little obvious deference to the woman's age or fragility. He kept his grip on her, steering her through the maze of tables, causing conversations to stop midjoke as the oddly matched pair walked past.

Imogene Farland was not known for frequenting any of the establishments in the neighborhood. In fact, few had ever seen her outside of official business, and even though the surrounding city blocks were rife with salacious vice, hers was a business that still invited a hushing of the voice.

"Miss Kassandra?" Sean said once he had navigated his way to the edge of her table, standing with his hat in one hand and Imogene in the other. "This is Miss—"

"She know who I be." The voice was at once high-pitched and lush, with a moist quality to it that made her seem to be constantly on the edge of an earth-shattering cough. "Now take your hand from off my person. You brought me where I go."

With a smile bordering on gallant, Sean loosed his grip on Imogene's elbow only to grasp her hand and bend low over it, depositing a quick kiss on the weathered brown skin. He offered a courtly bow to Kassandra, too, but she could not even look at him to acknowledge it.

He knows, she thought to herself, blushing. *He knows what I am. What I've done.*

Sean put his hat back on, tugged it low over his eyes, and strode out of the tavern. By the time the door had swung shut, the conversations had resumed, but with a loss of their previous volume.

Kassandra finally swallowed the bit of tart she'd had in her mouth since Sean and Imogene opened the door, but the remains of the treat had lost their appeal. She stared down into the plate, fork still clutched in her hand.

They all know.

"Of course they know."

Imogene's tone held no comfort or solace, but Kassandra felt obliged to look into the woman's eyes just the same. She stood right at Kassandra's elbow, and Kassandra's height while sitting in the chair brought the two women to eye level.

"What you care they know? How long you think something like this can hide?"

"I feel like I'm hiding all the time," Kassandra said, finding her voice at last.

"Well, that got to stop," Imogene said, "because no life can hide forever. Your Mister Ben tell me what you are. What you come from." She placed her elbows on the table and leaned in a conspiratorial posture, her feet nearly lifting off the floor as she stretched to meet Kassandra's avoiding eyes. "Your Mister Ben paying me a lot of money to take care of you. And it. He want this baby. He want it alive. He want it healthy."

Imogene's words brought Kassandra an unexpected rush of relief.

"And he want it a boy. Nothing I can do for that. It is what it is. But the rest…" she shrugged her miniscule shoulders.

"So you're going to help me?"

"Yes, child," Imogene said, her voice full of impatience rather than reassurance. "I be here to help you. Now take me upstairs."

"Upstairs? Why?"

"I need to meet the life I be helping."

Kassandra felt an immense sense of pride as she ushered Imogene Farland into the home she shared with Ben. The little flat was clean and tidy, the quilt stretched taut over the bed, the windows open to the afternoon sun, the table cleared of dishes. Imogene was her first chance to play hostess.

"Can I get you something?" Kassandra asked with the grand air she had heard Clara use with some of the reverend's visitors. "Maybe some tea?"

Imogene turned in a slow circle—seemingly taking in every nook and cranny of the tiny flat with her deep-set brown eyes— and came to a stop, her back to Kassandra. She turned her head to send Kassandra a measured stare over her shoulder.

"You think you quite the mistress of the place, don't you?"

Kassandra smiled self-consciously and simply stood, barely inside her doorway, and wiped her hands on the front of her skirt.

"Come in here, child," Imogene said, fully facing Kassandra and beckoning her in with the slightest movement of her little hand.

Kassandra took a few steps away from the door, feeling like an invited guest into Imogene's court. Solemnly, and a bit uncomfortable in her own home, she followed the older woman's silent instructions and sat down in the chair Imogene pulled out for her.

"Now I already tell you how Mr. Ben feel about this baby,"

Imogene said, standing directly in front of Kassandra, the volume of her tattered skirts keeping her quite a distance from Kassandra's own. "But now I got to ask you."

Kassandra had a sudden feeling of being back in school, straight and proper in her desk, prepared to answer any question the unforgiving mistress might toss her way.

"So, you tell me, child. You want this baby? You want it alive?"

"Of course I do! Don't be silly."

"*Phah*, no silly there. I see women every day don't care if their baby live. For that, I don't care if they live, neither."

"Well, I do," Kassandra said, offended at being lumped in with the tragic creatures she saw prowling the neighborhood streets every day.

A slow, thin grin spread across Imogene's face, causing one eye to close nearly completely while the brow of the other lifted like a thin brown cat arching its back. "You know, this baby tie you to Mr. Ben. This baby make you his forever. Makes this your home. Makes this your life."

"Of course it does," Kassandra said, wishing she could back away as the twisted brown face leaned ever closer.

"Mean no matter what happen, you can't ever just pick up and go back to that life you left behind."

"What do you know—"

"I know all about what you come from, child. How you got here. And I look in Mr. Ben's eyes and see there's times he's not such a good man."

"He is good to me."

"Always?"

"No man is good always."

"Nor is any woman, neither," Imogene said. "Now Mr. Ben, he want this child alive, and I got the skills to bring this child to this world alive. But I got the skills to make it happen other way, too."

"Don't even say that," Kassandra whispered.

"I can take this child from you today. Now. Free you up."

"No!"

"Why? Because you love Mr. Ben so much?"

"I—I think he would kill me if anything happened to this baby."

Imogene laughed. "You right about that," she said before sobering. "But that not enough to keep this baby strong. You got to want this baby alive because it a part of *you*." The last word was punctuated by the tap of a tiny finger right above Kassandra's heart.

"I know that."

"What you eat, it eat. Your blood, its blood."

"Of course—"

"You saying words like you understand." Imogene's voice was angry now, the tone pitched a bit higher. She stepped away from Kassandra and stomped her feet, invisible underneath the mass of skirts. "You think because you got a baby inside you, all you need do now is wait for it come out. Hand it over to Mr. Ben and say, 'See here, mister. What I done for you?'"

"That's not it at all—"

"You don't know what you got inside of you."

Kassandra opened her mouth to protest again, but snapped it shut.

"Right now, you don't feel it. You don't see it. But it got a soul." Imogene dropped to a whisper, causing Kassandra to lean in to hear. "It love the God you love, and that God know it same as He know you."

Kassandra held her breath. *He knows me.*

"That God watching this baby now. Even deep inside you. He watching every bit it grows. He want it safe. Mr. Ben, he want it born. Now you, I got to know. You want give this soul a life?"

"I've told you yes. I—I love Ben. Really," she added quickly as Imogene raised that brow again. "And this, I am sure, will gentle him a little bit. He wants a son so badly…"

Her words trailed off as a frown furrowed ever deeper into Imogene's face. The room was full with the sense that the fate of both Kassandra and the child within her rested completely in the miniscule hands of Imogene Farland—hands that were now resting on Imogene's childishly narrow hips, the first finger on each tapping impatiently against the patched fabric.

"I do not know what else to tell you," Kassandra said.

"Tell me you have joy."

"I can't say that."

"Tell me you are content."

"I have to be. I'm just"—Kassandra looked up—"scared."

Imogene broke into a smile that was almost reassuring.

"No need be scared," she said, giving Kassandra a friendly pat on the leg. "God watch your child. I watch you."

11

*F*or the next months, going into the winter, there were few steps that Kassandra ever took alone. Ben had appointed himself quite the protector, worried that some patch of ice or snow might cause the ever-expanding Kassandra to lose her footing and fall, and any time he could not hold her arm to navigate her through the city streets, he saw to it that one of his men was on hand to ensure her safety.

There were several occasions when Kassandra found herself walking alone—out on an errand or simply taking a brisk bit of air as relief from the claustrophobic warmth of their flat—only to notice that her shadow fell not on the street, but on some man in a cap and green kerchief, walking not two steps behind her.

Once, when her preoccupation with the soon-coming baby did cause her mind to wander and her body to misstep into a slick pile of waste just off the walkway, she felt as if her impending fall had been broken by the arms of an angel. Once secure, though, she turned around to see that it was only Sean, looking down at her with a serious expression. He gave a barely perceptible nod to her effusive thanks, and with a quick jerk of his head summoned another of Ben's watchmen to accompany her the rest of the way home.

Kassandra's other source of constant company was Imogene Farland. True to her word, the little woman had taken Kassandra under her care, ever mindful of the watchful eyes of Ben. She came to visit several times a week, often bringing mysterious packets of herbs and teas, with instructions for brewing and sprinkling, each designed to ease a specific ailment. Chamomile tea, laced with peppermint and sweetened with honey, kept Kassandra's stomach from lurching each morning or anytime hunger seemed a preferable alternative to eating. When she did eat, Kassandra grudgingly followed Imogene's admonitions that she couldn't construct an entire diet of apple tarts and cream.

"You got to know your blessings," Imogene said when Kassandra complained about the sickening taste of almost any food. "I take you out there, show you women with nothing inside them but a baby and stale bread. You got a man who take care of you."

And Ben did. Kassandra never allowed herself to question where the delicacies that graced their humble table came from. When Imogene suggested that Kassandra should eat more cheese, Ben brought in fresh rounds wrapped in bourbon-soaked chestnut leaves. The day after Imogene suggested that Kassandra have a glass of red wine in the evening to help her sleep, Ben came in with a rose-tinted bottle with French writing on the label full of a substance that bore little resemblance to the swill dispensed from the casks downstairs.

"Nothin' is too fine for my prince," he would say and drop a kiss on the top of Kassandra's head and give her expanding belly a patriarchal pat. Indeed, Kassandra felt like a queen, spared from the flashes of temper and sullen, seething anger. From the moment the first little bump appeared, Ben became the essence of humor and charm—every bit the man Kassandra dreamed he would be when he first lured her into this new life.

On a particularly blinding, bitter winter day, Kassandra sat on one of the wooden kitchen chairs, her swollen feet propped up on the other. The baby rolled and kicked fiercely within her, sometimes delivering a painful blow to the base of her spine. She winced and shifted her position, complaining loudly about the pain.

"You think that the pain?" Imogene said, her voice laced with a knowing condescension. "You just wait."

The little woman stood on an overturned apple crate, idly running a wooden spoon through a mass of boiling dandelion greens on the stove.

"Where in the world did you get dandelions in February?" Kassandra asked, eager to change the subject.

"I tell Mr. Ben I need them."

The little flat fell into companionable silence again, the only sound the scrape of the spoon against the pot. Occasionally Imogene would lift a mass of greens out of the boiling water, pluck one stem from the wilted bunch, and pop it into her mouth, chewing it carefully before leaning over to spit it back into the pot. Whether she was testing it for taste, temperature, or consistency, Kassandra had no idea. She had long ago given up on demanding an explanation for every broth, salve, and tincture Imogene Farland forced upon her.

Imogene reached, teetering on her toes, for a bowl on the shelf above the stove and laid a square of cheesecloth over the top. Half humming, half whistling a little tune, she spooned steaming heaps of stems onto the cheesecloth and pressed a bit with the spoon to strain away the water. When the last had been lifted from the pot, she grabbed the four corners of the cheese-cloth, formed it into a tiny bundle, and squeezed it over the bowl until not one drop more could be coaxed.

Going to tiptoe again on the apple crate, Imogene reached to the row of hooks on the wall behind the single-board counter and took down a bright blue mug. Into it she poured the green-ish contents of the bowl, careful not to slosh a single drop. All of this Kassandra watched without comment, knowing she would soon be sipping the mysterious broth. But when Imogene reached one last time for the large sealed jar on the shelf, Kassandra couldn't help but cry out

"Oh, no, Imogene. Please! No more of that, I beg you."

Undaunted, the miniscule woman wrenched the tightly sealed lid off the glass jar containing a beef shank bone submerged in apple cider vinegar. She dipped a spoon into the liquid not once, but twice, stirring the bone-infused vinegar into the dandelion broth.

"You want this baby have strong bones? Yes?" Imogene didn't bother to turn around to receive an answer from Kassandra. "Then you drink."

She tapped the spoon twice on the rim of the cup, hopped off the apple crate, and brought the cup over to sit in front of the now frowning Kassandra.

"Drink," she commanded.

Kassandra lifted the mug to her lips and wrinkled her nose at the bitter smell. "Do I have to?"

Imogene walked over to the window, opened it and, after leaning over the edge to see that nobody lurked on the sidewalk below, prepared to dump the water from the pot down into the street.

"Well, I am going to let it cool a bit so I can drink it down," Kassandra said.

Imogene put the pot back on the stove, braced her hands on the windowsill, and lifted her body up to lean further out the window. "What you say?" she yelled down into the street.

Kassandra heard a woman's thin voice through her open window.

"Tell her I be on my way." Imogene pulled herself back inside, shut the window, and turned toward Kassandra, rubbing her tiny hands in what seemed like gleeful anticipation. "Drink up, and get your coat."

"Why?"

"There's a baby to be born."

The two women made quite a sight striding through the doors of the Mott Street Tavern. Imogene, swathed in a rough homespun cloak wound three times around her body, and Kassandra—obe- diently following a few steps behind—towering over her, wearing Ben's heavy black wool coat. They weren't two steps out of the tavern when Sean, who had been waiting outside the building with a bag of hot chestnuts, fell in step behind them. The little parade traveled halfway down the block before Imogene turned around, pointed a gloved hand with a little brown finger popped out of the top up to his face, and told him to leave them be.

"But Mr. Connor says I'm to—"

"She safe with me," Imogene said with such authority that Sean tipped his cap to her and Kassandra before turning away.

Imogene resumed the pace that made Kassandra trot just to keep up. The winter air, laced with pungent smoke and ash, blew its bitter grit across Kassandra's face, and she lifted her muf- fler—nearly six feet of the softest wool she had ever felt—up to her nose to combat both the wind and the odor.

"Where are you taking me?" she asked.

But there was no answer from the scurrying bundle in front of her.

Before long the two women were in what was, for Kassandra, unfamiliar territory. Although she had spent many hours and afternoons patrolling arm in arm with Ben, Kassandra had never strayed more than three square blocks in any direction from Mott Street Tavern. Now, as she tramped behind Imogene, heading west on Bayard Street and turning south on Mulberry, it seemed as if she were watching the world itself decline. The relative afflu- ence of her own little neighborhood stood in stark contrast to what she saw now. The streets were narrower and darker and flanked by dilapidated brick buildings—some five or six stories high—largely unbroken by windows. What windows were there showed no sign of life or light. Piles of women and children hud- dled in doorways, stacked together against the cold, the occasional naked foot or face peeping through assorted shambled covers.

Every other door sported a shingle above it advertising the saloon within. Ram's Head Tavern. Georgetown Grocery. The Dark Corner. Raucous laughter and music spilled through their doors onto the streets that were clamped nearly silent under the weight of winter. Kassandra and Imogene seemed to be the only mobile people in the vicinity, with the exception of a few other women, their coats left open to expose nearly bare breasts, who strolled back and forth halfheartedly between the tavern doors.

Kassandra sprinted the few steps that separated her from Imogene, grabbed a handful of the woman's shawl, and forced her to turn around.

"I am going home," Kassandra said, stooping as much as her pregnant body would allow and whispering through the muffler she clutched against her mouth and nose.

"No," Imogene said simply.

"Watch me."

"I do watch you. You follow."

Imogene turned around and continued walking and, as if compelled by some predetermined force, Kassandra followed.

Just about half a block later, Imogene veered sharply to the left towards a dark, worn, three-story wooden structure that seemed impossibly suited to provide shelter. What windows it had were broken or cracked, and the gaps between the boards were so wide that tufts of material used to fill them poked out from the other side.

"Here," Imogene said, climbing the three short steps in the front and taking a hold of the door.

So this was darkness. Windowless. Airless. Immediately upon the closing of the door behind them, Kassandra felt as if her eyes may as well have been torn from her face for all the good they were in here. Soon after, the unbelievably acrid stench of human waste and unwashed flesh seeped through the layers of heavy wool bound over her mouth, and her ears were haunted by the sounds of soft moaning drifting through the darkness. She kept one arm outstretched, keeping her balance, running gloved fingers lightly along a wall that seemed slightly softer than a wall should be.

"Should we get a lamp?" Kassandra whispered into the blackness around her.

"There be a light for us," Imogene replied, her odd rasping voice eerily suited to the surroundings.

Soon enough Kassandra felt the floor beneath her become a set of stairs. She stepped onto each one carefully, one hand still guiding herself along the wall, the other holding tight to what she hoped was Imogene's skirt in front of her. She tried to count the steps, but the unfamiliarity of her surroundings was disorienting, and she soon lost count. At some point, though, the floor was once again level. She felt the turning of a corner and noticed a thin line of light several feet in the distance.

"Come, child," Imogene said, and Kassandra felt the tiny hand grasp her own.

When Imogene arrived at the door under which the light was streaming, she grasped the latch and swung it open. Kassandra followed her into the room, and the sight that met her took away what little breath she had left.

The flat was impossibly small—less than half the home that she and Ben shared—and completely bare save for a single chair acting as a table for the single kerosene lamp. Bundled as she was, the only witness to the bone-chilling cold of the room was her nose, exposed now as the woolen fabric was dislodged by her gaping mouth. She sensed rather than saw four sets of eyes staring at her from the dim shadows. Children, maybe, huddled in one corner, with one tiny arm pointing to the only other piece of furniture in the room. A sagging cast-iron bed stood in the corner, and the pile of fabric and rags on top of it was groaning loudly.

"Mrs. Fisher?" Imogene said, beginning to unravel her outermost shawl. "I here now, Mrs. Fisher."

The woman's reply was incomprehensible, a string of slackened syllables tossed out from her thrashing head.

Kassandra looked from Mrs. Fisher to the children to the lamp and back. "Why have you brought me here?"

"Time you see what new life is," Imogene said, reaching up to tug at Kassandra's wool muffler. "Take this off. Fold it up nice. Come see."

Kassandra had long ago accepted that she was taller than most other women she knew, but in this tiny space, seven months pregnant, she felt massive. Every move she made threatened to topple the lamp, and she slowly, gingerly, took off her coat, holding it aloft as she scanned the bare walls for a hook. Finding none, she laid it on the floor in front of the pile of children, one of whom snaked out a little hand and slowly inched it over to cover the bare legs of a smaller sibling. Something clutched in Kassandra's throat—a distant memory of being that small and that cold, creeping through the days and nights searching for warmth and comfort. The memory of it made her want to turn and run, but Imogene's commanding voice from the shadows stopped any serious thought she had of leaving.

"Come here. Hold the lamp."

Kassandra reached for the lamp's handle and lifted it off the chair, swinging it in the direction Imogene indicated, holding it high above the woman's gray head.

"Look. See."

Like most of the poorer women Kassandra had seen, Mrs. Fisher seemed to be wearing every garment she owned, piles of skirts and underskirts strewn around the legs Imogene worked to lift and open to make a way for the coming baby.

"Ach." Imogene looked over her shoulder toward the pile in the corner and summoned one child. "Lamp," she said, and Kassandra handed the light over to the small, genderless creature.

It soon became evident that Kassandra's role was to lift the listless Mrs. Fisher off her bed and hold her as Imogene worked to remove some of the woman's clothing. Mrs. Fisher seemed unaware of the importance of the occasion as her head fell back against Kassandra's shoulder, nearly sending the both of them staggering to the floor. She continued her incoherent moaning and muttering, her open mouth now inches from Kassandra's face; the odor was nearly as debilitating as her weight.

"I think she is drunk," Kassandra whispered, not wanting to speak ill of a mother in front of her children.

"Of course she drunk," Imogene said.

Along the opposite wall, the shadow of the child holding the lamp nodded in agreement.

Once Mrs. Fisher was stripped down to a practical, if stained, nightgown, she was redeposited on her bed. The child, ever shining the light, followed Imogene's most minute movement as she burrowed through her bag for a tiny glass vial. Once found, she dislodged its cork and waved it under the drunk woman's nose, saying, "Mrs. Fisher! Mrs. Fisher! Wake up now! It time!"

Mrs. Fisher regained a violent consciousness, lifting her body from the bed and swinging clenched fists at the closest target. But Imogene jumped back with a bit of a laugh and said, "Better now."

Mrs. Fisher, once again aware of her pain, abandoned her attack and emitted the most ear-wrenching scream Kassandra had ever heard; she echoed it with her own.

"Hush that!" Imogene said, whirling on her. "This not your time. Give me your hand."

Kassandra made her way to where Imogene was busy ministering to the now nearly frantic Mrs. Fisher, the lamp-wielding child moving silently out of her way. Imogene grabbed Kassandra's hand, bringing it to the relative warmth between Mrs. Fisher's splayed legs.

"You feel that?" Imogene said, her breath creating tiny puffs of steam. "The baby's head. Already here. That be a new life to join us today."

Kassandra felt the tiny life within her leap at the words, and she whisked her hand away from Mrs. Fisher to clutch at her own burgeoning stomach.

"I need a drink," the writhing woman on the bed said. "One of you," she turned toward the children still huddled in the corner, "go fetch Mama a drink."

Her voice was considerably weaker now, dwindling with each syllable as she repeated her request over and over. For the first time, Kassandra got a good look at her face. She looked far too old to be having a child. Her hair, lank and damp with the effort of labor, hung in loose strands, framing a face battered with scabbed-over blemishes and nearly concave in its toothlessness.

"Patty?" she said, capturing the full attention of the child with the lamp. "Go get Mama a drink?"

The child took one step toward the door, but a sharp look from Imogene and the bare foot jerked back to the floor. Soon enough, then, Mrs. Fisher was seized with another pain, and all need for the drink was momentarily forgotten.

"Patty, is it?" Imogene asked, her voice almost warm with affection. "Turn down the light so we don't waste the oil."

Young Patty turned the wick down until there was only the dimmest, dimmest light in the room.

"Can you see, Imogene?" Kassandra asked, still feeling the need to whisper.

"No. I touch."

"What can I do?"

"Whatever I say."

For a while Imogene said nothing, only hummed the strange little song Kassandra had heard so many times before.

Suddenly overwhelmed with fatigue, Kassandra sank to the floor, settling herself within striking distance of the sometimes flailing Mrs. Fisher. Little by little she scooted farther away from the bed and closer to the bundle of children. She snaked one hand off toward the right, where she knew she had draped her coat on the floor, and attempted to bring it up to cover herself. Her efforts, though, were met with resistance, a little force on the other end just as determined to keep the coat to itself.

"Now, push."

Imogene's voice brushed through the darkness, followed by the most startling scream yet to come from Mrs. Fisher. The moment that scream pierced the darkness, the little bundle that was Kassandra's coat leapt into Kassandra's lap, accompanied by two or three small creatures with bony arms and legs who piled, shivering, onto Kassandra.

"More light, Patty," Imogene said, and light flooded the room.

Kassandra could now make out the little woman, herself nearly wedged between Mrs. Fisher's legs, which were now bare to the thighs and spread wide across the bed.

"Kassandra, come."

Imogene's voice was tainted with urgency, but Kassandra felt herself rooted to the floor. The new light allowed her to distinguish two scabby heads plastered against her, eyes shut against the terror of the scene around them. Kassandra's arms encircled them, holding them near. She made no reply, only shook her head violently against the idea of leaving this spot.

"Come here," Imogene repeated, this time looking up from the impending birth to give Kassandra a pointed stare. "I need help."

"I—I would not know what to do," Kassandra said.

Imogene merely hissed—a sound that carried more weight than any amount of words possibly could. Kassandra carefully dislodged herself from the clinging children, tucked her coat tightly around them, and went to stand just behind Imogene.

"You see there?" Imogene said, gesturing for young Patty to bring the light closer. "Head. And part of shoulder."

Kassandra looked, and shuddered a bit.

"She not strong enough to push baby out. She need sit up to push down."

The women worked together to force Mrs. Fisher into a sitting position. Imogene grabbed her legs and turned her so that they dangled over the side of the bed, and Kassandra maneuvered the woman until her hips were perfectly balanced on the edge of the mattress.

"Hold her up," Imogene said.

Kassandra sat next to Mrs. Fisher on the bed, her strong hands firmly gripping the slack woman's shoulders.

"Now, sing."

"What?"

"Sing. It soothe mother." Imogene offered a slight glance around the shadowed room. "It soothe children."

"Why don't you sing?" Kassandra asked.

"I busy," Imogene said, settling herself on the floor at Mrs. Fisher's feet.

Sing. Kassandra didn't sing, at least she hadn't since coming away with Ben. She wracked her brain for a song, but only the bawdy tunes of the tavern came to mind. Even though Mrs. Fisher had spewed countless profanities from her toothless mouth, Kassandra wasn't about to contribute to the vulgarity with a ditty about Marie in her red petticoat. So she searched back further, back to her days with Reverend Joseph, her hours spent in the front pew, the voices of the congregation, and her heart became still.

"Praise God, from whom all blessings flow…"

The note lingered in the air, tremulous and uncertain, wrapped in the steam of Kassandra's breath. The sound of her voice in song was as new to this world as the babe attempting to be born, and at the sound of it, the faces of all of Mrs. Fisher's other children turned to look at her in wide-eyed wonder.

"That good," Imogene said, not looking up. "Sing that."

Kassandra didn't want to, but she cleared her throat and began again.

"Praise God, from whom all blessings flow
Praise Him, all creatures here below

Praise Him above, ye heavenly host
Praise Father, Son and Holy Ghost."

"Again," Imogene commanded.

"Praise God, from whom all blessings flow…"

She sang the chorus several times, each repetition urged on by Imogene, each repetition stronger and surer, both of the notes and the words and the wealth of history and comfort behind them. Her singing was accompanied by the intermittent screams and moans of Mrs. Fisher, forcing Kassandra to strengthen her voice to cover the sounds of agony that threatened to overshadow the blessing of the simple doxology. During one rendition, when Mrs. Fisher slumped silently against her, Kassandra noticed that her voice was not the only one in the room. She paused a bit in the third line and noticed that the clear, pure voice of Patty carried on—

"…above, ye heavenly host…"

And, encouraged by their sibling's courage, tiny mewling from the others—

"Praise Father, Son and Holy Ghost."

Just then there was a final, exhausted yelp from Mrs. Fisher, and a new voice entirely joined the room. This one was full and wet, and the shock of it silenced all but Kassandra and Imogene, who joined together in a final, whispered, "Amen."

"New sister," Imogene said, directing her announcement to the stoic Patty, whose arm was violently shaking now, casting erratic shadows along the bare walls of the little flat. "Put that down now. Bring my bag."

The child obeyed.

Kassandra continued to shoulder the weight of the now immobile Mrs. Fisher. She watched as Imogene reached into her bag, pulled out a length of clean white cloth, and handed the wet, squirming bundle of baby over to Patty, who held it with great reverence and skill. Imogene fished in her bag yet again to bring out some instrument with a sharp silver blade that winked in the waning light of the lamp.

Kassandra closed her eyes, the darkness a welcome change from the eerie shadows of the room. The body resting in her arms seemed every bit as helpless as the one beginning to quiet in Patty's. Imogene continued to hum the doxology, and Kassandra silently filled in the words, wondering how on earth God could be praised in this place.

"Lay her down now," Imogene said.

Gingerly, responding to Mrs. Fisher's wincing discomfort, Kassandra eased the woman back down on the mattress. No sooner had she done so than Patty deposited yet another bundle in her arms. Kassandra had never held a baby before, and the weight of it coupled with the weight within her took her last bit of breath from her.

"She is beautiful," Kassandra said after a time.

The tiny pink mouth pursed from side to side, then gaped in a yawn destined to overtake the newborn face. A little fist popped out of the bundle of rags encasing the child, and Kassandra brought her own hand to it, offering her smallest finger to be clutched.

"She is just perfect, isn't she?"

"Just." Imogene took the child—tugged, actually—from Kassandra and began to rub the tiny body vigorously with the clean cloth. "But cold. Too cold. Need wrap her up in something warm. And clean."

A thorough search of the flat revealed nothing appropriate, at least nothing up to the standards Kassandra instantly created for this new life. Nothing, that is, until her fingers grazed her wool muffler, still folded nicely, still lying where she had deposited it. She unfolded it to its full length, doubled the fabric, and handed it to Imogene.

"Here, use this."

Imogene took the muffler from Kassandra's outstretched hand, laid it on the bed and, after fastening the last bit of clean cloth around the baby's bottom, wrapped her tightly within it.

"You go now," Imogene said, never taking her eyes off the child. "It late."

"What about you?"

"I stay. Wait for mother to wake."

"How will I find my way back?" Kassandra had no idea how long they had been in this place, but she was certain any remnants of daylight were long gone.

"You find."

Kassandra nodded and bent to pick up her coat. The children beneath it were quite still, and closer inspection showed that they were asleep. The coat was still tucked snug around them, and the idea of dislodging it and exposing them yet again to the bitter chill of the room tore at Kassandra's heart.

"Take mine," Imogene said, nodding toward the pile of discarded garments at the foot of the bed.

Kassandra smiled, knowing that Imogene's coat would sooner fit Patty than herself. Instead, she picked up the rough-knit shawl that she had so fervently clutched in following Imogene up the dark stairwell and wrapped it as tightly as she could around her. Her gloves were hopelessly lost in the dark shadows, but no matter. She asked Patty to accompany her to the building's entrance, bringing the light so that she would not get lost within the bowels of the tenement, and the child—after looking to Imogene for permission—nodded and opened the door.

Just as Kassandra was about to step over the threshold, she turned to Imogene and said, "What kind of life is this for a child?"

Imogene surprised her by emitting a slight, rasping laugh.

"Maybe this one get lucky. Get kicked by a horse."

It was, indeed, dark. This was a street largely left without street lamps, and the minute Patty escorted Kassandra over the threshold of the building and onto the snowy steps below, Kassandra was disoriented. From which direction had they come? She took a few tentative steps to the left; then, unsatisfied, turned to walk in the opposite direction, coming into full collision with a tower of a man.

"You were right the first time," said a familiar voice, and she looked up to see Sean, whose firm grip steadied her. "Mr. Connor would want me to see you home."

"Does—does he know where I am?" Kassandra asked, overtaken with a new fear.

"Not exactly." Sean took her elbow and urged her to walk with him. "I only told him that you left with Miss Imogene."

"Oh."

"You're cold," Sean said as he unbuttoned his jacket.

"No," Kassandra said, stilling his motion with her hand. "Just…walk with me. I am quite fine."

"As you wish," he said, his dark eyes giving no hint of emotion.

They walked as quickly as the snow and the refuse of the streets would allow, dodging the occasional reeling drunkard and huddled body. She was grateful for the silence of her escort—just as grateful as she was for the steadying hand when she encountered the occasional patch of ice. The brisk walk did warm her somewhat, though the tip of her nose and ears burned with cold. Yet she harbored no regret for the loss of her muffler, only steeled herself to face the biting wind head-on.

Soon everything looked familiar, and just around the next corner would be the Mott Street Tavern, with its usual robust crowd filling a room that would actually be too warm, and above it, the flat that now seemed palatial. Before they actually turned the corner, though, Sean stopped straight in his tracks and grabbed Kassandra's arm.

"What is it?" she asked, looking up into his face that, for the first time, showed an expression close to fear.

"Mr. Connor would kill me for this, you know," he said.

"For seeing me home? I do not think so."

"Not for that," Sean said, glancing furtively around. "For this."

He reached for Kassandra's hand and, once it was firmly in his grasp, pulled her close.

"What are you—" Before she could finish, she felt something placed firmly within her hand. She glanced down and saw that it was a crumpled bit of paper. She unfolded it and saw the familiar handwriting on the outside of an envelope. The sight of it caused her legs to nearly buckle beneath her, and she would have welcomed Sean's steadying hand. But when she looked up, he was gone, his tall frame disappearing just around the corner.

She was standing just under a streetlamp, and with shaking fingers she opened the envelope and pulled out the single sheet of paper within.

My Dearest Sparrow,

I do not know when you will get this letter, or what state you will be in once you receive it. I only know that I pray continuously for your safety. Please do not feel that I have abandoned you. Quite the opposite. The minute I returned home to find you gone I began my search, but it was soon made clear to me, by persons of whom you are by now well aware, that any attempt to bring you home would be most unwelcome. I have been assured that you are safe and well, perhaps even happy, and while I cannot fully understand your decision to leave, I will trust that it was a choice made with the utmost prayerful consideration.

Please know that, should you ever decide to return, there is always a home for you here, warm and welcoming. And remember the conclusion to the Gospel of

Matthew, as our Lord promises, "Lo, I am with you
always, even unto the end of the world."

She should have felt something—relief at knowing his concern, regret for having left, joy at the possibility of return,
uneasiness at knowing she was at the end of the world. But what
she felt instead was an utter distance from the man who had
written this letter, as if it were a polite correspondence from a
long-lost relative. It had the formality and voice of a purely social
epistle. He wasn't begging her to come back, wasn't exhibiting
that he was beside himself with grief. It was months ago that
Kassandra gave up waiting for him to come pounding on the
door to take her home. Months, in fact, since she had thought of
his house as her home.

Sean seemed to think he risked his life to deliver the message. Kassandra smiled. How much greater that risk would have
been last summer. For now, she was nearly numb with cold, and
the thoughts of returning to Reverend Joseph were dulled
behind the impossibly long, cold journey it would be to get
there.

She took one last look at the letter before folding it into her
skirt pocket and pulling Imogene's shawl tightly around her.
There was no date on the letter; Kassandra had no idea how long
ago Reverend Joseph had written it, or how she would ever reply.

Right now, neither question mattered. Ben would have questions of his own.

❧ 12 ❧

The youngest Fisher was not the only child Kassandra would see into the world that winter. For the next two months she accompanied Imogene on countless visits. Sometimes the occasion was even a joyous one, as the resounding cheer of a celebrating father toasting his newest child streamed from the open door of a saloon down the street.

That will be Ben, Kassandra would think to herself as she walked past the lighted doorways on her walk back home. She pictured the Mott Street Tavern filled to capacity with well-wishers and Ben standing on top of the bar—glass high in the air—calling three cheers for the newly born prince.

She was a quick study of all Imogene had to teach her. The old woman had no written record of her treatments, but Kassandra listened closely to every word she said. In the blank pages at the back of Clara's Bible, she began a careful list of every herb in Imogene's cache. Chamomile, ginger, and peppermint to ease indigestion and heartburn. Also good for morning sickness. Rose hips to treat exhaustion. Nettles—boiled or steamed—to prevent leg cramps and anemia.

"What're you writin' in that book?" Ben asked on one of the rare evenings he was home.

Kassandra barely looked up to answer. "Things Imogene taught me."

"I don't like you spendin' so much time with her."

"*You* brought her to *me.* Remember?"

"To take care of you. Not to send you traipsin' through the city doin' God knows what."

Kassandra closed the Bible and carried it over to the bureau, placing it in the top drawer. "It is good for me, Ben. To see those other women."

"You're not like those other women. You're mine."

"I like feeling needed."

"I need you. That's enough."

In the final weeks of her pregnancy, Kassandra felt a surge of strength like she had never felt before. The rolling child within her was a constant reminder of her tie to Ben, and of the promise he had made to marry her upon its birth. More and more she felt a need to turn their little flat into a proper home, and she gave daily requests to Ben to bring in the necessary additions. Soon there was a tiny cradle tucked into one of the corners and a bright rag rug on the floor. A rocking chair—too cumbersome for the winding stairway—was hoisted through the third-floor window.

As her time grew closer, Kassandra made every effort to keep the apartment clean, lest Imogene be forced to deliver the baby in the midst of clutter and unwashed dishes. Having witnessed so many births, she knew to keep a ready supply of clean, soft cloths in a basket on top of her bureau, right next to her beloved porcelain sparrow. She knew to keep the kettle filled on the stove, ready to heat water for washing the new baby. She knew to keep the lamp filled, lest the child come in the middle of the night, and wood stacked next to the little stove so the new life would begin in a warm room.

What she didn't know was what happened to women in those moments or hours just before she and Imogene burst through the door ready to take matters in hand. When she asked Imogene, the old woman simply said, "You will know."

"How?"

"Your body tell you. Your baby tell you."

But the communication between Kassandra and her body and her baby was unreliable. In the first weeks of March, every twinge and spasm sent her flying to her window, calling downstairs to the man stationed outside to fetch Ben. Each time Ben stormed into the apartment, pushing Imogene through the door, only to find the crisis over, Kassandra's body at rest. Each time Kassandra would apologize, begging forgiveness of the unflustered Imogene after Ben, cursing, stormed right back out.

"It seemed so real this time," she'd say.

"It be real enough someday."

The real day came the third week in March, when bitter cold wind raced through the New York streets, cutting a path through the buildings, bringing with it stinging scraps of debris. The first pain hit just as Kassandra was clearing away the dinner dishes. Ben had made a courteous appearance, sitting with her for much of the afternoon, apparently to make up for the fact that he would be downstairs in the tavern most of the night.

"Big doin's this evenin', love," he said. "You best be plannin' on stayin' up here most of the night."

"And how would that be different from any other night?" Kassandra asked, feeling grumpy.

"No goin' off with that Imogene, for one thing."

"All right, Ben. But you will be just downstairs? Just in case…"

"I'll be busy, Kassie. Got a huge crowd comin'."

"For what?"

"Nothin' for you to worry your head about. You just stay up here."

He left soon after that, and just as Kassandra reached up to put the last dried plate on the shelf, she felt the familiar tightening across her belly.

"Oh," she said, letting the plate clatter to the shelf.

She grasped the countertop with both hands and stood there, waiting for the pain to pass. Once relieved of the contracting pressure, she took a washrag, dipped it in the water basin, and wiped the crumbs from the table. Next she took the broom from the corner and swept up the debris on the floor. Despite her valiant effort, no amount of bending would suffice to hold the dustpan for the little pile, so she lifted the corner of the rag rug, and with one good drag of the bristles, hid it away underneath. She still needed to refill the kettle.

Kassandra was on the second floor landing when the next pain came. No worse than the first, she simply stood on the step, clutched the banister until it passed, then gingerly made her way downstairs into the tavern to fill the kettle from the water pump behind the bar.

Ben's prediction of the big crowd seemed to be coming true. The Mott Street Tavern was rarely empty, but here it was not even four o'clock and already the place was teeming with men. Kassandra wedged her way through them, hating every moment her belly brushed against some natty vest, trying to ignore the callous comments blown through cigar smoke. She looked up just long enough to scan the crowd for a glimpse of Ben, hoping to ask him to fill the kettle for her and bring it upstairs. When she saw him standing at the tavern door, engaged in angry conversation with a strange man in a bright green suit, she thought better of it and made her way to the bar. Stymie, the barkeep, obviously irritated at the interruption, snatched the kettle out of her hand and gave it back with even less courtesy.

"Get back upstairs before you drop that litter on my floor," he said, drawing raised glasses and laughter from the men gathered at the bar.

Kassandra recoiled at his words. "What did you say to me?"

"I said get upstairs. We got fifteen girls workin' here tonight. You're gonna make the gents lose their appetites."

More laughter, and Kassandra spun with all the dignity her girth would allow and made her way to Ben.

"The deal we struck was thirty percent of the takin's," he was saying to the dapper man in the green suit, "and you won't go changin' that on me now."

The man took a long draw on his thin cigar before taking it out of his mouth. He held it almost daintily between his thumb and first finger and tapped the ash with his third. The other two sported heavy gold rings that clicked with the action.

"Mr. Connor," he said, "that was the deal made for the use of King Pit. But now I'm bringing in a Manchester terrier, the likes of which these people have never seen before. He'll bring in twice the money. Even at twenty percent, you'll be taking in more—"

"Thirty," Ben said. "Thirty or it's off."

"Not a wise threat, Mr. Connor. You'll have a lot of very disappointed men on your hands."

"And I'll see to it that you never—"

"Ben," Kassandra said, tugging his arm even as he pointed a finger that stopped just short of the dapper man's thick moustache.

"Kassie! What in blazes are you doin' down here?"

The dapper man smiled and chomped down on his cigar, stepping back to allow room for Kassandra to stand between them.

"The barkeep—Stymie, he—"

"Go back upstairs."

"He was very rude to me just now. Insulted me."

"I said get back upstairs."

"Ben, you have to know what he said."

"I don't have to know anythin', Kassandra." He glanced over her shoulder to the man standing behind her, then pulled her close. "Don't do this to me now."

"But Ben! You have to—"

"Not now."

Just then another pain seized her, and she inhaled sharply and gritted her teeth, focusing on the feel of the kettle's handle.

"Are you all right, Kassie?"

"Yes, I just…" She pulled him closer to her and whispered in his ear, "I think the baby might be coming."

Ben pulled away and looked at her with a suspicious glint in his green eyes. "Again?"

"Truly. It is different this time. It has happened three or four—"

"Mr. Connor? Sir?"

It was young Ryan. Kassandra had seen him often on the fringes of whatever activity surrounded Ben. He stood there now, next to a barrel that would have been nearly as tall as he was that afternoon in the back room. He had grown nearly three inches since then, and stood with his elbow jauntily perched on the barrel's rim.

"Are ya daft?" Ben said, impervious to the boy's wide smile. "Take that through the back."

"Hold up there, young man," Green Suit said. "How many have you got in there?"

"At least fifty," Ryan said, beaming. "And there's another kid comin' with more."

"Well, that's a fair job at least." Ben reached into his pocket and pulled out a wad of bills, peeling off two and handing them to Ryan. "See that James gets half of that. I'll be askin' him."

Ryan's smile grew even bigger as he stuffed the cash into his pocket.

"Now wait," the other man said, reaching into his own pocket and pulling out a gold coin.

"No, sir," Ben said. "I pay my men myself."

"Nothing says the lad can't accept a gratuity."

Ryan looked for Ben's nod of approval before snatching the coin. He dropped the barrel to its side, and a series of muffled scratches and squeaks emitted from within. Rolling it slowly, he made his way toward the alley. Behind him, Kassandra could see another boy engaged in a similar pursuit. He wore no cap, and the unruly brown hair was shaved clean to his scalp, but he wore the characteristic green kerchief around his neck. He looked up just as he passed the doorway, and she noticed a thin scar slicing one dark brow nearly in half, and a slight unnatural angle to his nose.

He's Ben's boy now.

"What is all of this?" Kassandra said.

"Ah, Kassie, haven't you learned by now not to ask me that?" Ben planted a quick kiss on the top of her head and, placing his hands on her shoulders, turned her away from him. "Now go on upstairs. Come find me if you need to."

Nearly an hour passed before Kassandra felt another pain. Changed into her nightgown, she was lying on their bed, head buried between two pillows to drown out the noise from downstairs. Just when it seemed the previous contractions had been yet another exercise in false labor, another came, stronger than before.

She had to find Ben.

She swung her legs over the side of the bed but found herself unable to stand. On her knees, her hands clutching Ben's mother's quilt, Kassandra waited for the contraction to subside. It lasted longer than the others, and as she knelt beside her bed, the memory of her long-abandoned nightly ritual of prayer seeped through the pain.

"Oh, God," she cried into the darkness. "I know You see me. You always see me. Help me, Father God. Give me strength."

When her body was once again relaxed, Kassandra stood and made her way to the table in the center of the room. She groped in the darkness, found the lamp and lit it, filling the room with soft light. She left it on the table as a beacon to lead her safely back and walked out of the apartment into the dark hallway.

A boisterous crowd in the Mott Street Tavern was not unusual, but Kassandra was little prepared for the onslaught of noise that greeted her as early as the third-floor landing. Even the clouds of cigar smoke seemed to have snaked their way up the stairway, stinging her eyes as she waded through it. Feeling weak, Kassandra paused just long enough on the second-floor landing to witness the crowd of men lined up in the hallway. She thought back to the barkeep's comment about her "spoiling the appetite" of the men who stood waiting for their turn behind the closed doors. She tugged the shawl she had thrown over her nightgown and kept her body close to the wall, hiding in the shadows as she turned the corner to descend to the first floor.

Kassandra remembered the eerie glow cast from the red-tinted globes that lined the walls of the back room behind the tavern, and she was surprised to see that crimson light waiting for her at the bottom of the stairs. For as long as she had been living with Ben, she had never known the back room to be in use, except for the afternoon's discipline of the young thief. Now she realized that the noisy crowd was not assembled in the tavern, but here in this back room, and as she reached the bottom step, what was normally a vacant, echoing chamber was now a sea of men. The density of their cigar smoke combined with the red hue, making it impossible for Kassandra to see clearly across the room. She called out for Ben exactly once, but her voice got lost in the smoky din.

Then suddenly the noise of the crowd came to an abrupt halt. Kassandra stepped back into the stairwell, allowing only her head to peek around the corner. Leaning against the wall for support, she felt the pain of another contraction coming on and stifled her cry with one balled fist brought to her mouth.

She soon realized that the silence had to do with a small procession making its way in from the door that opened to the back alley. At the front of the procession were Ben and the dapper man in the green suit, and they were carrying a small wire cage, about three-foot square. They came to the raised platform in the middle of the room, climbed over the wooden fence pickets, and deposited the cage onto the floor, the fence pickets obscuring its contents.

"Gentlemen!" Ben said, turning in a slow circle to take in the audience with a wide, sweeping gesture. "I give you Queen Sheba!"

With a flourish, the dapper man unhinged the top of the cage and lifted out a smallish dog, muscle-bound and writhing to get free. The crowd erupted.

Kassandra's pain intensified, and she sank to her knees, no longer worried, or hopeful, that her cries would bring Ben to her. She shouldn't be here. He had told her to stay away, and now she knew why. But until the pain subsided, she had no choice.

"Bring 'em in, boys!" Ben's voice somehow carried across the cheering crowd.

Young Ryan and James worked together bringing one of the barrels—now upright on a small hand truck—to the edge of the ring. Queen Sheba was returned to her cage, amid much canine protesting, and the two men stepped out of the ring. Ben produced a crowbar to pry the lid off the barrel, then using a set of metal tongs, he reached into the barrel and pulled out one screaming, squirming rat.

Kassandra knelt, breathless against the wall, her face pressed close to the rough plaster. She closed her eyes against the awful vision, but nothing could block out the sound. The frantic barks of Queen Sheba. The squealing rats. The voices of the men as they counted in unison—"Thirty-five! Thirty-six! Thirty-seven!"—numbering the rats to be killed by Queen Sheba. Kassandra counted with them, measuring the seconds left until the pain would subside, but when the men reached "Fifty!" with a resounding cheer, she was nowhere near relief.

"Now, gentlemen!" Ben called out. "The time to beat is three minutes! This man here will keep the time. All bets are in!"

The pitch of the screaming rats transcended the roar of the men, and no matter how hard Kassandra pressed the heels of her hands against her ears, nothing would block it out. The only blessing was the fact that the piercing of the screams distracted her from the pain of her own body. She curled herself closer to the wall, willing her senses to be deprived, and waited for the strength to stand.

Then, a new sensation, a new pressure, just between her shoulders. A new sound—"Miss Kassandra?"—barely discernible against the muffled, piercing screams of the rats.

"Miss Kassandra!"

She allowed one eye to open and turned her head. Sean knelt beside her, his long features a mask of concern. His lips moved, but she couldn't hear, so she gingerly lifted one hand.

"What are you doin' here, Miss Kassandra?"

"Get Ben."

Sean looked around nervously. "Can you stand?"

"Get Ben!"

"Come on." He grasped Kassandra's elbow and helped her to her feet. "Lean on me."

Kassandra's body once again relaxed just as a voice in the crowded room yelled, "Time!" Before being led up the stairs, she suffered one more look over her shoulder and saw the writhing dog, its muzzle covered in blood, being carried out of the ring to be put back in its cage. Meanwhile, a smiling Ben once again held the metal tongs and leaned over the picketed border of the ring to pull up one limp and lifeless rat.

"One!" the men began counting again.

Kassandra didn't know if she made it up the stairs under her own power or by the strength of Sean's strong arm around her waist. She did know that she had never seen a sight as welcoming as the light streaming from underneath her door, and nothing ever felt so welcome as the soft mattress beneath her.

"Now," she said, "go get Ben."

"Aw, he'll just be settlin' up." Sean wrung his cap in his hands. "I need to be down there wit' him, countin' the—"

"Listen to me! I am having a baby! I cannot do this alone!"

"I can send one of the boys. Young Ryan. To fetch Miss Imogene."

"Do that. But before you go, put some more wood in the stove and put the kettle on."

"Yes, Miss Kassandra." Sean's tall, lean form moved at her command.

"And Sean? In the top drawer of my bureau is my Bible. Will you hand that to me, please?"

"Are ya goin' to read right now?"

"I just want to hold it."

Sean nodded and walked over to the bureau. He opened the top drawer carefully, almost reverently, and took out the Bible. "D'ya want me to bring the lamp over here so you can see better?"

Kassandra offered up a weak smile, even as she felt the next contraction take over. "No, Sean. Thank you."

He nodded again and placed the Bible in her outstretched hands. Then, with unprecedented boldness, he reached down to smooth a lock of hair off her face and bent low to kiss the top of her head.

"If you was mine," he whispered, "I'd never leave your side."

"Go." She spoke through clenched teeth.

And he obeyed.

She tried to count the minutes between the birthing pains. Tried to measure their intensity counting up by fives as they progressed, then down by threes as her muscles relaxed. But all she could hear was the crowd downstairs tallying rats. Whether their voices were real or an echoed memory, she couldn't tell, but they were disturbing enough to make her resort to her childhood habit of naming the presidents. She cycled through the names twice before the pain finally reached its apex at Andrew Jackson.

When her body was at rest, Kassandra alternated between clutching her Bible close to her heart and listlessly thumbing through its pages. The room was too dimly lit to allow her to read, but the names of the books stood out as she riffled through: Samuel. Job. Proverbs. Matthew. How could it be that less than a year ago these books had such meaning? Reverend Joseph could call out a book, chapter and verse, and Kassandra—after just a moment's thought—could recite the Scripture to near perfection. Now, though, the words were as much a blur in her mind as they were on the page, but snippets of their truth came to her.

Lo, I am with you always.

Oh, Lord, my strength and fortress.

Deliver me from evil…

"Oh, God!" she cried out, whether in prayer or pain she was not sure, but before the escalating spasm could take all her breath, she spoke out into the empty room. "*Vater-Gott im Himmel.*" She had abandoned this language so long ago, and now, in an instant, she felt the comfort of childhood innocence as she called out to her heavenly Father, perhaps crying out the same prayers her mother had nearly sixteen years ago as she labored to bring Kassandra into this world. She begged for deliverance from this pain. She pled for the safety of her child. In a flurry of phrases barely comprehensible to her own ears, Kassandra begged God for His mercy, and called down His forgiveness for leaving the home He had provided, for coming to this place, for sharing a bed with this man.

Her body willed her to stand to relieve some of the pressure. Imogene would want her to walk. Kassandra herself had been the balancing force beside several women who paced through their labor, at least for those who weren't too intoxicated. Kassandra took inching steps, clutching along the top of the bureau, then palms-flat along the wall. Across the door. To the kitchen shelf where a glance at the stove showed the kettle to be simmering, but not yet boiling. She took one unsteady open step, practically falling against a kitchen chair, afraid to reach out for the table lest she topple it and break the lamp, setting the whole flat on fire. There would be no safe path across the room back to her bed, so she turned around, lurched back to the kitchen shelf, and made her way back to the bed.

Somewhere along the way, the intentions of her body took a turn. *Push.*

"*Ich kann nicht,*" she protested.

But her body would not be denied. *Push.*

Kassandra fell to her knees beside her bed. Everything she'd learned at Imogene's side, every trick and truth of childbirth fled her mind as she knelt there, her face buried in the soft mattress. She was conscious of a warm trickle along the back of her legs. She remembered Imogene telling her that that water was the life force of the baby in the womb. "When that water gone," she'd said, "time for baby to come out."

Push.

"*Nicht allein...nicht allein,*" she sobbed into the sleeve of her nightgown, but then she heard a voice as clear and distinct as if it had been spoken into her ear.

You are not alone.

Kassandra opened her eyes and looked around, but no one was there. Then her glance fell to the floor beside her, where Clara's Bible lay just where it had fallen. Sniffling, she wiped her sleeve across her face and picked it up off the floor. She held it in both hands and braced herself on her elbows.

"*Ich bin nicht allein.*" She dug her fingers into the leather and bore down.

❀ ❀ ❀

"Get off that floor. Into bed."

"Imogene! Where is Ben?"

"Into bed."

Kassandra felt herself being half pulled, half pushed onto the bed.

"Where is Ben?"

"Hush now."

"But he should be—"

"He downstairs. Waiting."

The brusque quality to Imogene's voice warned Kassandra against any further conversation. The little woman accompanied her ministrations with the same tuneless humming Kassandra had heard countless times. She lost herself in the notes, trying in vain to predict the next one when her body once again compelled her to push.

The humming stopped. The furrows that crossed Imogene's face deepened as she brought the light closer.

Kassandra took a deep breath and began to bear down.

"Stop!"

"I—I can—"

"I said do not push."

"Wh—"

But Imogene was gone. She threw open the door and ordered whatever sentry was posted there to go fetch Mr. Connor. Now. Returning, she positioned herself at Kassandra's feet.

"Tell me," Kassandra said.

"I see baby's head," Imogene said. "But something else, too."

"What?"

"The cord."

"*Oh, Gott.*"

"You keep pushing, not good."

"I didn't know…"

The final word trailed off in a shrill cry as Kassandra fought against her body's instincts to expel the child. In an instant, the heat generated during her fevered labor disappeared. She was overcome with chills as the sweat evaporated from her, the fabric of her nightgown clinging—clammy and cold—to her skin. It seemed her body would be trapped at this impasse forever. She reached toward Imogene, her hand floundering until it gripped the bony forearm.

"I need Ben."

"He downstairs. Smoking it up. Big man."

"Get him. Please."

But Imogene wouldn't go. Soon all thought of Ben vanished as Kassandra fervently worked to obey Imogene's quiet commands.

Deep breath. Hold. Little push, just tiny, tiny. Stop.

"Is the baby all right?"

"Don't know."

"If only—"

"Big push now."

The little woman all but disappeared behind Kassandra's raised legs and the now nearly sodden gown, but Kassandra smiled up to the ceiling, knowing that the "big push" always meant the end was near. She thought back to the miracles she'd witnessed, new beings thrust into the world. Maybe someday—

"Stop."

A tug, her body stretched, the pain beyond what she had ever imagined in all the times she'd stood by, watching new lives slide through almost effortlessly. She didn't scream, though. The time for calling out seemed long over.

"The cord. Around the neck."

Kassandra didn't scream then, either. There was no breath left in her to scream, or cry out, or voice a single prayer. Everything within her went numb. Her body fell away, dropped in pieces, floating detached from its core. The noise from the crowd downstairs dissipated, Imogene's instructions dropped to a whisper, and Kassandra allowed herself only the merest whimpering as she hoisted herself to her elbows and bore down with all the strength she could summon for the final push.

Then, the room fell into a silence as profound as she had ever experienced. There was no lusty cry from a newborn, no congratulatory pronouncement by Imogene as to the child's health and perfection. The old woman said just two words, "A boy," before placing the completely still infant in Kassandra's arms.

Neither woman spoke as Imogene attended to the final details of birth. She simply hummed her peculiar tune, bustling between Kassandra's splayed body and the washbowl on the table. Kassandra meanwhile studied every inch of the tiny boy—every wrinkle, every toe, every strand of soft hair that, even in the dim light of the room, showed every sign of being flaming red.

"He was perfect," Kassandra said, tracing a finger across her son's slightly parted lips.

"He was."

Imogene spoke more sweetly than Kassandra had ever heard as she reached down to take the little one from his mother's arms. She took him over to the washbowl on the table and, cradling him in one arm, brought the washcloth out of the warm water to gently wash the tiny body. From her bed, Kassandra watched as Imogene laid the child on a clean towel and gently patted him dry before taking a soft piece of flannel and swaddling him tight within it. Reverently now, she walked back across the room and handed the child to Kassandra again.

She looked down at the tiny face, infinitely peaceful, pale lashes dusting the tops of his cheeks.

"He looks like he is just sleeping," she said, after bringing the child close to kiss the top of his head.

"Always do." Imogene settled on the edge of the bed and reached out a stubby finger to caress the boy's face. "You want I go get Mr. Connor now?"

The idea of Ben storming into this utter quiet let loose the emotion gripped tight within Kassandra's chest. The first true tears flowed, and she brought the bundled baby close to her face, weeping into the soft blue flannel. Her shoulders heaved, but she made no sound until she voiced one long mournful sob.

"I cannot…cannot face him," Kassandra said once she had sufficient voice to speak.

"I tell him, Miss Kassandra. I tell him everything."

*F*ew people were able to mourn with the extravagance of Ben Connor. Even before the sun was up he had ordered a small, white, silk-lined coffin to be delivered to the little apartment, and trays of food to be laid out on the bar downstairs. All of the windows on all three floors were covered in black crape, clocks were stopped, and predawn revelers were unceremoniously ushered into the streets at the insistence of strong-armed, silent Branagans.

These same men returned later in the morning, this time to escort a few of the old women from the neighborhood who walked into Kassandra and Ben's apartment bowed with ceremonial grief and crossing themselves in nearly perfect synchrony. Under Ben's steely gaze, they took the baby from Kassandra's arms, unwrapped his tiny body, and began to wash it.

Kassandra managed to rouse herself from her numbed state, wanting to protest that he had been cleaned already, but Ben cut off any comment with a raised hand and soft thanks offered to the women. Kassandra watched silently from her bed as her son was washed, dried, and dressed in a beautiful gown of white cotton and lace and laid reverently on the kitchen table until the little coffin would arrive.

Kassandra spent the next few hours in fitful sleep. When she dozed, she entertained dreams of her son, floating just beyond her reach, resplendent in his white gown, its lace creating a cloud around his tiny body, wafting him further and further from her grasp. At the edge of this sleep, she heard conversations in the room around her. This is how she knew that her son would be buried behind St. Mark's, that the doors of Mott Street Tavern would open for the wake that afternoon, that the boy would be named Daniel after Ben's father.

When she came full awake, she wanted to ask Ben about all these things, but she found her voice stopped somewhere near the top of her throat, unable to call his attention away from the soft white bundle on the table.

He sat with his back fully to her, his head resting on his clasped hands. On either side of him stood an elderly woman, each with a gnarled hand resting on his shoulder. Even if Kassandra had been able to emit a sound, she doubted she would be heard over the deep, mournful sounds of these women—half crying, half singing Gaelic verse punctuated by wailing "Och, airiu…"

Kassandra watched, envious of their open grief. She hadn't shed a single tear since Ben's first arrival into that silent room, his face already ravaged with the pain of the news Imogene delivered to him. At the first sight of him, she had burst into sobs, crying, "I am so sorry, Ben," only to have him reach across the precious bundle in her arms and deliver a sound slap across her face.

"No sense weepin' over what you've killed," he'd said.

After that, every part of Kassandra—body, soul, and spirit—grew numb.

She was awake at noon when there came a knock on the door. Ben managed to tear himself away from the vigil he'd been keeping to open it and usher in two women Kassandra recognized from the second floor. Bridget had fiery red hair and a generous smattering of freckles across her nose, cheeks, and shoulders left bare by the flimsy chemise she wore tucked into a bright red skirt; Fiona wore a rich patterned wrapper cinched around her waist and loose black hair tumbled down her back. Both women smelled of sour alcohol and cigar smoke, and the stench of it awakened Kassandra's senses as the two women hooked Kassandra's arms over their shoulders and helped her out of her bed.

"Come along," Bridget said. "Time to get you up."

"What are you doing?" Kassandra said, finding her voice and the strength to struggle.

Bridget and Fiona loosened their grip on Kassandra's arms and looked questioningly over at Ben.

"Get her out," he said, and with new resolve, the women went back to their task.

"C'mon now, girlie," Fiona whispered into Kassandra's ear, her sturdy arm around her waist. "It'll be all right."

"I...I cannot leave him."

"We'll bring you back after a time," Fiona said, leading Kassandra in the first few tentative steps toward the door.

She was greeted on the second floor landing by a group of women—all vaguely familiar, though she would be hard-pressed to call most of them by name—in all sorts of ages, sizes, and stages of dress. They clucked and cooed as Fiona led her through them, doling small pats on her head and shoulders and muttered sympathies. Kassandra had been so accustomed to shunning their company that she could do little more than lean more heavily on the sturdy Fiona as she was conducted to the first open door.

A galvanized tub stood in the middle of the room, and one of the younger girls—probably close to Kassandra's age—was pouring a steaming kettle full of water into it.

"That'll do," Fiona said, and the girl offered Kassandra a tortured smile before scuttling out of the room.

Kassandra's nightgown was dropped to a puddle around her feet and, with the support of Fiona, she stepped out of its center and into the tub. Kassandra brought her hands to her empty stomach, and felt a new sense of mourning surge through her.

"Gone," Kassandra said. "He is gone."

"Yeah, it's always sad when a little one dies," Fiona said.

But Kassandra didn't detect any hint of sadness in her voice. The woman was all business, moving Kassandra's hands off her stomach so that she herself could press her hands against it.

"Miss Imogene told me to check your belly. Be sure it's flattened out. Soft."

"Where is Imogene?" Kassandra asked. "I would like to see her."

But before Fiona could answer, the door opened to let in Bridget bearing an armful of dark cloth and an equally dark expression.

"What's he got up there now?" Fiona asked, speaking over Kassandra's head after settling her down into the water.

"Two priests, would you believe it?" Bridget dumped her bundle on the neatly made bed and sat in a chair next to a tidy dressing table. "The man's heart is as black as sin, but he snaps his fingers and the clergy just flock to his door."

"Ben's?" Kassandra said.

"Never you mind," Bridget said, then immediately softened her look. "I mean, don't worry about nothin' right now. Poor thing. You have enough of your own grief."

Kassandra closed her eyes, leaned back against the raised side of the tub, and surrendered herself to Fiona's ministrations. Each limb was lifted out of the water and washed with a sweet floral soap before cascades of cleansing water—either from Fiona's own hands or the wringing of a soft cloth—rinsed her skin clean. For a brief moment, Kassandra was a child again—mute with shock, exhausted and alone, perched on the edge of a new life.

"You gonna wash her hair?" Bridget asked at the edge of Kassandra's darkness.

"Won't be dry before the wake," Fiona answered.

Then she felt her hair being lifted from her, and for a split second she feared that it would be shaved again. Instead, she felt the tug of a thousand bristles as knots and gnarls were smoothed against Fiona's palm. She felt her hair being plaited into two thick braids, then wound around the top of her head.

"Anything to pin it up with?" Fiona asked.

Kassandra willed her mouth to respond, but before she could, Bridget was saying, "I brought this from the top of her dresser." Soon Kassandra felt the familiar scrape of Ben's comb against her scalp.

"All right, now, girlie," Fiona said. "Let's stand you up."

Once again strong arms lifted Kassandra, and she stepped out of the tub into a large, luxurious towel that wrapped around her body. She obeyed Fiona's commands, arms up, now down, as she dried, the chill in the room turning her skin into goose-flesh.

"And this thing?" Fiona asked.

"Don't ask me," Bridget answered. "I never had no call to be a midwife."

The fog that had seemed so permanently settled around Kassandra's head lifted a little as she looked over at the bundle in Fiona's hand.

"Did Imogene send that?" she asked.

"Yeah," Fiona said.

"Have you boiled it? Steeped it?"

"Yeah. Just like she said."

"Then wring it out and bring it to me once it has cooled a bit."

Fiona and Bridget looked at each other and shrugged, then Bridget followed Kassandra's instructions while Fiona continued to rub the soft towel over Kassandra's warming skin.

"Where is Imogene?" Kassandra asked again. "I want to see her."

"Never mind that now," Fiona said. "Let's get you dressed."

She spread the damp towel over the bed to protect the

flower-sprigged coverlet and eased Kassandra to a sitting position upon it. Bridget brought the compress over and handed it to Kassandra, who took it and applied it directly where her body needed it. Soon, she knew, the lavender and comfrey leaves would bring some relief.

Next Bridget handed her a bundle of soft white cloth, folded into several layers, which Kassandra placed over the compress and held in place with a belt tied around her waist. Then, a pair of soft flannel pantalets and stockings, which were pulled on and tied by the much more willing Fiona.

"Don't think you need to bother with shoes," Fiona said. "Not like you'll be goin' out any time soon."

"I don't think you could get them on them feet anyway," Bridget said. "Be like puttin' slippers on a tree trunk way them feet are swoll."

Fiona sent Bridget a withering glance, but Kassandra found herself smiling for the first time in days.

"And apparently we're supposed to whip up a bunch of sauerkraut for the finishing touch," Bridget said, reaching into the bag she'd carried in and producing a head of cabbage.

"Now I know I heard you talkin' some of that kraut talk," Fiona added, "but I don't see how this is going to help."

Kassandra was amazed to find herself not only smiling but laughing, just a little. But her laughter soon died when she came to grips with what the cabbage was for.

"Tear off the leaves," Kassandra said, "the big ones. And wash them."

"I know, sweetie," Bridget said, sobering at the task. "Imogene told me everything."

Kassandra sat on the edge of the bed, Fiona at her side gently patting her leg as Bridget tore the outer leaves off the cabbage and dipped them in the same water the compress had soaked in. Once they were patted dry, she brought them over to Kassandra, who pressed them against her breasts. The pregnancy had made them full and round, and the impending milk for her stillborn child made them unbearably heavy. She stood then, holding the leaves in place, while Bridget and Fiona bound them in layer upon layer of a heavy cotton fabric, wrapping it tight until Kassandra's figure was completely disguised beneath it.

"Now the dress," Fiona said.

Bridget picked up the pile of dark fabric she had dumped on the dressing table when she walked into the room. It was a beautiful black silk, with a high collar and sleeves trimmed with matching lace. Once it was dropped over her head, Kassandra realized that even were her breasts not bound, her figure would be completely concealed in its shapeless cut as it fell in a straight line from her shoulders to the floor.

"And the picture of the grieving mother is complete," Bridget said with a sidelong glance to Fiona.

An unsettling silence fell between the three women, but it didn't last long as a wailing screech from upstairs cut through. Kassandra had never heard anything like it, and she started from where she sat on the bed.

"The baby!" she cried.

There was a split second when she feared her legs would give way, but she managed to take a few steps toward the door before Fiona caught her arm.

"Come, now," she said gently, leading Kassandra back to sit down.

But the wailing commenced again, a sound so sad it seemed to capture every one of Kassandra's unshed tears. Soon a soft vocalization of her own emerged to echo what she heard upstairs. The notes served as witness to her ravaged, unexpressed pain, and they were drawn from her, tugged hand over invisible hand, until she lacked the strength even to sit, and collapsed to her knees, her face to the floor.

"Now there's a keening true," Bridget said, her voice full of disgust.

"Hush, now," Fiona said, reaching a comforting hand to Kassandra's heaving shoulder.

"I mean it. She's the child's mother. She ought to be up there now."

"It's not our business, Bridget."

"Seems to me Mr. Ben could've saved hisself a few dollars there, anyway," Bridget said. "I could go up and screech like that, given a good reason—"

"Stop it!" Fiona said with a fierceness that jolted Kassandra out of her near trancelike mourning.

"She should be up there, Fiona. Up there with her son."

"And she will be—"

"But did you hear him? 'Keep 'er down with you, girls.' Like *she's* the one to bring shame—"

"Bridget! Hush!"

Kassandra looked up and wiped her eyes on the lace of her sleeve. "What are you talking about? What is happening up there?"

Fiona sent a pointed look to Bridget, then softened her gaze at Kassandra. "It's an old Irish tradition. They're keening. Songs for the dead. When someone dies, the old women in the family prepare the body and—"

"Those women are not a part of our *family*," Kassandra said. "I have never seen them before today."

"That's because Ben hired them," Bridget said. "He paid them to come, dress the body, to wail and keen and mourn."

"Why would he—"

"To make this all seem respectable. Like he has nothin' to hide."

"Ben and I, we have nothing to hide."

"What Bridget means—"

"I'll tell you exactly what I mean. Our Mister Connor wants to pass hisself off as the gentleman of the manor, with the wailin' upstairs and the beer flowin' downstairs. That way nobody will stop to think that the child's no more than some unbaptized bastard."

"Bridget!" Fiona's outrage took her away from Kassandra's side.

The two women let fly a barrage of words with a shrillness to rival the sounds from the apartment upstairs. Kassandra sat and let it all wash over her until she could bear no more.

"That is my child up there," she said, but neither woman responded, so she repeated, a little louder, "That is my child! And he is at peace now with God in heaven."

"He wasn't baptized," Fiona said in a pleading whisper.

"I do not believe God would cast away a child who never took a single breath in this world." Kassandra stood up, mustering all the dignity she could despite the soreness of her traumatized body. "I am going upstairs to be with my son."

"I don't think that's a good idea," Fiona said, offering a steadying arm. "Ben wanted to spare you—"

"He didn't want to spare you nothin'," Bridget said. "Hide you is what he wanted to do."

"From what?"

"Never mind that," Fiona said. "Bridget wouldn't have a kind word to say about Ben if it were painted on her tongue. If you want to go back upstairs, I'll take you."

"Don't you think you should put something on first?" Bridget asked with a pointed glance at Fiona's soiled chemise.

"Just help me up the stairs," Kassandra said. "I will be fine from there."

If it weren't for the fact that she walked through her own familiar door, Kassandra would not have recognized her little home. During the short time she was downstairs the apartment had been transformed into a shrine. No less than a dozen candles combated the onset of afternoon shadows. A tiny white coffin sat in the center of their table, flanked on either side by the old women—silent now—just as they had been when she left. Ben was no longer sitting vigil, though. He was engaged in earnest conversation with a rotund, red-faced priest who gripped Ben's hand and made conciliatory gestures with the other. As soon as the priest made eye contact with Kassandra, he excused himself from Ben and walked over to her, his pudgy hand outstretched.

"My child," he said as his eyes raked over her.

"No, my child."

Kassandra brushed past him and walked straight to the tiny coffin on the table. Nothing—not the silence of his birth nor the heavy weight of him in her arms—prepared her for this moment. Here was her son, nothing more than a tiny pale face surrounded by swathes of white cotton, silk, and lace. The topmost covering had a cross stitched in blue and gold thread, and a little rosary lay just over his heart.

She brought a hand to her mouth to trap what was left of her own breath.

"Oh, Ben."

Her fingers muffled her cry, but she turned, searching. For the first time she noticed all the other people in the room. Some she recognized—Sean with his bowed, shorn head, turning his hat in his hand; Mr. Kinley, the grocer—but there were many more, maybe a dozen, that were strangers to her.

"Ben?" she repeated after seeing him, his back to her, standing at their window looking out.

She took one last, lingering look at the baby's face before walking over to Ben and placing one hand on his shoulder. She felt his body tense against her touch.

"Father Michael," he said, shrugging her off and turning toward the portly priest. "Will you say the rosary?"

"Of course, son."

Father Michael thickly cleared his throat. Throughout the room, hands flew in one accord to touch foreheads, hearts, and shoulders, in the name of the Father, the Son, and the Holy

Ghost, Amen. Kassandra alone stood staunchly still, one hand still suspended where her touch had been rejected by the man who claimed to love her. Slowly she brought it down, to clasp the other just below her bowed chin.

"I believe in God, the Father Almighty," Father Michael said, launching into the Creed of the Apostles, while the room listened reverently to the recounting of the life of Christ. "...born of the Virgin Mary...suffered...died...ascended."

Kassandra listened as he listed everything he believed in— the Holy Spirit, the forgiveness of sins, life everlasting—and wondered if she could ever believe in any of it again.

"Our Father," Father Michael began before being joined by the others in the room, "who art in heaven, hallowed be Thy name..."

The familiar words rolled through Kassandra's head, though she did not speak them with the others. She picked through the sounds to find Ben's familiar voice, hearing him speak in prayer for the first time since she'd known him. She pictured his lips moving with the words of the priest. The last vestiges of a lilting Irish brogue clung to these syllables, just as it did in his everyday conversation, longing for the return of the kingdom of his hallowed Father in heaven.

"Hail Mary, full of grace, the Lord is with thee..."

Just as the Lord had been with her?

"...blessed is the fruit of thy womb, Jesus..."

And her womb?

"...who doth increase our faith..."

As hers waned.

"...who doth strengthen our hope..."

As hers fell.

"...who doth perfect our love..."

As she stood in a room full of strangers.

"And behold, thou shalt conceive in thy womb, and bring forth a son," Father Michael said.

Kassandra thought about the fear Mary must have felt at the angel's annunciation and about the spot of dread she had felt at the onset of her own pregnancy. Perhaps that was the moment God decided to take her son from her.

"...Hail, Mary, mother of God..." the strangers prayed to their sainted virgin as Kassandra stood alone. Silent and unworthy.

Father Michael recited the verses of Mary's visit to Elizabeth, the younger woman's confidante, and Kassandra looked out the window, combing the street below for the sight of her own dear friend in her floating ragged skirts. Her eyes darted back to Ben, and for the briefest moment, in the midst of all this prayer and meditation, her soul went cold.

"...lead us not into temptation, but deliver us from evil..."

Would she ever be so delivered?

"...pray for us sinners now and at the hour of our death..."

Father Michael spoke of the day Mary should be delivered, and Kassandra longed for one more day with her son inside of her. He told of the bringing forth of a son, and Kassandra remembered those final moments of hope. He told of wrapping the child in swaddling clothes, and Kassandra longed to trade her son's robes of silk and lace. He said there was no room at the inn, and Kassandra thought of all the children in the street below, wandering lost, just as she had. She remembered living just at the edge of acceptance in Reverend Joseph's home. And now, alone in this city, surrounded by people stealing her pain.

"Hail Mary, full of grace, the Lord is with thee..."

Father Michael told of Jesus' presentation at the temple. Would she have done the same for her son?

"...Thy kingdom come..."

He told of Jesus' teaching at the temple, sitting in the midst of religious leaders astonished at His knowledge.

She looked at the shorn heads of Ben's followers, their bruised knuckles and scarred faces. She thought about young

Ryan, taking such pleasure in his violence on Ben's behalf. She remembered the sound of the screeching rats, the roaring crowd, the music and whiskey and women and smoke that ruled their world just below this wooden floor. What chance had her son of being a scholar?

"…Thy will be done…"

Amen.

"Glory be to the Father, and to the Son, and to the Holy Ghost…"

Again the hands responded in perfect accord—head, breast, shoulder, shoulder—before they joined Father Michael in the final prayer.

"O, my Jesus, forgive us our sins."

And for the first time, Kassandra's and Ben's eyes met.

"Save us from the fires of hell and lead all souls to heaven…"

As they looked at each other across the room, Kassandra hoped to feel the first stirrings of shared grief and mutual comfort. But those hopes died as Ben's eyes narrowed to those green slits that could strike such fear within her, and his lips curled into a sneer as he held her gaze and prayed, "especially those most in need of Thy mercy."

❧ 14 ❧

The wake lasted until midnight. Kassandra chose not to join the revelers downstairs who were loudly celebrating the life of her son. What life had there been? She remained upstairs, sitting at the table, her forehead resting on the little coffin. Several women offered to spell her in her vigil—Fiona and Bridget among them—but Kassandra politely refused.

She had hoped to have a moment alone with Ben, the two of them in this quiet room consoling one another, but once he shuffled the little party out of the apartment after the time of prayer, he never returned.

The sounds from the wake wafted up through the floorboards and the open window, carrying the sounds of toasts and songs. Often Ben's name was called out in a raucous cheer, and uproarious laughter accompanied the antics of some of the games, but Kassandra felt no desire or obligation to join them. And, after a time, no one came up to cajole her.

When the little white casket was lowered into a freshly dug grave, Kassandra stood alone, looking at Ben on the other side of the chasm surrounded by a throng of solemn, bowed, shaved heads. After the final prayer, Ben dropped a handful of dirt into the grave. Kassandra heard it skitter over the casket below, and when Father Michael gestured for her to do the same, Kassandra merely let the clump of soil clutched in her fist fall to the ground by her feet. There was a brief moment of uncomfortable silence before Father Michael dismissed the small gathering, and everyone dispersed under the canopy of whispered conversation. Some shook their heads, *tsk*ing about the sadness of the death of a child; others murmured about the great loss this was for Ben, who so badly wanted a son.

Nobody offered a word of comfort to Kassandra. Indeed, few seemed to know who she was and why she was there. She'd searched the small gathering, looking for any sign of Imogene. As the closest thing Kassandra had to a friend, she should be here. Perhaps she felt at fault, but surely this wasn't the first child she'd lost as a midwife.

The shuffling crowd broke into groups of two or three. Ben continued to be surrounded by his men, all of them moving in one accord back toward Mott Street. But Sean lingered behind. He turned to find Kassandra's eyes, offering her a dark gaze laced with sympathy. And something else.

Kassandra made her way to him and reached out to touch his forearm. He took her hand in his—just for a moment—then released it.

"I'm so sorry about this, Miss Kassandra," he said. "Maybe if I'd—"

Kassandra silenced him with a gesture. "There was nothing to be done. It was the will of God. Somehow."

"But if I'd gotten Miss Imogene sooner—"

"There was nothing," Kassandra repeated with an air of authority and finality that surprised her. "But I want to ask you about Imogene. Where is she? Would Ben not let her come to the funeral?"

"Don't you know, then?"

She did, at that moment, but she looked up into Sean's eyes and shook her head.

"Imogene's dead, miss."

"No," Kassandra said, shaking her head more fervently now. "How could he do that?"

"She was an old woman. Old women die."

"But of course *he* wouldn't do it himself. That's why he has you…" Kassandra took several steps back, not stopping until she felt herself well out of his reach. "Was it you?"

"I couldn't do it," he said, rubbing his hand over his clean, dark scalp. "I couldn't do that to…her."

"Who, then?" Kassandra looked over her shoulder at the crowd following Ben. Bringing up the rear was young Ryan, who stopped to look back at Kassandra and Sean. "Was he here today?" Kassandra asked, keeping her eyes on young Ryan.

"No."

She turned to face Sean again. "Do you know how?"

"Quiet. Quick."

His coldness galled her. She felt sick, as if something besides her child had been ripped from her, leaving her hollow and weak. The dark wool coat of the man in front of her loomed closer as her legs gave out beneath her.

"Careful." Sean grasped her arms and stooped just a bit to come face-to-face with her. "Are you going to be all right? Should I get Ben?"

"I will see him hang for this," she whispered.

"No, you won't." His lips barely moved. "Forget you know anything. Forget I said anything."

He loosened his grip slowly, as if testing her steadiness. Seeming satisfied, he called young Ryan over, saying, "See that she gets home safely," before giving Kassandra a gentlemanly nod and setting off in the direction opposite Ben's.

Imogene's death became a local, ironic tragedy: The beloved and revered midwife, unable to bring the Five Points prince into the world, went to her home and died—quietly, naturally, in her sleep. Nobody voiced the least bit of suspicion. Why would they when Ben Connor himself footed the bill for her funeral? For the second time in as many days, the Mott Street Tavern played host to a good Irish wake, this one full of celebration of a long life. Once again, Kassandra sat alone in her room, listening to it all. But on this night, unlike the night she spent with her son, she was grateful for her solitude as she cried thick, silent tears until the last drunken mourner was tossed into the street.

Then, as empty as she had ever been, she slept.

For weeks after, Kassandra saw next to nothing of Ben Connor. On the occasions that she made her way through the tavern to venture out into the streets, he might be behind the bar or conducting some sort of business at one of the tables, but he never acknowledged her. He hadn't crossed the threshold of their flat since the funeral, and where he had been sleeping all these nights was a quandary answered by the excessive comforting offered to him by the second-floor girls as he made his rounds in the tavern.

Two of those girls, however, Bridget and Fiona, showed their allegiance clearly to Kassandra. In the early days, when Kassandra couldn't bring herself to get out of bed, they came to her with trays of food. They stayed to entertain her with conversation and news of the world outside, avoiding—after Kassandra's initial reaction—any mention of the baby or Imogene. After a time they convinced her to get up and join the world again.

"I do not have a world here," Kassandra said. "Ben was my world."

"That world's gone now, isn't it?" Bridget replied. "Time to make yourself a new one."

But Kassandra had no idea just how or where she was to fit in now. The more time she spent in the cozy little flat that had once seemed like such a nest and home, the more she felt like a guest who had overstayed her welcome. Each day she tidied it up, then sat—expectantly—at the table until it was time to go to bed again. Whenever her meager food supply was depleted, she went to the little jar on the kitchen shelf where Ben had always deposited a few coins for household expenses and fished out enough to get a few groceries at Kinley's. But after a week Kassandra began to wonder just what she would do when this little bit of money ran out.

"Why doesn't he just tell me to leave?" Kassandra asked Bridget and Fiona one day as the three women spent an afternoon chatting downstairs.

"He hasn't decided if he's done with you yet," Bridget said, casting the man himself a sidelong glance as he sat at the end of the bar, regaling a small gathering of men and women with some tale of import.

"If he is *done* with me?" Kassandra said. "He has not even spoken to me, not once, since—"

"He doesn't know what to do with you," Fiona said.

"Does he give you one more chance? Send you home? Or kick you downstairs?" Bridget ticked the choices off on her fingers.

"Well, he won't send her back home," Fiona said. "How would that look?"

"Wait a minute," Kassandra said. "What do you mean by kick me downstairs?"

"Where do you think we all started?" Bridget said. "Most every girl here was Ben's at some time."

"Now, Bridge," Fiona said, "that's not so. He might've brought them here, promised them things, but he didn't…"

"Have you two—been—with Ben?" Kassandra asked.

"No, dear, no," Fiona said, reaching a comforting hand to pat Kassandra's arm and sending a scathing look toward Bridget. "And Bridget hasn't, either. None of us has, no matter what it looks like." This, as one of the women gathered around Ben let forth a stream of gilded laughter and laid her head on his shoulder. "Ben's always made it very clear that he wasn't going to sully himself with any of the likes of us—"

"Yeah, the saint," Bridget said.

"He told me once that he thought I was pure," Kassandra said. "He wanted me because he knew I was untouched."

"Exactly," Fiona said. "We're all just people he's gathered around him. He gets a cut of the girls' money, and in return we get a nice place to live. The Branagans take care of his business and get a kind of respect they wouldn't get otherwise."

"The key," Bridget said, her voice maintaining that sour note it always had, "is that everybody gives Ben something. From you, he wanted—"

"A child," Kassandra whispered.

"That's right. Since that didn't happen…" She shrugged her shoulders broadly and settled back in her chair.

"Give it time," Fiona said. "He's mourning, too, you know. This has been quite a shock. Ben always gets his way."

"And I am supposed to just sit up there, waiting for him to decide what he is going to *do* with me?"

"You don't have to," Bridget said. "After all, you're a great big grown-up girl. How old are you?"

"Sixteen."

"Sixteen…" Bridget's voice faded to a nostalgic note. "You remember sixteen, Fiona?"

"Course I do. My father beat me till my teeth fell out, then took all the money I made whorin' for his friends."

"That is awful!" Kassandra said.

Fiona smiled, broadly enough that Kassandra could see the gaps of her missing teeth. "That's when Ben found me. Brought me here. Said if I was goin' to do a woman's work I'd be keepin' a fair share of the earnin's."

"See?" Bridget said. "A true saint."

"And your father? Did you ever see him again?"

Fiona's smile remained, but the slightest narrowing of her

eyes changed her countenance completely. "Oh, no. Ben took care of that, too."

The echoes of their conversation remained in Kassandra's mind as she made her way up to the third-floor flat later that afternoon. Had Ben ever loved her? Or was she just a kept woman to provide him with the son and heir he so desperately wanted? His passion had seemed so real when he first brought her here—his professions of love so emotionally charged. She'd truly believed that all of the excitement he'd shown over the coming child stemmed from his happiness at the thought of the three of them becoming a family. But, thinking back, there had never been any conversations about a future.

Or marriage.

She vacillated between feeling relief that she had no legal bond to this man, and wondering if, had she insisted that they follow what God commanded before ever sharing his bed, their son might have been spared.

She opened the door to the familiar room: the little table with its two chairs, dishes neatly stacked on the shelf, the bed covered with Ben's mother's quilt. Besides the little bird figurine perched on the dresser, the room looked every inch the way it had when Ben first ushered her in here nearly a year ago. There was nothing to say it was her home. Nothing to speak of the ghosts of joy or the shattering tragedy that played out within its four walls. Her clothes were hung neatly behind the blanket nailed to the wall, her other things tucked away in the dresser drawers just as Ben always liked—no, insisted.

She thought back to her room at Reverend Joseph's, picturing how it must look now after she had tucked everything she owned into the parcel she'd carried here. She imagined it didn't look a mite different than it had the moment she'd first opened her blinded eyes to it. No place, it seemed, had ever really been her own. Her life with Reverend Joseph and her life here with Ben weren't much different than the life she'd lived on the streets as a child. Just find a place to rest for a while, then move on. The only difference was that, as a child, she had been in control of where she chose to lay her head. She alone wandered the streets and alleys finding just the right shelter for her needs. Shady and cool in the summer, curled-up and soft in the winter. No one ever scooped her up or led her anywhere.

Well, she was now, as Bridget said, a great big girl. She wasn't about to sit at this table and wait for Ben to show up and decide just what he was going to do with her.

Moving quickly, she opened the dresser drawers and pulled out her clothing. Once again she took her best flannel nightgown and wrapped the precious sparrow figurine inside it. She took her dresses from the hooks on the wall, her brush and mirror from the top drawer. There, too, she saw Clara's Bible, with Reverend Joseph's letter tucked safely inside. She paused for just a moment to unfold it and brought to her lips a tiny lock of soft hair clipped from her son's head in the wee hours before his burial.

"Dear God," she prayed aloud, "guide my steps."

She placed the lock of hair back in the letter's crease, put the letter back in the Bible, and set it on top of everything she owned as she lifted the corners of Ben's mother's quilt to wrap up the entire bundle.

"That's when we get the best out of life, darling," she said to Ben's empty room, repeating the words he'd said to her in Reverend Joseph's parlor, "when we take a chance."

Of course, some chances were just foolhardy. So, once packed and ready, she settled down in one of the kitchen chairs to wait until dark.

Kassandra never was fully comfortable with the city at night. In truth, she'd been allowed very few forays into the dark streets, a fact that made her revel in her newfound independence all the more.

She strode as purposefully as the intermittent crowds would allow. Late spring still meant cold, damp nights, and her steps brought her weaving through clumps of people gathered around makeshift fires in iron casks on the sidewalks.

Habit had taught her to check over her shoulder frequently for the shaved Branagan heads following her through the streets, but even Sean's attentiveness had waned of late, probably fueled by Ben's own disinterest, and once she was out of Ben's territory, she felt no need to check behind her.

She took a deep, bracing breath and smiled. How could she ever have found the scent of the city distasteful? Yes, it was rancid and raw, but it was *life*. These were not people trapped in a little room waiting for someone to decide what to do with them. They were making their own way, surviving off the bounty of the streets.

When she was a little girl, all she ever needed was the occasional scrap of food and a quiet corner to settle down. And hadn't she been happy? Of course there had always been the tug of hunger, but that was just enough to keep her alive, alert. She hadn't been hungry—truly hungry—in years. No wonder she'd been lulled into such complacency.

She hazarded an occasional glimpse into the eyes of the women who stood, lounging and brazen on the street, their blouses open despite the evening chill, calling out promised favors to the men passing by. How different was she, really? Hadn't she allowed Ben—a stranger—to kiss her? Touch her? She'd gone into his bed as willingly as any of these women would, taking lies for cash and ending up back on the street with the encounter over.

She guessed it was about midnight. She'd been out of Ben's sphere for little more than an hour when the first twinge of regret hit. It actually hit her from behind, coming in the form of a man running at full speed who either didn't see her or didn't care that she was in his path when he slammed into her, sending her bundle of belongings into the street and Kassandra right on top of it.

"Get up, ya lousy jerk!"

Kassandra lay in the street, her face buried in Ben's mother's quilt, certain that the command was meant for her until a stream of curses erupted from the man who had knocked her down. She gingerly turned her head to see him hauled to his feet, and the voices that had been bellowing an exchange of insults were soon quiet as two men began exchanging blows instead.

She'd seen fights before. As a child, certainly, and from the safety of her third-story window she'd witness several displays of bravado fisticuffs and near-murderous violence. But never had she been close enough to feel the spray of blood from a shattered nose. In a frantic struggle to get out of the way, she found her legs tangled up with those of her earlier assailant, and within seconds the man was back on the ground, much to the amusement of both his opponent and the gathered crowd.

"Hey there, Bob!" an anonymous voice called out. "Not like you're the first one brought down by a whore's skirt!"

Raucous laughter followed as Bob disengaged himself and staggered to his feet. Kassandra, too, struggled up and was on her knees, her face bowed in shame as the crowd continued to shout its taunts.

"Whoop, look out, Bob! She's gettin' up now. Watch *she* don't knock you down this time!"

"Yeah, take 'er on." This the voice she recognized as Bob's assailant. "You might have a chance beatin' her."

"I'd take her on," another man said. "Lay 'er back down again and take 'er right now."

"Lay her down? She's already on her knees." And a chorus of low chuckles.

There was a palpable change in the crowd then. A primitive, canine-like quiet came over them—all of them—as the entertainment of an impromptu boxing match suddenly lost all its appeal. She still did not look up, but saw from the corner of her eye that the men were circling her. She saw filthy boots, dark pants—some nearly shredded—in a neat circumference around her. Then one pair of boots walked toward her and stopped in front. Soon she felt a hand at the back of her head, grabbing a handful of her hair, digging Ben's comb deep into her scalp, and yanking until she was forced to look up into a face so bloodied and raw it must be Bob himself.

"You knocked me down," he said through swollen lips.

"Get your filthy hands off me," she said, squelching any instinct she had to plead or beg.

An amused murmur resounded with the pack of men. Kassandra felt the release of her hair as Bob took a step away. The last thing she heard was "Slut!" before Bob's boot collided with her face, and everything went black.

*H*er first instinct, even before opening her eyes, was to run her tongue along her teeth to ensure that none had been knocked out. A small matter of vanity, perhaps, but one that seemed logical considering the crushing pain and the taste of blood in her mouth.

All there. A bit loose in the front, on the left, but none missing.

She was cold. Even without opening her eyes she knew it was that gray, predawn time in the city, a time when the streets were nearly thick with silence. Drunks and revelers were settled in their flats or in stupors along the streets; vendors hadn't yet brought out their carts and calls. The ground beneath her cheek was damp, and the chill of it seeped through her dress. She felt the hard-packed dirt beneath her open hand and gingerly patted it, reassuring herself that there was a solid world to carry her whenever she did choose to get up and join it.

The first sight to greet her when she opened her eyes was the distorted vision of colors gathered together with loving, precise stitching. The quilt from their bed. She groped across the bundle to find the rope still knotted at the top, seemingly undisturbed. She rose up just a little, running her hands, caked with mud, over the fabric, feeling the outline of Clara's Bible and the ridge of her hairbrush, taking comfort in the assumption that the bird figurine was still nestled inside.

Nothing missing.

But as she struggled to sit up, she felt a dampness in her skirt. Not anything seeped through from the street below, but something clinging against her very skin. That, combined with a tearing pain and a bunching of her underskirts triggered flashes of memory from the night before—flashes brighter than those first rays of sunlight piercing through the buildings looming over her.

They had taken what they wanted, after all.

The alley in which she revived herself—to which she had at some time, somehow been dragged—offered relative privacy from the stirrings on the street. The occasional passerby glanced in, but most ignored her as they would any other besotted mass. Kassandra herself had walked past and over countless such bits of humanity. Now she was thankful for the isolation as she crept further into its recesses, not yet trusting her legs to stand. There, hidden in the shadow of the tenement wall, she gingerly ran her fingers over her face. Swollen, yes, but no sign of any open wounds. Flakes of the crusted substance under her nose were dark, but the nose wasn't broken. She didn't doubt there was a fair amount of discoloration and bruising—she'd seen enough women with faces ravaged by their husband's fists to know that—but all bruises fade over time.

Then, her hands. The backs of them raw with cuts and scrapes, as though she'd valiantly defended herself. Closer inspection revealed dirt caked within the wounds, and she remembered. She hadn't fought back; she'd been pinned down. But still, these wounds were nothing that a little water, bandage, and balm wouldn't cure.

And the other…

Bracing herself against the wall she slowly stood up, then allowed herself a few steps, cringing at the chafing rawness. What had he—had they—done to her? She reached up her skirt and found the waist-tie of her bloomers, untied it, and let the garment fall around her ankles. After stepping out, she reached down and picked them up. The garment was smeared with blood, trailing halfway down the leg. She wadded up the material and tossed it to the ground beside her.

Once again, she reached up under her skirt and found the waist of her first petticoat, untied it, and let it drop to the ground. This, too, she lifted for inspection. This, too, bore the stain of her blood and brought it all vividly back. The fruitless struggle as her skirts were lifted. Hands gripping her feet. Whiskey-soured breath breathing into her mouth. Dirt in her hair. And one after another, after another. The seemingly endless lot of them in turn rutting and swearing and laughing.

Kassandra barely had time to take a few steps away from her precious bundle of belongings before bending over to retch against the wall, bringing up blood-tainted spit. She allowed herself a bitter laugh as she sought an unsoiled corner of her ruined petticoat to wipe the corners of her mouth when she was finished. So this, then, was the result of her first night of freedom from Ben. She imagined him somewhere—either holding court back at Mott Street Tavern or even just around the corner—sharing her low laughter.

How was it she had been able to live the earliest, smallest years of her life on these same streets in complete and utter peace? Had her survival instincts been completely eroded by years of Reverend Joseph's pampering and Ben Connor's protection? She reached into the deep pocket of her skirt and found the handful of coins taken from the jar on the shelf in the apartment. In her early, hungry days, this would have been a fortune—infinite bounty. Now, she wondered how it would get her through this day, let alone the next, or the next. Reverend Joseph and Ben thought they saved her, but they hadn't. They'd crippled her, made her unfit to live with either of them. Or alone.

She hadn't felt frightened as she strode through the streets alone last night. She didn't really feel frightened when Bob's drunken frame knocked her down. She'd been startled, then annoyed, but the reverend's assurance that God's watchful eye and his own careful training would always keep her safe in this world, coupled with Ben's reliably long arms, had kept her from ever feeling any real fear. It wasn't until this new morning, her face swollen and sore, her teeth loose, her hair and hands encrusted with filthy alley dirt, her underskirt streaked with blood, that Kassandra felt truly afraid.

She hugged her arms tight around her and folded herself against the tenement wall. *Dear God,* she began, then stopped. This was the God that saw everything, even the tiniest sparrow falling to the ground. Had He seen her last night? A new sense of shame enveloped her, dwarfing any she'd felt before, making her so small that she was sure she escaped God's notice. She couldn't pray. There, in that alley, cut and bruised and torn, she was overcome with such longing that she faltered a bit and fell to her knees. For a year she'd been vacillating between ignoring the growing emptiness inside her and placating it with the occasional prayer or glance at Scripture. Last night that emptiness became a deep, black, hopeless chasm.

She had to go back to him. But not like this.

Out of the corner of her eye, Kassandra saw, just next to where she'd been sick, a discarded, rusted tin bucket languishing on its side. There was a short, dull pain in her back when she bent to pick it up, and she wrinkled her nose a bit after sniffing inside. God alone knew what this bucket had last been used for. Left with little other choice, though, she picked it up and went to look for the closest water pump.

There was one not far—maybe half a block away—and she debated whether or not her bundle of possessions would be safe in that long of an absence. She took her chance and walked as quickly as her wounded body would allow without drawing attention to herself.

She rinsed the bucket twice before finally filling it. Then, she walked swiftly back to her little nest, keeping her head down and her eyes on the ground, though nobody seemed to take much notice of the bruised, bedraggled young woman fairly limping through the street.

Once back, she picked up her bloodied petticoat and tore off a sizable square. This she dunked into the water, wrung it out, and brought it to her face. She winced a bit as it made first cold contact with her bruised cheek, and though she hadn't brought out her mirror, she was increasingly satisfied as she saw the remnants of blood and dirt come off on the clean cloth. When at last the rag came away clean, she pronounced herself so, and tore off a second piece of the petticoat.

She dunked this new piece into the water and wrung it out, then brought it up under her skirts and scrubbed her legs and thighs, hoping to cleanse away every trace of her violation. The same cold water that had been initially uncomfortable to her face was somewhat soothing to her swollen flesh, though part of her wished to have a boiling kettle to submerge herself in a scalding bath. She longed for the healing of the lavender and comfrey compress she'd used just after the baby, and for just a moment she allowed herself the luxury of being glad the child was dead so he might never know the kind of world that would do this to his mother.

Once clean, she knelt in front of her little bundle and untied the knotted rope. She took out a small jar of a lavender and lanolin cream Imogene had given her to protect the newborn's skin and pried the large cork out of the jar's mouth. The healing properties of the cream were immediate, and she sent a silent, heartfelt thank-you to her caregiver and friend.

Kassandra dug into the bundle once again to find a clean pair of bloomers and debated whether to pull on another petticoat. She had several, as Clara had always told her a well-dressed young lady never wore fewer than three, but the idea of being such a slave to fashion seemed more ridiculous now than ever. He wouldn't care how many petticoats she wore. He had probably never noticed.

She once again tore strips of cloth from the petticoat, soaked them in the rapidly graying water, and wound them around her hands. Finally, she found her silver-handled hairbrush and brought it through her hair, dislodging tiny clumps of mud with its bristles. She began to plait it into the single braid she'd grown accustomed to wearing twisted into a knot and secured with Ben's comb. But she stopped herself and opted instead to leave it loose, with only the hair framing her face pulled away, as she'd worn it the day she left, hoping, somehow, to recapture just a bit of that innocence that now seemed to never have been. The comb was still lying in the dirt in the middle of the alley, where it had undoubtedly fallen the minute she hit the ground. As she took the few steps to retrieve it, she found herself in a much better state for walking, and the journey ahead seemed a little less daunting.

Her toilet complete, Kassandra noticed the handle of her hand mirror peeking out from the skirt in which it was wrapped. She debated for just a second on taking it out, but decided as long as she didn't look at herself, she could imagine she was much the same girl as she had been almost exactly one year ago.

Maybe he would think she was the same, too. And they could start all over again.

Kassandra folded the corners of Ben's mother's quilt around everything she owned and tied the little bundle securely. Then, standing, she picked it up and attempted to hoist it over her shoulder, without success. She slowly lowered her arm and took the first of many, many steps, willing her feet to bring her aching body to Park Avenue.

Back to Reverend Joseph.

Back home.

With each step she rehearsed what she would say when she saw him. From Canal to Grand she envisioned herself the weeping penitent. Unable to look him in the eye. She would simply walk, head bowed, into his waiting arms and listen to his whispered joy as he held her tight.

But as she grew closer, the anticipation of their reunion changed the scenario, and her steps took on a weightless quality. Each replay of it increased their joy, until her trudging reverie showed her to practically fly into his open arms, drawn through the air by the force of his smile. The thought of it would have brought an actual smile to her lips, had the expression not threatened to reopen the newly scabbed wound at the corner of her mouth.

Never mind that, though. Reverend Joseph wouldn't insist on a smile. Or even an explanation, she was sure. Not today, at least. They would have years ahead of them, Kassandra learning at his feet just as she had as a child. Reverend Joseph reading Scriptures, reintroducing her to the truths she longed to remember. He would drill her once more on her Bible, and to prepare for such tests—as well as to quicken her journey—she assigned a book to each step. *Genesis. Exodus. Leviticus. Numbers. Deuteronomy.*

Kassandra heard the bells when she hit the intersection of Broadway and Ninth Street, just as she cycled past Second Samuel for the third time. The sound of those bells was as familiar to her as the voice of their caretaker. She stopped dead and thought hard to calculate the date. The days had been somewhat of a blur since the baby—and truth be told for most of the months before—but she knew it wasn't a Sunday. And while any respectable-looking man with a watch fob shied away from her before she had the chance to inquire about the time, it clearly wasn't the evening, but it was long past noon. No reason for the bells of the Tenth Street Methodist Church to be ringing at all. The last time she'd heard the bells was the day she left, when Reverend Joseph ordered a mournful chiming chorus in honor of the late Clara. If the bells were ringing, then Reverend Joseph was there.

She took a brief detour on her path toward home, turning east on Tenth Street.

The crowd gathered around the church steps was massive, spilling nearly half a block and making any chance of reaching the door impossible. The first thought Kassandra had upon seeing them was utter relief, as nobody was dressed in mourning clothes and there was no hearse waiting at the front. There was a carriage, though, bedecked with flowers, and the general tone of the people gathered there was jovial.

A wedding.

Kassandra smiled—almost—and tried to imagine who would be coming through the church's ornate doors as man and wife. Who had been engaged when she left? Who had been slyly flirtatious? She allowed herself a private, youthful giggle, indulging in a one-sided schoolgirl conversation, trying to hearken back to that innocence when Sarah James had been her only link to all things carnal. She scanned the crowd now, looking for a glimpse of her childhood friend, wondering if she still wore her hair in sausage curls and silk ribbons.

Then the door of the church burst open, and the crowd made a path for the new bride and groom. The gathering was at least twenty people deep, and Kassandra had no chance of making her way through. But she would be patient. Soon the bride and groom would ride off in their carriage, the throng would disperse, and Reverend Joseph would be alone—in the good humor that weddings always put him in.

Then she saw him. As tall as she remembered and just as thin. Kassandra's breath caught somewhere just below her throat. She dropped the burdensome bundle she'd been carrying through miles of city streets and brought both hands to her mouth to stifle a scream.

Meanwhile, Reverend Joseph stood in the open doorway smiling as the bride, dressed in an elegant and expensive gown, appeared in the doorway as well. Kassandra craned her neck, straining to get a better fix on the woman's face.

It was that dull Dianne Weathersby. How many Friday afternoons had this woman spent in Reverend Joseph's parlor, while her conniving and desperate mother tried to manufacture a courtship between her daughter and the eligible young minister? Kassandra couldn't wait to see the poor man who had been coerced into such a union.

Reverend Joseph took the silk hat handed to him, put it on his head, and held out his arm to the former Miss Weathersby. Arm in arm they walked down the steps. When they reached the carriage, Reverend Joseph handed her up as if escorting a queen, then planted a quick kiss on her cheek when he sat beside her. He reached down and pulled out a large bag of sweets, throwing handfuls into the crowd to the delight of the children. With a good-natured command to the driver, whips were tapped to horses and the newlyweds drove away.

The carriage passed just in front of Kassandra. So close that one step would have taken her into its path. But the thought of it didn't occur to her until a corner was turned and they were gone.

"You can't very well go back to him now, can you, my love?"

It couldn't be. But she knew that voice as well as she knew the other.

"How did you find me?" She didn't want to look at him.

"Ah, now, Kassie." He grasped her shoulders and forced her to turn around. "Haven't you learned yet that nothin' happens to what's mine?"

"Plenty has happened to me, Ben."

She'd kept her eyes downcast, but Ben touched his hand to her chin and forced her to look up. He flinched a bit at what he saw.

"It wouldn'a happened if you'd stayed with me."

Kassandra left those words hanging between them, trying to sort out if they'd been spoken in compassion or as a threat.

There was nothing to confirm either one, just a chastising smirk that made her wish she could spit one of her loosened teeth into his face.

"I will not go back with you," she said.

"Ah hah!" He swept his cap off in a grand gesture toward the scattering crowd. "And how do you think the fine new Mrs. Reverend Joseph will feel about bringin' this fallen little angel into her house?"

"He will welcome me back."

"Are you sure of that? A woman can turn a man's head about things."

"I am like a daughter to him."

"Listen, Kassie girl."

He drew a protective arm around her, and before she knew it, she'd been herded off the sidewalk and around the back corner of the church, away from curious eyes.

"It's one thing to be the little girl back home after runnin' away with the handsome delivery boy."

"I no longer find you as handsome," she said.

"Nor, my love, are you so little."

"And who did this to me?" She felt tears well up in her swollen eye and tried to turn away.

"Aw, now, love," he said, lightly running his finger over her bruised face, "you can't be blamin' this on me, now. How many of them were there? Seven? Eight? That's more men in one night than most—"

Kassandra reached her bloodied, bandaged hand back and slapped Ben's face so hard the imprint was immediately visible among the freckles.

"Do you know what they did to me?" She was close to screaming, but the thought of the happy gathering just a few feet away brought her back to her senses. "Do you, Ben?"

"Kassie—"

"They—they *raped* me."

The sound of it, spoken aloud, made it real at last. She balled up her fists and pummeled his chest, over and over, repeating in a choked whisper, "They raped me. They raped me. They raped me."

He took the blows unquestioning, unflinching, until the pain in her hands brought them to a stop. He didn't try to comfort her in any way, never attempted to put his arms around her, draw her close, hold her. He simply stood—as unyielding as the solid wall behind her—until her hands were still, her breath steady.

Then, in a quiet voice of reason he said, "And just what do you think the reverend's wife will think about all that?"

"What can you possibly mean?"

"She'll want to know what you were doin' alone in the street at night, talkin' to a group of men—"

"I did not talk to them!"

"Of course you could always just keep it to yourself, but women have a way of sensin' these things…"

"No, Ben Connor," Kassandra said, shaking her finger in his face. "You will not do this to me again."

"And what am I doin'?"

"I will not let you seduce me again."

Ben threw his hands up in a surrendering gesture. "Kassie! I haven't touched you—"

"You know what I mean. It worked once before, but not again. I will not listen to your lies again."

"Now, love." He attempted to grasp her arms, but pulled away at her recoil. "Stop and think. Did I ever, even once, lie to you?"

"Of course you did!"

"Think, Kassie. I may not be the most honorable man in the world, but I am a man true to his word. I never lied to you."

"You deceived me."

"That's not the same." That grin was back, and the past few hours—the past year—was disappearing behind it. "Come back with me now, Kassie. There's nothin' for you here."

"There is nothing with you."

"You'll be safe. I promise you that."

"Is that all I am allowed to ask for?"

"You've seen this city," Ben said. "Bein' safe is more than a lot of women have."

He turned from her then and started to walk away, leaving her in the shadow of the church. It would have been a clean exit had he not stumbled over her bundle that she'd dropped sometime during their conversation.

"What's this?" he said, bending down to pick it up. "This looks familiar." He shot her a mischievous grin. "You're quite the thief, aren't you?"

"Please, Ben," she said. "I didn't have anything—"

"Now, you know I can't allow anyone to steal from me."

"I'll send it back."

"Oh, no, love. I might be offerin' you up to the reverend's new wife, but I'm takin' this with me."

Ben hoisted the bundle over his shoulder and started down the street. He had one hand in his pocket, and Kassandra swore she heard him whistling.

She stood alone watching, for the second time, any hope she had for a future disappear around the corner. She took one following step, then another, and when she, too, rounded the corner, she saw Ben standing next to a hired cab, her belongings in his mother's quilt strapped to the back, grinning like the triumphant prince.

"I know it's been a long day for you," he said, "so I figured to take you back in style."

Silent and sullen, Kassandra allowed herself to be handed up to the cab's seat.

It was late afternoon when the cab came to a stop in front of Mott Street Tavern. Ben stepped down and gallantly held out his hand to help Kassandra to the street, but she ignored him and did her best to breeze past him. When the cabbie unlashed her bundle and attempted to hand it to Ben, she shouldered her way between them, saying, "I will take that."

Ben shouldered her right back and handed the cabbie a substantial amount of cash and coin while taking the bundle from him in one smooth gesture.

The tavern was far from empty, but not a sound emitted from any of the people gathered there when Ben pushed through the front door and walked in with a sullen Kassandra lagging behind.

"Hallo, everyone," Ben said, oblivious to their gaped-mouth silence.

He walked straight through the tavern and out its back door. Kassandra followed into the horrid back room to the stairs, her eyes long accustomed to making a way through this darkness. She followed close behind Ben, her legs threatening to keep her from taking even one more step.

Ben stopped just short of the second-floor landing, and she collided with him in the utter darkness.

"I just want you to know, Kassie...I want you to know that I forgive you. For the baby."

It was the first he'd spoken about their child, and so shocked was she, she was unable to say anything in return.

Ben sighed and climbed on.

When they reached the second-floor landing, Kassandra reached round the corner to find the railing to guide her up to the third floor, but Ben's voice stopped her once again.

"No, Kassie."

She felt his hand grip hers, and he led her down the second-floor hallway—past girls who stood in their open doorways, whispering as she walked by. He took her three doors down, right next to Bridget's room, and opened the door. Inside were a plain iron post bed, a washstand, and a grime-covered window letting in the last of the afternoon light.

"Ben, you cannot mean—"

"You'll always be safe here, love," he said, not looking at her. "I'll see to that."

He walked over to the bed and put her bundle upon it. The knot gave him a little trouble, but he soon got it loose and untied the rope. Then, in one grand gesture, he took one corner of the quilt and flipped Kassandra's belongings onto the mattress, sending Clara's Bible and the silver-handled mirror clattering to the floor. The tiny bird figurine flew across the room, hitting the wall.

The sound of it caught Ben's attention, and he stooped to pick it up and brought it over to Kassandra.

"No harm to it," he said, grabbing her hand and placing the little statue within it. "Just a bit of a chip."

≈ 16 ≈

ever take 'em upstairs till you've got the money,"
Fiona told her. "Because then you're at their mercy.
They can do anything to you. Beat you. Worse."

"Not like they can't anyway," Bridget said.

"It's all different once you've got the money," Fiona insisted.
"I can take a smack across the mouth knowin' the man that give
it to me just put a dollar in my pocket."

"Dollar?" Bridget scoffed. "You've never taken a full dollar off
a man in all your days."

"What do you know what I take?"

"I know bloody well what Ben gets from us, and that doesn't
leave you with any dollar."

Kassandra listened to this exchange, her eyes bouncing back
and forth between the arguing women. They were all gathered in
her room on a muggy, early summer morning, nearly a month
after Kassandra's carriage ride home with Ben. Her face must
have registered something close to horror, as Fiona abruptly
hushed Bridget and gave Kassandra a comforting pat on her arm.

"This isn't anything for you to worry about right now," Fiona
said. "You know Ben'll keep an eye on what goes up to your room."

"And leave what for the rest of us, I ask you?"

Fiona shot Bridget a withering look.

"I'm just sayin'," Bridget pressed on, "that she's up here still
playin' the princess in the tower, and we'll have to send every
decent man up to her—"

"I will not ask you to send anything," Kassandra said with

an exaggerated air. "In fact, I would rather you keep them all to yourselves."

"Be careful what you ask for, girlie," Bridget said. "Keep yourself shut away like that and you won't ever get a man fed up to you."

"And before you think that's such a good thing," Fiona cautioned, "remember, those men are your survival right now. You don't find a way to get them upstairs and keep them there, you're goin' to find yourself back out on that street."

It turned out getting men upstairs wasn't much of a problem after all. Kassandra held no delusions that their attentions were due to her beauty. Many took a good-natured ribbing from their fellow tavern-mates for choosing her over some of the prettier girls trolling the tables. She was popular because she was—or had been—Ben's, and there was a certain prize attached to towing Ben's girl upstairs. The problem came once she had the expectant man at her threshold. Often they didn't get anywhere near her door before Kassandra, with a clipped apology, sent them straight back downstairs to find another girl. True to his word, Ben was her protector, of sorts. Any unwanted customer—and so far they were all unwanted—was firmly led away by one of the ever-present Branagans, who seemed no less attentive, no matter her change in status.

But that didn't prepare her for the evening she found Sean on the other side of her door.

"Miss Kassandra?" he said, with every measure of respect he'd ever used.

Her door was open, allowing a cross breeze from her open window to cool it from the stifling heat. She was sitting on her floor, elbows resting on the sill, looking out onto the street below when she heard a soft knock on the door frame and the low, familiar voice.

"Miss Kassandra?" He leaned forward, his dark brown eyes scanning the room. "Can I come in?"

Kassandra scrambled to her feet and grasped the door's handle, prepared to slam it straight into the man's face. "Does Ben know you are here?" she asked.

"He sent me."

As if by direct order, Kassandra backed away, opening the door wide with each step. Sean walked in, ducking his head though the doorway spared him more than an inch. She gave him a wide berth as she shut the door behind him, trying to ignore the knowing looks of the girls who poked their heads around to see who had been polite enough to knock.

"You look thin," Sean said, though he didn't seem to be looking at her at all. "Are ya feelin' all right?"

Kassandra could only imagine what a slatternly figure she cut, the material of her dress thin and soiled after more than a week's wearing, her hair lank and loose around her face. She tried to summon a reply, but was capable only of a brief nod and a vague gesture to sit down.

Sean glanced around, as if looking for someplace more proper to sit than her bed and, finding none, perched himself awkwardly on its corner. Kassandra noticed for the first time the sack he carried as he passed it from one hand to the other as he spoke.

"I can't tell ya how sorry I am, Miss Kassandra, about what happened. The baby, and then, the other…"

"You know about that?"

"I do. And I'd kill 'em all given the chance."

"How would you know who to kill?"

Sean set the sack beside him on the bed and looked straight at Kassandra. "I would kill anyone who hurt you."

"Ben has hurt me. Would you kill him?"

"There's not a one of us who wouldn't, given the chance."

She laughed at that and, emboldened by this new sense of camaraderie, sat down on the opposite corner of the bed. "So how does he command all of this…this—"

"Loyalty? I guess since Ben doesn't really believe any of us'll rise against him, none of us really believe it, either."

Kassandra rewarded him with a smile.

"He saved my life, you know," Sean said, his voice so deep it sent tiny rumbling waves through the mattress.

"He does think of himself as quite the hero."

"I was just a kid. Not much younger than him. My da beatin' the—well, beatin' me ev'ry day of my life. And Ben just tells me one day, tells me that ain't no way to live. That a boy can't grow up if he's beaten down. Can't ever be a real man, anyway."

"So what did you do?"

"I left. Came here."

"How old were you?"

"I dunno. Nine? Ten? This was just a burned-out lot. Ben'd got some boards from somewhere and built us—me and some other boys joined up with him—a little shelter. No one ever came forward to claim the land, so he built this place."

A comfortable silence settled between them as Kassandra envisioned that group of ragged boys building the foundation of Ben's empire. Soon, though, she became acutely aware of the stifling heat of the room.

"Let me raise up the window a bit more," she said, standing to her feet. But she felt her hand clutched in another, stopping her from taking even one step away from the bed.

"D'ya know why I'm here?" he said.

The grasp of her fingers in his was enough to compel her to turn around, look up, and be held there by the strength of his gaze.

"I cannot," she said.

"There's got to be someone, sometime," he said, inching closer.

"No, there does not. Ben said I would be safe here."

"Y'are safe, Miss Kassandra."

"He cannot expect—you, you cannot expect—"

"Wouldn't it be easier with someone who cares for you?"

"Ben cared for me."

"I'm not Ben."

He kissed her then, bending low to capture her mouth when she turned her head to avoid him. His lips were soft, and he moved them gently against hers, inviting her, nudging her to join him in their embrace. But she left her mouth stoic and slack, wishing she'd been allowed to cross the room to the window, that she'd been able to open it wide, that she'd been able to throw herself from it.

The panic didn't settle in right away, but welled up with each passing second. A little more as one hand crept around her back. A little more as she was drawn full against him. A little more as he dropped her hand and wound his fingers through her hair, tugging just enough to lift her face to ease his access, as he plunged in the moment she opened her mouth in protest.

She was back in that alley. Back, helpless, pinned to the street, rough hands holding her. Men laughing, tearing while she kicked and fought. She wanted to kick now. Wanted to bring her hands up as fists to strike this stranger, to rip her mouth away and scream until there was no breath left within her.

But she couldn't find the breath to utter the smallest whimper. Her hands dangled at her side, her legs unable to do more than carry her one small step away. Once that was taken, she found the strength for yet another and soon the hand at the small of her back fell away, and she was standing—quite shaken, but standing—alone.

"Please, go," she said.

"Not yet."

He took a knife from a leather holster clipped to his belt. Kassandra never took her eyes off its blade as he reached for the sack on the bed and cut through the twine cinching the top. He reached in and produced a small loaf of bread and something else wrapped in white paper.

"No one's seen you come out of this room for days. When's the last time you ate?"

He unwrapped the white paper to reveal a sliced ham and spread the fare out on the bed. With the same knife he cut the bread into rough chunks, placed a slice of ham between two pieces, and handed the sandwich over to Kassandra.

"I am fine," she said, holding the meal at a defiant distance.

"You're about to fall over. Sit down." He lifted the sack to make room on the bed and took two respectable steps away, standing to eat his own sandwich.

Trying not to appear as ravenous as she was, Kassandra sat down on the mattress and sank her teeth into the soft brown bread. After she finished the sandwich, she went over to the pitcher on her nightstand and poured water into her only cup. After drinking, she refilled the cup and offered it to Sean.

"No, thank you," he said, with a rakish smile she'd never seen before. He picked up the sack and reached inside again, bringing out a glass bottle of amber liquid. "D'ya mind if I drink this here?"

"Not at all," Kassandra said, wondering if all the men who frequented these rooms were this polite.

Sean dropped his unfinished food onto the butcher paper and wrapped the lot up before stowing it away in the sack. He uncorked the bottle, raised it to his lips, and took one long, seemingly satisfying sip.

"This isn't the swill from downstairs," he said, wiping his lips with the back of his hand. "This is pure Irish whiskey." He took another sip before offering the bottle to her.

"No, thank you."

"Ya sure?"

Kassandra nodded, never taking her eyes off the bottle as Sean took another long drink. When he was finished, he held the bottle out again. Kassandra reached for it.

"Maybe just a sip."

"Ya sure?" Sean repeated, smiling.

Kassandra nodded again and took the bottle from his hand. It wasn't the first liquor she'd ever had. Reverend Joseph had allowed glasses of wine on special occasions, and often treated stomachaches with brandy or gingered ale. Ben was never far from his own whiskey-filled flask and had often cajoled her into taking a sip or two. But nothing compared to what was in this bottle. The effect was immediate as she swallowed it down. Smooth, not burning as she had expected. Her head instantly felt a little lighter and her tongue a little heavier when she spoke.

"I have not seen you anywhere since—you remember."

"I've stayed away."

"So why are you here today?"

"It seemed…time."

She took another sip. "And did you bring this here hoping to get me drunk?"

"Not at all, miss."

She took another sip. "You didn't think it would make an easier go of it?"

He took the bottle from her and took another drink himself. "Easier, yes. But for me, not for you."

"What does that mean?" she said, laughing.

"You can't know how I feel bein' here. With you."

"How do you feel?" Kassandra asked, a flirtatious spirit taking over her.

There was a long pause while he seemed to search for the right word. Then he sank down onto the bed and looked up at her rather helplessly. "Scared?"

"Of what? Of me?"

Sean laughed and raised the bottle to his lips again, but Kassandra intercepted it and took a long drink. She felt the beginnings of protest from the ham and bread below, and while she waited to be sure all was settled, Sean took the bottle back.

"No, not of you."

He bowed his head, and Kassandra found herself fascinated by the perfect, clean plane of it. She had the distinct feeling that the room was shrinking all around her, as if she were being surrounded by cotton batting, and all that seemed in clear focus was the sight of this head and the amplified sound of her own voice.

"Does it hurt?" she asked.

When he looked up at her, puzzled, she attempted to steady herself and asked again, "When you shave it. Does it hurt?"

"No," he said, running his hand along the top of his head. "Not as long as it's done right."

"Can I touch it?"

"Of course."

She placed her hands on the top of his head. The skin was warm, but not as smooth as she'd imagined, as tiny shoots prickled against her palms.

"Was it dark?" she asked, a bit surprised at the slurring of her words.

"Black as sin."

She was drawn to that head, somehow, and before she fully realized what she was doing, Kassandra leaned forward and planted a slight kiss right on top of it. She felt his sharp intake of breath and stood there, her lips soft against his scalp, savoring this new sensation. Power. The room and the world had gotten so much smaller in the last few minutes. If there were fears out there, they were pushed aside by the ever-growing fog inside her own head—the same fog that was slowly dissolving the hardness inside her.

She moved her hands to the side of his face and tilted it back to look up at her.

"Tell me, Sean. One more time. Did Ben really send you?"

"Does it matter?"

"What would he think, seeing the two of us here like this?"

Sean grasped her hands and kissed each palm. "Part of me thinks it would kill him."

Part of her thought so, too, and the thought of it knocked down the last wall of protest as Sean pulled her to the bed beside him.

Drop Thy still dews of quietness,
Till all our strivings cease;
Take from our souls the strain and stress,
And let our ordered lives confess
The beauty of Thy peace.

~ 17 ~

Stymie lined the shot glasses along the bar—twenty in all, each full of dark amber whiskey. Side by side in the center of the row of glasses stood two frothing mugs of cold beer. A hush fell over the crowd gathered at Mott Street Tavern as Stymie held his hand high above the bar, sending officiating glances to the two figures poised over the first shot glass at each end of the row. At one end, a fellow named Burly Joe, fresh from the docks, still reeking of whatever vile cargo he'd hauled onto shore. At the other, Kassandra, her head just foggy enough to muffle the sound of Stymie's hand slamming down on the bar and the explosion of voices that accompanied it.

She reached for the first glass and tossed the drink back, barely feeling the bitter burning of the whiskey slide down her throat. She slammed the empty glass down on the bar with one hand and picked up the next shot with the other—a nifty trick she'd mastered months ago that shaved a second or two off her time. The floorboards buckled a little bit with the sixth shot, and Kassandra grabbed the edge of the bar to steady herself, holding on long enough for Burly Joe to turn and share a laugh with his buddies. She snuck down nine and ten while his back was still turned. Her head was full and ringing, barely registering the last shot, by the time she reached for the beer. After the harshness of the whiskey, it tasted cool and smooth. She tilted her head back and took long, deep swallows, ignoring the spill down her chin. She slammed the mug down in triumph before bringing her arm up to wipe off her face with her sleeve.

The fellows who had come in with Burly Joe declared they'd been swindled as they handed over money lost betting on their most dedicated drinker.

"It is all right, boys," Kassandra said, encasing the last word in a reverberating belch. "Next time you will know better."

There was much muttering that there'd never be a next time to come into this swindling snake pit, but soon their anger melted under the flirtatious persuasions of Bridget and Fiona. Even Kassandra took Burly Joe's unfinished beer out of his hand and offered to dance with him if he'd buy her just one more drink.

The small gathering of musicians struck up a lively jig and tables were shoved to the side to make room for the men and women who paired themselves off with little discrimination and even less decorum. The room was a spinning mass of music and bodies, and Kassandra found herself bounced and tossed and flung from one man to the next, pausing just long enough to rest against the bar and convince one man or another to buy her a drink, too, if he was to have one. She tipped Stymie a wink and a smile with each nickel handed across the counter before whirling off again on some other broadcloth arm.

At some point she broke away and walked over to the fogged over window to rest her head against the cool glass. Kassandra brought her sleeve up to the glass, wiped a clean, imperfect oval, and peered through to the other side. There she saw Sean and a small gathering of Branagans standing around a fire built high in a steel drum. They all assumed an identical posture—hands shoved deep into pockets in an attempt to appear impervious to the bitter cold, caps pulled low over their eyes, green mufflers wound right up to their chins.

She saw young Ryan, too. Of course he wasn't so young any-more. He was nearly as tall as Sean and probably sixteen—almost the same age she'd been when Ben first brought her to this place. That was two years ago? Three? She'd have a better idea this spring, on the baby's birthday. Or even tomorrow morning when her head wasn't packed with whiskey batting.

A rough tugging on her waist caused her to turn and face head-on the barreled chest of Burly Joe.

"I'm taking you upstairs," he said, baring a mouthful of sparse brown teeth. "Gunna try and get some of my money back."

"You need to settle up with Ben."

"We're settled," Burly Joe said, moving his hand from her waist to grab her upper arm. "Let's go."

"Buy me a drink first?"

He laughed at that. "I've bought you enough drinks."

"Just one more. It is cold upstairs and—"

"I ain't buying you no drink. Come on."

Burly Joe pulled her through the crowd, their conversations and laughter washing over her like one continuous wave. As she passed by, she tried to latch on to someone to anchor her to this place. She wasn't going upstairs with this man until she saw Ben. He always screened her men. Certainly he wouldn't approve of this loathsome fishmonger.

When they got closer to the bar, she saw Ben standing behind it, drawing a beer. He always liked to help out on busy nights like this, saying it helped him keep in touch with his people. Burly Joe was trying to steer her past the bar, towards the door at the back, but Kassandra veered resolutely and pounded her hand on the counter, trying to capture Ben's attention.

"I ain't buying you no drink," Burly Joe said, leaning his body against hers, trapping her against the bar.

"You need to settle up with Ben," Kassandra said. She continued to pound on the bar, rattling the empty glasses littering its surface. "Ben! Ben!"

"I told you I already settled with Ben."

"That is impossible. Ben!"

He heard her that time and, after handing the beer across the bar, excused himself from his conversation and walked toward Kassandra.

"What's the problem?" Ben asked, looking right over Kassandra at the man standing behind her.

"You tell me," Burly Joe said. "Your girl here ain't being much of a sport."

"There's no problem, Kassie," Ben said, still not looking at her. "We're good."

Ben turned to walk away as Burly Joe reached his hand between her body and the bar and began to pry it loose.

"Ben, wait!" Kassandra thrust herself forward and grabbed a handful of Ben's shirt.

"What are ya thinkin'?" he said, turning and wrenching himself out of her grasp.

"Come closer." She crooked her finger, beckoning him. "Closer." He brought his face nearly next to hers. "I am not going upstairs with that man tonight."

Ben smiled at her—the smile that never quite reached his green eyes. "He's already paid for ya, Kassie. Go."

"I will not," Kassandra insisted. "He stinks of fish."

The smile now crept up to his eyes, and Ben laughed. "Have ya taken a whiff of your own self lately, love? That's hardly a reason for turnin' anyone away."

Ben was still chuckling to himself as he set out two glasses on the bar and poured three fingers of dark liquid into each one.

"This one's on the house, friend," he said, pushing the glass toward Burly Joe. "And one for you, love. I forgot that it sometimes takes a little more to warm y'up."

Burly Joe reached around Kassandra and picked up the glass, thanked Ben by raising it to him, then downed the drink in one full swallow.

Kassandra stared at the glass she held, surprised at the appearance of her fingers—red and rough, the nail beds encrusted with grime. Her hand shook just a bit, though not enough to slosh the liquid over the side. She took a breath to steady the glass before raising it to her lips. She'd never developed a taste for swill—traces of wine and scotch and gin dumped together when there wasn't enough of any one to tap from its keg. But it was one more drink. Kassandra braced herself against the bitterness and tipped her head back, filling her mouth with the vile stuff.

When she looked straight again, there was Burly Joe, smiling at her with that mouth half full of rotted teeth. He was laughing—probably at something Ben just said—because the two of them were sharing a conspiratorial look. For just a moment, Kassandra considered spitting that mouthful of swill right into Burly Joe's face. Maybe that would get him to close that mouth, make him angry enough to leave her alone. If nothing else, it would mask the smell. But who knows what he might do to her once he got her upstairs? And Ben would see to it that he got her upstairs.

So she turned and spat it on Ben instead.

The ensuing silence didn't fall all at once, but began with those closest enough to see the drink hit Ben's face, and spread layer by layer through the crowded tavern until the only sound was a single fiddle note that screeched to a halt at someone's nudging insistence.

The initial angry curse was the only emotion Ben showed. Even as the droplets of his tavern's swill dripped down his chin and clung to his pale eyelashes, his expression remained passive as he calmly took the bit of towel Stymie offered him and wiped his face dry. But Kassandra knew—saw it in the narrowed slits of his green eyes—just how angry he was, and she wasn't fooled for a minute by the unruffled timbre of his voice when he said, "Go upstairs."

"Not with him."

"Find another girl," Ben said to Burly Joe. "Got plenty of 'em here."

"Don't want no other girl here," Burly Joe said.

There was a soft, unison gasp from the crowd at the challenge in his voice.

"Well, then." Ben folded the towel neatly and set it down on the bar. He reached into his pocket and pulled out the ever-present bundle of folded bills, pulling two off the top and setting them down on the bar next to the towel. "Go somewhere else. Go hit the places on Centre Street. Girls there dance with bells on their feet."

The man actually seemed to be considering whether to take Ben's order, but to Kassandra's relief he soon swiped the pile of bills off the bar, dropped them in his own pocket, and went out into the cold night.

"Now," Ben said, capturing Kassandra's attention once again, "go upstairs."

Without a word, Kassandra turned away from the bar and made her way through the crowd to the door at the back and up the stairs to wait in her cold room.

It turned out that she had quite a bit of time to wait. Long enough to run her brush through her hair and put a cleaner skirt on over the two she was already wearing. She dropped a bit of lavender water into her washbasin and splashed it over her face and clothing. The icy water may have stung her skin, but it also cleared her head—so much so that she subjected herself to a few more splashings long after she felt clean. She plaited her hair into a soft braid that she coiled and secured at the back of her head with the one comb he'd given her.

All of this she did by the dim light of a single candle. She hoped the softer light would lend warmth to the puffy pallor of her face and hide the cluttered corners of the room. Ben always did hate a messy room. She puttered for a few minutes, straightening the cover on the bed, hanging up her discarded clothes, laying her brush and mirror straight on the bureau top. Then, with one short, bitter breath, she doused the candle, saving it to light the room when Ben came to see her.

The sudden darkness caused the room to spin, and she staggered a bit before the backs of her legs found the edge of her mattress and she fairly fell down upon it. Groping around the end of her bed she found the shawl Imogene had given her the night Kassandra first helped bring a child into the world. She never let the garment leave this room, but kept it close by for those times when she needed the comfort of its warmth around her shoulders. She needed that comfort now—though it did little to ward off the bone cold of the room—and she pulled the edges of the shawl tight against her as she lay down on her bed, curling her legs up against her body.

She must have dozed off, because the minute she heard the knock she was fifteen years old again, racing down the back stairs to open the kitchen door. So great was her haste to get to the door before Clara, her legs became tangled up in her skirt and her arms were pinned helplessly to her side by the corners of the shawl. She lost her direction in the blackness of the room and fell against the bureau in her quest for the door. The knocking continued, giving her a target to aim for, and within two steps she found the latch.

He wasn't the only man in the hall. The space was packed with men jostling each other good-naturedly for position. The walls were lined with kerosene-fueled flames ensconced in glass globes. The light behind him, coupled with her own bleary vision, swept away his features in dark silhouette, but his stance was unmistakable. Chest puffed up. Arms straight at his side. Fists clenched. Legs anchored as if ready to withstand an attack.

"Ben?" The word was thick in her mouth.

"Were you expectin' some smelly fishmonger?"

She laughed and opened the door wider to let him in.

He walked through the door, rubbing his hands together. "It's freezin' in here. Colder than a—"

"Let me get a light."

She took the candle from the bureau top and dipped it in

one of the glass globes in the hallway to catch a flame. She closed the door behind them, and without invitation or request they sat side by side on Kassandra's bed.

"I was not expecting you."

"Liar," he said, reaching over to smooth the strands of hair torn loose during her waking.

"You have not been up here in a long time, Ben. Months."

"I shouldn'a started up again with you at all."

"But you did."

"I did," he said before kissing her with the hint of soft penitence that always lurked behind the first kiss.

When Kassandra allowed her mouth to open to his, she imagined him cringing at the stale whiskey on her breath and tried to pull away, but Ben clapped his hand on the back of her neck and pulled her closer. Deeper.

She was alive when he was here. She imagined these kisses held the same promise as their first ones, and sometimes the same girlish flush came to her cheeks. Everything—memory, pain, disappointment, loss—disappeared behind this embrace.

It was much the same feeling that she had when she reached the end of a drink, only instead of staring into the bottom of an empty glass, she kept her eyes firmly closed, trapping her in darkness where she and Ben swirled together. Shadows of the people they might have been. Before he took her breath. Stopped her heart. Dropped her in this cold, dark place.

The muted sounds of gathering outside continued to seep through the walls, little more than some harmless rumble until something—or someone—collided with the door, threatening to tear it from its frame.

Kassandra jumped up from the bed. "What was that?" she said, heading toward the noise.

Ben caught her hand. "Leave it," he said, pulling her back. And she obeyed.

She settled next to him again, and they sat in companionable silence, holding hands and staring at the floor.

"I am sorry," she said after a time, "for spitting that drink in your face."

He chuckled. "You know, I woulda killed any man that did that to me."

"But you would not kill me?"

"No." He brought her hand to his lips.

"Well, of course not *you*. But you might send someone else to do it for you."

"Stop it, love," he warned.

"Maybe it is time for young Ryan to get his first kill."

"Wouldn't be his first."

"Oh, Ben," she said, her bravado deflated. "He is just a child."

"No such thing as a child here. You should know that."

"You could send—"

"D'ya really want to talk about this?"

"Of course not," she said, embarrassed that her levity had taken such a turn.

"Well, then…" He put his arms around her and eased her down on the mattress. She wound her fingers through his curls and tugged him down.

The fracas in the hallway continued at a constant, harmless volume, though occasionally there would be an insult or curse that would distract Ben, stopping his hands midcaress and lifting his head to listen. A particularly thunderous crescendo punctuated by the sound of shattering glass prompted him to disengage from Kassandra entirely—amid a cloud of his muttered curses—and tear across the room to throw open the door. The human missile aimed to collide with it flew through, landing with a *thud* on Kassandra's floor.

"Hold your noise out there!" Ben called out into the hallway. He bent over to grab the fallen man by his collar and hauled him to his feet. "Get out of here, y'idiot," he said, thrusting him out the door. "An' quiet down before I wipe the floors with the whole lot of ya!"

The responding laughter proved that the only blows Ben would be throwing tonight were those delivered good-naturedly to the back of the ousted intruder.

"Lousy drunks," he said, closing the door.

"There are enough of them here," Kassandra said, scooting away from the bed's edge as Ben sat down. "In fact, had I swallowed that drink instead of spitting it in your face, you would have no reason at all to send someone to kill me."

"That bad, is it?"

"Awful."

"Well, I've seen you drinkin' enough of it."

"What does that mean?" She sat up, dodging his lunging embrace.

"I just don't like what it's turned ya into."

"I am exactly what you made me, Ben Connor." She inched further away.

"I never set out to make you a drunk."

"You put me here," she gestured to the small, dark room. "This after a promise to take care of me."

"Would you rather be out in the streets?"

"I had other options."

"But you made this choice, love. You made the choice to come back here with me, and you made the choice to pour whiskey down your throat every night."

"It helps me," she said, consumed with the need to justify this to him. Wanting, like she never had before, to make herself seem worthy and blameless.

She knew he wasn't a man drawn to compassion, but he was prone to pity. And, under the right circumstances, guilt. She knew that was why he ever came to see her at all. Not out of love, not any lingering feelings from before. Not even because he was an equally miserable soul seeking comfort. It just so happened that every now and then he remembered her exile and took a passing shot at absolution by coming to her like this—sharing a laugh, sharing a bed—before turning back to the less bothersome realm of his conscience. She wished she could hate him for it.

"Drinkin' never helped anybody," he said, settling in to untie his shoes.

"It helps me forget."

"It's makin' you fat."

Had he thrown his discarded shoe at her he could not have shocked her more. "I am no such thing!"

"It happens to drunks. They tend to get a little puffy—"

"I am not *puffy*! I might seem that way because I happen to be wearing three skirts."

"So now you're one of them, the walkin' poor, goin' around wearin' everything you own, all your worldly possessions on your back?"

"What I am," she said, "is cold. This isn't your flat. We do not have the luxury of a nice little stove in every room on the second floor."

"But you have those other options, don't ya?"

"Which I do not care to—"

"Ah, but you care when it's me." He reached for her.

"Stop it."

"Or Sean."

"Do not talk about Sean."

"He cares for ya, you know."

"Does he?" Somehow she was lying down beside him again.

"I worry sometimes that he might take you away from me."

"What if he did?"

"You wouldn't go."

"He has not asked," she said, quickly learning that a multitude of skirts posed no problem to a determined man.

"An' I haven't heard any of the others complain."

"You are a pig."

"Ah, but you love me."

She wanted to tell him that no, she didn't, but before she could utter anything at all his mouth covered hers.

They were, by now, able to ignore the concert of voices on the other side of the wall, though when they heard the sound of another broken glass, Ben wondered out loud if he was going to have to beat the life out of them. This time, however, the sound of the broken glass was followed by shouts of panic. Fear. A solid mass of terrified noise with one discernible word rising above all the rest.

Fire.

*B*en was out of bed and at the door in an instant, throwing it open, allowing Kassandra just a glimpse of the pandemonium before slamming it shut again. What she saw terrified her—the opposite wall with a blaze snaking up from the carpeted floor, consuming the pattern of the papered wall. All of this subdued behind a thick haze of black smoke that billowed through her door even as Ben slammed it shut.

The sounds from the hallway proved just as frightening as the sight of those flames: screaming women and shrieking men; shouts to get out of the way; pleas to come back and rescue; footsteps pounding over wooden floorboards and—from the sounds of the cries—over fallen bodies. There was a pounding on doors—"Get out! Fire! Get out!"—and Kassandra could think of nothing else than to obey those voices. She got up from her bed and ran to the door, but Ben caught her round the waist and flung her away before her hand reached the latch.

"You can't go out there!" he shouted, though she could barely hear him over the screaming crowd outside. "Open your window!"

She went to the window and raised it up. The air outside was crisp and cold, and she took in great gulps of it. She knew she should cry out for help, but nothing would come out of the tightness of her throat.

Ben pushed her aside, leaned out over the edge, and called to the street below, "Oy! We've got fire here! Send for a truck!"

He managed to deliver this directive while putting on his shoes, balancing on one foot at a time.

Kassandra stood numbly in the center of the room watching the smoke creep in through the crack above the door.

I am going to die.

It was just a matter of time before the smoke would be followed by flames, eating a path across her wall, jumping to her bed, making it a blazing testament to the sin committed there. She shouldn't be here. She should never have been here.

I am going to die here. I am going to die tonight.

She felt the smoke lodge in the back of her throat. The fire didn't seem as dangerous now, not nearly as dangerous as this solid suffocation

I am going to die.

She was brought to her senses by a stinging slap across her face.

"Get down!" Ben was screaming, only inches away. He put his hands on her shoulders and pushed her to her knees. "Stay there."

He grabbed the towel she'd been washing up with earlier and tore it in two, placing one scrap of it over her mouth and nose and the other over his own. She felt a bit of relief from the choking smoke, but her eyes still stung. A solid band of orange lined the space under her door, and the fire roared on the other side. She was never going to get out of this room. She had landed herself in hell, and God was watching her burn.

"You have to get out of here." He had taken one of the thin blankets off her bed and was plunging it into the water in her washbasin.

"I am never getting out of here," she said, feeling her words trapped inside the cloth she held to her mouth.

"Come on." He crouched down to grab her arm and help her to her feet, but Kassandra wrenched herself out of his grip, shaking her head violently.

"I will die out there!" she screamed, taking the cloth away from her mouth.

"Don't be silly." He moved her hand to cover her mouth again. "The window. C'mon."

He dragged her to her feet and hauled her over to the open window. The street below teemed with activity—people poured from the tavern, shoving each other aside, knocking one another down and scrambling over the sprawled bodies. Faces appeared in the doorways and windows of neighboring buildings, casting worried glances towards the roofs lest the flames leap from Ben's building to their own. Children ran around in manic glee. Nothing was quite so exciting as a fire—the breaking glass, the clanging bells, the chance to go in for treasure once the smoke was cleared.

"Go on," Ben said, giving Kassandra a little nudge.

She whirled to face him. "What do you mean, *go on*?"

"Jump."

"I will break my neck!"

"It's only the second floor, Kassie. And thank the Lord you got so fat. You'll have something to cushion the fall."

He spoke from behind the rag held to his mouth, but she could tell that he was smiling. She could tell, too, that this was one of the smiles that didn't reach his eyes, because they were too red and full of tears to hold any humor.

"What about you?"

He put his hands on her waist and guided her two steps back until she sat on the windowsill facing him.

"I've seen worse than this, love." He leaned forward to place a kiss on her forehead. "Let's go."

The bulk of her skirts did little to ease the process of turning her body within the confines of the narrow window, but Ben held her steady whispering bits of encouragement in her ear. Kassandra numbly resigned herself to his manipulations until she was balanced on the sill, her legs dangling over the side of the building, and a crowd gathered below shouting for her to jump.

She braced her hands on the inside wall on both sides of the window. "I cannot do this," she said.

"Be sure to tuck up your legs on the way down. Try to roll once you hit the ground."

"My boots?"

"I'll toss 'em down to ya. Wait right here." He was gone for just an instant, and when he returned he draped Imogene's shawl over her shoulders. "Ready?"

"No."

"It's got to be now, Kassie girl."

She took in a deep breath of snow-filled air and nodded her head.

"One more thing. The minute you have your boots, go back home."

"What?"

"Go back to Reverend Joseph." He held her close, his words warm on the back of her neck. "There's goin' to be nothin' left for you here."

Then she was lifted up and off, and before she had even enough time to turn her head and call his name, she was on the ground, rolling on her shoulder just as he'd said, covered in the slush of snow and mud and dung. The gathered crowd cheered her safe landing, but it was Ben's voice that she heard above them all.

"Kassie!"

She looked up to see him leaning out the window, dangling her boots over its side. One by one she watched as they dropped to the ground beside her.

"Now, go!" he shouted.

When she looked up again, he was gone. Her window, which had been a solid mass of black smoke, turned bright red with heat and flame.

She stood, watching and waiting, as the first fire engine

arrived. Fewer and fewer people were streaming out of the first floor of the building, and still no one emerged at her window, which was now bordered with licking flames.

Firefighters shoved her aside, running toward the building with their leather hose from which, at some shouted command, a steady stream of water burst forth. It seemed little match for the ever-growing conflagration that seemed to engulf the entire street in its heat, burning Kassandra's face.

She sat down in the muck, right in the midst of the ever-growing crowd, to put on her boots. When she attempted to put the right one on, her foot collided with something hard inside. She reached her hand in and ran her fingers along a familiar surface. She gripped the porcelain wing and carefully pulled her sparrow figurine from her boot.

Thank you, Ben.

Bathed in the flickering orange glow, just next to where the firemen's engine pumped water through the hose, Stymie had two whiskey barrels set up on chairs dragged out of the tavern and was offering a drink from the spigot for just a penny a piece. "We'll save some for you boys when you're done!" he said, clapping each passing fireman on the back.

Ousted prostitutes languished on the arms of would-be heroes. Violence erupted as the Branagans formed a line around the parameter of the crowd, keeping everybody at bay and protecting the property while the firemen fought the flames.

Kassandra walked through the crowd, hearing snatches of conversation about how it all started. About the scuffle in the hallway that knocked the lantern off the wall, the flame spreading to the room with the little kerosene stove. Probably Bridget's. She hated the cold.

Nobody mentioned Ben's name.

Nobody called out to her.

Having shouldered her way through the worst of the drunks and the crying women, Kassandra found herself on the other

side. Out of the crowd. She took a deep breath, felt a light, stinging sleet on her face. The tiny sparrow was tucked in her pocket,
Imogene's shawl tucked around her shoulders. She could still
hear the roar of the flames behind her, could see the shadows
cast by its tremendous light.

But she also heard Ben's voice in her head. *Go.*

And go she did, never once looking back.

❧ 19 ❧

She stood outside the iron gate just as the sun was peeking up over the roof of Reverend Joseph's house. The
day of Clara's funeral she had stood here with
Reverend Joseph and the disapproving Austine sisters with
their baked beans. She wondered what they would think of her
now—her skirt caked with mud, her face streaked with soot
and snow. No coat, no hat, disheveled hair clinging to her skin.
She was, indeed, what Ben had called the walking poor—two
blouses, three skirts, four socks, one small bird. How they
would hate her.

Her hands were numb as she fumbled with the icy latch. The
gate's scraping against the cobbled sidewalk echoed in the empty
street, and Kassandra looked over one shoulder to be sure that
she hadn't roused the entire neighborhood. She never heard this
kind of silence in the Points.

She walked up to the house and paused at the front door.
Clara had always been adamant about people knowing their
place and which door they belonged at; there was nothing about
Kassandra this morning that merited acceptance through the
front door. Besides, all the windows were dark, and Reverend
Joseph had never been an early riser. She turned and made her
way round to the back of the house.

Not surprisingly, the kitchen windows were all aglow, and
Kassandra saw a small, dark woman puttering around in Clara's
kitchen. She stepped as close as she dared, peeping over the window box filled with iced-over soil. In the spring there would be

gardenias here, assuming this woman in the kitchen cared for such things.

Nothing else, it seemed, had changed. The table was laid with two places for breakfast; jars of marmalade and a mold of butter sat square in the middle of it. The kettle was steaming on the back burner. The only real change was the woman in charge. She wasn't nearly as round, but she was short, like Clara, and black, like Clara. Right now she was slicing a loaf of bread to make Reverend Joseph's toast, but she lacked the irate sawing motion of Clara, who always took to the task like a victor in battle taking the head of a fallen enemy. Kassandra hoped she had a kind heart, both for the reverend's sake and for her own.

She stepped away from the window, walked over to the back door, and poised her hand to knock. Once she did, nothing would be the same again. She could, of course, just turn and leave. Never let anyone know she was even here. But that option was torn away as the woman in the kitchen turned around, saw Kassandra's face through the pane, and furrowed her brow in a glare of suspicion and concern.

Knife still in hand, she walked calmly to the door and opened it. "Who are you?"

Her voice was high, yet not shrill, and it took a moment before Kassandra realized that the knife was no real threat.

"Please," Kassandra said, her own voice still a bit hoarse from the smoke, "I have come to see Reverend Joseph."

"Like this? Sneakin' up the back porch at the crack of dawn?"

"I...I did not think—"

"I'll say you didn't think. What kind of civilized person—" She looked Kassandra up and down. "Well, I'm freezin' standin' here talkin' to you like this, so you may's well come in and set while I figure out what to do with you."

"I do not think I should—"

"Now, ain't no puddle that a mop can't clean. Come on."

Kassandra barely got across the threshold before her legs

melted beneath her and she grabbed the woman's arm for support.

"Lord help us," she said, helping Kassandra to a waiting chair. "You're chilled clear through. Let's get you some tea."

"Thank you."

Kassandra was barely able to get the words out through her chattering teeth. When she tried to still them, her whole body responded in tiny convulsions. She closed her eyes tight, willing her body to stop, knowing she couldn't even attempt to pick up the delicate china cup until she'd regained some measure of control, no matter how enticing the steaming tea in front of her seemed. Then, a warm, dark hand enveloped her own.

"You're her, ain't ya?"

Kassandra opened her eyes and saw the woman sitting across the table from her.

"You the girl. His girl. He pray for you every night, pray that you'll come home."

"He prays?"

"Like I say. Every night. I feel like I know you already."

"Can you tell me your name?"

"I'm Jenny. You remember Miss Clara?"

"Of course."

"I'm her cousin. Now you drink this, and I go tell the reverend you're here." Jenny gave her hand a little squeeze. "He'll be so happy!"

"And his wife?"

A slow shadow passed over Jenny's face. "She know how the reverend feels about you."

"Wait," Kassandra said as Jenny rose from her chair. "Please, do not say anything yet. Just give him this." She reached into her skirt pocket and pulled out the sparrow figurine.

"All right," Jenny said, turning it slowly in her hand. "You drink your tea."

Soon after the chattering and shaking had stopped, her

hands curled gratefully around the steaming hot cup. Just yesterday morning she'd been deep in drunken sleep—just as cold as she was now—hours away from waking in her small, dark room. She would never get used to how drastically the world could change with just one setting and rising of the sun.

She brought the cup to her lips and took one small sip, savoring the bittersweet flavor. A slight sound to her left caught her attention, and she turned toward the door leading to the parlor.

He hadn't changed. Not a bit. Neither Jenny's cooking nor the contentment of marriage had put a single pound on his thin frame. His hair still hung—straight and blond—to his jaw. His skin still pale, his arms and legs endless in his black suit. He held the door open with one hand and nestled the tiny bird in the other. When he spoke, she heard the same voice that had come to her in the darkness so many years ago.

"Well," he said, his quivering lip hiding the gap between his front teeth, "what have I done to deserve such a present?"

In an instant, the cup crashed to the table, Kassandra was in his arms, and he held her up as the years melted beneath them.

"*Mein kleinen Spatz,*" he said.

The sound of that special name brought fresh tears to her eyes, and she sniffled loudly against his shoulder. Reverend Joseph gently kissed the top of her head.

"Fire?" he whispered.

Kassandra nodded and sniffed again. He pulled away to look down into her face, and brought one long thumb up to wipe the streaming tears. To Kassandra's embarrassment, she saw that his thumb was nearly black with soot. She started to apologize, but was interrupted by a most ladylike cough just behind the reverend's shoulder.

"Am I to be introduced?"

"Darling."

Reverend Joseph stepped away from Kassandra, who was further chagrined to see the damp grime all along the front of his suit.

"Kassandra, I'd like you to meet my wife."

She was small and slight, barely reaching past Reverend Joseph's elbows, not quite meeting Kassandra's shoulder. Her features seemed all to be pinched in the middle of her face—eyes, nose, and mouth surrounded by vast planes of white, white skin. Her deep brown hair was parted straight down the center, with two perfect wings swooped over each ear. The high ridge of her collar was rimmed with stiff ivory lace, and the wide bell of her sleeves ended in the same, nearly hiding the tiny hands clutched at her waist.

"We have met before," Kassandra said, trying to remember the rules of social decorum. "It is Miss Weathersby, isn't it?"

"Not for quite some time, actually," she said. "It's Mrs. Hartmann now."

"Of course. How stupid of me."

"This is a rather unusual hour for a social call, isn't it?" Mrs. Hartmann asked, tilting her head up toward her husband.

"Kassandra's come home, Dianne," Reverend Joseph said. "At last."

"Well, she does seem to be the worse for wear," Mrs. Hartmann said, alternating a pointed glance between Kassandra and the stain on Reverend Joseph's suit.

"Dianne, can't you tell what the child's been through?"

Kassandra found herself becoming less and less with each word. The melting sensation that was so warm when she was in Reverent Joseph's welcoming embrace seemed to be dissolving her now, and she wished she could become one of those puddles that Jenny could just mop away.

"I should not have come here," she muttered, already wondering if she had the strength to make it back to the steaming rubble on Mott Street.

"Don't be ridiculous," Reverend Joseph said, though it was unclear for which of the women the remark was intended.

"Indeed." Mrs. Hartmann laid a comforting finger on

Kassandra's arm. "We don't need to make any decisions right now. Jenny?"

The woman couldn't have been far, because she was in through the door almost before the second syllable of her name.

"Yes, Mrs. Hartmann?"

"The reverend and I will take an early breakfast in the dining room. Please see to it that our guest is served in here."

"Yes, Mrs. Hartmann."

"Then the reverend and I will leave together to make his morning calls. Will you please help our guest clean up a bit?"

"Yes, Mrs. Hart—"

"And take her clothes to the laundress at Woodbridge. You simply won't have the time to wash them here today."

"Yes, Mrs.—"

"In the meantime, do you have a sleeping gown she could wear? I certainly don't have anything that would fit—or suit her."

"I'll take care of everything, Mrs. Hartmann," Jenny said.

The whole conversation took place in such rapid-fire succession that neither Kassandra nor Reverend Joseph had any chance to intervene. By the time it was over, Reverend Joseph was somehow on the other side of the kitchen door, Jenny was at the stove, and Kassandra was sitting at the table again, teacup in her hand.

"Then," Mrs. Hartmann said, poised at the swinging door, "take her up to the guest room to lie down. Poor thing looks like she hasn't slept all night."

"Yes, Mrs. Hartmann," Jenny said to the swinging door.

She poked her arms out from under the pile of soft quilts to indulge in a long, back-arching stretch before burrowing down deep again. There was no separating the initial thrill of being here—being back—from the tragic contrast of what she left behind and the uncertainty of what lay ahead.

Once Mrs. Hartmann had swept Reverend Joseph into the

dining room for breakfast, Kassandra had no opportunity to see or speak with him again. After she had wolfed down plates full of warm food in the kitchen, Kassandra had been taken back to the washroom where a new linen-draped tub awaited. There, in an eerily familiar reenactment of her first arrival to this house, she submitted herself to Jenny, who scrubbed her skin and washed her hair—rinsing and rinsing and rinsing until every trace of soot and smoke and city was washed away.

She'd confessed to Jenny that it had been over a year since she'd taken an all-over bath, and the woman scowled her acknowledgement when Kassandra stood up for her final rinsing, leaving below a tub full of water so thick with grime she could not see her own feet.

But she was deliciously clean now, wearing somebody's warm flannel nightgown. She studied the slit of morning light peeking through the curtains and decided she must have been asleep for nearly twenty hours.

The soft knocking she heard on the door was a mere formality because it swung open before the third rap and Jenny stepped through. She was carrying a breakfast tray with a pretty china teapot and cup, which she set on the small table next to the bed before going back to carefully close the door.

"Miz Hartmann's gonna be in here in just a minute. Wanted to make sure you was awake."

"And good morning to you," Kassandra said, sitting up.

"Well, ain't you the sassy one?" Jenny took a muslin-wrapped warming brick off the tray and slipped it under the covers near Kassandra's feet. "If I was you, I'd lose some of that sass before talkin' to Miz Hartmann. She don't go much for that."

"Does he love her?" Kassandra asked. "Do you think he is happy?"

"She's a good wife, don't you worry about that. You got your own business to worry 'bout. You ain't gonna be able to hide that much longer."

"I am not trying to hide anything."

"Guess you didn't have time to mention it yet." Jenny poured tea from the china teapot into a matching cup and handed it over to Kassandra, who was surprised to realize her hands shook a bit, causing the cup to rattle against its saucer. "But if I was you," she continued, with a pointed glance at Kassandra's shaking hand, "I'd wait and tell him first, once you get a chance to talk to him alone. He's got a soft spot for you, girl. The wife might throw you right straight out again."

"Just what are you talking about?" Kassandra demanded, lowering her voice only at Jenny's warning *hush* to do so.

"The baby," Jenny said. "Now, like I told you—"

"I…I do not have a baby. My baby died three years ago."

"I don't know nothin' 'bout that. I'm talkin' about this baby right here." She poked her long brown finger into the comforter, just above Kassandra's stomach.

It was a lucky gesture as it put her hand in the perfect place to catch the teacup and saucer when Kassandra's body went numb and she lost her grip.

☙ 20 ❧

here never was any question that Kassandra was a welcome guest in Reverend Joseph's home. She was, after all, given her old room, a place at the table, and an open invitation to join the reverend and Mrs. Hartmann when the couple spent a long winter evening in the parlor. Mrs. Hartmann was quite deft at keeping the conversation lively, speaking at such a quick pace and of such trivialities that the life Kassandra had been living never became a focal point. Too often, Kassandra's contributions made it obvious that she had lived too long outside the influence of genteel company, and she would interject a comment or a laugh too bawdy and loud for a fireside chat in a reverend's parlor. At these times, Mrs. Hartmann would deliver a silent, smirking admonition— though Reverend Joseph often seemed to be both captivated and relieved at Kassandra's outbursts.

When not engaged in artful conversation, Mrs. Hartmann pursued her second talent, which was keeping Reverend Joseph out of the house. Several times each day he was summoned from his study, from his bedroom, from the kitchen to the front parlor where Mrs. Hartmann stood holding his coat, ready to stand tiptoe and smooth it over his slim shoulders. The Ladies' Aid Society was waiting for him to test its cookies for the baked goods sale in the church kitchen. The ailing Mrs. Farnsworth was depending on a visit. The Christian Temperance Union needed someone to deliver the opening prayer for its meeting.

During her moments alone—and Mrs. Hartmann saw to it that she had several moments alone—Kassandra would sit in the pretty wing-backed chair in front of her bedroom window, or on the comfortable horsehair sofa in the dayroom, or in the warm, fragrant kitchen, wondering how she would possibly tell Reverend Joseph about this baby. It was enough that he had welcomed her into his home unquestioningly. How could she expect him to accept an illegitimate child as well? And, even when she was alone, Kassandra's face stung as a preview to the humiliation she would feel when Mrs. Hartmann received the news.

For nearly a week, Kassandra had to carry this burden under the watchful eye of Jenny. And it was getting harder to carry.

It wasn't until a Saturday afternoon when, according to Jenny, the ailing Mrs. Farnsworth would take no comforting visit unless it was the delightful Mrs. Hartmann, that Kassandra had a moment to talk alone with Reverend Joseph.

He invited her into his study, a privilege not offered to her since her return; neither, as far as she could tell, was it ever offered to Mrs. Hartmann. Kassandra hesitated at its threshold. She would be more worthy of walking into the house of God Himself than into this shrine. There was the rug on which she had learned God's Word. There, the desk and on it his well-worn Bible. And on the bookshelf—where it had been the first time he'd taught her about God's watchfulness—the tiny sparrow figurine.

"Come sit, Sparrow," Reverend Joseph said, gesturing to one of the deep leather chairs flanking the fireplace.

She did, and he settled himself across from her. He picked up his pipe and tobacco pouch from the small table between the two chairs.

"Dianne won't have me smoking in any other part of the house," he said, lighting the pipe.

"It is a different household indeed," Kassandra said, smiling.

"My darling Kassandra, I have been waiting for an opportunity to speak with you. I must ask you, will you ever—" his lips quivered in their perch around his pipe, "will you ever find it in your heart to forgive me?"

"Forgive you? What could I ever have to forgive you for?"

Reverend Joseph clamped his jaw on his pipe and looked away for just a moment before answering.

"For weeks before you left home, Clara had been warning me about that young man. She said he was entirely too familiar with you, and she had great concern for your virtue as far as he was concerned."

"She was—"

"Please. I have waited years to tell you all of this, Sparrow. Let me speak. The moment I realized you were gone, I knew that young man had some hand in it. Had I taken my carriage and left the house immediately, it is likely I could have overtaken the two of you on the street and brought you home. Indeed, that is exactly what I planned to do."

If only you had . . .

"But I allowed myself to listen to the counsel of others who, I believe now as I did then, spoke to me out of a genuine, if misguided, concern. I allowed them to turn my heart against you. They convinced me that you were ungrateful and undeserving. They led me to believe that you were a young woman of questionable morals even at that age, and that having you under my roof would be a liability to my ministry and to my own status in the religious community."

The exact lies I was told . . .

"And so you must forgive me for not being willing to risk my life for your sake as you were for mine."

"But . . . your letter. You said that you did try to look for me."

"And so I did, but I allowed myself to be detained for several days. I did know where to find you, my darling child. Indeed, I was quite close to you at one time, in my carriage."

"When was that?"

"It was summer, more than a month after you left. I saw you

walking with that young man. I must say you seemed quite happy and content, but I wanted to be sure, so I left my carriage and attempted to capture your attention."

Kassandra closed her eyes and tried to remember such a moment. She remembered the first summer with Ben, their walks around the neighborhood as he introduced her to the people and places. Surely she would have noticed the tall figure of her beloved caregiver calling out her name.

"Of course," Reverend Joseph continued, "you didn't see me. As soon as I was close enough to call out to you, a tall man with a shaved head came to me and—*suggested*—that I leave you two alone. There were others with him—"

"The Branagans," Kassandra said.

"Hmm? Yes, well, they were quite insistent that I leave their neighborhood quickly, and that it would be best for all concerned—myself especially—if I were to leave you alone."

Kassandra heard the shame in Reverend Joseph's voice, and she reached across to lay a comforting hand on his arm.

"I was happy then. I probably would not have gone back if you asked me."

He smiled. "I intended to go back frequently, hoping to catch a glimpse of you alone. But soon after that first encounter I was struck quite ill with fever, and by the time I had recovered sufficiently to permit another visit, it was late in the fall."

When I was pregnant.

"I was met just outside of your building by one of those men—quite tall, he was, with a kind face and a rather hooked nose—"

Sean.

"—who made it quite clear that it was your own safety at stake if I were to try to contact you and bring you home. I had written the letter and asked if he would be so kind as to give it to you at some opportune time. I see he did."

"He did."

A few minutes passed as they sat quietly, lost in their own thoughts. Reverend Joseph puffed on his pipe; Kassandra picked at her skirt.

"It is never an easy thing for a man to admit to being a coward, Kassandra."

"Now, stop that. You did what you thought was best."

"No, I did what I thought was safe and convenient. But to do what is right in this world, to follow God's directive is rarely that."

He studied his pipe for a moment before setting it down on the table next to his chair. Leaning forward, he reached for Kassandra's hands and held them tightly as he spoke.

"I have already asked God to forgive me of my shortcomings, for my failure to care for what He entrusted to me. But I must know that you forgive me as well."

"How could I—" she began, though her throat was nearly too choked to speak, "how could I ever be one to forgive? I am so..." *Defiled? Beaten? Unworthy?*

"Do not forget, my child, that no matter what you may think of yourself, you are still a child of God. Do you know that?"

"No," she said, her eyes burning like they hadn't since the fire.

"Then there is another way I have failed you, if I did not instill that truth."

"You do not understand," she said, tearing her hands from his grip and pressing the heels of her palms into her eyes in a vain attempt to stop her tears. "You don't know what all I've done. Been."

"You've nothing to confess to me, Kassandra. And there is no sin too grievous for God to forgive. He loves you."

"He could not possibly love me."

"Remember what the Bible tells us: *It is of the Lord's mercies that we are not consumed, because his compassions fail not. They are new every morning.* We may feel that we have failed Him, but—"

"I mean He could not possibly love me and allow such horrible things…"

"Oh, now, Sparrow…"

He reached for her hand again, and she took it, allowing herself to be pulled from her chair and brought closer to him. Then, just as she had all those precious evenings as a child, she sat on the woven rug at his feet, her head resting against the cool leather of his chair, and every bit of the past four years poured out of her, unchecked. She told of dancing with Ben in the parlor the afternoon just before she left. That he hadn't married her; that she hadn't insisted. Imogene and the babies—all those beautiful, poor, doomed babies. And her own. Not the one inside her now—there would be time enough for that later—but Daniel. The screeching rats in the cellar the night he was born. The horrible silence the morning he died. His funeral; her flight. Rape.

"Child. My child," Reverend Joseph said, his long fingers gently stroking the top of Kassandra's head. "Why did you not come home to me?"

"I was at the church the day you married Mrs. Hartmann," Kassandra said, taking a moment to wipe her tears and blow her nose with the handkerchief Reverend Joseph had given her some time ago. "But Ben was there, too. And I just could not imagine how I would fit into your new life."

"How did you fit into his?"

"I am sure you know."

She couldn't give voice to the humiliation of her years spent above Mott Street Tavern. Couldn't bring to life all of those men—those who survived her alcohol-clouded memory.

"So you see," she said, shrugging, "I do not see how God and I could ever truly love each other."

Reverend Joseph laughed. "Aren't we lucky, then, that God is capable of so much more than we are?" He leaned forward in his chair and, with one finger hooked beneath her chin, forced Kassandra to turn and look at him. "We can never be sure why

God doesn't choose to rescue us from our mistakes. But we can be sure it's not for lack of love for us. There is always a reason, *kleinen Spatz*, for the trials we endure, even if those trials are the consequences of our own poor judgment."

"And do you really think He can forgive all I've done?"

"If He could not, the death of His Son would have been in vain. You are His child, Kassandra. You prayed to Him in this very room many years ago and made Him the Lord of your life. He has never left you, not in all this time."

She tried to look away, filled with shame at all she had asked God to endure with her, but Reverend Joseph would not allow her to.

"I came to you this afternoon," he continued, "asking you to forgive me for my sins against you. I did that knowing you would. You must believe, too, that God will grant you grace, my child. Then simply confess to Him and ask for His grace to bring comfort to your heart. I am guessing that your heart has not known such comfort in quite some time."

"Not since…not since Ben."

"And can we expect that Ben will be coming back to reclaim you?"

Kassandra closed her eyes and saw the blazing inferno that had consumed what had been her home for so many years. For just a moment she could once again sense the acrid smoke at the back of her throat and feel the heat on her face. Most of all, though, she saw Ben leaning out of the little second floor window to throw down her boots, then disappearing into the black.

"No," she said.

"Well, then," Reverend Joseph said, holding his smile long enough for Kassandra to notice the deepening of the lines at the corners of his eyes, "you must remember that when God forgives our sins, He takes them from our hearts and throws them as far away as the east is from the west. You must try to do that, too, Sparrow. Hold on to the fond memories, but toss the others away. You are home again now. This is a new life for you, if you would like to make it here."

"I would," she said, standing.

Reverend Joseph stood with her and folded her into his long arms. She felt like a very little girl again—exhausted from crying, weak from confession—being held aloft by a father's embrace.

"Reverend Joseph?"

He moved his hands to her shoulders and stepped back to look down into her face. "Yes, my child?"

"Will you pray with me?"

"Nothing else could be such an honor."

She felt a twinge of guilt as Reverend Joseph braced his hand on the back of the chair to lower himself to his knees on the rug, but that feeling soon disappeared when she felt the enormous power of having him there beside her as she lifted her voice to God.

"Heavenly Father," she prayed. Then stopped.

How could she begin to list all she must confess? Her body went cold though her face was flushed, and soon the hands clasped so fervently at her breast could no longer stay interlocked. She felt her fingers unclasping, felt her arms unfolding as she lifted her hands high above her head. An offering. Of herself. Of her sin.

"My Father," she began again, "You know my sins. You know even those I cannot name..."

With each word of contrition she felt her body grow lighter, as if her uplifted hands could somehow pull her from her knees. She felt it, then, starting at the base of her spine and rolling across her shoulders. Light. And lightness. Years of hatred for herself and for God simply sliding away. It was a feeling of pure joy, pure relief. Like that first gasp of air when she escaped the fire around her.

Then she felt something else entirely. Something deep within her. A tiny flutter, like a tiny, cool, flickering flame.

She opened her eyes. "Reverend Joseph?" she said, then

politely waited for his *Amen* before continuing. "There is one more thing I must tell you."

They agreed it would be best if the reverend himself broke the news of Kassandra's pregnancy to Mrs. Hartmann.

"She'll be just as thrilled about it as I am," he'd said before ushering Kassandra out of his study so he could resume planning his sermon for the next morning. Though he had been nearly unflinching and gracious at her announcement, his reserved nature gave little evidence that he was "thrilled," and Kassandra had no delusions that his wife would be, either. To avoid any awkwardness, Kassandra requested that she have her supper in her room that evening.

Reverend Joseph hadn't tried to pin down a month for the baby's arrival, and Kassandra hadn't tried to give him one. Each time she had tried any sort of calculation, she'd been so overcome with pain she had to shut down the very memories that would give her the answer.

Last night, though, after her prayer, everything changed. For years she'd lived with shame so close to her that it was like some fuzzy image held flush to her nose. But through her prayer, and through God's forgiveness, she'd been able to take a step back. And another. And another, each breath taking her further away until every significant moment since Daniel's death lay mapped out and clear before her.

She was a prostitute. She was pregnant. Two facts that could never be changed. But *she* was changed, was forgiven, and nothing would ever make her go back to that life again. And nothing—*please, God*—would take this child from her.

When Kassandra walked into the kitchen the next morning, Reverend Joseph was quietly sipping his tea and looking over his sermon notes while Mrs. Hartmann slathered jam on her toast with such ferocity that the soft swoops of hair over her ears quivered with the effort.

"Well, good morning," she said, pausing in her task and smiling at Kassandra with a visibly valiant effort at cheerfulness. *She knows.*

"Mrs. Hartmann," Kassandra said, slowly approaching the table and stopping just short of pulling out a chair. "I...I understand if this upsets you."

"Upsets me?" She set her knife down with deliberate gentleness. "Why, don't be ridiculous. The Lord hands us all kinds of things in life, doesn't He? What's the sense in getting upset?"

"Good morning, Sparrow," Reverend Joseph said. "You look very nice this morning."

"Thank you." At the reverend's gesture Kassandra sat at the table and smiled over her shoulder when Jenny came to fill her teacup. "I am so looking forward to going to church with you this morning, Reverend Joseph."

"When was the last time you've been to church?" Mrs. Hartmann asked, her smile never leaving her face.

"Not since...I left."

"Doesn't matter a mite," Reverend Joseph said, laying a comforting hand on her own. "God hasn't changed a bit."

"That may be," Mrs. Hartmann said, "but I think it would be best if we didn't rush right out and make this news known to everybody in the neighborhood."

"Not tell everyone that the child's come home?"

"Well, certainly we'll let them know that Kassandra has returned," Mrs. Hartmann said, "but there is this other...business."

Kassandra looked down into her empty plate and folded her hands in her lap.

"This other *business*, Dianne, is a child. We above all people should realize what a blessing it is."

"A blessing, of course, Joseph. But there are circumstances to consider. What might people—"

"I do not mind staying home this morning," Kassandra said, looking up in time to catch the look of relief on Mrs. Hartmann's face before she switched it to match the look of concern on her husband's.

"But, my dear," Reverend Joseph said, "you know you are most welcome in the house of God."

"I know that, but I am a little tired, still. And my dress—"

"Do you see?" Mrs. Hartmann chimed in. "The poor dear would feel miserably out of place."

Kassandra nodded along, though she couldn't imagine feeling more out of place in God's house than she did in this one.

"Well, if you're certain, Sparrow," Reverend Joseph said. "I've kept your prayer book all these years. If you like, you may read from it, and this afternoon I can share my sermon with you."

"That sounds just lovely, doesn't it, Kassandra?"

"It does," Kassandra replied, trying her best to smile warmly at Mrs. Hartmann. "And I must tell you that my Bible—well, it was Clara's Bible. And the fire—"

"Think nothing more of it," Mrs. Hartmann said, picking up her spoon and digging into the bowl of warm porridge Jenny set in front of her. "I have scores of lovely Bibles, and I'd love to give you one to have as your own. Now, isn't it nice to have everything settled?"

The usual stream of after-church callers flowed through the front parlor of Reverend Joseph's home, and though Kassandra was not instructed to stay in her room, she was not invited to join in the visit, either. She spent much of the afternoon alternating between sitting in her chair, looking out the window, and dozing on her bed. She also took time to open the Bible Mrs. Hartmann had handed to her before bundling into her fur for the walk to church. The words were so familiar, even as they flew past her eyes, but she could not settle her mind or her spirit to find any true meaning.

I want my child to grow up knowing Your Word, Lord. From the day it is born. Before it is born, even, so it can be so much stronger than I am.

Finally, remembering a buried teaching from Reverend Joseph, she leafed through the pages to find the Psalter and began to read aloud the first psalm.

"Blessed is the man that walketh not in the counsel of the ungodly, nor standeth in the way of sinners, nor sitteth in the seat of the scornful. But his delight is in the law of the LORD*..."*

The words were unfamiliar on her tongue, speaking to the truth that she'd turned her back on, if she'd ever fully embraced it at all. She realized she had become like the ungodly—the chaff driven away by the wind. Blown from Fifth Avenue to Five Points and back again. No direction, just at the mercy of the winds.

"Not for my child," she prayed aloud. "Not for you, my little one."

21

*S*he tried not to feel like a prisoner. During her life at Mott Street Tavern, she'd met a lot of prisoners, and she knew they didn't sleep between crisp linen sheets with their heads on soft feather pillows. Prisoners didn't push themselves away from the table, too full to eat another bite. Prisoners didn't complain when their only venture outside consisted of strolling through a lush, albeit dormant, garden, sitting on stone benches with their faces lifted up to the warm sunlight of emerging spring.

Yes, there was an iron gate at the front walk, and she was being asked—nicely—to stay behind it. But Kassandra knew the life that waited on the other side of that gate, and though the constant company of only Reverend Joseph, Mrs. Hartmann, and Jenny sometimes grew tiresome, she knew enough to thank God every day for this haven for her and her unborn child.

By the end of March her pregnancy was obvious, and her presence in the house was by no means a secret to anybody. While she was still not invited to join in any of the social calls paid in the front parlor, she knew she was often the topic of their conversations since she spent many afternoons in the kitchen with Jenny helping her prepare the trays of tea and cookies.

"Ooh, you should hear her," Jenny said, coming through the swinging kitchen door with a tray of empty cups. "She's goin' on 'bout how good it is that you've come home. An' how good *they* are for takin' you in, knowin' the life you fallen into."

"They have done a good thing, you know," Kassandra said

with an indulgent smile. "They did not have to take me in."

"It's just nothin' gets me more than Christians boastin' 'bout doin' good."

"Perhaps, but that is better than not doing good at all."

"I don' know 'bout that," Jenny said. "Sometimes you gotta wonder if things wouldn't be well enough just left alone."

The women chatted companionably, working together to tidy up the kitchen. While she was putting the leftover pastries into the pie safe, Kassandra caught her sleeve on a jagged edge of one of the shelves, tearing a nearly three-inch gash.

"Oh, bother," she said, pleased with herself at having refrained from cursing. It was one of only two dresses Mrs. Hartmann had requested of her seamstress, and the other was out at the laundry. "Do you have a mending basket handy, Jenny?"

"Well, yes," the woman said, furrowing her brow with disapproval, "but we can't be mendin' that dress while you're still wearin' it, 'less you want that baby to grow up and get its eyes poked out."

Kassandra laughed. "Now, Jenny. You cannot believe that."

"Indeed I do. Had a cousin carryin' a child. She darned up a tear in her sock without takin' it off. Said it was too cold. That child was born—a boy. He was helpin' in the workshop, went runnin' to bring his daddy a hammer, tripped over a wagon spoke and fell down. That hammer handle went clean up into his eye, dug it right out."

Kassandra cringed at the image. "Now Jenny, you expect me to believe all of that, yet you will not let me boil up some of the herbs I need for myself and the baby?"

"It ain't me sayin' you can't cook up your dandelions," Jenny said, wiping the last dirty cup. "That's Miz Hartmann's doin'. I told her what you wanted, and she said she wasn't goin' to have no witchcraftin' in *her* house. Says that's what probably—" She stopped abruptly and turned away from Kassandra, seeming to concentrate very hard on wiping the cup dry.

"Probably what? Jenny?" Kassandra grabbed the woman's arm and stopped Jenny in midwipe. "What did she say?"

Jenny sighed and looked at Kassandra with her warm brown eyes. "She said that's probably what killed your first baby."

Kassandra felt as if her breath had been batted away. "How…how does she even *know*?"

"Did you tell the reverend? Then, he told her."

"And she told you?"

"Not really. She just talk. She talk all the time like I ain't nothin' more than a little brown piece of furniture pickin' up after her all the time."

"Do you think she has told…everybody?"

"Who?" Jenny gestured toward the parlor. "Them? What do you care if she does? There ain't no shame in losin' a child. Just gives you twice the love for this next one."

Kassandra had hoped to be invited to accompany the reverend and his wife to church on Easter Sunday, but she overheard Mrs. Hartmann telling her husband that the seats would be full to the rafters, and surely such a large crowd would make them all uncomfortable. Reverend Joseph's attempts to sway her opinion were no match for her rapid-fire logic. So on that holy morning, Kassandra sat at her window, watching Reverend Joseph in his best black suit and his wife in a new plum-colored silk gown walk through the gate to join the morning promenade towards the church.

Jenny had been given the day as a holiday, and Kassandra found herself alone in the house for the first time since Clara's funeral. She wandered from room to room, running her fingers over the highly polished furniture in the front parlor, pausing to look into the faces of the portraits hanging in the hall. She stood in the doorway of Reverend Joseph's study, too respectful of his privacy to enter the room. She did, however, poke her head in and allow herself to breathe in its aroma—books and pipe smoke and leather. Even with no fire in the grate, the study always carried a warmth not found anywhere else in the house.

Thank You, God, for this man. I would be dead without him; I wouldn't know You.

She walked up the main staircase, her palms gliding along the silky intricacy of the carved banister. How different this was from the dark and twisting stairs of Ben's building—from any of the tenements she'd been in. These stairs were wide and covered with a patterned carpet to muffle the sound of clomping steps. She had noticed, though, that she was the only one in the household who tended to clomp. Reverend Joseph moved with the lightness of a long-limbed waterfowl, and Mrs. Hartmann never seemed to walk anywhere. She merely appeared from place to place. Lately, with her ever-protruding stomach, Kassandra felt more ungainly than ever, and she took these unwatched moments to practice taking the stairs with a light step.

Upstairs the two unused bedrooms stood ready for any guest. The beds were made with linens and blankets as fine as any in the occupied rooms, and it was Jenny's task to air them out weekly, along with running a dust rag over the bureaus and washstands within. When Kassandra lived here before, these rooms were frequently occupied. Sometimes with other children Reverend Joseph took in en route to finding them a permanent home, or by visiting ministers and their families. In the months since she'd come back, however, they had remained vacant. Once, when she was helping Jenny air the bedding, she asked if her presence in the house was the reason for the lack of visitors.

"Oh, no," Jenny had said. "Miz Hartmann don't care too much for comp'ny. Likes to keep the reverend to herself."

Though her room was just across the hall and two doors down, Kassandra had rarely gone near Reverend Joseph's bedroom—both as a child and now. While he had always been kind and generous with her, he had also maintained a palpable formality. On this morning, though, she found herself on the threshold of that room he now shared with Dianne Hartmann. There were two large mahogany armoires against the far wall, no doubt full of beautiful gowns suitable for any social occasion. In front of the velvet-draped window, two chairs sat facing each other as if in companionable conversation. At the foot of the bed was a large cedar trunk, and the bed itself loomed nearly a foot over the trunk's lid. High off the ground and wide, its four posts were bare, and the mattress was covered with yards and yards of a rich, emerald green quilted duvet. Before she had time to be shocked at her boldness, Kassandra was trying to picture a passionate embrace beneath such luxury. Reverend Joseph with the long, skinny legs and Mrs. Hartmann with her nervous flitting fingers conjured an image of a stork and a squirrel locked in a fierce connubial battle.

She smiled. Ben would have laughed at that.

Just then she felt a forceful jolt from the baby. This wasn't the soft, slippery movement she'd grown accustomed to, but a purposeful call for Kassandra's attention. She ran her hands over her stomach. As the child made its presence known more and more each day, her heart and mind constantly returned to little Daniel. She remembered this time with him, the excitement and anticipation of a new life, Ben showering her with attention and affection, Imogene's careful wisdom and ministration.

But this child was rarely acknowledged at all. Reverend Joseph avoided looking at her stomach, and though Mrs. Hartmann's gaze often lingered there, her mouth was usually set in a thin-lipped frown. It was only with Jenny, in their cozy afternoons in the kitchen, that Kassandra ever had a chance to muse and wonder at the changes in her body and upcoming promise.

This morning's impromptu tour of the reverend's home brought to light one aspect that she hadn't taken time to consider yet. Where would the baby live? Her room was certainly large enough to accommodate a bassinette, but what then? Reverend Joseph made it a daily ritual to tell Kassandra how glad he was to have her home. But the three of them never discussed any plans beyond what Jenny would be preparing for the next meal. No one had ever said that she would ever have to leave, but no one ever said that she and the baby would stay forever. She didn't feel like an intruder, but she did feel like she was hovering, always just on the outskirts of truly belonging.

Reverend Joseph and Mrs. Hartmann took Easter dinner in the home of a prominent city councilman, and Kassandra treated herself to a Sunday afternoon nap. Jenny had been thoughtful enough to set up a cold dinner of sliced ham, pea salad, rich buttery rolls, and a fresh strawberry pie, but it was so late in the afternoon when Kassandra finally went downstairs to claim it that the meal was really an early supper.

She was just heaping a mound of pie onto her plate when the little bell rang, indicating that the front door of the house was opening.

"Hellooooo?" Mrs. Hartmann's voice sang from the front door.

Kassandra sighed and put her fork down, wondering if secondary household servant was going to be her place after all.

The woman did manage to put away her shoulder wrap without assistance (unless Reverend Joseph did that for her), and she breezed into the kitchen resplendent in her Easter finery.

"Are you just now having your dinner?" Mrs. Hartmann asked, her disapproval thinly veiled behind a Sunday smile, which seemed quite genuine by the time Reverend Joseph entered the room.

"Good afternoon, Sparrow," he said, briefly laying his hand on top of her head. "Is that strawberry pie?"

"It is, and it's delicious. Can I cut you a slice?"

"Of course not," Mrs. Hartmann said. "We've just come from a lovely Easter dinner."

"Where the carrot cake was as dry as dust." Reverend Joseph took a plate down from the cupboard and cut himself a thick slice of the pie, spooning out extra filling. "Tell me, Kassandra dear, did you enjoy your day of rest?"

"I did. In fact, I spent most of the day resting."

Mrs. Hartmann poured two cups of tea and set one in front of Reverend Joseph. She pulled out a chair and took her accustomed place to his right.

"I suppose it's easy to forget that this day was also meant to be a day of worship," she said.

"I was not invited to church," Kassandra said, regretting it immediately. "And I'm…I'm just a little more tired these days."

Reverend Joseph broke the awkward silence that followed with a gushing compliment about the pie, for which Kassandra took credit for slicing the strawberries. When Reverend Joseph noted that one particular strawberry looked much like the hat Miss Austine wore to church that afternoon, Mrs. Hartmann launched into a report on every dress and bonnet in attendance at Tenth Avenue Methodist Church, and Kassandra found herself surprisingly entertained by the narrated parade.

The three enjoyed companionable chitchat and silence as the kitchen grew darker with the coming evening. After a time, Mrs. Hartmann took a sip of her tea and set her cup down. "Kassandra," she said, running her finger along the cup's rim, "I think we should get you away from here."

Kassandra's held her breath, as if it might be her last.

"Now, don't look so shocked, dear," she continued, with the nerve to look amused. "I don't mean to put you out on the street."

"Listen to her." Reverend Joseph laid a reassuring hand on Kassandra's. "We just want the best for you, my dear."

"My family has a house in Cape Cod," Mrs. Hartmann said. "That's in Massachusetts, dear."

"What could that possibly have to do with—"

"It is a fact that women in your…condition benefit greatly from being by the sea. In truth, I should have taken you there right away, but there have been so many obligations here. But now I am offering to take you to my family home where you can have ready access to that fresh, salty air. You'll be able to walk on the beach every day. It's the best thing for you and the baby. Very healthy. All the experts say so."

"Am I to live there?" Kassandra asked, turning back to Reverend Joseph and searching his clear blue eyes for a sign of disapproval, of being sent away.

"Don't be silly, Sparrow." He looked at her intently, every feature set in a promise. "While you're away, we'll be making some changes here."

"What kind of changes?"

"You know we have the little shed at the far end of the garden, but I've never taken to employing a full-time gardener. Right now it's full of some tools and other odds and ends."

Kassandra remembered it well. She and Sarah James had often played in that cottage, pretending they were princesses locked away, waiting to be found by a handsome, roving knight.

"While you're gone I'll have it cleaned out and painted. We'll put a little wood-burning stove, some furniture. It will be a lovely little home for you and the child."

Kassandra's hope and heart swelled with each word. Her breath quickened until Reverend Joseph could barely finish his last word before she burst forth with a cry of utter joy. "I can stay then? With you?"

"Of course, my dear, of course," he said, squeezing her hand. "It's just going to be time for my little Sparrow to have her own nest."

"And you are not worried about what people will think?"

Mrs. Hartmann gave a little sniff. "The time has long passed for us to worry about that. You're not exactly a secret, you know.

We think this is the best way to make sure you feel you are a part of our…family, but still on your own."

"I…I don't know what to say. I will do all that I can to help you here. I'll work with Jenny—"

"Now see here, Sparrow," Reverend Joseph said, "you are not a maid. You are not a servant."

"But I am not your daughter, either."

"I failed you miserably enough once before. I don't want to make that mistake again."

"So why must I go to Cape Cod?"

"It's just as I told you, dear," Mrs. Hartmann said. "Everybody says the sea air is best for a woman in your delicate condition. It opens the lungs. You'll be far better off there than here, surrounded by all those hammers and nails and paint. Besides," her voice quickened, "think of the surprise waiting for you when you return!"

"And you think this is best?" Kassandra said.

She turned all of her attention to Reverend Joseph, who remained silent as, just over her shoulder, his wife prattled on and on about the virtues of the sea, the spaciousness of the house, the health of the baby, the privacy for the mother, the stillness of the neighbors, the brightness of the future. Not once during the litany did Reverend Joseph's gaze waver. He continued to hold her hand tightly, as if to transfer to her the strength to make this decision. Kassandra hated the idea of leaving him again—just as much as she hated the idea of spending months alone with Mrs. Hartmann. Even more, she feared what might happen if she refused to take them up on this generous offer. The more Mrs. Hartmann talked, the less likely it seemed that anyone had planned for an alternative.

"When will we be leaving?" Kassandra said.

"I have a hired coach scheduled to come for us Tuesday morning," Mrs. Hartmann said.

22

The sand was warm in the late afternoon, and Kassandra never tired of the glorious feeling of it between her bare toes. Her walk down the beach was a daily ritual, greatly encouraged by Mrs. Hartmann, who seemed to share with Kassandra a need for solitude. The only sound was the constant exhalation across the sea grass; when the wind was high, this breath drowned out even the lapping of the sea, and this day the wind was strong enough to keep the grass bowed down, creating soft, rolling green waves as far as Kassandra could see.

All the promises of the improved well-being for both herself and the baby proved to be true, as Kassandra fell in love with the salt-ridden sea air the minute she stepped out of the hired coach in which she had spent too many uncomfortable, claustrophobic days.

The home Mrs. Hartmann brought her to spoke of her family's fortune, gained during her grandfather's Chinese shipping trade with Perkins and Company. Now, with the family's fortune dispersed into a local mill and three small freight ships operated by Mrs. Hartmann's uncles, the family home—willed to her at her father's death—sat vacant for most of the year.

"I've tried to get Joseph to come here every summer," she'd told Kassandra as the women alighted from the coach, "but he simply won't tear himself away from the church for that long."

"Why would you ever leave this place?" Kassandra asked, enthralled by the expanse of grass and beach and sea.

"The people here are essentially animals. No culture. No

breeding. I wasn't about to spend my life wondering if my husband is coming home at the end of the season."

"But why New York?"

"It was my mother's choice," Mrs. Hartmann said in the clipped manner she had of closing conversation.

The Weathersby home was deceptively worn on the outside with its battered clapboard exterior. A single, narrow door sat in the exact center of the front of the house, and four dormer windows jutted in perfect symmetry under the steep, black-shingled roof. There was no ornamentation on the house—no gables, no porch. Even the shutters had been taken down, Mrs. Hartmann observed, to be repaired during the summer season.

It wasn't until the women walked through the front door that Kassandra had any clue as to the wealth the house represented. Inside, floors she would later learn were solid oak shone to mirrored perfection. The walls were pristinely whitewashed and interrupted by aesthetically spaced oak paneling. The entryway seemed to run half the length of the front of the house, with a stairway at the far end leading to the second floor.

"We'll go upstairs in a moment," Mrs. Hartmann said, walking briskly through the door leading to the front parlor. At a loss, Kassandra remained in the entryway until her hostess's voice beckoned.

"We keep help year-round," she said, her little footsteps echoing on the wood floors. "The Brown family has been here in service to our family for as long as our family has had the house. Why nobody was out to greet the coach I simply can't understand. Mariah?"

Mrs. Hartmann continued calling out the name of the elusive Mariah throughout the tour of the first floor. Just half a step behind her, Kassandra poked her head into a dining room fashioned after how she had always imagined a ship's galley to look, with a mahogany table big enough to sit twelve people dominating the room. Hanging just over its center was a crystal chandelier, and at the far end, a sideboard boasted a set of gleaming silver serving dishes. They zipped past and through an elegant front parlor with an ornate fireplace inlaid with marble, and a back sitting room where a series of four French doors guaranteed light and air on even this warm summer day. Still, no Mariah.

The kitchen was small and designed for utility, for it had only a small table tucked into a back corner. A pot of something wonderfully fishy bubbled on the black iron stove, prompting Mrs. Hartmann to observe that Mariah mustn't be too far off, unless she'd purposefully left the oyster stew to boil over and burn the house down. She even gave a couple of brisk raps to the door that led to Mariah's room off the kitchen, calling through the wood, but no answer there, either. Up the back stairs the women went, to a rather narrow hallway dimly lit by the two windows at each end.

"Well, I guess it's up to me to show you to your room," Mrs. Hartmann said, as if the chore were tantamount to chopping the wood for the morning fire. "You'll be in the last on the left."

Kassandra followed, her stomach rumbling after having had a whiff of the stew. All of the upstairs doors were shut, so she had no idea what to expect when Mrs. Hartmann opened the door to her future room.

"Mariah!"

Kassandra, ever on Mrs. Hartmann's heels, stumbled over the room's threshold in time to see the supposed Mariah lounged on the bed, deeply engrossed in a book. Judging by the swiftness with which she stashed the tome under her apron, it must have been one of the French novels Mrs. Hartmann's Ladies' Society spoke so vehemently against.

"Mrs. Hartmann!" said the flustered woman, scrambling to get off the bed. "I wasn't expecting you so early."

"I find that hard to believe, considering I sent you a letter nearly a month ago telling you we would be here on precisely this date."

"I guess I was thinking it might be a little later in the afternoon."

Mariah was smoothing her hair back now. She was pretty if plain and probably around thirty years old, not much older than Mrs. Hartmann. And she was not nearly as flustered as Mrs. Hartmann would have wanted her to be. In fact, Mariah had quite the mischievous glint in her eye.

"But you know how it is, Mrs. Hartmann. You've always enjoyed a leisurely afternoon."

Mrs. Hartmann seemed to be trying her best to remain composed. "Please go downstairs and get our bags. The driver has been paid."

"Yes, Mrs. Hartmann," Mariah said, affecting an exaggerated curtsy. "But knowing you I'll get some money from the kitchen jar to tip the driver."

Mariah Brown's speech was an exaggeration of the same pattern that sometimes overtook Mrs. Hartmann's before she caught and corrected herself. *Jar* sounded like *jah*, and this dialect combined with the woman's lack of repentance gave her an air of unabashed cheekiness that Kassandra found amusing.

"And you must be the little mother?" Mariah said, reaching out to pat Kassandra's stomach on her way out, ignoring the fuming Mrs. Hartmann.

That afternoon had been nearly two months ago, and the memory of it still brought a smile to Kassandra's face. She looked back over her shoulder and saw the roof of the house peeking out from behind the grass-covered dunes. If she stayed out much longer, walked much farther, Mariah and Mrs. Hartmann would be in a state when she got back. The baby—according to the pompous Dr. Hilton, who had been the Weathersby family physician for two generations—was due any moment, though Kassandra felt she had nearly a week left before she would hold the child in her arms.

She bent down the little she was able and gathered her skirts around her knees before taking a few steps into the ocean water. She closed her eyes and concentrated on the feeling of the wet sand being washed away beneath her feet—the little bit of sinking each time—then more again. This is what it felt like to be restored to God. *His goodness is new every morning,* and every morning she woke up with the memories of those torrid years with Ben washed further and further away.

Out on the horizon she saw ships, and the Weathersby family docks were visible just a few miles down the beach, though none of Mrs. Hartmann's family had ever come to pay her a visit.

"I've chosen a life apart," Mrs. Hartmann had said when Kassandra questioned her about their absence, her Cape Cod shipping roots coming to life in her speech. *Apaht.* Kassandra hadn't asked again.

The sun was beginning to disappear over the dunes, so she turned and headed back home. She walked through the grass on her way up to the house, scooching her feet to dislodge as much sand as possible and walked inside.

"You shouldn't stay out so late," Mrs. Hartmann said. She was sitting in the front parlor at the window, reading by the waning light. "It's nearly dark."

"I know," Kassandra answered. "I am sorry if I made you worry. It just feels so good to walk." She sat down in the chair opposite Mrs. Hartmann and waited for the other woman to look up and give her full attention. "Thank you so much for bringing me here."

"I simply thought it would be best." Mrs. Hartmann took off her reading glasses and set them aside. "Mariah has already gone home for the evening, so if you want a snack before you go to bed you'll have to get it yourself. There's a bit of sponge cake left from supper."

"I am not very hungry," Kassandra said.

How could the two of them still be so wary of each other after all this time together? When they left New York, Kassandra hadn't entertained any visions of their becoming bosom friends, but Mrs. Hartmann barely showed any less disdain than she had that first morning in her kitchen. So in the growing shadows of the front parlor, Kassandra stood up and said, "Good night."

She must have slept through the first pains, because the one that finally did wake her was so severe she nearly cried out into the darkness of her room. She lay in bed, long enough to clear her head, to make sure what she'd felt wasn't a dream. She heard the clock downstairs chime the quarter hour. Then the half. When it chimed again, her body seized up in that tight band that could mean only one thing.

It was time.

Her window was wide open, and the white lace curtains billowed with the sea breeze. When the contraction subsided she climbed out of bed and walked over to the window. She knelt in front of it and propped her elbows on the sill, clasped her hands together, and bowed her head.

"This is the day, Lord, that my child will be born." The lapping waves filled the silence as Kassandra searched for words. "You have my son. Please, my Father, let me bring this child into the world."

Her answer was the continuous motion of the sea.

She thought about that night, months and months ago, when she knelt at another open window, flames raging behind her, smoke filling her lungs. Not a day went by that she didn't thank God for saving her that night—saving her from the hell she had created for herself. Every day she thanked Him, too, for His forgiveness for the sin that nearly consumed her every bit as much as that fire. Now she asked to be saved one more time.

"Protect me, Lord," she prayed, "from the pain of losing this child. Keep me strong, and bless me with this life."

She felt the tugging of the next pain across her back and

braced herself to stand, clutching her bedpost and breathing deep, until it subsided. The moon was bright and full, casting an iridescent glow on the sandy beaches. She thought back to all those other women she and Imogene had helped through their labor, and one directive was constant. Walk.

She knew the plan was to call for Doctor Hilton, even though Kassandra said time and again that she would be fine, as long as Mrs. Hartmann was present to assist. But Mrs. Hartmann said she had no intention of helping with the birth of this baby, and Mariah Brown's offer to be of support was overlooked in favor of calling in the trusted family physician. But Kassandra did, after all, know a few things about the progression of labor, and as her water hadn't yet broken, there might still be hours before the doctor's presence would be needed.

Kassandra took Imogene's shawl from the chair it was draped on and wrapped it around her shoulders. She made no noise on her way through the house, pausing just long enough to smile at the slight snoring coming from the other side of Mrs. Hartmann's door.

Outside, she promised herself that she would not walk far, always keeping the house in her sight. The sand was cool beneath her toes, and the effort it took to walk through it ener- gized her muscles. She counted the laps of the ocean between contractions, their numbers decreasing as the sky grew gray. She walked, her hand braced to her back when the pain intensified. Then, just as the first pink of dawn peeked into the sky, she made her way back to the house and into the kitchen where Mariah was already up, making breakfast.

"Mariah?" Kassandra said, surprised at the calmness of her voice. "You need to go into the village for the doctor."

"What were you thinking? Out there on that beach all alone in the dead of night? With the…the baby coming?"

"Walking is good, Mrs. Hartmann," Kassandra reassured the pacing woman. They were in Kassandra's room now, and Kassandra was safe in her own bed, obeying what Mrs. Hartmann was sure would be the doctor's orders once he arrived.

"You'll have to forgive me if I don't acknowledge you as an expert on such things," Mrs. Hartmann said.

"I think I know more than—"

Kassandra's words were lost in the onslaught of a new birthing pain, the strongest one yet.

God help me, God help me, God help me.

She distinctly remembered those hours alone in her flat, waiting for Imogene, not knowing the grave danger her baby was in.

"Mrs. Hartmann," she managed to say as the contraction subsided, "I need you to look. To check and see that the baby is—"

"I'm not your midwife," Mrs. Hartmann snapped, stopping midpace to face Kassandra with her hands on her hips. "Perhaps if you'd called for the doctor earlier, you wouldn't be relying on me now."

"I just need to know if the baby's head—"

"Don't speak to me of babies' heads. Leave that for the doctor."

Just then there was a clamor downstairs, to which Mrs. Hartmann exclaimed, "He's here! Thank God!" and left Kassandra alone in the room to run downstairs and usher Dr. Hilton in.

She had met him just once before, shortly after her arrival, in a very proper interview in the front parlor. The only other doctor she had ever known was the kindly physician who nursed her back to health after being struck by Reverend Joseph's horse. He had been full of humor and life. Doctor Hilton, however, was nothing like that. Elderly, yes—nearly seventy, he had been present for the birth of Mrs. Hartmann herself—but there was no humor about him. His first visit with Kassandra consisted of little more than a tremulous grip of Kassandra's hand and an assurance that everything would be fine. Just fine.

Now here he was, the sky outside not yet bright enough to constitute true morning, and he was as perfectly attired in his suit and hat as he had been on that first conversation in the parlor. He walked in, discarding his jacket and rolling up his sleeves.

"Well, now, miss Kassandra," he said, adding an *r* to the end of her name—*Kassandrar*—"it seems it's time to have this baby."

Mariah followed close behind him with a kettle full of warm water that she poured into the basin on the washstand. Doctor Hilton washed his hands and positioned himself at the foot of Kassandra's bed, where he drew aside the covers and lifted her gown. Mrs. Hartmann, who stood just in the doorway, gave a little gasp and turned away.

"I hear you went for a walk this morning?"

Kassandra nodded and made an affirmative noise, the current contraction making conversation uncomfortable.

"Best thing to help the labor along as far as I know." Dr. Hilton continued in his conversational tone, sometimes talking to her, sometimes to Mrs. Hartmann, but always in such a flat, pragmatic tone that no one overhearing the conversation would ever be able to guess at the momentous event taking place.

When Kassandra told Dr. Hilton she felt it was time to push, he merely said, "Well then, push." When she felt the need to stop, he said, "Well then, stop." At times he seemed nearly as puzzled at his presence there as she was.

After nearly thirty minutes of Kassandra's attempting to push the baby, Dr. Hilton took one peek under the sheet, and his demeanor changed. "Well, now, from the looks of this here, we have a baby."

Kassandra's groans throughout had been matched by those of Mrs. Hartmann, who was eager to be sent on any minor errand. Now, at Dr. Hilton's announcement, she left to fetch the bag he'd left in the parlor and to alert Mariah to heat more water.

Kassandra barely heard any of the words spoken by Dr. Hilton, and their atonal quality gave her no indication as to the progress or health of the baby. She was certain only of the commands of her body and the prayer in her heart that had been reduced to only one word. *Please.*

She heard the doctor say something about the head, and then the *sholdahs.*

Then, the healthy, piercing cry of her child. Her daughter, according to Dr. Hilton.

The baby's cry brought Mariah clattering into the room. She elbowed her way past Mrs. Hartmann, who hadn't taken a single step into the room in all this time.

"Oh, she's beautiful." Mariah held out a clean linen towel into which Dr. Hilton deposited the wet and squirming baby. "She's a keeper, this one is."

Kassandra lay back, exhausted on her pillow. "Thank You, God," she said, over and over, tears flowing freely and puddling in her ears. "Let me see her," she said, holding out limp and exhausted arms to receive her child.

"Let me clean her up first," Mariah said, "so you can meet her proper."

"No, please, please—"

"There's time enough for that later." Dr. Hilton redirected Kassandra's attention to the aftermath of her labor.

Kassandra propped herself up on her elbows and struggled to get even a glimpse of the baby girl who continued to fill the room with her welcome wails. She saw nothing but Mariah's back, bent low over the dressing table now covered with a thick towel. Mrs. Hartmann, though, from her vantage point of the doorway, would have a clear view, and Kassandra looked to her to ask about her daughter. But the expression on Mrs. Hartmann's face stopped Kassandra from asking anything. Her eyes, so fixated on the child, bore a longing that Kassandra had seen only in the eyes of the starving children in the streets of the city.

"One last push," Dr. Hilton said, and Kassandra complied.

"May I see her now?" Kassandra asked.

Mariah turned around with the blanketed bundle. "Of course you can."

"I think you should rest first." Mrs. Hartmann walked into the room and stood in front of Mariah, blocking Kassandra's view. "Don't you think, Dr. Hilton?"

Dr. Hilton exchanged a pointed look with Mrs. Hartmann before opening the large leather bag on Kassandra's bureau and rummaging through its contents.

"No!" Kassandra ignored the pain in her body and worked to sit up in her bed, even attempting to swing her legs over the edge. "I do *not* need to rest! I need to see my baby!"

But her weakened body would not obey. She felt paralyzed, and the helplessness took on the tinge of panic as she saw Dr. Hilton dip a bottle of clear liquid over a clean white handkerchief and approach her.

"Now, Kassandra," he said in that matter-of-fact manner of his, which sent chills through her body. "You've been up most of the night. You'll need your sleep."

"What are you doing?" Kassandra said.

She wasn't referring to the doctor's suspicious ministrations, but to the vision of Mariah Brown handing her child over to the waiting arms of Mrs. Hartmann. That was the last sight Kassandra had before the handkerchief was placed over her mouth and nose, and all conscious thought disappeared.

❦ 23 ❧

The second time she woke up, she was on the floor. Mariah knelt beside her, wiping her brow with a cool cloth as she held Kassandra's head in her lap.

"There now," she was saying, "that's it. Wake up. Help me get you back into bed."

Kassandra didn't want to get back into bed. Even in this groggy state, she wanted to find her daughter. But Mariah was not one to be denied, and the two women struggled together until Kassandra was back in the bed, sitting up on newly propped pillows.

"Where is she?" Kassandra asked, surprised at the thickness of her voice.

Mariah busied herself helping Kassandra take a sip of water and smoothing out the covers. "I'll get Mrs. Hartmann in here," she said.

"Not her. My baby."

"You just rest," Mariah said, patting Kassandra's leg before leaving the room and closing the door behind her.

"No!" Kassandra's voice croaked with the effort, but Mariah didn't return. Kassandra continued to holler—calling for Mariah, calling for Mrs. Hartmann, calling for her baby—until her throat was raw and the door opened again at last.

This time, it was Mrs. Hartmann who came through, scowling and asking Kassandra if she had gone quite mad.

"Where is my baby?"

"Calm down, Kassandra."

"I will not calm down. Where is my daughter?"

"We need to talk."

"We do *not* need to talk. I need to see my daughter."

Mrs. Hartmann moved a chair close to the bed and sat on it. She reached for Kassandra's hand, which was clenched into a fist, and covered it with her own. The gesture was fraught with such unwarranted and unprecedented affection that Kassandra dreaded what she had to ask next.

"Is she…is she all right?"

Mrs. Hartmann looked at her, seeming to deliberate her answer. How many answers could there be? Yes, she's fine. No, she's sick. She's sleeping. She's—

"I've hired a wet nurse from town," Mrs. Hartmann said, as calmly as if she were announcing that they were having pork chops for supper. "It's really the thing to do. All the experts say so. The baby is with her."

Kassandra tried to wrap her mind around what Mrs. Hartmann just said, but it didn't make any sense. She had been prepared to hear the worst—had steeled herself against the idea that this child, too, had died before she got a chance to hold her. But that she had simply been taken away? Why would she hire a nurse when Kassandra was perfectly capable of taking care of her child? She stared at Mrs. Hartmann and inwardly, silently, begged for an explanation.

"I didn't want to say anything until after the baby was born," Mrs. Hartmann said, "knowing what happened to the first one. I didn't want to get our hopes up too high, just to be disappointed."

She spoke in that fast, almost manic way she sometimes did—as if terrified of the interruption that would send her hopelessly off track. The rapidity of her speech made it difficult for Kassandra's muddled head to make sense of all of it, but one phrase stood out. *Our* hopes.

"Maybe I was afraid you'd run away before I even had a

chance to explain things. You have a history of that, you know, my dear. Running away. Of course, I don't know where you would have run to, exactly…"

"You aren't making any sense," Kassandra said, her tongue thick behind her teeth.

"Joseph and I, you see, will never have children."

"You and Reverend Joseph?" Kassandra tried to attach meaning to the abrupt change in focus. "He loves children."

"I know he does, but we'll never have children of *our own*."

"You have been married only a few years," Kassandra said. "It takes time…sometimes."

"It's not a matter of time." She still held Kassandra's hand, and now she worked her thumb underneath Kassandra's clenched fingers and gently pried them open, until there was a flat, open palm to cover with her own. "Dr. Hilton has assured me that it would be quite impossible for me ever to carry a child. I haven't told Joseph. I'd been praying for the right words, the right time…then you showed up. It was like an answer to prayer."

Kassandra withdrew her hand and laid it protectively on her empty stomach. "That is why you decided to let me stay. My child—my daughter and I—in the carriage house?"

"Not exactly," Mrs. Hartmann said, looking down at her empty hands.

Kassandra clutched at the bedclothes and closed her eyes, wishing she could make Mrs. Hartmann disappear as quickly as her baby apparently had. "You cannot mean…"

"We would give her everything, you know." Mrs. Hartmann was fidgeting now, looking around the room, perhaps remembering how wonderful it was to grow up with everything. "We could provide for her in ways you never could."

"I know what Reverend Joseph wants." Kassandra hoped the slowness of her speech would make her meaning more clear, both to herself and to Mrs. Hartmann. "He wants all of us together—"

"That will never work."

Mrs. Hartmann stood and walked over to the window. It was getting dark again, and Kassandra wondered if more than one day had passed since that first birthing pain. Mrs. Hartmann busied herself lighting the lamp at Kassandra's bedside as she talked.

"It's no way to raise a child. She'll never really know her place. If we provide for her, is she ours? If she calls you 'mother,' is she yours? Children are either raised by their parents, or they are adopted outright. That place in the middle...well, you know better than anyone how unbearable that is, don't you?"

How well she did. It was being in that place in the middle that drove her into Ben's arms. That need to belong somewhere—to have a place—that allowed her to find contentment in the most wretched of circumstances. But now she did belong to somebody. She belonged to her child; they belonged to each other.

Kassandra scrutinized the profile of Mrs. Hartmann's fussy face, grotesquely illuminated as she adjusted the lamp's flame. This was not a woman who appreciated God's gifts. Why light a lamp when the full gray moon could bathe the room in nearly as much light? No, any minute now she would make some disdainful remark about the maddening monotony of the crashing waves. How could such a woman ever truly love a child? Especially one conceived in such blatant sin.

"I cannot," Kassandra said at last. She wasn't begging; she wouldn't plead. "Will you bring her back to me now?"

"I'm not some kind of goblin, you know, stealing babies away."

"I know that," Kassandra said, feeling the tendrils of compassion snake through the dissipating fog in her head. She tried once again to stand, but felt the shadows of a weakness she didn't want Mrs. Hartmann to witness. Softening her tone, speaking calmly as if to a madwoman, she said, "Please, please bring her to me."

"If that's really what you want, of course."

Kassandra heard her quick little footsteps disappearing down the hall. She reached for the glass of water on the table beside her bed, took one cautionary sip before quenching her dry, sore throat with its coolness. She ran her fingers through her matted hair, drawing it behind her head and plaiting it loosely, leaving it unfastened at her back. Soon she heard the little footsteps again, this time much slower and measured, and when Mrs. Hartmann bent low to deposit the bundle into Kassandra's waiting arms, there was the briefest moment when she wasn't sure if the other woman would let go.

The tiny girl was wrapped in a soft yellow blanket, swaddled tightly, with just one tiny fist escaping from the confines of the fabric. Kassandra caught that fist between her finger and thumb and brought it up to her lips, delivering a series of kisses on the baby's red, wrinkled knuckles. The child was fast asleep, pale eyelashes flush against soft, blotchy cheeks, but Kassandra didn't need to see her eyes to know who had fathered this little girl. On the top of her head, hair the color of glazed carrots lay in soft, wispy strands. She let go of the little fist and ran her fingers across the scalp, remembering the tuft of her son's hair tucked into her Bible and lost to the fire. This hair she would live to see grow. She lifted the baby to plant a soft kiss on top of its head.

"Isn't she a precious lamb?" Mrs. Hartmann said, speaking just over Kassandra's shoulder.

"She is," Kassandra said, pulling the blanket away to lay her palm against the infant's strong, beating heart.

"However will you be able to care for her alone? Especially back in that horrible neighborhood. By the Bowery, wasn't it?"

Kassandra felt her blood turn cold. "I...I do not want to go back there."

"Well, darling," Mrs. Hartmann said, moving from behind Kassandra to sit in the chair at the bedside. "We don't always get what we want in life, now do we?"

"I thought I might stay with you—"

"I already told you that would be impossible."

"Not forever. Just until I have a chance to get back on my feet."

"Now, now, darling. When have you ever *been* on your feet?"

Kassandra felt as if she'd been thumped between the eyes. "I just meant until I can find a job."

"And who would be so quick to hire a young woman who came along with her illegitimate child?"

"You cannot make me go back there."

"No, I can't," Mrs. Hartmann said. "I can only try to speak to you as one woman to another. Can't you see how hard it would be to have you there—living with us—a constant reminder of what I am unable to give my husband?"

"Does Reverend Joseph know about all of this?"

"He is completely blind when it comes to you." Her words revealed a vulnerability that reached far beyond her inability to have a child. "He's never forgiven himself for letting you get away the first time. Given the choice," she laughed nervously, "I believe he'd have me out on the street and you and the baby cozied up by the fire."

"Surely not."

"I abhor gambling, Kassandra. I won't take that risk."

Just then there was a soft knock on the door before it opened to allow Mariah, carrying a tray, to enter the room.

"Doctor says you shouldn't eat just yet," she said, setting the tray on the bureau top. "Said that medicine he give you to help you sleep might make you sick if you eat too soon. But I brought some tea—oh, there's the precious one."

"Not now, Mariah," Mrs. Hartmann said. "Kassandra and I are speaking."

"Is that so?" Mariah stood just behind Mrs. Hartmann's shoulder, hands on her hips, staring right into Kassandra's eyes. "Is there anything else I can get you?"

"Could you open the curtains? And the window? I would like to look outside," Kassandra said.

"All right." When Mariah was finished, she turned and said, "If there's anything else, I'll be just downstairs."

The two women sat in silence for several minutes after Mariah left.

With just a bit of a stretch, Kassandra could see the now full moon over the ocean. The sand was iridescent in its glow, and she thought back to those early hours of her labor, staring at the same beach, under the same moon, so full of hope and life. She wished she could take the baby now, straight down to the beach, and walk along the shore, holding the child in her arms as carefully as she'd held it in her womb.

"Couldn't we just stay here?" Kassandra asked, the idea forming even as she said the words.

"What do you mean? *Here*?"

"Here. At this house. Leyna and I—"

"Leyna?"

"I thought if I had a girl, I would name her Leyna," Kassandra said, almost shyly. "I used to think it was my mother's name."

"My mother's name was Charlotte," Mrs. Hartmann said, her tone distracted.

"That is lovely," Kassandra said, tearing her eyes away from the view to find a connection to this strand of the conversation.

"This house was hers—actually in her name. It's been in her family for generations. When my uncles inherited all the ships from our family's shipping business—not to mention the millions of dollars that went with it—she got this house. And she left it to me. What makes you think I would hand it over to you?"

"I would never claim it as my own," Kassandra said, choosing her words carefully. "I simply thought we might stay here. Help with the upkeep."

"Why?"

The question stunned her. Who wouldn't want to stay here? Who, if given the choice whether or not to rise and sleep to the sound of the ocean, would ever willingly walk away?

"I just...I am just so happy here. So much at peace. I love it."

"You think this will give the child a family?"

"I will be her family. And Mariah."

"Servants are not family."

"I would be a servant, too."

"People here will know exactly who you are. What you are. This is a small town, Kassandra. A little shipping village. Your child will grow up victimized by gossip." Mrs. Hartmann's voice grew almost frantic as she spoke. "We have standards here. We don't forgive."

"I have done nothing to require your forgiveness," Kassandra said. "God has forgiven my sins. I need nothing else."

"Perhaps you don't. But what about your daughter?"

"I will take care of her."

"There's nothing in your life that has prepared you to raise a child, Kassandra. You simply don't have the wherewithal to do it properly." For the first time, Mrs. Hartmann's voice rose in accusation.

"You have no right to take my child from me," Kassandra said, matching Mrs. Hartmann's volume. But one look down showed the little one to be wincing against the noise, and she lowered her voice to a whisper. "She is mine. I will raise her."

"Kassandra, please. Can't you try to think beyond your own selfishness?"

"When...when have I ever been selfish?"

"Think about it. You had a good home, and you left it. Why? Because something better came along. Something a little more exciting."

"That's not why—"

"And not a word. Not a single letter to the man who raised you, gave you everything. You can't imagine the heartache and guilt he carries with him because of you."

"You do not understand—"

"How do we know there won't be some other man who'll come along and you'll go running off with him?"

"I would never do that."

"You simply aren't stable, constantly roaming from one life to another. Now you've come traipsing back here—for the second time, I'm told—"

"I didn't stay the first time because of *you*. I did not think I would be welcome."

"You probably wouldn't have been." Mrs. Hartmann shrugged her shoulders, as if she were as disappointed at this as Kassandra was. "And now, well, you'd be more like an obligation. A chance at his redemption."

"You are lying." Kassandra's whole body was shaking now, and she clutched the child closer to her until she could be still. "Reverend Joseph does not feel that way."

"He'd never say so, of course. He might not even realize it. But really, what other explanation is there?"

"I cannot go back to the Points."

A hint of victory crept into Mrs. Hartmann's eyes. "I know Joseph would hate that for you, too."

"But perhaps," she gulped and felt her pride fall to her feet, colliding with the rising shame, "I could stay here. Alone."

Mrs. Hartmann shook her head slowly. "No, my dear. Next summer I'll insist Joseph come for the season. This will be our home, too, for part of the year."

Kassandra's mind entertained first one vision and then another. A little redheaded girl rushing into Reverend Joseph's arms; a little redheaded girl dirty in the alley behind Canal Street. Her child's eyes watching the full moon dance on the water, hearing the waves lap on the shore; her child's eyes looking up through a haze of soot and smoke as she tries to see the sky; this bundled baby nestled in Mrs. Hartmann's arms, sitting in the cozy back parlor by a roaring fire on a cold winter night; this bundled baby in her own arms, huddled in a doorway, hoping not to freeze before finding shelter.

"Well then," she asked, "where would I go?"

Mrs. Hartmann burst into a smile. "I have given this some thought," she said. "San Francisco. It's just perfect for you. It's a brand-new world for your brand-new life. Just full of promise. Everybody there is starting over, building a new country. Nothing but gold and opportunity—"

Kassandra laughed out loud. "How in the world would I get to San Francisco?"

"My Uncle Hiram. He's run a clipper ship round the Horn to San Francisco several times already. He says he can have you there by the end of October. Just about three months from now."

"You seem to have given this *a lot* of thought," Kassandra said.

"I simply wanted you to know your options." Mrs. Hartmann reached over to stroke the sleeping child's head.

Kassandra looked down at the face of her sleeping daughter. All at once, her tiny mouth opened for a face-scrunching yawn, though her sleep remained undisturbed. "If I did this," she said, speaking to the child rather than to Mrs. Hartmann, "I do not know if I could ever live with myself. This is exactly what my mother did to me, you see? She just walked away. I have never really forgiven her for that."

"This isn't the same thing at all," Mrs. Hartmann said. "Think of Samuel's mother and the strength of character it must have taken for her to leave her son, even if she was leaving him to the house of God for His service."

"She was fulfilling a promise. I have made no such promise to God."

"Or Moses' mother, who had the faith to set her child adrift, knowing that God would take care of him."

"Only it is I who will be setting sail."

Mrs. Hartmann offered a weak smile. "You have my word, as a Christian woman, that your daughter will be raised with love. She will have everything a little girl could ever want. You know how much Joseph loves children…he's helped so many of them before. Given so much. Think of what he will do for this little one that he has chosen to be his own."

"*He* has chosen?"

"Joseph would never be strong enough to ask you to do this, even though it's clearly what is best for both you and the baby."

"And how is this best for me?"

Mrs. Hartmann crossed back over to the window and looked outside. "Do you realize, Kassandra, that when you get to San Francisco you will be looking at an entirely different ocean? The waters from this one will never touch it. Ever."

My sin as far as the east from the west.

"It's really quite simple, Kassandra. Do you love this child so much that you would take her to the streets just to have her at your side? Or do you love her enough to spare her from that life?"

"Would you call her Leyna?" Kassandra asked.

"Will that make your decision any easier?"

"Nothing about this is easy," Kassandra said, wondering just what color eyes hid behind those soft pink lids. "Just let me hold her a little longer."

Breathe through the heats of our desire
Thy coolness and Thy balm;
Let sense be dumb, let flesh retire;
Speak through the earthquake, wind, and fire,
O still, small voice of calm!

assandra's utter hatred for sailors had been finely tuned during her years working on the second floor of the Mott Street Tavern. They bore with them always the putrid smell of bile and fish. Their skin was blistered and torn from the sun. Indefinable crusts formed in the crevices of their necks and hands, and their clothes—if such rags could be called such—were stiff with seawater and salt.

It frightened her at the time to realize that Mott Street, being so far from the docks, actually attracted a higher class of maritime clientele. These were the captains, the first mates, the officers who had enough money to bypass the Water Street whores to venture farther inland for their pleasure. Given that, she couldn't imagine the condition of the common lout fresh from the decks. Why, they must have been little more than half-rotted carp in trousers.

Trade the trousers for a skirt, and they must have been in much the same shape that she was in now.

During her first week at sea, Kassandra managed to keep an air of hopeful decorum. It wasn't easy, watching the land slip away as the ship left the dock, knowing somewhere her newborn daughter rested in the arms of a stranger. She'd stood on the deck of the ship, the rails pressed to her empty body, her breasts—still aching and heavy—wrapped tightly beneath her blouse, willing herself with each passing moment not to jump into the ocean and make her way back to shore, to Mrs. Hartmann's house. To her child. The fact that she couldn't swim was a minor matter. Surely God would protect her, send a tide to wash her safely onto the beach, a whale to spit·her whole upon the sand.

Then she heard Mrs. Hartmann's words lodged into her very soul. Didn't she want the best for her daughter? Wouldn't she want her little girl to grow up with every advantage? Shielded from the ugliness of this world, protected from the diseases of poverty. Did that baby deserve to grow up in the shadow of illegitimacy and prostitution?

The only answer, then, was to cross over to the other side of the ship and gaze at the horizon. Focus on that thin, straight line where the sea met the sky, and pray that God was on the other side of it, waiting to reward her for her sacrifice.

That was the first week.

After that, there was nothing but ocean, for days and weeks and months. Sometimes smooth and glassy, which Kassandra enjoyed despite the crude dissatisfaction such conditions inspired among the sailors. Sometimes wild and tumultuous, tossing her from the bed in her cabin.

Not that the word *cabin* did any justice to the tiny space allotted to her on the *Sea Crest*. A narrow cot was bolted to the floor, with merely a door's width between it and the opposing wall. There would have been no place to store any extra clothing, had she brought any. As it was, the few things she had in her bag—one other dress, three pairs of stockings, a nightgown, and Imogene's shawl—remained folded in her small bag and stored underneath the cot. She hadn't bothered to change her clothing since boarding, as the room afforded no space for the maneuvering required to do so. There was no ventilation, and the recurring images from the Mott Street inferno kept her from bringing any open flame into such a coffinlike box.

Uncomfortable as the cabin was, she knew she was lucky to have it at all. The *Sea Crest* was a clipper ship, not a passenger vessel, and her presence in this room left the first mate to sleep dangling in a hammock next to his subordinates. That was the first hint that her presence wasn't entirely welcome.

Hiram Weathersby, captain of the *Sea Crest* and Mrs. Hartmann's uncle, had taken great pains to make Kassandra's voyage as pleasant as possible. A tall, broad-chested man with neatly trimmed whiskers framing his otherwise clean-shaven face, he had introduced Kassandra to the crew gathered on the dock for their instructions before the ship launched.

"This woman here," he said, his Massachusetts accent adding to his air of authority, "is traveling as a personal guest." The lascivious nudging and laughter by the men gathered on deck was soon quelled with a single glare from Captain Weathersby's piercing eyes under thick brows. "She is not to be harassed or molested in any way, do you hear?"

"Aye, aye," the crew replied, though halfheartedly.

"As far as you are concerned," Captain Weathersby continued, pacing back and forth in front of his assembled men, "she is another bit of cargo. I've been charged with her safe delivery to San Francisco, and she will be delivered. Is that clear?"

"Aye, aye," they chorused, with slightly more enthusiasm.

At first the men fairly ignored the order, and she was met daily with crude remarks and propositions any time she found herself alone on deck or in some dark crevice below. But when these elicited neither her interest nor her ire, the remarks disappeared. After a while Kassandra moved about freely as if surrounded by an aura of inaccessibility.

Most days the sea was choppy, juvenile waves slapping at the sides of the ship, giving continuous bits of encouragement as it followed its course. The older men said they'd never seen such a fine stretch of good sailing, gloating as if they had some hand in creating the favorable conditions. The fastest ship ever to make this voyage was the *Flying Cloud*—just eighty-nine days from Boston to San Francisco. The sailors figured if the weather would hold, the *Sea Crest* just might beat it.

Kassandra wasn't interested in breaking any records. As far as she was concerned, they could never spend too many days at sea. Yes, reddened skin pulled away from her face after hours in the sun. Yes, her eyes burned from the glare off the water. The steady diet of weevil-infested biscuits and dried beef left her weak and listless. She'd grown tired of picking insects out of the foul-tasting water dipped from barrels in the bowels of the ship and diluted with molasses and vinegar. Now she simply swallowed them, trying to ignore the passing scratch of a wing or leg in her throat.

None of this, though, would she trade for the uncertain future awaiting her once they reached land. None of Mrs. Hartmann's conversations—or any of her own thoughts—extended beyond disembarking in San Francisco. As long as she was on the *Sea Crest,* she was under God's care. There was no bustle of humanity to obscure her from His view. Surely He could look down from heaven and see her, a tiny speck surrounded by miles and miles of ocean. Not lost. She'd been lost in the city, out of His view, out of His care. She'd had to look straight up to see a patch of sky, and that was often black with smoke and sick with smell.

But here, the sky was endless and clear and blue. She didn't have to look up at all. The humblest glance to the left, to the right, and the majesty of God's presence unfolded. Perhaps she couldn't see Him, but when she stood alone and exposed on the deck, *He* could see *her*, and she relished that exposure even if it meant the burning and tearing of her flesh from the sun and salt and wind.

One hundred and twenty-eight days later, the *Sea Crest* sat in perfectly still water just off the coast of California, waiting for one last good wind to usher her into the San Francisco Bay. Everybody on board carried with them a disposition as sour as the small, tart fruit they picked up after a brief stop on the St. Christian Islands.

Captain Weathersby occasionally allowed Kassandra to look through his glass at the bustling port, and each time she did, her heart sank a little. Back east, California was thought to be paradise itself, a land of golden opportunity. Perhaps she'd been spoiled, misled by the exotic ports on the journey here, where beautiful brown-skinned men and women appeared on the beaches like characters in some glamorous dream. She saw nothing dreamlike through Captain Weathersby's glass. Row upon row of cheap-looking wooden structures lined the shore just past where what seemed like hundreds of ships choked the harbor. It seemed that once the *Sea Crest* came alongside the outermost ship, Kassandra could simply hop from one to another until she reached land, the muddled, muddy mess with no beach to speak of, no trees, no grass.

Kassandra hadn't stepped a single foot off the boat, and already she was lost.

There was no ceremony afforded to the docking of the *Sea Crest*. Kassandra had been asleep in her cabin and woke up to the shouting of sailors about to shed themselves of the sea.

Four purposeful raps sounded at her door. "Miss Kassandra?" Captain Weathersby paused for just a few seconds before knocking again. "Miss Kassandra, we've made shore."

The thin slits of light streaming through the cabin's wall did little to illuminate the room, so Kassandra made her preparations in the dark. It had been months since she'd bathed, days since she'd combed her hair, years since she had any real reason to care about her appearance. The only mirror on board had been crowded by the sailors, shaving their whiskers in anticipation of a day's leave on shore. No matter. She fumbled through her bag and found her brush, raking it through her ratted locks before braiding, coiling, and securing it with the tortoiseshell comb Ben had given her.

There was neither light nor room to change her dress, so she simply smoothed the material as best she could, mindful of the odor she emitted even to herself. She'd overheard the men talking about the bathhouses—perhaps that would be her first stop.

The weather had turned cool of late, so she wrapped Imogene's shawl around her shoulders, grateful to have at least that to hide some of the more prominent stains and mending places of her tattered dress. She squeezed her swollen feet into shoes for the first time in weeks, tapping the heels on the floor to reorient herself to the feeling of a false sole.

The shouts of the sailors outside became more urgent and purposeful. They were eager to unload their cargo—including her, she was sure—and disembark.

When she emerged from below deck, the crew shouldered past her, carrying crates and boxes, rolling barrels, marching them down a feeble-looking wooden plank that extended between the *Sea Crest* and the dock. Nobody took any notice of Kassandra at all, unless she stood squarely in his path, in which case she was shoved aside with a muttered curse mixed with a profane prayer of thanks to be rid of her.

After one such assault, she found herself stumbling backwards until she collided with Captain Weathersby, who reached for her arm to steady her.

"Miss Kassandra," he said, tipping his cap, "you are hereby delivered."

He kept hold of her arm as he escorted her down the plank, through the milling wharf where well-dressed merchants met with the cargo-toting sailors to purchase their goods sight unseen for prices that made Kassandra turn and gasp. One crate full of men's shirts was handed over for five hundred dollars. A case of straw-packed dinnerware went to a dapper man in a tall silk hat for over a thousand dollars. One man sat with a basket of tiny mewling kittens, lifting them up by the scruffs of their necks to start an impromptu auction with the bids starting at ten dollars each. There could be only one reason for such a price: a city full of rats.

Captain Weathersby kept hold of her arm, steering her through all of this, until they were no longer on the dock at all but squishing through mud. At the edge of the first solid structure they came to, he tipped his cap again, turned, and disappeared into the crowd.

Kassandra clutched the shawl a little more tightly to her, gripped the handle of her bag a little stronger, and backed against the wall. She looked up the street and down and saw nothing but one unadorned building after the other standing sentry over a wide, muddy street. She tried to keep count of the people who passed by. Men dressed in brushed wool coats and silk brocade vests crossed with thick watch chains; men dressed in filthy, torn shirts and tattered boots; the occasional Chinese with his long, thin braid—all rushing by, calling out to others just beyond her sight. Nobody offered her so much as a passing glance. Even if she found the courage to reach out, touch an arm…what would she ask? She had nowhere to go. Knew no one.

Lord, she prayed, *You have brought me here. Help me now.*

She closed her eyes, hoping that blocking out some of the chaos would help her focus on what direction to take. The steadying arm of Captain Weathersby had helped ease the transition from so many months walking the deck of a ship, but now Kassandra felt herself on the verge of collapse. She reached out her hand to try to regain her balance, but drew it quickly back as it encountered something soft and fleshy.

"If you was a fellow I'da charged you ten bucks for that." The voice was deep and husky, almost like a man's.

"I am so very sorry," Kassandra said, opening her eyes to the largest woman she had ever seen. Not tall, as Kassandra stood nearly a head taller, but wide. From hip to hip she was the width of three women, and her depth was no less impressive. Her hair, an unnatural shade of red, was piled haphazardly on top of her head, and the highest frizzy mound of it threatened to tickle Kassandra's chin as she leaned in close.

"You're lookin' like you lost your best friend."

"I haven't got a best friend," Kassandra said.

"Well, that ain't no surprise, smellin' the way you do," the woman said, wrinkling her powdered nose after a brief, too-close inspection.

"I just got off a boat," Kassandra said, wondering why she was so quick to confide in this woman.

"Well, didn't nobody tell you this was San Francisco? California? If you're lookin' for Ellis Island, you sailed the wrong ocean."

Kassandra laughed despite herself, despite the dizziness and the strangeness of the city. She felt an eerie ease with this woman, something she hadn't felt since her first year with Ben, and the realization caused her to catch her breath up high. The painted face, the tinted hair, the plunging neckline. She knew exactly what this woman was. Certainly God didn't bring her halfway across the world just to drop her in another brothel.

"Oh, now come on, girl, don't look so scandalized. I ain't gonna eat you up. Hiram pointed you out to me. Told me to help you out."

"Captain Weathersby?"

"The one and the same. My name's Jewell, by the way. Jewell Gunn."

"I am Kassandra."

"Good. I got the right girl. Now," she reached over and took Kassandra's bag before Kassandra had a chance to protest, "what'll it be? Bath, then dinner? Or other way 'round?" Jewell started walking up the street, leaving no choice but to be followed.

They passed one building after another advertising every kind of good and service imaginable. Just like the city back home, every other establishment boasted liquor and women. This far from the docks, there weren't many street vendors, but the air was alive with every kind of scent pouring from the restaurants lining the street. Pungent noodle shops, savory roasting sausage, yeasty baked goods—all seemed to vie for Kassandra's palate, practically pulling her from the path she followed behind Jewell's voluminous skirts.

"You're prob'ly pretty hungry," Jewell said, glancing over her shoulder without breaking stride.

"I am," Kassandra said, already near breathlessness after what she estimated was merely half a block.

"Well, tell you the truth, the shape you're in, you wouldn't be welcome in none of the establishments I care to frequent."

"Sorry?"

"I'm just thinkin' it would be best to get you cleaned up a bit. Don't you worry, the food's not goin' anywhere. Our first stop needs to be a bath."

Kassandra followed without question, already feeling inextricably linked to the waddling woman in front of her. The crowd was such that if she lagged behind one step or took one to the left or the right, she would be swallowed up. There was a strange sense of comfort in how every third person they passed saluted Jewell—men tipped their hats, women called out greetings—like she was the flagship of the San Francisco Armada and Kassandra the tall tugboat behind.

They came to a stop in front of an impressive-looking four-story building with arched windows along the top story. Several well-dressed men loitered at its doors, and Jewell pushed through them with good-natured ribbing and an open invitation to visit her later in the afternoon.

She led Kassandra through an ornate front door and into the most sumptuous room she had ever seen. The grand, open floor was a checker-pattern of different carpets. No fewer than a dozen chandeliers hung from the vaulted ceiling, and groupings of overstuffed sofas and chairs were scattered throughout.

Kassandra stopped dead just inside the door, her eyes opened so wide she felt she'd never close them again. "What is this place?" she asked.

"This is the finest hotel in San Francisco," Jewell said. "They got a public bathhouse downstairs. Hot water, imported soap. Just ten dollars."

"Ten dollars? I do not have ten dollars to spend on a bath."

"How much you got?" Jewell asked with a sly wink.

Kassandra reached down to pat her skirt pocket. Just a few dollars there. Mrs. Hartmann had given her a soft leather wallet with fifty dollars cash. It was snugly wrapped within a pair of stockings. In her bag. In Jewell's hand.

"Let me tell you this," Jewell said with a conspiratorial air. "They got huge vats of steaming water ready to fill up a porcelain tub. Perfumed soap imported from France, make you smell like the sweetest woman you ever hoped to be. Soft towels, big enough to wrap you up like a baby."

"Please give me my bag back," Kassandra said, reaching for her case, amused at Jewell's juvenile attempt to hold it out of her reach.

"Oh, come now. Wouldn't you like the chance to take off them rags, have 'em washed at a Chinese laundry?"

"I simply cannot—"

"Then they'll give you a fine silk robe—not to keep, you understand—and let you wear it upstairs to the softest bed you've ever set your bones on."

The images swam in Kassandra's head. Her skin grated against the fabric of her filthy dress, and she could feel the prickling grime at the back of her neck, exposed by her greasy, upswept hair. More powerful than the vision of such an experience, though, were the disdainful looks she drew from all who walked past her. At first she thought maybe the disgusted glances were more for Jewell and her ostentatious display, but the upturned noses and muttered insults were proof enough that it was she who offended. For just a moment, she wished to be invisible again. But certainly such luxury must come with a price. If a bath cost ten dollars, she couldn't imagine the price of a bed.

"Now if it's just a matter of the money," Jewell said, her voice taking on a teasing quality, "don't let that bother you. I'm more'n happy to help out a new girl in town."

This was it. Seduction. Rather than being fifteen and poised for love and adventure, she was twenty and tired from unwanted battles. The lure of luxury, the promise of protection. She closed her eyes. Surely God had some other plan for her. She sent up a silent plea for rescue. A four-piece band struck up a lively tune somewhere in the recesses of the main hall, and a group of men raised their voices in a cheerful toast. She heard the *clink* of glasses and opened her eyes to see Jewell's face, oddly comforting in its multitudes of painted, folded flesh.

"Why would you do this for me?"

"Why, you're nothin' but a poor little lost sparrow, ain't you? Blown in from the storm. Come on, let's get them feathers cleaned up."

She nudged Kassandra toward a stairwell to their left above which a sign read, *Public Baths for Hotel Patrons Only*. Kassandra followed a few steps, then stopped.

"Why are you doing this for me?"

Jewell smiled, a big grin that showed her teeth to be small and yellow framed by her crimson-smeared lips. "This is a big ol' scary world, darlin'. A girl oughtn't go through it without her mama. And if she ain't got her mama, she at least needs a friend. And if she ain't got a friend," she winked, "at least she got me. Now, come on, Sadie, let's get you cleaned up."

"My name is Kassandra."

"I like to name my girls myself." Jewell transferred the bag to her other hand and took Kassandra's arm to lead her through the stairwell door. "No better way to start off a new life than with a new name."

As they took the stairs down into the dark basement, Kassandra had the feeling of her life being a book, flipped back to its first page to be lived again. Another tainted savior, and her with no doubt what the price of such salvation would be.

25

*N*ot three days after her rescue in the street, and Kassandra was wearing new clothes, had been given a new name, and occupied a moderately sumptuous room on the second floor of Jewell Gunn's red-roofed brothel. The modest bit of cash she'd arrived with wouldn't have supported her for a day in this city, and Jewell had been more than happy to extend her credit.

She'd never before worn gowns tailored to her frame; she'd never had her hair arranged in painstaking curls, fussed and fretted over by some of the younger of Jewell's girls. The first night she'd been primped for an evening in Jewell's parlor, she stood in front of the full-length gilded mirror (the first of those she'd ever seen, too) and marveled at her own reflection. She felt beautiful. Looked beautiful. The décolletage made her broad shoulders seem anything but manly, especially with the single spiraled curl draped artfully over one of them. The redness brought on by so much exposure to the sun had faded to a healthy bronze, nothing like the ghostly pallor on every face in the sun-starved streets of New York. She used a bit of powder to disguise some of the darker blotches, and there was a definite new crinkling at the corners of her eyes. But with the tiniest dot of rouge applied to her lips and a brush of beeswax on her lashes, her face took on an exotic appeal she'd never anticipated.

Jewell let out a long whistle the first evening Kassandra descended the stairs into the parlor. "Lookee here, girls," she said in that deep, rasping voice of hers. "We got us a genuine Amazon."

Kassandra smiled, pleased at the admiring consent of the other women gathered in the room.

There was a chorus of masculine laughter just outside Jewell's ornate door. It opened, and a group of men—all in freshly laundered shirts and slicked-back hair—tumbled over the threshold. Once inside, they immediately took off their dust-covered hats and looked almost shyly about the room.

Jewell sidled up to Kassandra and motioned for her to lean down.

"You ready to jump in there?" she whispered into Kassandra's ear.

"Almost," Kassandra said, taking a breath so deep it strained against her corset. "Maybe, though, I could get a drink first?"

Her favorite restaurant came to be a small German eatery tucked away on the eastern edge of Portsmouth Square. The thick noodles and tart cabbage made her think of how her mother would have cared for her if she'd ever had the chance. She liked to go early in the evening, before the streets were full of revelers. On many days she didn't see first light until well after noon, and the early supper at Klausen Haus was the first food of the day. She always dressed carefully, and today the warm spring sun called for her new lavender silk gown, its neckline low and square.

"Afternoon, Sadie." He was dressed in a sage green broadcloth suit, a watch chain stretched across his ample stomach. The bright sun glinted off his spectacles when he looked up into Kassandra's face, but she could well imagine the sprightly squint behind the glare.

"Hello, Jimmy." She offered the affected smile that brought a pink tinge to his broad, wrinkled neck. "Are you staying out of trouble?"

"At least until later on tonight." Jimmy made a clicking sound inside his cheek and reached a pudgy arm around to pat the cascade of ruffles at the back of Kassandra's dress.

"Well, then I guess I'd better go inside and have a good dinner," she said, maintaining a flirtatious air as she wormed away from his grasp. "Get my strength up."

The man pulled out an impressive gold timepiece from his strained vest pocket. "Maybe we can make a go of it now. I've got a little time—"

"Now, Jimmy, Jimmy." She patted the top of his balding head. "A girl's got to get some rest some time. You let me go get my dinner, and I'll see you later tonight. The bank won't run itself, you know."

The smile he gave her made it seem as if a twelve-year-old boy suddenly took possession of his mind as he fumbled putting the watch back into its pocket and pulled out a bulging leather wallet from the lining of his jacket. It was thick with bills, and his stubby fingers worked furiously to pull out an impressive pinch of cash. "Well, at least let me buy you your dinner. It's the least I can do, knowing you're fattening up for me."

She matched him in his laughter and offered a quick kiss to the shiny pate as she took the bills from his hand.

"Thank you, Jimmy. I'll be thinking of you with every bite."

He blushed beet red then and seemed suddenly in a rush to get back to his business. Kassandra kept the smile on her face until he had rounded the corner. Once inside, she headed for her favorite table—tucked into the back corner with a clear view of the street through the large plate glass window—nodding a greeting to several of her fellow patrons.

Frederik, the owner, cook, and waiter to the more important clients, was at her table steps before she was, holding her chair out with a flourish and offering a slight bow as she settled in.

"Fraulein Sadie?"

"Hallo, Frederik," she replied. Slipping into her native tongue had been awkward at first, after so many years of disuse, but now it came to her naturally, bringing with it an inexplicable sense of

comfort. She asked him what was on the menu for the day.

"*Wurst-und Gerstensuppe,*" he said, indicating a sausage and barley soup that was a favorite of Kassandra's.

"*Das klingt gut,*" Kassandra said, offering Frederik the remnant of her earlier smile.

"*Und ein Bier?*"

"*Ja, bitte.*"

The second Frederik turned his back, Kassandra let her face relax, only briefly offering up a thankful grin when Fredrik returned with a mug of beer. "*Danke,*" she said, sliding her fingers around the cold glass, lifting it to her lips, and taking a long, deep drink.

Frederik brought her a second with her soup.

like he was a California sultan, greeting him at the door with a smile and cajoling him into buying drink after drink in the parlor before adjourning upstairs. Whenever the men weren't around, she sharpened her verbal wits sparring with Jewell, swapping stories about the colorful life in the slums of New York for those about the adventure of building an empire on the opposite coast.

She kept her fashionable clothes neat and clean and varied, never allowing any former or would-be customer to see her looking slatternly. She maintained her figure despite all the culinary temptations of the city and, recalling Ben's accusation that alcohol made her "puffy," she avowed her limit to be no more than three drinks a day.

If Jewell wanted her girls to be attractive, Kassandra made herself beautiful. If she wanted them to be friendly, Kassandra was effusive. No one had ever asked her to be strong, but if doing so would keep her in Jewell's good graces, Kassandra was more than prepared to become a woman of power. When a seventeen-year-old chippie from a rival brothel accused Kassandra of stealing her favorite customer—calling her a stinkin' kraut—Kassandra calmly grabbed the girl by her auburn hair, hauled her into the alley behind Jewell's house, and hit her exactly once, breaking the girl's nose.

"Well, well, well," Jewell said, surveying the scene of the fray with frank admiration, "what brought on this bit of inspiration?"

"Today is my daughter's first birthday," Kassandra said, wiping the girl's blood off the back of her knuckles on a silk handkerchief pulled from her pocket. "I was not in the mood for another insult."

"A year old? Now that's somethin', isn't it? That merits a drink."

She held out her silver flask to Kassandra, who took it without question and offered a quick salute before tipping it to her lips.

"Tell you what," Jewell said, recapping the flask upon its return. "Why don't you take the night off? Go see a show?"

"I think I will," Kassandra said, immensely satisfied. God had dropped her off in this place, wobbly and nearly unable to stand, but today she summoned her strength and found her legs. If she couldn't trust her Lord to lead her, she'd make her life her own.

Unlike many of the young women who spent their time working for Jewell, Kassandra had no desire to find a man and fall in love. She was too engrossed with falling in love with the city. Though theaters and music halls were in abundance back in New York, she had spent her life being either too sheltered or too poor to enjoy them. Not so here. Just as Kassandra was working to create a new identity of confidence and beauty and breeding, so also was the city of San Francisco.

Every day new improvements were made—the streets paved with cobblestones, ground broken to begin the construction of more sophisticated, aesthetically pleasing buildings. She learned there had been a horrific fire just a few years before her arrival, but there was no evidence of any such destruction. It had sprung back to life, resplendent in its resilience, and in that Kassandra felt a kinship and a sense of belonging she never had before.

She went to the theater on the arms of some of the wealthiest men in the city—bankers and merchants, shipping moguls and politicians. Often the show was a comedy burlesque, a broad satire of the plight of the earliest gold-seekers played out in a melodramatic frenzy. Other times, singers would take the stage performing sentimental songs that reduced the room full of men—from the gritty to the groomed—to sniffling into their handkerchiefs. Once she saw a beautiful little girl sing and dance into the hearts of the audience, and Kassandra wondered what songs Reverend Joseph and Mrs. Hartmann would teach her daughter.

By far her favorite evenings were those when a traveling troupe came to town, and she had the chance to see the works of Shakespeare—known to her only as those words studied in her schoolbooks—come to life on the stage.

During the day she delighted in exploring the city on her own. In no time at all it seemed unreal that she had ever found it frightening.

She especially loved poking through the more exotic shops of San Francisco's Chinese district. There she found many of the different plants and herbs that she had learned about under Imogene's tutelage. Besides the familiar chamomile and lavender, Kassandra learned—through arduous conversations consisting of shouted short phrases and emphatic gesturing—about new remedies the Chinese proprietors had brought from their native country. Many of these were known to ease the monthly trials of womanhood, and Kassandra brought them back to the skeptical Jewell, who couldn't imagine anything worthwhile coming from that bunch of pigtailed heathens.

But the other women eagerly embraced such exotic cures for their regular womanly discomforts. Under Kassandra's careful guidance, they made teas from red sage root that was meant to nourish their blood and encourage mental tranquillity. They made tinctures of the herb called *dong guai,* which seemed to put each of them on a more regular, predictable cycle. Even if Jewell never openly endorsed the Chinese invasion under her red roof, she did seem to enjoy running a productive, unruffled establishment, for which she openly credited "Sadie and her potions."

All of this would seem to solidify Kassandra's status and position with Jewell, but there was one condition Jewell would not tolerate, and as Kassandra entered her second spring in San Francisco, she knew she was in violation of Jewell's most emphatic edict.

She was pregnant again.

The idea of a new baby—the feel of it—filled Kassandra so she could hardly bring her mind to focus on anything else. Unlike before, where the earliest months were lost either to inno-

cence or ignorance, she was immediately aware of the changes in
her body. And, though she knew she had to keep the information to herself, the revelation seemed always to be just a breath
away. When she first walked downstairs every morning, her
stomach churning, she had to stop herself from announcing her
news to the still-sleepy women lounging on the sofas. She loved
knowing there was a baby under all the layers of silk as she
strolled through the city streets. *Be careful with me,* she wanted to
say to every gentleman who followed her upstairs from the parlor, *I am carrying a child.* With this baby she felt every bit of the
hope and promise she'd carried with Daniel, and a chance to
recapture what she'd abandoned with her daughter.

She hadn't prayed much since her arrival in San Francisco,
but she did so now—every day—thanking God for giving her
another chance to be a mother, asking Him to keep her and the
baby strong, hoping her prayers weren't trapped under the red
roof of Jewell's fancy house.

Pregnancy was, in Jewell's estimation, illness, weakness, and
betrayal all in one. She was militant in her insistence that her
girls take all measures necessary to prevent it, and had been
known to patrol her own carpeted hallways replenishing each
room's vinegar jar. Every new recruit received instruction in how
to insert the acidic suppositories that allowed a working girl to
keep working all year long.

Because of her obsession, it was a rare case who slunk away
from Jewell's parlor with empty pockets and a bulging belly—for
there was never a question of the girl's staying on to have the
child in her upstairs room.

"I put up enough with Millie and her brat daughter," she
would say whenever the subject came up. "I ain't one to turn
away a girl in need, but a screamin' kid is bad for business."

As much as Kassandra had worked her way into Jewell's

good graces, she still took great pains to find the perfect time to put her head on the chopping block. She wanted a time when they could speak alone, but those moments were rare. Jewell had ten girls working for her these days, and with only seven bedrooms in the house, there was always somebody about. If Jewell were to react with her usual bluster, Kassandra would have no chance to appeal to the woman's well-hidden sympathetic nature. Her best bet was to get the two of them away from the house for the afternoon. One day, wearing her new green walking dress, Kassandra asked Jewell to accompany her on a little shopping excursion and maybe a spot of lunch.

"Come on, Jewell," Kassandra said, "we can have a champagne lunch at the Parker House, and I'll get me a hat tall enough that all the men there will be able to follow me straight back here."

"I guess it has been a while since we had any new blood," Jewell said, though Kassandra knew the true selling point was the roast duck and oyster platter at the Parker House Hotel.

They made quite a vision, walking together. Kassandra, a full head and shoulders taller than Jewell, glided down the walkways while Jewell puffed beside her with visible effort. Several times Kassandra stopped, supposedly to admire some item in a shop window, and allowed Jewell to catch her breath before pressing on.

A number of men recognized them and tipped their hats as they walked by. A fair amount of women knew them, too, though their greetings weren't nearly as friendly.

"You know, when I got here in '49, I had the only house in town. The others were workin' outta tents. But I had me built a great big house, bright red roof, stocked it full of the best lookin' women I could find." They passed a trio of haughty, painted women as they walked through the hotel door. "Now you can't swing a pickax without hittin' some cheeky whore in this town."

"Well, there are certainly enough men to go around,"

Kassandra said, smiling at a hungry-looking miner, probably fresh from his claim, who held the door open for her and offered a charming smile through the layer of grime on his face.

"That ain't the point," Jewell said.

She ignored the maitre d' and headed for a prime table in the center of the room. She didn't pick up the conversation until they were settled in their seats and had caught the attention of at least a dozen other patrons.

"There's just no sense of adventure anymore. No fun."

"Everybody certainly seemed to be having fun last night."

"I'm talkin' about for me. I like the idea of makin' somethin' outta nothin'. Bein' somebody. Now these girls are just usin' me as some quick path to get rich."

"None of us are exactly rich, Jewell."

"Yeah? What did you have when I met you?" She summoned the waiter and brusquely ordered a bottle of white wine and a platter of oysters. "Now we got these girls comin'—they're nothin' but starvin' trash where they come from. Livin' a couple o' months in my house, gettin' sacks of gold for the same tricks that'd go for two bits back home."

"You certainly don't seem to complain when you are taking your share," Kassandra said, thinking of those settle-up sessions where Jewell sat with her tabletop scale, carefully calculating her percentage.

"I'm sentimental, Sadie girl. Not stupid." She poured a second drink and shot a pointed look at the string quartet in the corner that abruptly ceased the sprightly tune they were pursuing and opted for something softer. "I got all these girls thinkin' they're workin' independent. And I say fine, go on out into the street and see how long you last there. I just want a little loyalty. That's all."

This wasn't the turn of conversation that Kassandra wanted, and deep in the pit of her—just where that tiny life settled—she prepared herself to fight.

"Jewell," she said, just as the woman was downing her third glass of champagne, "I am pregnant."

"I know." She finished her drink, slurped down another oyster, and dabbed the corners of her mouth with the starched white linen napkin, leaving a trace of red lip rouge on the fabric.

"How could you know?" Kassandra asked, not sure if she believed Jewell at all.

"It's my job to know about my girls."

"I do not want to leave," Kassandra said, feeling irresponsible warmth at being one of Jewell's girls.

"No reason you got to. Bein' pregnant don't have to be permanent." She belched in the most ladylike way she was capable of and dabbed her mouth again. "It's early yet."

"No," Kassandra said, loud enough to call the attention of some of the other customers. Then, lowering her voice, "I have lost two children already, Jewell. I cannot lose another."

Jewell arched her thin brows at this revelation, but remained unmoved. "I'm not talkin' 'bout hackin' it out of you."

"But you have before."

"We've all done things before," Jewell said. "You wanna do an open confession of your sins?"

"Of course not."

"I'm just sayin' that you ain't the only one who knows about all those fancy herbs and whatnot. Get you some black cohosh—"

"No, Jewell."

"Well, then." Jewell bristled and picked up another oyster. She offered it up to Kassandra, who shook her head, her stomach lurching at the sight of the cold, gray, moist meat within the shell. "Looks like you're gonna have to find yourself a new place to live then, don't it?"

"Jewell, please—no, hear me out. I have never belonged anywhere. Never felt like I had a real home before this."

"You're kiddin' me?" Jewell said, making no attempt to stifle a laugh. "Well, sorry to bust your dreams, girl, but no matter how much you feel like *home*, what I got is a place of business. Pregnant women and screamin' kids don't exactly make for good business."

"This baby means the world to me."

"Well, that's just great to hear." Jewell made a toasting gesture with her newly refilled glass. "You willin' to pack up your stuff and make your life out on the street?"

"That's just what Mrs. Hartmann said," Kassandra muttered.

"Sounds like a woman after my own heart."

"I was not strong enough then. But now—"

"It seems you're waitin' for me to give you a blessin'."

"The first day I arrived here, you told me I needed a friend. You have become that friend for me."

"Well, I'm sorry for misleadin' you 'bout that," Jewell said. "Besides, there's one other side to this story we haven't talked about yet. Who's the daddy?"

"You know better than to ask that."

"Well, I know it can't be a certain science, but you got to be able to narrow it down to a few. You have your regulars, you know. Don't tell me you ain't even thought about this yet."

"What difference could that make?" Kassandra asked.

"As much difference as you want it to. It don't mean a thing if you decide it's some poor panner who just came in to dump his gold dust on the town. But if you get it in your mind it's that rich banker—"

"Jimmy?"

"Now, don't look like you just stepped in a pile of horse patties. He might be a bit pudgy—"

"And short, and old, and awful."

"And rich. An' smitten with you, if you wanna know the truth. You could waltz right up to him with any man's kid in your arms, and he'd take you in a heartbeat."

"You cannot be serious." This time it was Kassandra who

laughed, and the outburst once again drew the attention of their fellow diners.

"Mark me, girl. You just wait until you've got yourself a nice little bulge—just enough to round you out a bit, leavin' no room for questions—and then march down to that bank of his and announce it to anyone who's there to listen."

"You are terrible!"

"I'm smart. It'll work one of two ways. He'll either be so proud of himself he'll parade you around that bank like a farmer with a prize turkey. Or he'll be so shamed he'll grab you aside and propose just to shut you up."

"And how would I ever be able to convince him that the child is his?" Kassandra asked, as the plan started to take on an edge of feasibility.

"That's easy. Take one look at the kid when it's born. See if it looks like him. If it's fat, bald, and wrinkly, it's his."

"You know, Jewell, only a true friend would come up with something like this."

"This ain't the workin's of a friend, missy. It's the dealin's of a businesswoman, plain and simple. Now where's the waiter with that duck? I'm like to starve to death."

❦ 27 ❧

*A*lthough Jewell's idea may have had its origins in jest, it wasn't long before the idea of marrying Jimmy the banker took true form. Jewell steered any client other than he away from Kassandra, allowing her to focus her attentions and concoct her affections for the pudgy little bald man who showed his appreciation with lavish gifts and frequent visits.

"Just look at our Sadie," Jewell would say the minute Jimmy stepped into the parlor. "Doesn't she look lovely today?"

Jimmy would rub his pudgy little hands together, looking at Kassandra the way she imagined he looked at a nicely charred steak. "She sure does, Miss Gunn. She does indeed."

"You might say she's positively glowin'," Jewell would add, sending Kassandra a broad wink behind Jimmy's back and erupting into her trademark wheezing laughter when Kassandra narrowed her eyes in silent chastisement.

"Do not listen to her," Kassandra would add, taking Jimmy's arm in fawning possession. "I'm the same old horse-faced girl I ever was." Then, having settled up with Jewell, she made her way upstairs with Jimmy following close behind. After Jimmy's almost ritualistic visits, Kassandra would open her window and look out in the street just in time to see him leaving the house. She never called out to him or made any noise she could remember, but he'd turn anyway and see her leaning against the sash.

"Good night, my love!" he'd say, blowing her a broad kiss. "Until we meet again!"

Kassandra would smile in return, put her hand to her breast in a pantomime of a grand romantic flutter, then step away from her window and put out her light, wondering just how she could resign herself to joining her life with this man.

"It seems wrong," she said to Jewell late one night when all the other girls were either working or sleeping and the two women sat together on a large wooden swing on the front porch. Jewell's weight caused it to sag a bit on one side, so Kassandra sat with her back flush against the opposite end, one leg keeping her braced upright, the other guiding her bare foot against the smooth porch floor as she kept the swing moving in a slow, creaking motion. She didn't feel well—just a little stomach bug, some cramping—but enough to have begged the night off. Jewell, in a rare moment of understanding, agreed, and the two women had spent the better part of the evening sitting out on the swing, talking. And not talking. The summer night was chilly, and Kassandra wore Imogene's shawl wrapped around her shoulders over her nightgown.

"I do not like deceiving him."

Jewell laughed as she exhaled a puff of smoke from her cigarette. "You're a whore, honey. It's what you do."

"I hate that word," Kassandra said, shivering and pulling the shawl close about her.

"Don't matter if you hate it. Don't change what it is."

"I was thinking tonight that if I go through with it, it won't change anything. I don't think I could ever love him—or even like him any more than I do right now. I will just be sharing his bed. Every night. I just won't be getting paid for it."

"Oh, you'll be gettin' paid all right, missy," Jewell said, "an' a fine sight more'n what you're gettin' now. Think of it. A house. Carriage. Whatever that heart of yours desires. Plus a good daddy for your baby. I think women like me would be flat out of business if all these girls grew up with a good daddy."

"I grew up with a wonderful father." Kassandra looked up at the moon, a wide gray smear behind a haze of clouds.

"He know you're here?"

"I don't know." He was on the other side of the country, looking up at the same moon, wondering why she had left her newborn daughter in the arms of a relative stranger.

"I bet he don't," Jewell said. "If he's as good a daddy as you say, he wouldn't be able to live with himself knowin' you're here."

"He was not exactly a daddy."

"Then what exactly was he?"

"If I knew that, I don't think I would be here."

Jewell chuckled. "I think we can pretty much all say that."

"How did you get here?"

Jewell took another long drag on her cigarette, grimaced, picked a fleck of tobacco off her lip, and flicked it away before answering. "That's too big a question to answer in any one night."

"You know," Kassandra said after a few minutes of silence broken only by the creaking of the swing, "he might not want me."

"He wants you now 'most every night."

"There is a big difference between being a mistress and a wife."

"Mistress?" Jewell tossed the remnant of her cigarette out into the street. "Don't flatter yourself, missy."

"If he refuses me, will you still make me leave?"

"I ain't one for makin' promises. When're you plannin' to spring the good news on him?"

"I have not decided. Maybe to—"

The word was lost as Kassandra became distracted by a pain that seemed to be knotting her very core.

"Sadie? You all right?"

"I'm not sure."

Kassandra closed her eyes and held her breath, trying to

relax. Her ears began to ring, and she felt her entire body grow cold and clammy. She shivered against the breeze, pulled the shawl even tighter against her, and tried to find a more comfortable position.

That's when she felt it. Wet and sticky between her legs.

Please, God! No!

"Sadie! What's wrong, girl? You're white as a ghost."

"I—I—"

But she couldn't bring herself to say a thing. Surely God wouldn't take this child from her. Not when she had already lost so much. Given up so much. Not when she intended such a sacrifice of herself to provide for it. To surrender her life to a man she didn't love to see that it was cared for.

"Let's get you upstairs."

Kassandra lurched with the swing as Jewell stood up. She opened her eyes and saw Jewell looming over her, taking her arm and helping her stand. The pain increased, keeping her from being able to stand upright, making her face level with Jewell's— so close she could smell the stale tobacco and gin on the woman's breath.

"Oh, Sadie."

Kassandra looked down and saw three drops of blood fall between her bare feet. She felt her nightgown, wet and cold, slap against the back of her legs.

"Jewell?" Kassandra grasped the woman's hand. "What have I done? What have I done?"

They bypassed the parlor and went directly into the kitchen, taking the back stairs up to Jewell's room. The girls were rarely allowed in here—the gentlemen even less frequently. Compared to this chamber, the other rooms in the house, lush and lavish as they were, may as well have been convent cells. In here the carpet was thick, the walls were pink, the lampshades covered in lavender silk, the chairs upholstered in a red velvet that matched the voluminous drapes held back from the window by gilded tassels. On one wall was an enormous painting titled "Lovers' Embrace" featuring a nude man and woman under a fruit tree. The bed was low to the ground and wide.

"Can you stand there for just a second?" Jewell said.

Kassandra nodded and held to the post for support as Jewell opened a trunk at the foot of the bed and took out a thick, dark quilt. In one large gesture, she swiped the silk coverings off the bed and spread out the quilt. Then, with a tenderness and concern that spoke to just how grave the circumstances must be, Jewell took the shawl from around Kassandra's shoulders and helped her into bed.

"How're you feelin'?" Jewell asked, wiping Kassandra's brow with a soft cloth wrung in the silver washbowl.

The pain was duller now. "Maybe it will be all right."

Jewell continued to stroke her brow. "It ain't gonna be all right, girl. You know that."

"I know…"

Kassandra's eyes filled with tears that ran down her face. Jewell caught what she could with the cloth, but soon Kassandra's entire body was heaving with pain and sobs. Jewell set the cloth beside Kassandra's head and held her hand.

"What do you want me to do?"

"Make it stop," Kassandra said.

"I wish I could."

"That sounds like something a friend would say."

"Yes, it does."

Jewell gave Kassandra's hand a few friendly pats before releasing it. She walked over to the washstand, knelt down, and opened the cabinet beneath. After a little rummaging, she came out with a black leather bag. She groaned a bit getting back to her feet, then returned to the bed and set the bag down at the foot of it.

"What is in there?" Kassandra asked.

"Somethin' to help you."

Jewell took a small bottle full of a clear liquid, then walked over to her bureau to take a clean white handkerchief out of the top drawer. She placed the handkerchief over the bottle's open mouth and quickly tipped it, holding both the bottle and the handkerchief away from her face as she reapplied the cap and set the bottle on the bureau.

Kassandra watched all of this in wonder, but as Jewell came closer, the odor from the soaked handkerchief grew familiar, and she turned her head violently.

"No!"

"Let me help you through this, girl."

"Last time someone made me breathe that…they took my baby."

"This baby's gone. Now, I don't know why it's happenin', but it is. There's no need for you to suffer any more'n you have to."

Kassandra reached up and knocked the hand that held the handkerchief away. "Get it away from me. You have no right—"

Jewell dropped the handkerchief. Bitter fumes drifted up, burning Kassandra's nose and eyes.

"I want to keep this baby," she cried, clutching Jewell's hand.

"There's nothin' to keep," Jewell said, squeezing back.

"Because God is punishing me."

"Shucks to that. God's got lots more important things to do."

"He knows—" She closed her eyes, crying out against the pain, and turned to her side facing Jewell, still clutching her hand. "He knows my sins, Jewell. He is punishing me, making me pay—"

"Shh, shh now." Jewell stroked Kassandra's hair, then settled on the bed beside her and reached a hand around to rub her back. "Now, I ain't been in a church for quite some time, but I don't remember it workin' like that. God don't have to punish us for our sins, girl. We do enough of that ourselves."

Kassandra continued to sob—deep, loud cries that seemed to be pulled from her very soul. Her body, from the moment she stood on the porch, was one continuous twist of pain, and at the same time, she felt almost nothing. She contracted her muscles, wanting to hold on—to hold the child in, keep it just a while longer—but when the cramping pain subsided, she relaxed and fell limp against the mattress.

"Let me take a look," Jewell said.

She helped Kassandra roll to her back and positioned her legs, lifting Kassandra's gown over her knees.

"We got to be careful, or you're gonna bleed to death."

"I don't care."

"Well, I do. No sense losin' two lives here tonight."

Jewell reached over to the black leather bag and took out a long metal instrument. The handle appeared to be ivory; the lamplight flickered off the silver hook.

"What is that?" Kassandra whispered, drawing her body up close again.

"You ain't the only one that has sins to answer for."

"But you can't mean—"

"It's all we can do now."

"You don't think there's a chance…"

Jewell shook her head slowly. "The only question now is whether or not you're goin' to live through this. Why don't you let me put you under? Ease up the pain a little. You can wake up—or not. Either way it'll all be over."

"No," Kassandra said, gritting her teeth. "I deserve to feel this. To remember this."

Jewell sighed. "Suit yourself." She moved a pillow within Kassandra's reach. "But if you got to scream, scream into this. Don't need nobody thinkin' I'm killin' you in here."

❧ 28 ❧

S he didn't leave Jewell's bed for nearly a month. A raging
fever brought nearly daily visits from a doctor, who
more often than not took his fee from the woman in the
next room. In the early days, when Kassandra was aware of little
more than the occasional voice and an insatiable thirst, it was
Jewell who sat by her side, her pudgy hand on Kassandra's, her
cigarette smoke wafting through some ever-present darkness.

Later, when she began to sit up and was able to talk, there
was at least one girl from the house who came by and played a
round of cards or brought in the latest fashion magazine. And
even after she was feeling relatively fine, when she was able to
walk across the room unassisted, when she could wake up in the
morning and relieve herself without crying, she still crept back
to the comfort of this bed, refusing to open the curtains, keeping
the room dark and close.

"Get up outta there," Jewell would say, throwing back the
covers, yanking open the curtains, and shoving the window
open as far as she could reach. "There ain't nothin' you can do
for yourself lyin' in here all day."

"Tomorrow," Kassandra would say, burrowing under the
sheets, trying to lose herself in the thick feather ticking. "Tomorrow,
I promise."

Then somebody would come upstairs with tea and toast.
Kassandra wouldn't eat. Another would come with a small plate of
sandwiches and milk. Kassandra refused it. Finally, in the evening,
someone would bring up a tray with a cooled bowl of soup, which

26

*M*aintaining employment with Jewell Gunn was tricky at best. Any sign of weakness, illness, or disloyalty, and a woman could find herself kicked to the center of Chatham Square with nothing but whatever clothes she'd arrived in and enough money to buy a week in a wharf-side flophouse.

"You ain't exactly a guest in my home," she'd say whenever one of the girls declared she'd rather spend a quiet evening alone in her room rather than entertain the men downstairs.

"I'm not aimin' to be no matchmaker," she'd say whenever she caught one of her girls sneaking around the city, offering her services to a favored customer free of charge.

"Does this look like a hospital to you?" she'd ask whenever a lingering cough or unexplained rash overstayed its welcome.

New girls were arriving in the city every day, she warned them. They hopped off the Sacramento stage or hit land from the passenger steamers making more and more regular deposits in the San Francisco Bay.

"Now I'm not sayin' I'm ready to stock the place with a bunch of Frenchies," she'd say, rolling one of her cigarettes. "Just mind you don't think you can't be replaced."

Kassandra took her warning to heart. Never again would she allow the course of her life to be determined by her frailty of body or spirit. She would not cower in the corner, waiting for the scraps of acceptance to be tossed her way. Trying to recreate Ben's easy way with people, she made every man who came into Jewell's feel

Kassandra would slurp hungrily—to the last drop—before curling down into the darkness to try to get through another night.

Jimmy came one more time. He stood outside Kassandra's door, twirling a new summer boater hat in his hands, refusing to go away no matter how many times he was told that Kassandra just wasn't fit to see him. Finally, after listening to hours of muffled conversations on the other side of the door, Kassandra sat herself upright, gathered her hair it into a loose knot at the nape of her neck, and beckoned the man to come inside.

He was smaller than she remembered, less grotesquely fat. He seemed sad, humble, and terrified of what he was facing.

"Miss Sadie," he muttered, trying to find some comfortable place for his eyes to land. He glanced at the washstand, saw the chamber pot, zipped over to the bed, saw Kassandra, roved over to the wall, saw the nude painting, and finally stared at the ceiling. "Miss Sadie, I'm glad to see you looking so—"

She remained silent, feeling something between amusement at his ineptitude and annoyance at his intrusion.

"Well…fine. You're looking just fine."

"Thank you, Jimmy," she said, surprised at the kindness in her voice. "I am feeling much better."

He crumpled a little then, smiling shyly. The room remained cast in shadows, but knowing Jimmy, he was blushing clear across the top of his bald head. He dropped his eyes to look at her, and she motioned to the chair near the foot of the bed, inviting him to sit down.

"Jewell told me what you've been through," he said. "Do you think…was it really my child?"

Now it was she who looked away.

"Because I would've married you, you know. I would've been proud to have you as my wife."

"That is very sweet of you. You are a good man."

"I'd still take you, you know," he said, fidgeting with the hat in his lap. "That is, I mean, if you'd let me."

"No, Jimmy."

"I know I'm not the youngest one around, nor the most handsome—"

"Jimmy—"

"But I'd take good care of you, Sadie. Give you everything you ever wanted."

"There is nothing that I want."

There was nothing left to say. Jimmy stood, leaned over, and kissed Kassandra tenderly, fatherly, on the top of her head.

"We're gettin' outta here," Jewell said.

"Tomorrow," Kassandra said.

It had become their routine, but this day there was a new sense of urgency. Usually Jewell would simply rip the covers off, but today she took hold of the sheet beneath Kassandra and effectively rolled her onto the floor.

"Jewell!"

"Ah, would you smell 'em?" Jewell said, wadding up the fabric, sniffing, and turning away with an offended face. "How can you sour up good silk like that? Do you have any idea what that cost me?" She yanked the curtains open, threw open the window, and leaned out over the sill. "Hey! Pin-Pin! Me throw! You wash!"

While Kassandra was still on the floor, rubbing the sore rump she had landed on, Jewell took up the bundle of sheets and tossed them out the window.

"Have you gone mad?"

"I don't like the Chinks roamin' 'round my house." Jewell yanked the cases off the feather pillows and tossed them out as well. "Now, take this off," she said, grabbing at the sleeve of Kassandra's gown.

"No!" Kassandra clutched the fabric to her.

"It stinks, girl. You've been wearin' it a solid two weeks now. Take it off."

Kassandra lifted the gown over her head, exposing her naked body—thin and soft. Jewell was right; the gown *did* smell awful, as Kassandra concluded she must, too.

"Maybe I will go and get a bath later," she said, reaching for the silk dressing gown Jewell was holding out to her.

"Not maybe," Jewell said. "Go. Get yourself cleaned up. Drop that."

Kassandra walked over to the window and saw the little Chinese man below, dressed in brown pants and shirt, his long, thin pigtail falling down his back. Next to him was a large wicker basket overflowing with the bedding Jewell had tossed down. Seeing Kassandra, he lifted his hands high to catch whatever she might throw.

"Now, really, Jewell," she said over her shoulder, "haven't you ever heard of the dangers of airing your dirty laundry?"

"Since when have I had anythin' to hide?" She shoved Kassandra aside, took the gown from her, and tossed it out the window. "You go washee now," she yelled. "Me pay tomorrow."

Jewell was short of breath after the exertion, and she settled herself heavily on the corner of the bed. "I meant it," she said, wheezing a little. "'Bout gettin' out of here."

"I know. And you are right. It's time. I think maybe I will feel better if I get out a bit."

"I don't mean you," Jewell said. "I meant us. We've got to get out of here."

"Your house?"

"This town." Jewell came back over to the window and stood beside Kassandra. "You see that over there?" She pointed to a wooden platform being built. "You know what that is?"

"No."

"There's gonna be a big meetin' there on Saturday. Lots of speeches."

"So?"

"Lookin' for reform. Law and order. Close down the saloons and clean up the streets type of talk. Next thing that happens? All the men start shorin' up wives. Wives don't like women like us. So they tell their men to round us up. Put us in jail. Next thing you know, an honest workin' woman is spendin' half her life in the slammer, and half her money goes to payin' off the people to keep her out of it the other half."

"You are getting all of this from a platform?" Kassandra said.

"It ain't just the platform. They've got pamphlets, too. And givin' little talks to anyone who'll gather to listen."

Kassandra watched as Jewell made her way back to the bed, then went awkwardly to her knees to rummage for something underneath it. After much huffing and puffing, she finally produced a small leather-bound case, which she handed up to Kassandra.

"Set that on the table for me, would you? Now help me up."

Kassandra reached down and gave her arm to Jewell and braced herself to help the woman back to her feet. Jewell reached down and dusted off the front of her skirt, then pulled the little stool out from underneath her dressing table and draped herself over it. After searching for a few minutes through a little dish of hairpins, she found a small key that she fit into the tiny lock on the case's latch.

"You finally trust me enough to let me see where you keep the money?" Kassandra asked.

"Money, nothin'," Jewell said, leafing through the papers in the case. "I keep my money stored up where it's safe from the thievin' mongrels around this place."

"Then what is all this?" Kassandra moved closer to look over Jewell's shoulder.

"It's the deed to the house. Jimmy says he's got a buyer."

"A what?"

"I told you it was time to get outta here. What did you think I meant?"

"Well, not this. Where are we going to go?"

"*We?*" Jewell said, twisting her neck to look up at Kassandra. "You girls can fend for your own selves. Don't know what the new owner wants to do with the place."

"Who is the new owner?"

"Don't know. Don't care. It's gettin' me a fair price. What with the rest I've got, I'll be able to start up fresh right away."

Jewell set a few papers aside, then snapped the lid on the leather case, dropped it on the floor, and sent it skidding back under the bed with a perfect kick.

"Now I gotta find me somethin' respectable to wear down to the bank. Maybe that black number with the fancy red jet beads on the sleeves."

She was up again, flinging open the doors of the giant armoire and rummaging through the dresses.

Kassandra felt as though her head were flying downhill completely independent of her body, as images and ideas roared past in a barely acknowledged blur.

"So after—everything, you are just going to throw me out?"

"Girl, when did this get to be about you?" Jewell located the black beaded dress and tossed it on the stripped bed.

"But…it is just so sudden! I wake up and find out I am losing my home?"

"First off, it ain't so sudden. If you hadn't been so holed up in here feelin' sorry for yourself, you woulda known what was comin' round the bend."

"Feeling sorry for myself? I lost a child, Jewell."

"Yeah, that's just what every workin' whore needs, some brat to drag with her from place to place. Because *second*, this ain't your home."

"Where are you going to go?"

When Kassandra had walked on the beaches of the cape, she loved the feeling of sand being slowly washed away from underneath her feet. Now it felt like a massive wave surging up from behind, leaving her suspended above some cold, wet hole.

"Things are slowin' down around here, anyway," Jewell said. "Gold's been taken over by all these big operations. Used to be we'd get these great kids comin' in, spillin' gold dust out of their pockets. Just ain't fun."

"So where are you going?"

"Someplace new."

"Where?"

"Wyomin'."

"What?"

"It's what California was back in the beginnin'. Got silver and gold poppin' out all over the place. And best of all, there's nobody there."

"Why is that a good thing, exactly?"

By now Jewell had peeled off the simple cotton day dress she'd been wearing and dropped an impressive whalebone corset around her waist.

"Help tuck me in, will you?" She turned her back to Kassandra, who took hold of the laces and pulled with all her might. "No civilization. No laws. Tug it again."

Kassandra wrapped the ends of the laces around her hands and doubled her efforts.

"No civilization means no women," Jewell said, her words sounding as strained as the laces of the corset. "Get it again."

"Can you breathe?"

"Course I can breathe. No women clears the path for a good business-minded woman."

Kassandra tied the corset off and watched for several seconds to be sure Jewell could breathe. Satisfied, she obeyed the woman's silent request and picked the black dress off the bed and dropped it over her shoulders. Jewell turned around, and Kassandra began the task of fastening no fewer than twenty red bone buttons.

"Take me with you," she said, glad to be able to ask the question without having to look Jewell in the eye. It was bad enough feeling her shoulders stiffen at the request.

"I'm not takin' any of the girls with me, Sadie."

"Why not?"

"Just let me get myself set up, and I'll send word for you. If we all go out together, there's no real knowin' who's headin' the place up."

"I have no desire to act as madam."

"Besides, I like to set up a class operation. Build up some anticipation. Get me a nice place built up, then bring on the women."

"But what am I going to do here? Who is buying the house?" She tugged the fabric across the widest point of Jewell's back. "Where would I go?"

"Now stop that whinin'. You sound pathetic. You think you'd be able to just pack up everything and head out just like that?"

Kassandra chuckled. "That is all I have ever done."

"So tell me. Does that make me Naomi? Or Ruth?"

"What are you talking about?"

"You know, from the Bible? *Whither thou goest…*"

"Of course I know it, but I did not expect you—"

"You don't think I've ever been to a Sunday school?" Jewell asked, sounding genuinely annoyed.

She walked over to the full-length mirror next to her armoire and studied her reflection, running her hands down the bodice of the dress and turning to check herself at all angles.

"I'm a sinner, missy. Don't mean I'm a heathen. You wanna go? Fine. Get yourself cleaned up. If all goes good at the bank, we're leavin' in three days."

In simple trust like theirs who heard,
Beside the Syrian sea,
The gracious calling of the Lord,
Let us, like them, without a word,
Rise up and follow Thee.

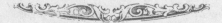

29

*J*ewell's plan of heading up the first, best, and biggest brothel in Wyoming territory met with a few setbacks along the way. She and Kassandra left San Francisco, a wagon train of two—one actual wagon laden with trunks full of gowns and lamps and various luxuries to deck out the new place, and one stagecoach with velvet-lined seats in which the two women spent hours and days and weeks jostling along the trails carved out by the rush to find California gold. They still came across the occasional hopeful prospector—sometimes with a family in tow—but it was obvious from the dereliction of some of the more popular stopping posts that the traffic had slowed considerably and that Kassandra and Jewell were going in the more sensible direction.

They'd gotten as far as the City of the Rocks in Utah Territory when the drivers they'd hired advised against continuing on with winter so fast approaching.

"Well, I ain't payin' you one dollar more than what we agreed on," Jewell told them, but she did lay out the money to rent the drivers a winter's bed in an abandoned fur trapper's cabin and a relatively comfortable room in the settlement's best hotel for herself and Kassandra.

They spent their days downstairs, in the hotel's dining area, playing cards with other emigrants shoring up for the winter. Kassandra was amazed at the ease with which Jewell was able to turn new acquaintances into old friends, always ready with a joke and advice for those living with unrealistic expectations for the California gold fields. Although she'd always expressed disdain for what she called "decent women," she talked to them with such an air of compassion and guidance that they turned a blind eye to the obviousness of Jewell's profession, though they did take pains to keep a great distance between Jewell and their husbands and children.

As soon as was deemed safe, Kassandra and Jewell rounded up their drivers—who had spent much of the winter hopelessly drunk—and continued their journey east. The information gathered from other travelers indicated that South Pass in the Wyoming Territory would be a likely place to set up housekeeping. But when they arrived at the settlement, nestled in the center of the mile-wide mountain pass, they found it to be a continuous bustle of activity, with a well-established, if understated, brothel. Jewell would have none of setting up a second house.

"Besides," she said after spending only a week scouting out the territory, "this place is too transient. Everybody's on their way to someplace else. All the money's in repeat business."

If Jewell had a mind for money, she also had an ear for opportunity, and she soon came to Kassandra with the news of a tiny pocket of silver about five miles up a narrow, winding pass.

"We'll be the first ones there," she said, tossing garments into trunks to be loaded by their ever more disgruntled drivers. "The way I hear it, the men ain't even there yet."

"Wouldn't it be better if there *were* men there?" Kassandra asked.

"This way, *we'll* be there waitin' for 'em." Jewell said. "Nobody spends money like a man after his first big strike. We'll be the only women, the only booze…"

And so Kassandra and Jewell spent a second winter together, but this time there was no luxury of a warm hotel with hot meals and entertaining conversation. Rather, when the first storm hit the nascent mining camp in early October, the two women were sentenced to seven months of solitude, virtually trapped in the tiny cabin meant to be a temporary shelter while Jewell oversaw the construction of her house. Not an inch over a hundred square feet, they could not cross the room without their skirts brushing against each other.

The first day of the new year brought the last day of civil conversation. Whenever the sky was clear and the temperature poked above zero, Kassandra would wrap herself in the bearskin coat she'd charmed out of a trail scout in South Pass and spend as many daylight hours as possible clambering through the snow.

That spring, Jewell laid out every last dollar she had to have her house constructed right in what she swore would be the center of the Silver Peak mining camp. Fewer than a dozen men had joined the original prospectors, and the yield from the ground was slow but promising. With lumber and labor that seemed to appear out of myth, Jewell's two-story, four-bedroom, downstairs parlor and kitchen, whitewashed, red-roofed house was built.

Then came the furnishings. Loaded wagons scrambled up the narrow pass full of lamps and linens, sofas and side tables. Case after case of every liquor imaginable and whiskey barrels strapped to lumbering mules. Jewell gave herself the largest of the four rooms, with a window overlooking the main road into the camp. Kassandra was across the hall and down a door, ever grateful for any distance between them after their winter of forced camaraderie. Enough lumber was left over to build one or possibly two little one-room cabins behind the main house.

"In case I get enough girls to expand," Jewell said, making frantic notes in the ledger she kept with her at all times.

"Expand?" Kassandra said.

They were puttering around the new parlor, laying lace doilies on the end tables and filling the lamps.

"Well, I ain't exactly goin' to make a fortune off of you, now am I?"

"I don't think you are going to make any money off of me,"

Kassandra said, running a dust rag over the intricately carved arm of the overstuffed sofa.

"I'd better make enough to pay back what it cost to drag you out here." Jewell had opened one of the straw-packed cases of gin and poured herself a third glass. "I wasn't plannin' on makin' you a business partner."

Word began to spread about the promise of Silver Peak, and soon the vision that Jewell had all those months before came to fruition. Men hungry for money coaxed it out of the earth, and by the time they'd amassed some semblance of personal fortune, they made their way to the red-roofed house. They may have poured in to satisfy thirst, but they showed little evidence of being driven by lust. Jewell attributed their lack of interest to the lack of choice, and she remained doggedly optimistic that once word spread of the trickling silver, the women would come along, too. Soon enough, things began to look up.

Her name was Mae, and had Kassandra not seen her take the stairs with one or another man in tow, she would never have believed this woman was a prostitute. Mae was plump and pretty with chestnut brown hair and dancing brown eyes. Though she was twenty—just four years younger than Kassandra—she seemed much more juvenile. Perhaps it was her high-pitched laugh, never far from being a giggle, that made her seem like such a young girl. Or the ever-present dimples in her soft, round cheeks. Or the habit she had of clapping her hands in quick, happy demonstrations whenever she was even slightly pleased. Whatever the reason, Kassandra felt an immediate envy of the woman who could demonstrate such blatant joy in such bleak circumstances.

For Mae did take joy in everything. When the sun was out and warm, she would run outside, turn her face to the sky, and say, "Is there anything more wonderful than the feeling of sunshine on your face?" When the first snow of the winter fell, she would run outside and catch snowflakes on her tongue, saying, "Isn't snow the most beautiful thing on earth?" When she walked through mud, she tried to make a tune with the little sucking noises her boots made; when the wind howled, she tried to match its pitch with her own.

When she wasn't extolling the beauty of creation, she was playing the role of pampering mother to Jewell and Kassandra. She mended their worn clothing, created scrumptious dishes from their meager supplies, kept every inch of the house neat and tidy. And for the few men who frequented Jewell's house, she offered such an enticing balance of exuberance and warmth that hers was the only company sought upstairs.

"I never seen nothin' like it in all my days," Jewell said one night after the last stammering man set down his empty glass, tipped his hat, and beat the trail back to his little place high up the mountain. "These men are actin' like we ain't got anything to offer 'em at all. Now, I understand them stayin' away from me— I'm too much woman for most men to handle, but you, Sadie? You ain't the prettiest thing I've ever seen, but with pickin's this slim, I can't see why they wouldn't want a go with you."

"No one can give a compliment quite like you, Jewell," Kassandra said.

She picked up a half-empty bottle of whiskey and went behind the mahogany bar built across the shortest length of the room. She took a short swig before putting the bottle on the shelf. The drink was surprisingly good—not the smooth quality available back in San Francisco, but miles above the swill she'd downed in the Mott Street Tavern.

"Be careful with that stuff," Jewell said. "I don't like my girls bein' drunks."

"I think I have moved beyond being one of your 'girls,'" Kassandra said.

"I'll let you know just what you are and what you aren't. Don't forget who paid for this place."

"I know very well who paid for it. You earned a good portion of it off my back, if you remember."

"So you think you oughta be entitled to a cut of what we make here?"

"There is nothing to cut," Kassandra said, deciding to pour herself a proper drink. "Ten percent of nothing is still nothing—not that you have ever limited yourself to ten percent."

"A woman don't get where I am by bein' nice."

"Well, right now it looks as if you and I are in the same place." Kassandra poured a drink for Jewell and slid it down the bar with a panache that old Stymie back in New York would have appreciated. "Plus, I have not seen you taking anything from Mae."

"Aw, Mae ain't brought in enough to make it worth my time. You'd think as cheap as she lets herself go, the guys would be linin' up at the door."

"Maybe they are just good men," Kassandra said. "There are a few of them out there, you know. They might have wives back home."

"I ain't never known a wife to stop a man before," Jewell said, downing her drink. "If this was California, those pockets would be empty before the next sunup."

"This is not California."

"Nope," Jewell said, sliding her glass back down the bar. "There'll never be another one like that."

30

*B*efore turning in for the night, Kassandra wrapped Imogene's tattered shawl around her shoulders for one last trip to the outhouse beyond the piles of lumber that would become Jewell's one-rooms when the weather turned warm.

She inhaled sharply at the first blast of air when she opened the door. It was the tail end of her third winter in Silver Peak— spring, really, being nearly April—and she still could not fathom the cold. It felt as if her very bones were exposed to the howling wind and spattering snow. True, she'd be warmer if she'd worn the bearskin, but that was too bulky to maneuver in the out-house, and she had learned that any temperature hovering near zero could be tolerated for a short time with a minimal wrap. Besides, she had the last few drinks still warm in her belly.

She bent her head low and kept it down as she scrunched through the snow across the yard to the outhouse. Once fin-ished, she followed the same path back to the kitchen door.

The snow was falling harder now, steady and with obvious intent. Kassandra paused at the door and looked back at the path of footprints. It wasn't perfectly straight and direct—in fact, there were all along it a few meandering steps—but it was clear and distinct. *The straight and narrow,* Kassandra thought, remember-ing back to Reverend Joseph's sermons. *Always stay on the straight and narrow path, and you will have righteousness. Well, look where this straight and narrow leads.*

She laughed out loud, all alone there in the yard behind

Jewell's house. There'd been nothing straight about her life. No plan, no direction. And narrow? Only insomuch as she was utterly alone.

She looked back and saw that, just in the time she'd hesitated at the door, the path to the outhouse was covered with a dusting of snow—like the sprinkled sugar on the molasses cookies Mae baked whenever they had a fresh load of supplies. In the morning the path would be obliterated. She looked out into the dense darkness of the woods surrounding the little camp clearing and thought—not for the first time—of what it would be like simply to walk into them and disappear. She would leave no trace; her steps would be lost by dawn.

And who would know? Reverend Joseph probably thought she was dead by now; Mrs. Hartmann would be quick to encourage such a thought.

And her daughter? Somewhere out there her little girl was five years old, learning to read, writing her name, and Kassandra had no idea what letters the child would use for that purpose.

She clutched her hands around her stomach and remembered those warm, stuffy mornings, curled under the massive pile of Jewell's silk bedding, hiding from the daylight. She could hear Jewell's voice chiding her for slacking in bed, urging her to get up, and meet her own promise of *Tomorrow*.

It seemed now that the woods beckoned her. The woman who'd stood alone on the ship's deck at sea, so sure that God could see her and would direct her path, now stood in a tiny clearing in the middle of a wintered forest, obscured by snow so thick that the stars were lost to her upturned eyes. She put one raw, cold hand on the kitchen door handle and looked back over her shoulder to the waiting woods.

"Tomorrow," she said.

That was when the woods answered back. It was long but not low—the sustained sound of pain. Not an animal; most of the creatures were still dormant. This was a human cry, but the falling snow made it difficult to determine from which direction the cry came.

"Hello?" Kassandra called to the darkness. "Who's out there?"

There was no other sound, and Kassandra began to wonder if the woods and the wind had concocted the cry. If so, the memory of it was so strong and clear that she couldn't simply go to bed. She went inside, grabbed the lantern hanging by the kitchen door, and lit it with a long match. Upstairs, she went first to Mae's room, then to Jewell's, shaking both women out of an early sleep to tell them there was something out in the woods, and she was going to investigate.

"Whadya want me to do about it?" Jewell asked, her words slurred from sleep and scotch.

"Just listen for me," Kassandra said. "And maybe watch out the window. Holler if you see anything."

"I'm fixin' to holler at you now," Jewell said, reburying her smeared face in her pillow.

Mae's only response was to hop out of bed, run downstairs, and put a kettle on lest anyone need tea later.

Kassandra had also instructed Mae to put a lit candle in at least one window in each wall of the house. She was now wearing the big bearskin coat, and her boots crunched twenty paces out from the house. Turning west, she began walking in what she hoped was a consistent circle around the house. If she found nothing when she got back to this point, she would take twenty more paces out and repeat the cycle. All the while, she swung the lantern out in front of her, calling, "Hello? Is anyone there? Do you need help?"

She was making her third widened lap when the light from the lamp revealed a dark form in the snow, covered with a light dusting of flakes. She set the lamp down and bent beside the figure. Long skirt, long, loose hair. It was a girl, not little but young. Kassandra bent over the face, pale in the lamplight but not blue.

Yet. She looked to see if any puffs of steam came from the girl's opened mouth and saw none. Ripping the glove off her hand, she gently patted the girl's face, but got no response.

"All right, little one," she said, scooping the girl into her arms. "Let's take you home."

Kassandra had lifted sacks of flour that weighed more than this girl did, but she couldn't carry both the girl and the lamp. Luckily, she could still see the dim light of the candles burning in Jewell's windows, so she left the lamp to be retrieved after the thaw and headed back toward the house.

Jewell met her at the door. "Now what is goin' on here? You've got Mae worked up into an absolute fit."

Kassandra pushed Jewell aside and carried the tiny form to the parlor sofa. The girl was pale—whiter than any living person Kassandra had ever seen—with the faintest tinge of blue around her lips. Whether or not that blue came from exposure to the cold was impossible to tell, however, because the little face was covered with one bruise fading into another. Her hair was wet, and spread a damp circle on the cushion underneath it. Her dress was wet, too, with rips on the front of the skirt. She'd been crawling.

Kassandra had seen girls like this before; they turned up regularly on the sidewalks and in the alleys between the tenements back in New York. She reached out and touched the girl's cold, cold face, letting her fingers linger just under the nose to feel for breath.

"Who do you suppose this is, Jewell?"

"Oh, my word. Tell me she ain't dead."

"Where could she have come from?"

"I thought I heard somethin'. Cryin' and such. Ah, Sadie, is she goin' to be all right?"

Kassandra took her eyes off the girl and looked at Jewell. In all the years she'd known this woman, she had never seen her so distressed. Even when Kassandra lost the baby, Jewell had been rather detached and practical. But now she stood actually wringing her pudgy hands. Had she not known better, Kassandra would have sworn that the woman was praying.

"She is alive, but she is very, very cold. We need to get her upstairs. You and Mae need to build up the kitchen fire and get the warming pans out of the beds. Heat up some water—not too hot, just warm. Bring it all to my room. I will take her upstairs and get her out of these wet things."

Kassandra scooped the girl up in her arms and took her to her own room, pleased to see bits of movement coming from the slight, sleeping form.

"You are going to be all right," Kassandra said, smoothing the bruised brow.

She laid the girl—child, almost—on the floor so as not to dampen the bedding. She first tugged off the wet boots, then the damp stockings. The child whimpered and made a feeble attempt to pull away, but Kassandra made soft, soothing sounds. She lifted the girl to a sitting position and began unbuttoning the bodice of her dress, only to find that many of the buttons had been torn away and the front of it merely wrapped one side over the other. It fell open at Kassandra's touch, as did the heavy woolen chemise under it. This girl was years away from needing a corset.

Kassandra peeled away the wet clothing and saw clearly what she had feared. Bruises, deep and black, shaped with such perfect symmetry Kassandra could imagine the strength of the hands that left them behind. Still holding the girl upright, she eased the fabric off one thin shoulder, then the other, revealing open, raw-red bite marks in the hollow of her neck.

The skirt was a high-quality wool—perhaps blue, but the wetness of the material and the darkness of the room made it impossible to tell for sure. It was fastened by a single button at its back, and Kassandra lifted the girl off the floor just enough to reach underneath her to unfasten it. She knew what she would see before moving the skirt even an inch, but the fore-knowledge could not prepare her for the sight. The girl wore a soft wool petticoat under the skirt. Kassandra found the tie that fastened it around the barely defined waist and pulled the skirt and petticoat off in one gentle motion.

Her legs were thin and, like the rest of her body, they were ghostly white and bruised. There were finger marks here, too, and deeper, darker marks accented by the dried blood on her inner thighs. Kassandra had seen wounds like this before, on her own flesh that morning in the alley.

"*Oh, mein kleines,*" she said, drawing this little one up in her arms. "Who has done this to you?"

But the girl said nothing, not even a moan, and as Kassandra felt the chill of this tiny body seeping through her clothes, she knew how imperative it was to get her warm. She wrapped the girl in her own flannel nightgown, laid her on her bed, and hollered downstairs for Jewell and Mae to hurry with the warming pans. In the meantime, she worried especially about the girl's hands—hard and waxy. She held them in her own, careful not to rub, and waited for the warm water.

"Here's the first one," Mae said, bringing the bed warmer into the room. Kassandra lifted the girl up again, holding her aloft as Mae ran the hot iron pan between the sheets.

"I'm not sure if it had time to get hot enough," she said.

"It will be fine," Kassandra said. "We can bring up the others later." She laid the girl back down on the mattress and tucked the sheets tight around her. "Go ask Jewell about that water. Get some towels and soak them in it, but not too hot, remember. Bring them up here to wrap her hands and feet."

"What do you think happened to her?" Mae asked, her voice wide with awe.

"We will ask her when she wakes up."

"And you think she'll be all right?"

"Go see to the water, Mae. Getting her warm is the first thing."

Mae paused just long enough to touch the girl's brow before nearly running out of the room.

The girl's hands were already showing signs of blistering healing just from being covered by the warm blankets. When Kassandra reached under the covers to check the rest of her body, however, she was worried to find it still so cold. She took off her own damp clothing and wrapped herself in her softest woolen robe. Then, she lifted the covers and crawled into bed with the girl, reaching an arm around and drawing her close, willing the warmth of her own body to reach into this other cold one.

"Get warm, little one," she whispered into the girl's ear, mere inches from her lips. "Get warm, but keep sleeping. Sleep as long and as deep as you want. Because nothing will be the same when you wake up."

31

The girl did wake up, though she didn't speak. Not for days, then weeks on end. She made no sound to tell them that the blisters on her hands were uncomfortable and oozing. They never knew when she was hungry; she simply ate when she came into contact with food. They never knew if she was in any pain; she simply allowed her body to be manipulated in the bed, then out, then walking, leaning heavily on Kassandra's arm. They never knew her name, but Jewell declared she would not go around calling her "girl" all the time.

"You're a tiny little thing," she said one morning after the girl had been led—without protest—to join them for breakfast in the kitchen. "I'm gonna call you Biddy."

"No, Jewell," Kassandra said. "This one isn't yours to name."

"Well, we got to call her somethin'."

"She is not one of your girls."

"It's all right." They almost didn't hear the voice; it was almost as small as the girl. "I like that name."

"There, you see?" Jewell spoke through a mouthful of porridge and reached across to tap Biddy's hand. "She likes it."

Mae dropped her spoon and clapped her hands.

Kassandra just smiled. "Well, then, that is who you shall be."

As far as Kassandra was concerned, every man in the vicinity was a suspect in Biddy's rape, and because of that, she had insisted that none of them be admitted to the house.

"Now, that is just ridiculous," Jewell had said. "I ain't never in my life seen a bunch of men so uninterested in sex. Mae can't hardly get one to go on up with her."

"Trust me, Jewell," Kassandra said. "I've known a lot of good men who were quite capable of terrible things."

"No, you trust me. I'm gonna find out who did this. And when I do, I'll see to it he ain't never gonna walk again."

With the onset of spring came the final thawing of the snow, and an onslaught of new men ready to try their luck at striking silver in the Wyoming mountains. More and more tiny shacks were being built up the side of the hill, and pack mules loaded with supplies became a regular occurrence.

These events brought the whole settlement together. Jewell set a plank across two whiskey barrels and opened up a bar in the yard. Having decided there were two things a man would pay for—and the other one was food—she bought up as much of the foodstuff as she could to assemble into meals to sell to the hungry miners before the next shipment arrived.

Biddy watched from the safety of an upstairs window, with Kassandra's arm firmly around her.

"Is that him?"

"They won't come back here."

"Just look."

"It's not them."

From the yard, Jewell caught Kassandra's eye. "Psst! Sadie! What about that one there?" She pointed none-too-subtly to a tall man at the edge of the yard. His hair hung long beneath his hat, and he seemed to keep his distance from the other miners.

"MacGregan? What about him?" Kassandra said, feeling silly trying to whisper from another story.

"Remember him? He was in prison when we was in South Pass. Killed a guy."

"So what?"

"So, maybe he's the one—"

"It isn't him," Biddy said quietly to Kassandra, who relayed the message to Jewell.

"Is she sure?"

Kassandra looked at Biddy who was nodding emphatically. "She is sure."

Jewell shrugged her shoulders and walked back to the crowed of men gathered around her newly purchased keg of beer.

"I've told you," Biddy said. "They won't come back."

"We just want you to be safe, little one."

Their surveillance complete, Kassandra and Biddy returned to the task at hand. The room they were in was to be Biddy's, who finally felt secure enough to venture away from sharing Kassandra's bed. A new mattress stuffed with clean straw had just been brought up and laid on the bed frame, and a pile of linens freshly hemmed by Mae lay folded on a straight-backed chair near the window.

"I'm not worried," Biddy said, taking the first sheet and spreading it over the ticking. "The Lord will keep me safe."

"How can you say that, knowing where you are?" Kassandra moved to the other side of the bed and tucked under the corners of the sheet.

Biddy smiled for the first time Kassandra could remember.

"Don't you realize, Sadie? He brought you to me."

"Me, you can count on. God? I am not so sure."

Kassandra picked up the second sheet and unfolded it with a snap. She looked over to see Biddy's eyes gone wide in her face, her expression grave.

"Oh, Sadie, we should never doubt that we can trust in God. If we doubt, what else do we have?"

"How old are you, Biddy?"

"Fourteen."

"I had faith like yours when I was fourteen, too." Kassandra busied herself spreading the second sheet on the bed, reaching across the mattress to smooth it on the opposite side. "I knew God as my Savior. Prayed to Him every night."

"What happened?"

"I *trusted* Him," Kassandra said, standing upright, barely able to keep the sneer out of her voice. "I trusted that He would watch out for me. That He would take care of me, no matter what. I left my home hoping He would show me that my decision was the right one, that He would *make* it the right thing to do."

Biddy smiled a little, then seemed embarrassed and turned to take the covering quilt from the chair and, keeping her back turned, slowly unfolded it.

"What?" Kassandra asked, defensive.

"I'm sorry," Biddy said, still fighting the smile that curved at the corners of her lips, "but that sounds a little silly."

"Silly?"

"You can't just make your own decisions and then hope that those were the ones God wanted you to make. The first time my Daddy decided he wanted to move out west, he practically started loading the wagon that same night. He said all those trails opening up had to be a sign that people were supposed to head out to Oregon. But Mother? She just told him, 'Everybody isn't us, Robert, and we're not budging an inch until we know what God wants *us* to do.'"

Usually, when Biddy spoke about her family, her voice became even softer and smaller. But this time there was a powerful wistfulness to her words. She didn't look away, keeping Kassandra's eyes locked with her own.

"I remember praying every night for months, until both of my parents were sure that this was what God wanted them to do."

"And where are they now?" Kassandra asked softly.

"They are with the Lord," Biddy said, her voice a bit less confident.

She handed two corners of the quilt to Kassandra, and together they spread it over the bed. Kassandra recognized it as one Mae had pieced together over the winter, some of the swatches cut from the tattered remains of the skirt she had worn on her voyage to San Francisco.

"And do you really believe that is what God would have wanted for your family?"

Biddy ran her hand over and over the quilt, tracing the pattern as if trying to choose her words carefully.

"I didn't ask for what…happened to me. None of it was by my own decision, or my own choice. None of it."

"I'm sorry, Biddy. I did not want to make you—"

"So that means," she said, holding up her hand to cut Kassandra off, "that means I must have been in His hands."

"Why would His hands drop you here?"

"That's just it," Biddy said, beaming again. "That's exactly what it's like. It's like waking up and wondering, 'How did I get here?' Do you ever feel that way?"

"Sometimes," Kassandra said. "But I know exactly how I got here. I can remember every single step."

"You see?" Biddy said. "I can't. I really don't remember… much."

"So how can you still trust Him?"

There was a single pillow stuffed with all the goose down collected last fall. Biddy picked it up, fluffed it, and handed it over to Kassandra to slide into its case.

"There's a verse of Scripture," she said. "I can't remember it exactly, but it talks about how God cares about even the most worthless sparrow—"

Kassandra could not contain her laughter then, and surprised herself at its bitterness.

"What's so funny?" Biddy asked.

"*Are not two sparrows sold for a farthing? And one of them shall not fall on the ground without your Father.*"

"You know it?"

"You seem shocked." She tossed the pillow onto the bed.

"I just…"

"Somebody very special taught me that verse. He used to call me his *kleiner Spatz*. Little Sparrow." Kassandra's entire body warmed with the memory.

"Your father?"

"Something like that."

"Then, see? God is my father, too." Her voice dropped to a whisper. "And yours."

"He used to be."

"He still is. My mother says we can never stop being God's children. No matter how far away we go, He always hears us."

Kassandra could not imagine how so much faith could reside in such a small person, and she cringed in a mixture of envy and shame. How far away had she gone? The city. The ocean. The mountains. And each time God's voice got dimmer and dimmer, until now, even when the woods were thick with silence, she could hear nothing at all.

"I do not think He would hear me." She sat on the bed to ensure its comfort and patted the mattress, inviting Biddy to sit next to her. "Not anymore."

"Of course He would," Biddy said, sitting down. "You're just not talking to Him."

❧ 32 ❧

Jewell spent most of the summer in a bad temper, much to Kassandra's amusement. When the days grew crisp, Kassandra prepared to buckle down for another long winter. Most of the miners packed up what belongings they had, along with whatever money they'd been able to keep, and headed for a warmer climate. Others crammed together in their little makeshift cabins to ride out the cold.

Jewell had ordered an ample amount of booze to be delivered in the final supply drop-off, and the downstairs parlor became a makeshift saloon. To Jewell's continuing consternation, however, the men who stayed behind refused to make her red-roofed house into any kind of a bustling brothel, preferring the company of each other as they gathered around makeshift tables to play cards.

"You could always go back to California," Kassandra would tell her whenever she was in the midst of one of her pouts.

"Life ain't about goin' backwards," she would reply. "That's why God made our toes stick out front."

This was just the kind of philosophy that delighted Mae to no end, and she would spend the rest of the day muttering Jewell's latest gem under her breath.

"Pretty soon they're gonna be thinkin' they're in Monte Carlo," Jewell said.

"Oh, what do you know of Monte Carlo?" Kassandra asked.

"I know plenty."

Even Biddy was wooed by the friendly atmosphere and had ventured down from the room she'd been given to talk and serve drinks to the miners. In truth, they seemed far more terrified of her than she did of them, and on odd occasions Kassandra even heard her laughing at some joke or another. She thought of herself when she was just seventeen serving up drinks to the men in Mott Street Tavern. *Oh, Biddy,* she thought, *faith can slip away so quickly. We have to get you out of here.*

But there wouldn't be any leaving now for any of them, not anytime soon. Leaving took money or a willingness to walk alone down the mountain, and right now Kassandra had neither. She'd given everything she had to Jewell to move them here and build this house, and she hadn't earned a dime since then. Part of her was at peace with that, knowing that her body was her own, living with an invisible, impenetrable hedge, completely undesirable to the few men who did come to Jewell's house seeking a woman's affection. Since leaving San Francisco, she hadn't once painted or powdered her face, and the blotches and wrinkles were exacerbated from months of exposure to the Wyoming winter's air.

No, where Jewell found aggravation, Kassandra found tranquillity. As Jewell bemoaned their poverty, Kassandra enjoyed a manner of prosperity. Never before—not since before leaving Reverend Joseph's house—had she felt such control over herself and her life. There had been a few moments there, during her conversation with Biddy, when she had felt a little sorry for herself. A little bit abandoned by God. A little lost. But if Biddy could take comfort in the fact that God dropped her here, she could take pride in having gotten here on her own. Here, nobody would hurt her. Here, she had nothing to give, so there was nothing to take. In Jewell she had someone who watched out for her, and in Biddy she had someone to watch over. She was, at last, a mother and a daughter.

It seemed they were doomed to repeat a winter identical to the previous one, just Jewell and Kassandra and Mae—with the welcome addition of Biddy—rattling around Jewell's house, getting poorer and poorer as they passed late nights drinking coffee and swapping stories.

Then one afternoon, just before dark, Kassandra heard an elated *whoop!* come from Jewell's room.

"What is it?" Kassandra clambered through the doorway to find the woman wearing her silk dressing gown and leaning out her window.

"Come look at this," Jewell said, beckoning Kassandra over her shoulder.

Kassandra stood and looked over Jewell's shoulder. Her window faced the little path that led into the Silver Peak camp and directly into Jewell's yard. In the distance, she saw a woman emerging up the path. She carried a small green case, wore no coat, and looked like she might collapse at any step.

"I wonder what she wants," Kassandra said.

"Her name's Gloria."

"You know her?"

"I knew her ma," Jewell said, not turning around. "Millie Marsh. Best whore that ever worked for me."

"The one that got sick? How can you be sure that is her daughter?"

"Looks just like her ma. Beautiful woman—one of the most beautiful you're ever gonna see. If that girl woulda stuck with me, we'd both be knee-deep in rich by now."

"Why didn't she?"

"*Hmph.* Some sense of loyalty to that mother of hers. Look," she turned around and gave Kassandra a light push away from the window, "you stay away from her."

"What?"

"I don't want you turnin' her off with all your gloom and doom. One look at that long face and she'll haul herself right out of here."

Kassandra let forth an incredulous laugh. "Am I to be banished to my room?"

"I'll bring her up here, let her get some rest. Just wait in the kitchen for now," Jewell said, giving her another little push. "She might want somethin' to eat."

It was Biddy who came into the kitchen a little while later, her eyes wide. "Oh, Sadie, she's lovely."

"Is she, now?" Kassandra replied, both amused and concerned at Biddy's sense of wonder.

"I'm to fetch her tea and toast."

"Fetch? Are we her servants?"

"Nothing like that. I think she's really quite hungry."

Hours later, Kassandra and Mae ate their own late supper. One of the men had managed to shoot a late migrating goose, and the two women were heartily enjoying it when Biddy came back in the kitchen, this time lugging Gloria's green case, her eyes downcast.

"What's the matter?" Mae asked, licking her fingers as she jumped to her feet to put a comforting arm around the girl.

"Jewell told me I was to go through her bag and look for money," she said quietly. "She wants me to be a thief."

"Well, don't do it," Mae said, drawing Biddy close.

"Tell her you looked and found nothing," Kassandra said.

"Then that would make me a liar," Biddy said.

"Then tell her you gave it to me." Kassandra reached over to take the bag out of Biddy's hand. "I have no problem lying to her."

Still later that night, after all the company had gone away, Kassandra picked up empty glasses and bottles and took them to the kitchen. The room was a mess from supper, but she was too tired to face it now. Her bed beckoned, and taking a single candle for light, she went back through the dark, abandoned parlor and headed up the stairs. There she saw Jewell, coming out of her own room, looking as downcast as Biddy had when sent to do a thief's errand.

"How is she?" Kassandra asked, opening her bedroom door and stepping inside, giving a silent invitation for Jewell to follow.

"Pregnant."

"Really?"

Kassandra attempted an air of nonchalance, though for some reason this news quickened her heart. She sat on the edge of her bed, set the candle on the table next to it, and bent to untie her boots.

"Why would she come here?"

"Your guess is as good as mine," Jewell said, depositing herself on the other end of the bed. "But I'll lay ten to one she wants me to get rid of it."

"She told you that?"

"She didn't even tell me she was pregnant."

"Then how do you know she is?"

"I stripped her down. Woman that good-lookin' is bound to have some cash on her."

"You should be ashamed."

"No, what I should be is rich. Anyway, when I got her down to nothin', I seen she wasn't but skin and bones, with that perfect little tummy bump."

"You won't do it, will you? You would not…hurt that baby."

"Well, I don't know," Jewell said, taking a huge, stretching yawn. "She ain't much value to me in that condition."

Kassandra caught Jewell's arm midstretch. "Don't do it," she said, more strongly than she had intended. "You have seen what can happen."

"You talkin' about you?" Jewell tugged her arm out of Kassandra's grasp. "Missy, I seen lots worse than you went through. Even had to do it once for Gloria's ma—at her request, of course. You know, it ain't every woman as keen as you to lug some brat around all her life."

"Do not talk to me of children," Kassandra said, fully angry now, but speaking in a sharp whisper so as not to disturb the others. "You have no right."

"This ain't about you."

"How far along do you think she is?"

"I'd guess four months."

"Think of how dangerous that is."

"Look, Sadie, she ain't even asked me for nothin' yet."

"But if she does, what will you say?"

Jewell let out a sigh, as if feigning disappointment. "I ain't decided."

"Jewell, she is young and beautiful." Kassandra's voice rose, and she found herself speaking through the threat of tears. "Don't take away all of her chances to have a beautiful child."

"She can always have more kids if she wants. Later."

"Like I can?" Kassandra asked, holding Jewell's gaze and using all her strength not to erupt into wailing. "Tell me, Jewell. Am I ever going to be able to have more children?"

"I don't know. I ain't God and I sure ain't no doctor."

"Then remember that tomorrow morning when you talk to this—Gloria."

"It ain't my call."

Kassandra reached down to take off her second boot. "Of course it is your call. When have you ever answered to anybody?"

❧ *33* ❧

I t didn't take long for Gloria to fit in with the rest of the house. Obviously no stranger to the brothel life, she seemed to appreciate the camaraderie of the other women, and Biddy seemed fascinated with her every move.

Despite several offers from Kassandra, Mae, and Biddy to share their room with her, Gloria insisted in staying in the little one-room cabin built behind the main house—the evidence of Jewell's long-abandoned dream of expansion.

"I like having a house to myself," she'd said upon each invitation. "I never have before." None of the women could argue with that.

To the delight of everybody—even Jewell, Kassandra suspected, though the woman would never admit to it—Gloria's pregnancy blossomed before their very eyes. When Gloria's clothes no longer fit, Mae generously shared hers, and Gloria good-naturedly wore the voluminous material draped over her belly, exposing her legs halfway up her shins.

"Jewell's changed," she told Kassandra one day when the two women had a moment to chat alone.

"How so?"

"She used to be the biggest madam in town," Gloria said. "San Francisco, during the rush."

"Do not remind her," Kassandra said. "She would never admit it, but I think she is just a little bit happy."

❀   ❀   ❀

The only place Gloria didn't seem to feel comfortable was in the parlor where the men were, and truth be told, they seemed to shy away from her, too. No one would dispute that she was the most beautiful woman in the house, with a perfect cascade of blond curls and eyes the color of the lakes that formed from the melting snow on the surrounding mountaintops. But their eyes were inevitably drawn to her protruding belly, and the sight of it made them squirm. So she spent a lot of time in Jewell's kitchen, tidying up, washing dishes, but leaving all the cooking to Mae.

In fact, Mae's cooking had added quite a few pounds not only to Gloria, but to Biddy as well. Kassandra took a maternal satisfaction in seeing the two grow healthier, sturdier with each meal, and she silently marveled that Jewell's own girth had not been affected.

"I got nowhere else to go," Jewell had said one time when Kassandra commented on the subject. "And I figure tall as you are, you're just startin' to fill up at your toes and work your way up."

They estimated that the baby would be born late in March, and Kassandra assured Gloria that she could be counted on to act as midwife when the time came. But nothing seemed to put the younger woman's mind at ease. During several late-night chats, sometimes in Jewell's kitchen and other times sitting together on Gloria's bed, Kassandra told her everything to expect. How awful the pain would be, but how soon it would be forgotten. How cumbersome her body would become, but how much she would miss carrying that child.

She had been reluctant to give all the details of her own children, afraid to squash any joy that Gloria would feel about the impending birth of her child. She told her that her first child had died, but not the grisly circumstances. She told her about her daughter, born healthy and strong and living with a loving family, in the hope that should Gloria not love this baby, she would seek such a home for it. And she told her about the horrible loss of miscarriage in the hope that Gloria would in some way see her full pregnancy as a blessing.

"How old are you?" Gloria asked, as if to calculate how one woman could have so much loss in one life.

"Twenty-five," Kassandra said after a moment's hesitation.

"Oh. You...you seem...older."

Kassandra smiled reassuringly. "I got started very young."

"Didn't we all?" Gloria said with a sigh.

Kassandra often caught glimpses of Gloria running her hands over her stomach, a slight smile on her face. She wished—not for the first time—that she had access to all the herbs and ingredients Imogene had taught her how to use all those years ago. Instead, she dispensed what advice she could, telling Gloria to sit with her feet elevated whenever possible, to try to walk a little every day, and to keep track of when and how often and how vigorously the baby moved. She took great satisfaction for herself with every bit of counsel, and felt a tiny bit of the sadness at the loss of her own children melt away with the hope of bringing this one safely into the world.

That January saw a warm spell, with several days in a row inching well above zero. Much of the snow melted, everybody's spirits lifted, and an unexpected supply train made a surprise visit up the narrow mountain pass. Word spread quickly, and soon Jewell's yard was teeming with men ready for anything fresh, food or drink. The women of Jewell's house made a party of it with sandwiches and cookies and a tap in the last keg of beer.

Kassandra saw Gloria watching the festivities from behind the curtained window of her little cabin, but soon urged her to come out and join the celebration. She had taken the iron to her own hair for the first time in months and created curls that spilled over her shoulders. And when Gloria asked for help with her own, Kassandra was more than happy to comply.

That was the day she learned that Gloria was not the only expectant mother in Silver Peak. The man she and Jewell had known as the killer from South Pass made a rare appearance with his wife. Mrs. MacGregan sought no friendship with the women of Jewell's house, and they sought none with her. In fact, Mrs. MacGregan rarely came down to the central part of the camp, and when she did, she clung to her husband's arm, looking as if she wished the ground would open up and suck her down.

It was Gloria who pointed out that the woman was pregnant. "You should talk to her," she said. "Offer to help."

"But of course," Kassandra said. "Then maybe we will drink some tea and tell each other secrets."

"Listen," Gloria said. "She's going to need a midwife."

It was the idea of being needed that drew Kassandra toward this sickly, sour-faced woman, so she took Gloria's arm, and together they crossed the yard to introduce themselves.

After several awkward exchanges, during which Mrs. MacGregan seemed determined to deny her condition, Kassandra finally blurted out, "I am a skilled midwife." She had never identified herself as such, and the sound of the words coming from her mouth made her feel the pride of it. True, it had been nearly ten years since she had helped deliver a baby, but the notes copied in the back pages of Clara's Bible were at that moment as clear to her as if she had them folded in her pocket.

"When your time comes, just send your husband down, and I'll be right up to help you."

"That's good to know," Mr. MacGregan said.

He held out his hand to shake hers. Kassandra stood for just a second, not knowing what to do. No man had ever offered her his hand before; her hand had always been taken, to be led up a flight of stairs to some upstairs room or held tight lest she try to squirm out of an embrace. Men had used their hands to stroke her shoulders, pinch her body, hold her down. But a handshake? This was a gesture of equality. This was an acknowledgment that she was a person worthy of respect.

Nervous, actually afraid that she might do something wrong, she reached her hand out. His grasp was firm and strong, and the touch of it gave Kassandra a sense of satisfaction she'd never imagined for herself.

Then it was gone.

"He will not be darkening the door of your house," Mrs. MacGregan was saying, having slapped her husband's hand away from Kassandra's grip.

Mr. MacGregan apologized profusely for his wife's behavior, but his wife showed no sign of contrition. Kassandra heard very little of the exchange, her head ringing with the shame of Mrs. MacGregan's judgment. How silly she'd been to think that she could ever rise above this pit she had dug for herself.

"Well then, good day to you," she said, her words sounding hollow, as if spoken from a well.

She turned and walked back to Jewell's house. Back to her place.

～ 34 ～

I t was a snowy night late in March when Gloria's baby arrived. The women had been enjoying a quiet evening in the kitchen when Kassandra noticed Gloria wince just a little, not calling for any attention, then leave her companions early to retire to her little cabin out back.

"I think the baby is coming," Kassandra told the others, watching through the kitchen window to see that Gloria made it safely across the yard.

"Really? Tonight?" Mae clapped her hands and broke into an impromptu jig.

"Shouldn't you go help her?" Biddy asked, straining to see out the window for herself.

"Not right now," Kassandra said, remembering her solitary midnight walk on the beach nearly five years ago. "Let her enjoy her last few moments alone with the child inside of her. The hard work will begin soon enough."

There were a few men visiting tonight, but Jewell kept them occupied with round after round of cribbage in the parlor. Mae mixed and baked a spice cake in the kitchen, and Kassandra stood watch at the window, looking for any kind of sign.

"Are you going to go check on her?" Biddy asked each time Kassandra looked out the window.

"She will know when to call me. I will be right there for her."

Then, a little over an hour after Gloria left the main house, Kassandra saw a light appear in her cabin's little window. The snow was falling thick by now, and the pinpoint of light was somewhat obscured, but Kassandra knew it was a summons. She repeated the instructions she'd given the girls earlier about boiling water, finding clean towels, and making regular visits out to the cabin to check on Gloria's progress. Then, wrapping Imogene's shawl around her shoulders, she headed out into the yard.

She paused in the clearing and held her head up to the sky. Snowflakes wafted down, landing on her nose and lips, bringing small stings of cold into her eyes. Nearly a year ago, on a night much like this, she'd stood in this very yard contemplating her disappearance into the woods, being lost forever, knowing nobody would know or care. Then she found Biddy. And Gloria. And Gloria's coming baby. People who needed her. A purpose.

"Father in heaven," she spoke to the sky, not sure if her inner voice would be heard, "help me to—"

"Saideeeeeee!"

When she turned, she saw Gloria collapsed in the doorway of her cabin.

The labor progressed well, considering it was Gloria's first pregnancy. Months of Mae's cooking had given her strength to endure the pain, and she was quick to comply with all of her instructions. Kassandra was surprised and comforted at how quickly she was able to recall all the aspects of midwifery—how to make Gloria feel more comfortable, how to measure the strength and endurance of the contractions.

The two women were able to chat in bits and pieces along the way, but when the hardest part of the delivery arrived, Kassandra remembered Imogene's advice to sing to the laboring mother. That same song she sang at the very first birth she attended had become her song of choice, and as the looming shadows of her deft movements dominated the tiny cabin lit by a single light, she reached inside of her to pull out those words again.

"Praise God, from whom all blessings flow—"

Before she could continue another line, her throat closed on her. When had she last praised God for anything? When had she ever?

She had a cool, wet cloth—lately delivered by Biddy—which she absentmindedly dabbed over Gloria's contorted brow. For the briefest of moments, her mind was torn away from the scene at hand, and try as she might to conjure up some sincere connection of praise to God for the miracle she was about to witness, she could not. She felt her heart constrict within her, puckering to some dried thing.

Still, though, the occasion demanded a song, so she reached to a part of her memory more worthy of the person she had become. A song from years spent hearing drunken sailors staggering through the streets of the New York slums. The ideal summer at a beachfront paradise. Months on a ship, at the mercy of the relentless sea and sun. A city built on the docks of the opposite ocean, where ships choked the harbor.

"Deserted by the waning moon,
When skies proclaimed night's cheerless noon,
On Tower Fort or tended ground,
The Sentry walks in his lowly round
The Sentry walks his lowly round…"

"Sadie?" Gloria's voice spoke through the song.

"Yes, honey."

"You're singing?"

"Yes."

"I've never heard you sing before."

"I don't do it very often."

"You should. It's beautiful. What is it?"

"It is just a song I remember growing up. Sailors sang it."

"Where did you grow up?"

"New York." This was the delirium of labor. How many hours had they spent talking about Kassandra's life?

"How did you get here?"

"Long story," Kassandra said, thinking of all the details she hadn't shared. She gladly complied when Gloria asked her to sing again.

"And should a footstep haply stray
Where caution marks the guarded way
Stranger quickly, tell a Friend
The Word good night all's well
All's well, all's well…"

The final, heroic push on Gloria's part ushered a healthy, squirming baby boy into the room. Into the world. Kassandra caught up the tiny wet thing in a clean, folded blanket, and had to will her arms not to collapse under the onslaught of grief that infused her. How would her life have been different if Imogene had taken into her arms a living, breathing baby boy? How many lives were lost at the moment of Daniel's silent birth? That, Kassandra believed, was the moment she herself died.

Now she felt alive again, more alive than she had in years. It was as if she'd taken a deep breath high up a mountain and felt her ears clear of the pressure. A part of her wanted to run with this baby boy into the woods, to keep him as her own, to get back what she'd lost at sixteen. But Gloria was asking questions about the baby, *her* baby, and Kassandra realized her blessing would come from handing the child over to his mother.

"He's here," she said to Gloria, and laid the squirming baby on his mother's breast.

She'd named the boy Danny, in memory of Kassandra's own lost child, but his arrival did little to change the day-to-day life of the women of Jewell's house.

Nearly a month after his birth, Kassandra sat in Jewell's parlor, pouring her third shot of whiskey into a glass and slamming it down before dealing another hand of cards. She rarely drank these days, if nothing else because each sip seemed to earn a disapproving glance from the ever-watchful Biddy. But tonight Biddy was out in Gloria's cabin watching the baby so Gloria could get some sleep, and the amber liquid warmed her against the cold, wet draft that invaded the room each time the door opened. Outside, sleet hammered at the widows, and just the thought of its stinging made her shudder. One after another, men came down from the mountain, braving the conditions for a little companionship and to escape their leaking roofs. After a while there was a coziness in the little parlor, accented by lots of laughter and swiftly emptying bottles.

"Where's Biddy tonight?" The question came from a young man named Ben Danglars. The men in camp called him Buck, in reference to both his native Virginia and the fringed coat he wore. A handsome boy, he had hair the color of wet sand, and it would stick straight up from his head whenever he pulled off his hat.

"She is with Gloria and the baby tonight," Kassandra told him, sending a sly smile that caused him to blush and turn away.

Kassandra was just judging the hand she'd dealt herself when the front door to the parlor burst open. Filling the doorway entirely was Mr. MacGregan. He was soaked through from his walk down the side of the mountain, and droplets of cold rain dangled from the brim of his hat as a puddle formed just at the edge of Jewell's imported Spanish rug.

"I need you," he said, directing his hooded gaze to Kassandra. "My wife. Somethin's wrong. With her. With the baby."

The whiskey she'd been drinking fogged Kassandra's mind just a bit, but not enough to block out the response she'd been given when she last offered to help MacGregan's wife.

"I don't think so," she said, reaching for the bottle and pouring another drink. "Your wife is a good woman. Good women have good babies all the time." She downed the drink with a shaking hand.

"I'm not askin' for my wife." He still hadn't stepped foot in the parlor, and the room was growing colder with each passing minute. "I'm not askin' for myself, either. But the baby. There's just so much blood."

Kassandra set her glass on the table. "Blood? How much blood?"

"I don't know," MacGregan said. "I don't know about these things. But somethin' just doesn't seem right."

"Let me get a few things," Kassandra said, rising from the table. "Wait outside. You are making a mess."

She hadn't expected the cabin to be so small, and given it size, she was surprised at its tidiness and functionality. It was, quite simply, a miniature house, with a plank for a kitchen, a plank for a table, two chairs, and a bed—all within a space so small it was impossible to move from one point to another without bumping into something or someone.

Mrs. MacGregan didn't look much better than she had that afternoon at the supply train, still pale and drawn…and still. Too still for a woman in labor. There were a few soft moans escaping, but nothing that would indicate the continuance of two healthy lives in that bed.

When Kassandra pulled back the covers and lifted the woman's gown, she saw the reason for the woman's weakness. Blood. Something had ruptured. She had seen this before with Imogene, and the chance of the mother surviving was almost nonexistent. Not without a miracle anyway. But the way MacGregan's lips moved in obvious prayer, maybe there was a miracle in store.

In the meantime, she knew of only one way to save one

life—that of the child—and she was glad to not have to be here alone. She directed MacGregan to get behind his wife and hold her somewhat upright as she turned to her supplies.

"You must have put the water on before you came to get me," she said, nodding toward the hissing kettle on the tiny stove.

"She told me to."

"Smart woman."

Kassandra opened her bag and rummaged through the contents instinct had directed her to put inside. She was glad to have had the bracing walk from Jewell's house as a chance to clear her head. She knew she would need both it and a steady hand as she took the knife out of the bag and held it over a bowl on the table-plank, pouring boiling water over its silver blade. Upon seeing it, the man began to pray aloud.

When she moved to Mrs. MacGregan's body and sat at the foot of the bed, she wished she had the chloroform Dr. Hilton had given her after the birth of her daughter. She could only hope that the delirium of the woman's existing pain would be enough to mask some of what was to come.

Mrs. MacGregan moaned. "Get that whore out of my house!" she said, accompanying her disapproval with a few thrashes and kicks.

Kassandra was grateful to have the woman awake, though she knew she would never have the strength to push the child out on her own. Upon closer inspection Kassandra saw that much of the baby's head was still hidden. The mother had lost so much blood already that her life was surely waning. If she died before the baby took its first breath, chances were it never would.

Kassandra instructed MacGregan to place his hands on his wife's stomach and, when he was told, help her push. At her command—over and over—both MacGregans seemed to yelp together, and Kassandra saw a bit of the baby's head emerge. But it wasn't enough.

She'd seen Imogene do what she was about to do, but

she'd never attempted it herself. Every time she watched the procedure, she had sworn to herself that she would never be capable. The mother and baby would just have to die.

Never before had anything felt as heavy as the knife she held in her hand. She ran the blade across the soft skin below her thumb to be certain of its sharpness, took a deep breath, and made a tiny cut in Mrs. MacGregan's flesh. Just enough to allow the safe passage of a beautiful, squalling baby.

"It's a little girl," Kassandra said. "Leave your wife for now and come help me with the baby."

She handed the newborn over to MacGregan and instructed him on how to wash and wrap her. Then she lifted the frail woman—too weak to protest—and stripped her of the bloody gown. She found the cleanest parts of it, tore them into strips, and soaked them in the distilled witch hazel she'd had delivered on the last supply drop. She used these strips to pack the wound and found another gown in a trunk in the corner for Mrs. MacGregan to wear. Then she picked up a brush and began to run it through Mrs. MacGregan's jet-black hair, chanting to herself, *Genesis, Exodus, Leviticus,* just as she had as a child, counting her own brushstrokes. She plaited the hair into one long braid and fastened it with a curling scrap.

This, without the acute pallor, was how Kassandra pictured Mrs. MacGregan looking the night this new daughter was conceived. Somewhat pretty, waiting for her groom to join her in her bed. Kassandra led him there now and gave instructions on how to bring the baby to her mother's breast to suckle.

Then she packed her things back in her bag and left the little family alone. If the woman lived until dawn, she might be that little girl's mother forever. If not, MacGregan would be back at her door, ready to fight for the life of his daughter…or to look for a place to dump her.

When Kassandra came out of the woods and walked into the

clearing, she found that the rain had stopped and everything was a cold, soggy mess. She thought back to Biddy's statement that God had saved her life by bringing her here. What an unlikely place for such a rescue.

❧ 35 ❧

*T*he death of Katherine MacGregan was barely noticed by the residents of the Silver Peak camp. There had been a brief service, of course, attended by a few of the miners and the women from Jewell's house. Gloria had stayed away, saying she wanted to keep her son out of the sharp, chill wind, but MacGregan stood at his wife's graveside, holding his newborn daughter in one arm, dropping a handful of earth into the open grave with the other. Afterwards they retired to Jewell's house for sandwiches and coffee—all but MacGregan.

"Looks like she was loved most by those that knew her least," Jewell said as the little party made its way down the path to the red-roofed house.

"Hush that," Kassandra said, nearly elbowing the woman off the path, but smiling a bit at the comment.

As the weather grew warmer, rumors persisted that the lode at Silver Peak was about tapped out, but that didn't stop a new influx of men who came to coax out what little might be left. With them came two new women to work in Jewell's house— Yolanda, a lovely, dark-eyed Mexican girl, and Donna, a dark-skinned quadroon from the brothels of New Orleans.

"That's what we're needin' around here," Jewell said, tickled at their arrival. "A little more color."

And the men couldn't have agreed more. The simple, quiet evenings at Jewell's house were soon a thing of the past. There was dancing to the music played on the piano that had recently made its precarious ascent up the pass. Whiskey and beer flowed more freely than ever, and more and more miners' boots tramped up the parlor stairs to the second floor. It was obvious in no time that Yolanda and Donna would each need a room of her own, and Kassandra graciously took Biddy back into hers, if for no other reason than to protect her from an inevitable fate, given her fascination with the music, dancing, and increasing attentions of Ben Danglars.

Mae moved in with Jewell under a fair amount of protest—surprisingly from Mae.

One person not caught up in this new burst of life was John William MacGregan. And Gloria. He'd given over the care of his daughter to her, and according to the men gathered at Jewell's, he'd been selling off a lot of his mining equipment, making trades for a wagon and a team of horses.

"He is going to leave that baby here," Kassandra hissed into Jewell's ear one night after hearing that MacGregan had just purchased a leather driving harness. "How can he do that?"

"When you find somethin' better, you walk away," Jewell said, pouring a drink. "You know all about that, don't you?"

But it turned out MacGregan wasn't leaving. Not alone, anyway. One afternoon, after watching fitfully from Jewell's kitchen window for MacGregan to leave Gloria's cabin after his daily visit to his daughter, Kassandra ran across the yard to ask Gloria what his plans were.

"We're leaving on Saturday," Gloria confessed after some attempt at being coy. Kassandra felt a pang of envy as she took in the news of Gloria's life to come. Two beautiful children. A strong, caring man.

"It's not forever," Gloria said, as if trying to comfort her friend.

Kassandra felt immediate shame for not rejoicing in this, another life saved.

"Nothing ever is."

❀   ❀   ❀

The rush to get everything ready for Gloria's departure was unlike anything Kassandra had ever seen. Mae immediately took to making Gloria some new clothes from the bolts of calico that had been delivered on the last supply.

"We don't want her going off to Oregon looking like some tart he picked up at a whorehouse," Mae had said, using her arm to measure out lengths of a serviceable brown sprigged print.

"Oh, no. We would not want that," Kassandra said, cutting her own bed quilt in half to make a soft lining for the babies' baskets. She knew the scraps from Gloria's new clothes would be made into a new quilt for her before the winter came.

Biddy was beside herself with happiness, and she found every available bit of cloth to cut and hem into diapers for the babies. One night, as she and Kassandra sat up in bed, she whispered in the dark, "You know, I wish they would take me with them. I could be an awful big help with the babies—I've taken care of lots of them. I wouldn't be any trouble at all."

"Have you asked her?" Kassandra couldn't imagine a more wonderful means of escape for this child, who seemed to daily become more enticed by the life Jewell had to offer.

"No," Biddy said. "I figure if it's God's will that I go, He'll lay it on Gloria's heart to ask me."

Kassandra smiled into the darkness. "I would not bet on that, *Liebling*. I'm not sure Gloria has a heart for God to lay anything on."

"Of course she does. Everybody has a heart for God. She just hasn't found it yet."

The night before Gloria was to leave, Kassandra, Mae, and Biddy squeezed themselves into Gloria's tiny cabin for one last evening of chat like they used to enjoy before the new women came to turn Jewell's house into Jewell's dream. Mae brought over the new clothes, and Gloria tried them on right in front of the other women, transforming herself into a pioneer before their very eyes.

"All you need now is a sunbonnet and a hunched back," Kassandra said, laughing through a mouthful of one of Mae's cookies.

"Let me just take up the hem on this one," Mae said, taking the brown skirt covered with scattered red flowers. "I don't want it to get dragged through the mud and ruined."

Gloria tried to stop her from leaving, but Kassandra knew Mae wouldn't want to be a part of the conversation should it turn maudlin. For as long as Kassandra knew her, Mae had found true comfort in serving others. Besides, she had a suspicion that some of the leftover fabric would soon become a sunbonnet for the trail.

Later in the evening, after an uninvited and rather unpleasant visit from Jewell, Kassandra and Gloria sat in the darkness of the little cabin. They talked a little about their pasts, but often they were silent, listening to the sounds of sleeping babies nestled in baskets around them.

"You're the only friend I've ever had, Sadie," Gloria said wistfully. "I'd almost want to stay just for that."

"Nonsense," Kassandra said. "You have a child. You have to do what is best for him."

"Do you miss your little girl?"

"Yes. I wish I could say every day, but I don't. Sometimes— and this is terrible—but I will think about her and realize it is the first I've thought about her in perhaps a week or more."

"I hope I'll be able to be that strong," Gloria said, "when it's time to leave Danny."

"Oh, Gloria, why would you even think about leaving him behind?"

"Because I don't know how to live that life." Gloria gestured to the pile of clothes strewn across the chair. "This is what I know. This is all I've ever known. It's what I was born for."

"Nobody is born to be a whore," Kassandra said. "It's something that happens when your choices are taken away. You have a choice now."

Early the next morning they all gathered to bid farewell, and a definite sadness was left in Jewell's house. Yolanda and Donna missed the send-off entirely, sleeping late into the afternoon, but the rest of the women puttered around the parlor and kitchen as if in constant search for something.

"I think I'm even gonna miss them babies," Jewell said, smoking a cigarette and staring out the kitchen window.

"You won't think that way tonight when you get to sleep through without hearing one of them crying," Mae said, punching down a lump of bread dough.

"I'll miss all of them," Biddy said. Her fondness for Gloria had grown akin to hero-worship, and only Kassandra knew how badly disappointed she was at having been left behind. "Mae, do you think tomorrow you could start working on the dress?"

"Of course I can!" Mae reached out and left a floury pinch on Biddy's cheek. "We'll start first thing."

Gloria had given Biddy her best dress—a beautiful green with black velvet trim—and Biddy's grateful reaction to it worried Kassandra even more that she was becoming enticed by the life that accompanied it.

The house was quiet that night. Jewell imposed a sense of mourning. Whether it was the loss of Gloria or the reminder of the life none of them would ever have, she didn't say. She declared she wasn't in the mood for music and fun tonight, and therefore nobody else was, either. Yolanda and Donna simply took the festivities up the mountain to the miner's cabins, accompanied by several bottles of whiskey.

"I'm movin' them two out back first thing in the mornin'," Jewell declared, watching them cross the yard, looking like two bright silk birds picking their way across a barren field. "I want my own bed back."

And so she did. That same evening, they all worked together lugging trunks full of dresses and arms full of various other luxuries out to the two cabins behind the main house. Jewell was all for dumping the mess in the middle of the cabin floor and letting them sort it out later, but Mae and Biddy insisted that they put the rooms together nicely, giving the girls something pleasant to come back to.

Kassandra noticed the curtains hanging in the window of Gloria's cabin and remembered a promise she had made to Gloria. "Don't let Jewell have them," she'd said. "Take them to your room and keep them for yourself." At the time such a promise seemed silly, but now, with the void left by her departure painfully raw, she took the yellow sprigged fabric down and clutched it to her.

Later that night, as Kassandra lay in bed, there was a knock at her door and Biddy stepped in, carrying a candle that took the room from darkness to a soft, promising glow.

"What are you doing here?" Kassandra asked, scooting over and patting the mattress beside her. "You have your own room now. Don't tell me you have grown afraid of the dark."

"Oh, no," Biddy said, setting the candle on the table by the bed and crawling under the covers. "I was just thinking, then I got a little sad."

"What were you thinking about?"

"Would you ever want to leave this place, Sadie?"

"Yes."

"Where would you go?"

"I have not given it that much thought," she said, though the seeds of her desire had been planted the night Gloria's Danny was born, and she'd thought of little else since. "I think I would like to go back to New York. To my daughter."

"That sounds wonderful," Biddy whispered. "I wish my mother could come back to me."

"I do not know if my daughter even knows that I am alive," Kassandra said. "Or what she thinks of me. But I need to find out."

"Do you want to get married?"

"No, no, *Liebling*," Kassandra said, laughing. "Not any time soon."

"Why did you become a prostitute?"

"Ha! That is a very good question. And one with a very long answer. Too long for this late hour."

"I'm not sleepy."

Kassandra sat up in bed, and Biddy did the same, tucking her thin legs underneath her, facing Kassandra in the candlelight.

"I was not much older than you, dear. And I felt I didn't have any choice."

"Do you…do you think I'll have a choice?"

Her eyes were huge in the dim light, her soft brown hair loose in waves around her narrow shoulders. Though hidden now beneath the loose nightgown, her body had developed quite womanly curves, and the men who came down from the mountains were beginning to notice. Some were new arrivals, ignorant of the taboo against touching Biddy; others had been around long enough to have forgotten. The easy antics of Yolanda and Donna had fueled their lust, and it was a common occurrence now to hear some whoops and whistles whenever Biddy entered or left a room.

"Of course you'll have a choice," Kassandra said, reaching out for Biddy's hands. "Don't get into this life, Biddy. You will never be able to leave it behind if you do."

"There's that boy, Ben Danglars—"

"My life was ruined by a boy named Ben. Stay away from him."

"He seems nice."

"They all do. But when they see you here, in a place like this…"

"Is that what happened to you? Were you a prostitute when you met Ben?"

"No, dear, I was just a young girl like you. A good Christian girl in a good Christian home, waiting for something exciting to happen to me."

"Isn't that what you are now?" Biddy asked with a coy smile.

"I guess so, minus the Christian home. And being young."

"You are younger than my mother was when we left."

"True, but I do not think I could ever go back. Not really. I cannot imagine facing…him."

"The man who raised you?"

"The man I disappointed. Again. He forgave me once for falling into this life. I don't know if he would forgive me again."

"I don't mean any disrespect," Biddy said, "but he doesn't have to forgive you. Only God does."

"But when I confessed to him last time, and we prayed together"—she clasped Biddy's hands tight—"it was just such…peace. I don't know if I could ever feel that way again."

"But Sadie, surely you know that feeling of peace came from God's forgiveness, not your reverend's."

"But how much can I ask him to forgive me? And my daughter? How can she ever…" Kassandra's voice trailed off at the thought of someday explaining to her daughter just where she had been for the first five years of her life. "The thought of it alone makes me never want to go home."

"Saint Peter once asked Jesus how many times a sin should be forgiven," Biddy said, her voice slow and patient, as if she were talking to a child. "Jesus said until seventy times seven. That's a lot of forgiveness we should have for each other. Imagine how much more than that our Father has for us."

Kassandra looked into Biddy's smiling eyes. "You, my child, have an old soul. How did you get to be so wise?"

"My mama taught me. And my papa. But it's nothing you don't already know, Sadie. God loves you. He sent His Son to die because He loves you so much. But you know that."

"Yes, I know all of that. I know what it means to have a Father in heaven. But I also know what it means to disappoint Him. You are such a fine young girl, Biddy. I'll bet you never disappointed your parents even once."

Biddy gave a small laugh and looked away. "I don't know about that. But my mama always let me know that I had my God to answer to—even besides them. And now that they're gone…well, I still have Him."

"And that brings you comfort?"

"That's what kept me alive," Biddy said, with a countenance far beyond her young years.

"But you see?" Kassandra looked beyond Biddy's face, unable to hold up under her gaze. "I do not feel like I have Him anymore. Or that He has me."

"There's another verse," Biddy said, thumping the palm of her hand against her head. "Oh, I wish I had my Bible. Jesus is talking, and He says something about His sheep hearing His voice—"

"*My sheep hear my voice,*" Kassandra began. She closed her eyes, and the words poured from her as naturally as any thought. "*And I know them, and they follow me: And I give unto them eternal life; and they shall never perish, neither shall any man pluck them out of my hand. My Father, which gave them me, is greater than all; and no man is able to pluck them out of my Father's hand.*"

She opened her eyes, and Biddy was smiling at her.

"You know that one, too?"

"Reverend Joseph would give me candy for reciting Scripture. It is how I learned to speak English."

"So, it's all in your head, but we are supposed to hide His Word in our hearts so that we do not sin."

"It is not that easy, child. After everything that God has done to me—"

"Stop that, Sadie!"

Biddy's reproach was so strong that anybody listening in on the conversation would have been hard-pressed to know which of the two was the adult.

"You said yourself that you could remember every step of your life that brought you here. You said that we always have choices. You and I are both here at the same place, at this same time. But *I* know that my God *brought* me here. I didn't have anything to do with it. And I don't know why He wants me here, but He does. And I'll stay until He finds a way for me to leave. But you—"

She jumped off of the bed and paced the room with her hands balled into fists punching the air.

"*You* got yourself here. You can get yourself out."

"You think it is that easy?" Kassandra said, feeling a bit ridiculous defending herself to this child. "How do you think women get here in the first place? They do not have any money. They do not have any means—"

"God will provide, Sadie. If you ask Him to. If you stop blaming Him for bringing you here and start asking Him to forgive you for getting here on your own. No father can deny his child—mine never could."

Biddy stood in the middle of the room, looking so small despite the power behind her words, and something in Kassandra broke. There was always a morning, after the night of the first snow, when she would walk out of the house and be nearly blinded by the whiteness. The air was so clean and clear she felt she would shatter it like glass if she spoke even a single word. And so she would add her own silence to the silence around her, becoming as still as the branches too laden with snow to move.

She felt that still now. As if her heart had stopped. As if every drop of blood rushing through her veins had paused, poised to be given the order to move on. One word out loud, and that clarity might disappear.

All of a sudden, she didn't care that she'd been brought down by a child. She wouldn't waste another breath defending her sin. Stripped of any shred of dignity, she fell to her knees, her face buried in the mattress, in the prayerful position she'd assumed every night as a child. She reached up a hand, silently imploring Biddy to pray with her.

"No," Biddy said, bending down to kiss Kassandra's hand before placing it gently on the mattress. "You need to come to God alone."

Kassandra didn't know how long she stayed on the floor by her bed, and she could never clearly articulate—even to herself—the words that went through her mind as she knelt there. There was just a sense of begging. For forgiveness. For cleanliness. To take the last ten years of her life and cast them away. To take her back to the day she left with Ben Connor. No, the day she kissed Ben Connor. No, the day she felt that the home God had given her and the earthly father He had provided for her were not enough. Better yet, to the joy she felt when she first prayed and knew she was a child of God, never wanting that joy ever to be overshadowed by anything again.

She stood up after a time and walked over to the window. It was open to the night air that cooled the stuffiness of the room in the summertime. She laid one hand on the sill, then the other, and knelt beside it, her elbows braced in prayer, her tear-stained face drying in the breeze. She looked up and could see every single star with such distinction; they appeared as close as flickering candles on the lawn. The wind blew through the trees, making a constant sound that she knew would carry her words clear up to heaven.

"Father God," she said, feeling her words carry up and up and up. "You know my sins. You know my heart. You trusted me with this body, and I sold it away. I have never turned to You. Never trusted You. You said, *My thoughts are not your thoughts, neither are your ways My ways,* and I have made every decision in my life based on my thoughts and my ways. Forgive me now, my Father. Draw me close to You again."

She paused and felt her spirit being lifted up with her words. There was a lightness to her that she hadn't felt since she was a child—even when she was a child of the streets, oblivious to the idea of sin and shame. She felt clean and whole and new. Restored.

"Thank You, Father," she said, unclasping her hands and opening them wide, holding them out the window as if to cleanse them in the beauty of His creation.

Now she could go home. Now she could face her daughter, face Reverend Joseph, face Mrs. Hartmann as a restored child of God. She would take her little girl's hand, and together they would seek God's direction, wherever that might lead.

Exhausted, she stood to her feet and closed Gloria's curtains across the open window. She got back into her bed, pulled the covers just up to her chin, and was about to drift off to sleep when an unusual noise got her attention. It was a *slap, slapping* sound, and it was coming from the window. Looking over, she saw that both of the curtains were fluttering in the breeze, but one side seemed weighted down, and it was the sound of its hem hitting the wall that had captured Kassandra's attention.

She got out of bed and once again knelt at the window. She took the curtain in hand and saw that the hem was at least two inches wider on this curtain than the other; the stitches were wide and loopy, made with a dark thread—it looked blue in the moonlight—against the pale yellow fabric. How had she not noticed that before? She was just about to go back to bed when she realized something wasn't quite right about the texture of the material. No, not the texture, but the weight of it. She pinched her fingers around the edge and realized there was something sewn in the hem.

She went to her bureau and got out the little pair of scissors from her mending kit. Back at the window, she knelt down, looped one stitch over the scissors' blade, and ripped. Then another, and another. As each thread fell away, Kassandra's mouth grew wider and wider.

Cash. This was the money Gloria spent months promising to give to Jewell, the money little Biddy had been sent to steal. And it had been given to her. Just to her, with the promise between friends to take a pair of curtains.

"*Oh, danke, mein Gott!*" Kassandra said, clutching the bills to her breast.

She got to her feet again and padded to Biddy's door. She knocked softly, then opened the door to the darkness of Biddy's room.

Amen.

～36～

The house hadn't changed much, besides seeming a bit smaller than she remembered. The trim around the windows needed painting, and the steps could use washing, but the iron picket fence still stood out front, and the gate still creaked when she grasped the handle and opened it.

She stood at the door for what seemed like an eternity.

Her dress was a deep blue wool with a high neck and tight-fitting sleeves. The hand poised to knock was encased in a tan kid leather glove, and her hat was woven straw with a ribbon tied just under her left ear and a long feather dyed to match drifting down her back.

Part of her was ready to walk away, but she paused, bowed her head, giving her hand over to God.

And knocked.

She heard a series of quick little footsteps on the other side of the door and saw nothing but the entryway behind it when it swung open. Then she looked down, and the hand that she had used to knock now grasped the door's frame.

The child was beautiful. Looking into her eyes, gray and spaced a bit wide above her nose, was like looking into Kassandra's own. Her hair spilled in perfectly curled ringlets that sprang naturally from her head. She had a smattering of her father's freckles, too, just across the bridge of her nose.

"Yes?" the child said, catching the tip of her tongue in the gap where her two front teeth should have been, making the word sound like *Yeth*.

"I...I..." In all the travels she'd taken to get back to this place, she'd never once taken the time to think about what she would say when she actually got here.

"Leyna!" The familiar, authoritative voice boomed from the back of the house. "Haven't I told you not to open that door?"

"It's a lady," the child said, using the doorknob to support her slight weight.

"I don't care if it's—" Jenny took one step into the entryway and stopped with her jaw unhinged. "Oh, my Lord..."

"You don't care if it's your *Lord*?" The child laughed, tickled at her joke.

Kassandra laughed too, if at nothing but the child's delight.

"Now what would the reverend say if he heard such blasphemin' in his house? Get yourself back in the kitchen. I made some scones."

"Yeah!" the girl said, and without another glance at Kassandra, clattered back to the kitchen.

"Well, well," Jenny said, leaning against the open door. "I was always wonderin' when you would show up. Come on in."

"For scones?"

"But not in the kitchen. You sit yourself in the front parlor. I'll bring in a tray."

Kassandra had never been a guest before—anywhere. She sat now in Reverend Joseph's front parlor, not sure how to conduct herself. She tugged her gloves off her hands and took off her bonnet, laying both on the sofa beside her.

"The reverend's not home just now," Jenny said, entering with a tray laid with tea, scones, and little dishes of jam. "But he is sure to bust somethin' when he sees you."

Kassandra didn't want to pass the afternoon in idle chitchat. She wanted to run into the kitchen, take the child Leyna into her arms, and run away.

"And how is Mrs. Hartmann?" she asked, pasting on her best polite smile.

Jenny set the tray down on the table. "She passed," she said, standing upright again.

The news wiped the smile off Kassandra's face, leaving her with just enough breath to stammer, "What?" before pointing to a chair on the other side of the tea table and saying, "Please, sit down and tell me everything."

Jenny checked over her shoulder before smoothing her skirt and sitting down to pour Kassandra a cup of tea.

"Not much to tell," Jenny said. "'Bout two years ago, she took sick. It got into her lungs, she took to her bed, and never got up again."

"Reverend Joseph must have been heartsick."

"Yeah, he took it hard. She wasn't the easiest person to love, but he did somehow. Course Mrs. Hartmann always did have it in her head that he had strong feelin's for you. He was fit to be tied when she came back alone with that baby."

"And the little…Leyna?" Kassandra asked.

"Well, she was so young. She don't have much of a memory of her ma—of Mrs. Hartmann, that is."

"It is all right, Jenny. I know my daughter knew Mrs. Hartmann as her mother, but tell me—was she a good mother?"

"Mrs. Hartmann? Oh, she was lovely with her. Always had her dolled up in the prettiest little dresses, all kinds of ribbons in her hair. She'd sit and play tea party with that child for hours at a time, singin' silly songs and carryin' on."

"So Leyna was…is happy?"

"Oh, yes miss. The reverend, he just took up where the missus left off, and that child don't know what sadness is in any way."

Kassandra looked around the room where a few scattered toys bore witness that a child lived here now, and she wondered just how she would ever fit in with such a family. She was, in fact, sure she wouldn't—just as Mrs. Hartmann had predicted the day Leyna was born. She put her cup back on the tray and began to pull her gloves back over her fingers.

"Well, then, Jenny, I will not keep you any longer. I just wanted to see—"

"Ah, don't go yet, Miss Kassandra. The reverend will have a fit knowin' he missed you."

"Then do not tell him," Kassandra said, feeling the collar of her dress constrict her neck.

Jenny chuckled. "That little one seen you, and she'll describe you to the last detail. He'll know exactly who was here visitin'."

Just then, Leyna came bounding into the room, red curls flying, and ran right to Jenny's side, laying her head on the woman's shoulder.

"Miss Leyna," Jenny said with exaggerated politeness, "how would you like to take our visitor up to show her your room?"

Leyna turned to look at Kassandra with just a hint of suspicion. "Would you want to see it?"

"Very much." Kassandra nearly choked on the words, but soon composed herself.

She followed Leyna up the stairs and to the very room that had been hers so many years ago. The door was open, and white lace curtains fluttered in a late autumn afternoon breeze. The coverlet on the bed was lace, too, and the bed skirt a deep pink velvet. On the walls were a series of small paintings depicting all kinds of woodland creatures—rabbits, skunks, raccoons—wearing waistcoats and top hats.

"My mother painted them," Leyna said proudly.

"They are quite beautiful," Kassandra said, wondering what she could ever have created for this little girl. "Do you like to paint, too?"

Leyna nodded vigorously. "My father says I have a gift."

"Your father is a very wise man. You should always listen to him."

"Do you know my father?"

This time Kassandra nodded, afraid to speak lest she burst into tears.

"Well," Leyna continued her tour, "this is my bed. And that is my chair. And this is my table where I have tea parties. That is my window. This is my carpet. And that is my bureau."

Kassandra spun slowly, taking each element in and emitting hums of admiration with each revelation. But when she came to the bureau, there was no patronization to her gasp.

"Oh, Leyna, look what you have!"

Its porcelain feet clung to a branch, legs poised and wings spread out as if on the edge of flight. There was a tiny chip on the tip of its beak where it had flown against a wall so many years ago, but other than that, the piece was perfectly intact.

"That is not a toy, so be very careful," Leyna said. "My father gave that to me. He said it used to belong to a very special lady. And that she had gotten lost in a storm and couldn't find her way back right away, but that she would come back someday for the gift she left behind."

"And this is the gift?" She could barely speak.

"Mm-hmm. Are you the lady?"

"I…I think I might be."

"Oh." The child's face dropped in profound sadness. "Are you going to take this away with you?"

"Well, I don't know, Leyna." Kassandra turned the figurine over and over in her hands. "Would you miss it very much if I did?"

Leyna nodded gravely. "Yes."

"Then you must keep it," Kassandra said, setting the bird back in its place of honor on the bureau. "We must learn always to hold on to those things that are precious."

There was a sound of a bell downstairs, the one Kassandra remembered being attached to the front door.

"Father's home!" Leyna shouted, and tore out of the room.

"Father! Father!" she shouted all the way down the hall and stairs. "The lady's here! The lady for the bird!"

Stunned and a little embarrassed, Kassandra took a few seconds to compose herself before walking out of the room.

He stood at the foot of the stairs, unchanged. Although it had been just a few years since she had last been here, she fully expected to see an old man. Perhaps she'd always seen him as an old man. But here he was, as tall as ever, his blond hair still hanging straight, though maybe slightly more receded. He was still bone thin, but strong enough to hold Kassandra's daughter aloft over his head, letting her red curls fall down to tickle his face, before taking her in a big hug and setting her down at his feet.

"Well, well," he said, still not turning to acknowledge Kassandra as she eased down the stairs. "You say the bird lady is here?"

"Yes, but she says she isn't going to take the bird away. She says it can stay right here."

"Is that right?" Reverend Joseph stood up, turned around, and looked straight into Kassandra's eyes. "Well, well," he repeated, giving her his smile with the same gap between his front teeth that she always found endearing. "What have I done to deserve such a present?"

In an instant, Kassandra took the final step and found herself locked in Joseph's embrace. His arms were stronger than she ever imagined, and she felt his lips in her hair, kissing the top of her head gently.

"You've come home to stay?" he said, stepping back and looking deep into her soul with his soft brown eyes.

"If you will have me."

He embraced her again, while little Leyna danced in circles.

Reader's Guide

1. Throughout much of the book a little bird figurine acts as a symbol of Kassandra herself. Do you have a little trinket that represents who you are?

2. Of all the reasons Ben gives to convince Kassandra to run away with him, which do you feel was his most compelling?

3. Would you say that Kassandra is a strong woman? Why or why not?

4. Consider what we know of Biddy by the end of the book. What future can you predict for her?

5. Consider the relationship between Kassandra and Jewell. Would you classify Jewell as a mother? A sister? A friend?

6. What is your opinion of Mrs. Hartmann? What do you think was the motivation for her actions and decisions?

7. Kassandra first appears in the novel *Ten Thousand Charms* (Book 1 in the Crossroads of Grace Series). What new insights into her character do you gain from reading this book? Is your perception of her changed?

8. How would you classify Ben Connor? Is he purely a villian? Tragic figure? Hero? Why?

9. The lyrics of the hymn, "Dear Lord and Father of Mankind" (appearing at the front of and throughout the book), echo

Kassandra's pleading, conviction, and repentance at several stages of the story. Is there a hymn that brings you particular comfort? One that brings you to a sense of conviction?

10. Revisit the first chapter of the book. In what way is it a snapshot of all that is to come?

11. Lamentations 3:22 (NIV) says, "Because of the LORD's great love we are not consumed, for his compassions never fail. They are new every morning; great is your faithfulness." What message of hope is in this verse for Kassandra? For you?

Ten Thousand Charms
Crossroads of Grace Series, Book One
ISBN 1-59052-575-2

Wyoming Territories, 1860.

Gloria is in trouble. A mining camp is a merciless place when you're young, pregnant…and a prostitute. No matter. Life will not defeat her.

John William McGregan is in despair. His beloved wife died in childbirth. And while John is a resourceful man, raising an infant daughter on his own seems impossible.

Thrown together by a seemingly cruel fate, Gloria and John William make a pact: She will nurse his daughter; he will raise her son. Neither asks for marriage. They are joined by necessity, nothing more.

But after a move to the new Oregon territory, facing John William's faith day after day, and receiving an older woman's motherly mentoring, Gloria longs for something more. For the love she's been denied all her life. If only that life hadn't made her unfit, not only for John William…but for God.

Then tragedy strikes—making even the resolute John William question his faith. Terrified, Gloria turns to the One she has never been able to trust. But can even God save what now means more to Gloria than life itself: her newfound family?

*Here's an excerpt from book 3
in the Crossroads of Grace series*

COMING SPRING 2008!

I wasn't asleep—wasn't even pretending to be—when my cousin Phoebe slipped into my room. Her white nightgown fought through the darkness until her body settled on the edge of my mattress, creating such an imbalance that I rolled toward her, giggling as our bodies collided.

"Ssh!" Phoebe hissed into the shadows. "Do you want to wake the whole house?"

"Sorry," I whispered.

"Do you have everything?"

I nodded. She gripped my hand with her soft, pudgy one and led me across my own bedroom floor. I held my other hand out, gingerly searching out the familiar obstacles, and stopped when my fingers brushed the corner of my bureau.

"Wait." I slipped my hand out of her grip and walked my fingers along the grain of the wood and brass pulls of the top drawer. It opened smoothly, silently—trademark of a quality piece of furniture, Mother said—and I had to stretch up to my tiptoes to feel inside.

Normally I would be sifting through a collection of rolled stockings, cotton chemises, and ruffled pantalets, but all of those things were packed away, wrapped protectively around porcelain figurines. Now the cavernous top drawer was empty, and after just a few searching pats my fingers closed around the stump of a white tallow candle and the gilded handle of the mirror I received as part of a matching set for my twelfth birthday.

"Very well," Phoebe said, squaring herself in front of Ida. "But remember, you must follow the instructions exactly."

Ida nodded.

"First, light your candle." Ida touched the black wick of her tallow stub to the flame. "You must stand on the top step, with your back to the cellar, and say, 'I descend into the darkness to see the face of my true love.'"

We all shivered at the word *darkness*.

"Then," Phoebe continued, "you walk down the steps, backwards, to symbolize that you are able to trust yourself. You mustn't try to steady your steps by clinging to the wall, or else you will never fall in love. Hold the candle and mirror in front of you. Do not look down, or your husband will find an early grave. Do not look into the flame, or your true love's eyes will burn for another. You must look only into your own eyes, the reflection you see by the light of the candle. In this way, you are looking into your very soul."

By the time she finished speaking, her voice was a mere whisper, and we all might have stood there in our little semicircle until dawn if Augustine, the littlest one of all, hadn't piped up to ask, "Then what?"

"Then," Phoebe continued, her voice even deeper, "when you know you are on the cellar floor, without taking your eyes off your reflection, blow the candle out!"

We gasped.

"In that split second, before everything goes completely dark, you will see the face of your true love reflected in the glass."

All of us, Phoebe included, burst into nervous giggles. When we had sufficiently hushed ourselves, Phoebe asked Ida if she was ready to take her journey down the steps.

"Yes," Ida whispered. She held her lit candle in front of her and walked toward the cellar door. It was closed but not locked, and there was an unspoken understanding that I was the one who should pull it open. Our candles illuminated only the top

"Let's go."

When we came to the top of the stairs, I transferred the stub of candle to the hand that was holding the mirror and used the other to grip the banister. I'd been running up and down these stairs at least twenty times a day for most of my life, but never in the dark. I gripped the varnished wood—slick enough to slide on if Mama wasn't around—and used my toes to search out the edge of each step before moving down. Phoebe was behind me, breathing impatiently down my neck, occasionally tapping her knees into my spine to hurry me along.

Once safely on the ground floor, she brushed past me and took the lead, her white gown iridescent in the night shadows of my family home. It never occurred to me at the time to wonder why I was following her, why she took the lead in navigating through our front parlor, our morning room, our receiving hall. I suppose her frequent visits—sometimes lasting for weeks on end—made her feel less like a guest than did my other cousins who were all gathered in what used to be our formal dining room. Where twelve perfectly carved and upholstered high-backed chairs once stood, a litter of bedrolls and blankets covered the floor. When Phoebe and I walked into the room, the bundles sprang to life, and six girls were up on their feet, hair streaming unplaited down their backs. They burst into whispered anticipation, then exchanged even louder admonitions to be quiet until Phoebe had to actually raise her voice to achieve silence.

"Is everybody ready?" Phoebe said.

"Yes, yes!" they chorused, first quite loud, then softer in response to Phoebe's scolding finger.

"Come on, then." The pack of little girls—the youngest not quite eight years old—followed us out of the dining room and into the kitchen.

This is where I took over. Phoebe might have been able to stride her way through the vastness of our rooms, but she knew nothing of the intricacies of the working part of the house. After handing her the mirror and candle, I reached into the box on the shelf above the stove and took out a match, drawing it swiftly across the striking surface attached to the wall. The sulfurous odor leant an additional air of mystery to our little adventure, and the girls let out a spontaneous collective gasp and shiver at the ordinary spark and light. I touched the new flame to the stub of candle Phoebe held, then brought the match to my lips to blow it out.

"No," Phoebe said, her tone insistent enough to stop me.

"You can light the other candles off this one," I said, not happy about being in a power struggle in front of these younger girls.

"Each candle must have its own flame." Her voice took on a deep, earthy quality, and I could sense the excited shivers of my younger cousins. I, however, was not impressed.

"It's going to burn my fingers."

"Only if we waste time arguing about it."

"So we'll stop arguing." I gave a decisive snap of my wrist, extinguishing the flame. The only light in the kitchen came from the candle Phoebe held close to her face, her pale skin now ghostly, her blond hair transparent. She narrowed her perpetually pink-rimmed eyes to angry slits.

"You're going to ruin everything." She shouldered in close so the other cousins wouldn't hear.

"We shouldn't be doing this anyway, and you know it," I said, matching her tone. "Mother would skin us all alive if she knew."

"That's why nobody is going to tell her." She slowly turned and faced the whole group. "Nobody's going to tell anyone." The cousins took a collective step back, twelve wide eyes nodding in pale faces. Then she turned directly to me. "Now, what can we use to break the mirror?"

"Isn't that bad luck?" I asked.

"Only if you believe it is."

"I got this for my birthday."

Phoebe leaned in close. "Listen, Belinda, you chicken out on me now, and I'll march right upstairs, wake your mother, and tell her this was all your idea."

I believed her threat, so I snatched the candle out of her hand and used it to light my search for any leftover tea towel and some heavy utensil not yet confiscated by a needy neighbor. I quickly found a scrap left crumpled on top of the counter after being used to wipe it clean, and a rusty potato masher left to languish in a drawer.

I offered these to Phoebe, who took them with the solemn air of a presiding priestess. As the girls craned to see over her shoulder, she placed the mirror on the kitchen counter, covered it with the tea towel, and with one decisive *whack* of the potato peeler's handle, produced the distinctive sound of broken glass. We all jumped back at that moment, as if expecting the shards to fly straight into our faces, but surged forward again when Phoebe removed the towel to reveal the broken surface of the mirror. She gingerly poked around and handed me the largest piece.

"For your soul and your soul mate," Phoebe said in that eerie voice she seemed to have affected just for this evening. She repeated the gift and the incantation until each—even the youngest—held a sharp-sided piece of mirrored glass. "Now, whoever goes first will have to be very, very brave. I'm sixteen, the oldest, but I can't go because I'm holding"—she looked pointedly at me—"the first flame."

"So Belinda's next," my cousins chorused, pointing slender white fingers at me.

"No! I, um, I gave the sacrifice of the looking glass." I tried to sound as eerily authoritative as Phoebe. "In fact, I can choose not to participate at all."

Before Phoebe could argue, my cousin Ida—just a month younger than I—stepped forward, holding out her candle stub. "I'll go."

two steps; after that it was a dark, gaping maw.

"You don't have to do this if you don't want to," I told Ida, looking into her wide, staring eyes.

"We all promised we would," Phoebe said in that bossy tone nobody ever seemed to have the will to fight against.

"I'm fine," Ida said. She positioned herself at the edge of the top step against a canvas of black and took a deep breath. "I descend into the darkness to see the face of my true love."

Step by careful step, she drew away from us. We all gathered at the doorway, so close we could each feel the heartbeat of another. Nobody said a word, and Ida's gaze never left its target. She grew smaller and smaller, the darkness seeming to crowd around her, then finally she stopped. We heard the sharp intake of her breath, and at once the tiny flame that revealed her to us was gone, and Ida was consumed.

Silence, and then a voice from the abyss. "I saw him!"

The girls nearly threw themselves down the stairs, exhaling the common breath we all held. For the briefest moment, I doubted my own disbelief, wondering if there might be something to this voodoo folderol that my cousin Phoebe had roped us all into. I made my way to the front of the crowd, cupped my hand to my mouth and said, "Who'd you see?"

"Michael Foster!"

Phoebe caught my eye and sent me a look of smug confirmation, but I was nowhere near convinced. Cousin Ida had been talking about Michael Foster in her letters to me for at least three years. His father owned a textile mill, which Michael would surely inherit. I met him once when we went up to visit; his hair stood on end like porcupine spikes and his hands were softer than mine, but Ida had her heart and mind set on marrying him. I would have been more surprised if she *hadn't* seen his face in the glass.

Ida's supernatural success infused all the girls with anticipation—except Augustine, who, being not quite eight years old, insisted she was too little to have a true love.

The honor went to Lillian, who had just turned thirteen, but had the face and figure of a much older girl. She and her family lived twenty miles away, and Mother often said she was glad, because Lillian had all the earmarks of a girl who would grow up too fast, and a girl like that could ruin the reputation of an entire family.

As Lillian poised herself at the top of the stairs, saying, "I descend into the darkness to see the face of my true love," Phoebe elbowed me in the ribs and muttered something about being certain Lillian had descended into darkness before, causing me to giggle and draw a reproachful glare from the other girls waiting their turn. When her little light extinguished below, we once again leaned forward, waiting.

"I definitely saw someone," Lillian said, "but I couldn't make out the face clearly. He had curly hair, though."

"Maybe it's someone you haven't met yet," Ida's voice chimed in from the darkness.

"Maybe there's just too many for the fates to choose from," Phoebe said, and all of us upstairs laughed.

Next were the twins—first Violet, then Virginia—twelve years old and identical with the exception of the scars each one sported after an agreed-upon wounding to establish separate identities. Violet swore she saw a distinct face in the glass, but refused to divulge a name until Virginia had descended. Nobody was surprised to learn that both girls saw the same face—some boy named Virgil who worked as a day laborer on a neighboring farm. The ensuing squabble might have lasted until dawn if a mysterious scuffle hadn't brought it to an abrupt halt.

Then came Rachel, eleven, a levelheaded girl who must have shared my skepticism about the night's events. When she delivered her line about descending into the darkness, she did so in a warbled falsetto, dragging out the word "loooooove" for at least the first three steps. When she hit the bottom and doused her candle, she swore she'd seen the face of Thomas Jefferson.

That left only Phoebe, me, and little Augustine at the top of the cellar steps, and when Phoebe tried to maneuver the girl into her starting position, she was met with a swift kick in the shin.

"I said I didn't want to!" Augustine stamped her little foot and settled her face in a determined pout.

"And I said you have to. Otherwise, you'll be left up here all alone in the kitchen. Is that what you want? To be the only one in here when Uncle Robert comes down to see what all the ruckus is?"

Phoebe's Uncle Robert was my father, and the thoughts of facing him in a dark kitchen in the middle of the night with a bevy of would-be witches tucked away in the cellar was not a soothing one. It was some kind of miracle that he hadn't heard us at all—yet.

"What if we let Augustine go down face forward?" I nudged Phoebe. "Just let her keep her candle lit, walk down the stairs holding on to the wall, and join everybody else at the bottom."

"Yeah," Augustine said. "I don't want no true love anyway. Boys stink."

Phoebe rolled her eyes at the grand concession. "Just go."

I watched little Augustine make her way down the stairs, feeling guilty for having brought her into this mess. I also knew there was no way that little girl would be able to keep this a secret for long, and I was glad to know that I would be deep into the Great Plains before she cracked.

"All right, Belinda," Phoebe said, holding out her candle to me. "Now it's your turn."

"Ah, Phoebe, you know I don't believe any of this. It's…it's evil, it's witchcraft."

"It's not *witchcraft*," Phoebe said, her voice full of disdain. "It's just, it's—"

"Wrong. It's just wrong. It's sinful."

"So you're perfectly fine with letting the rest of us sin, but you're too good?"

"You're welcome to do what you want, but I can't."

"You promised."

"I didn't know what it would be like. I thought it would just be like the apple peels." That was another of Phoebe's favorites: peeling off a strip of apple skin and seeing what letter it formed when dropped into a dish of sugar. Mine was always a *J*; hers a *C*.

"This isn't any different," Phoebe said. "Besides, if you don't believe, it won't even work for you. It will just be a walk down some stairs."

Compliance seemed to be the only way to bring this wretched night to a close, so comply I did. I tipped my wick into Phoebe's flame and stood at the mouth of the cellar. "Idescendintothedarknesstoseethefaceofmytruelove."

I could have cheated, could have stumbled into the wall and used it to guide me down, could have cast my eyes down to follow my feet, but once I saw my reflection, illuminated by that small flame, I had an overwhelming desire to know if what the other girls experienced was real. The piece of glass I held was almost a perfect triangle, curved slightly along its longest side, and it afforded me a full view of just one eye obscured by a few strands of long, loose hair. I kept my focus on that eye, seeing not my soul, but something completely detached. A tiny flame dancing in a deep, dark orb.

The cellar steps were rough and cool beneath my bare feet— a marked change from the soft carpets of the house and the smooth finish of the kitchen floor. I put one foot gingerly down behind me, fought for balance, then brought down the other. I told myself I was just playing a game, appeasing my cousins, participating in a ritual as harmless as tossing spilled salt over my shoulder.

The whispers petered into silence, and one final toe-reaching behind me confirmed that I was on solid ground. Never taking my gaze away from my piece of the mirror, I took a deep breath, puckered my lips, and extinguished the flame.

And, nothing. Nothing but the darkness wrapped close around me. I kept my eye trained toward the shard of mirror until the glowing tip of my candle's wick was swallowed by black.

"Well?" The girls gathered around me spoke as a chorus.

"I told you this was a bunch of nonsense," I said, not allowing a drop of disappointment to come through.

"Or maybe you're just never going to have a true love," Phoebe taunted from the top of the stairs.

"Or maybe God knows the plans He has for me and He's not going to reveal them through some childish, evil game."

"Aw, save your Scriptures for Sunday school." Phoebe positioned herself at the top of the stairs and intoned the fateful phrase with more conviction than any of us had mustered.

I felt my cousins gather around me, and Augustine's small hand slipped into mine. My failure to see an image hadn't shaken their faith; with the exception of the good-humored Rachel, they were believers.

Phoebe came down the final step, and we took a collective step back. I heard her sharp intake of breath, then a puff into darkness. Nobody broke into the silence that followed, but Augustine did squeeze my hand a little tighter, and I felt her shifting nervously from foot to foot.

"Thank You, God," Phoebe whispered.

"You leave God out of this," I said. "There's nothing of God in this. It's just, just—"

"You know who I saw, don't you?"

"You didn't see anybody. None of us did."

"Who was it?" The eager voices of my cousins overrode my singular voice of reason.

"Chester," Phoebe said in triumph.

"*Cousin* Chester?" Rachel voiced everybody's concern, but none of the girls could possibly have the same sick, seething stomach that I had.

"Not by blood," Phoebe said, reminding all of us of her adopted status—the very factor that gave her such mysterious appeal and power. "Now all of you get back upstairs before we all get in a world of hurt."

There was a shuffle as the girls found their way back to the stairs, and excited whispers as they made their ascent. I made my way to join them, but was detained by a grip on my sleeve.

"Now do you see?"

"This doesn't mean anything."

"It changes everything." She jerked me hard against her and stood so close I could feel her lips moving against my ear. "Talk to your father again. Tell him I have to go with you."